Praise for Mercy's Legacy

Mercy's Legacy is such a timely piece. without giving platitudes or easy-peas fly in real life. I particularly enjoy how current racial issues with historical ɪ With every chapter, I couldn't wait to find out what happened next. It's challenging and encouraging—a book you won't want to skip.

~Gretchen Hoffman, writer

Sarah Hanks takes you on a journey that will grasp at your heartstrings. A brave crossing through a land divided by freedom and slavery, life and death. As a white woman married to a black man and the mother of a biracial child, I felt this story through and through. Above all, it is an account of hope, faith, and grit that I found to be a must-read!

~Amanda Speights, writer

Mercy's Legacy is a heart-tugging tribute to redemption. So many of us need it, but so few are willing to simply accept it. The stories of Natassa and DeAndre are beautifully intertwined with a past that informs not only their lives, but the roots of our nation. Racial tension, a mother's love, and a father's heart follow Mercy as she helps everyone rediscover the meaning of family. A timely book, written by Sarah Hanks' talented hand, is an excellent choice for your next book group.

~ Kristine Delano, writer

Mercy's Legacy will leave you deeply satisfied and with a renewed hope in the power of forgiveness. In her third installment of *The Mercy Series*, Sarah Hanks takes readers on another journey of faith, struggle, heartbreak, and grace, where history mingles with the present, speaking truth in the unlikeliest of places. Sarah's authentic characters resonate from the first page to the last in this beautifully and intricately woven story of redemption.

~ Alyssa Schwarz,
Author of The Glass Cottage

They say all things must come to an end. However, after crying over and cheering on these characters, I'm not ready to say goodbye. Sarah has continued her stellar character development, and we see our favorite characters maturing in their relationships and their faith. Another well researched and accurate historical journey is a special treat. I always learn something new when I read Sarah's historical stories. *Mercy's Legacy* won't disappoint!

~Dr. Rene Burress

Sarah tackles some serious topics in her telling of Mercy's story. In navigating such difficult terrain, she draws the reader into Mercy's world, allowing us to feel her struggle. We also gain insight into the choices the adults in her life have made, and how those decisions affect Mercy in her battle to find her identity in a world and family that make her feel like an outsider simply because of the color of her skin. The historical accounts tie in very nicely to the overall story showing similar struggles generations before we meet Mercy. Throughout both storylines, we see God's hand in these characters' lives and how He brings about restoration, healing, and reconciliation in the most difficult of circumstances. Mercy's story is definitely one you want to read.

~Andrette Herron

In the last installment of the Mercy series, Sarah does a beautiful job of pulling everything together. With her modern timeline, she weaves the intricacies of the story into the present complications of our COVID world. If you wondered what kind of young woman Mercy would become, or how the family would handle raising her—here it is, with surprises you wouldn't expect. And *I loved* learning more about Liberty in the historical timeline, giving us another glimpse into the original Mercy's world and her next generation. Another beautifully written book by Sarah Hanks!

~Janell Harris

Once again, Hanks has used a historical narrative to add perspective to present-day issues. The characters, both past and present, are relatable and real. The story is powerful.

~Pamela Baker, writer,
Goodreads reviewer

In *Mercy's Legacy*, Sarah Hanks carries us into the story of Mercy's daughter, Liberty, and Thaddeus, a discharged Union soldier making his way home. Hanks grabbed me in the first couple pages of the historical line with a lynching. From there, we follow Liberty as she searches for hope, equality, and respect in the Reconstruction-era South, a world where the promises of the war have fallen short. Will Mercy find her grandmother and the answers she seeks as she traverses the boundary of color? And what about Thaddeus, who travels at her side? Is there a place in this world where they can be friends or even more? Will Mercy's heart be broken? I devoured the pages in my quest for answers.

~Sherry Shindelar, Author,
ACFW First Impressions Winner

Sarah has, once again, effectively woven the past and the *very* present into a tapestry that teaches without preaching, while drawing the reader along on a journey. Through the process of reading these books (this one in particular), I've found myself questioning biases, racism, the legal processes, & social justice. What is redemption, what is "moving on," and how far are we willing to trust the power of God in forgiveness? These are all recurring thoughts in *Mercy's Legacy*. The stories themselves create a juxtaposition of the same concepts through history and challenge our perceptions. I have found myself so emotionally invested into these characters; I'm sorry to see their stories end, but I am so grateful to have read their journeys! I will say that many authors start their series off with a "bang," but quickly descend into boredom and repetition. Sarah has kept these multiple stories going full throttle, and I've been captivated throughout. I highly recommend this series, and I'm so pleased that Sarah wrote their conclusions as well as she wrote their beginnings.

~Cassidy Cooley

Sarah has done it again! *Mercy's Legacy* will make you smile, cheer, frown, and think deeply about your own bias. I love how the storylines of all my favorite characters have been intertwined once again. This book brings a beautiful and, in some ways, very unexpected conclusion to the people I have come to know and love throughout these three books. The way this all comes together into a beautiful tapestry was a surprise in many ways, but it brings a fullness to the story that I found very enjoyable. Again, Sarah draws the reader in right away. Make sure you have time to read more than one chapter because you will not want to put this book down!

~Melissa Jacobs,
Author of *Livin' the Dream*

In the midst of modern-day events, I couldn't help but find myself smack dab in the middle of this story. Hanks doesn't hold back in wrapping up the Mercy Series. I have asked God to break my heart for what breaks His, and He did through this story.

~Brittany Roach

MERCY'S

LEGACY

MERCY'S

LEGACY

SARAH HANKS

This is a work of fiction. Names, characters, places, and incidents either are the product of the author's imagination or are used fictitiously. Any resemblance to actual persons, living or dead, events, or locales is entirely coincidental.

Edited by Janice Boekhoff

Cover by Samantha Fury of Fury Cover Designs

Dedication

This book is dedicated to all those who have prayed, worked, and bled for justice in His name.

Acknowledgements

This is the end of an incredible journey. When these characters were but a dream in my heart, a community of people surrounded me to help breathe life into them. I could not have done this alone.

Thank you to my dream team of readers—Melissa, Janell, Rene, Shannon, Cassidy, and Brittany. Your insight and feedback each step of the way has strengthened this story and this author. Thank you to the sensitivity readers—Anne and Llechor—who lent their time and life experience to help ensure that this novel helps to heal instead of wounding further. Thank you also to the Scribes Critique Group of AFCW. I've learned so much from the fellow writers there. All those red lines and comments paid off. This story is immeasurably better because of them.

To my husband Kevin and all eight of my beautiful children, thank you. You've been my biggest fans and I appreciate your support more than words can say.

And to my Lord who has blessed me abundantly and loves me unconditionally, thank You.

1

September 2016
On the road to Chicago, Illinois

"A re you sure she's going to like me?" Janell Scott flexed her left hand on the steering wheel, angling her fingers toward the afternoon sunlight. Her diamond ring cast glittering sparkles on the roof like a dome of stars.

No, DeAndre thought, but he said, "Of course," and smiled at her. To reassure her that his mama would welcome his new wife with open arms. That she'd pour love upon her and treat her like the daughter she never had. If he was sure, he would have waited to marry her until they arrived in Chicago. Until Mama could be there for the wedding, handkerchief in hand.

But no, he couldn't be certain of Mama's reaction. Would she call him a fool to his face, right in front of Janell? So he'd told his girl he couldn't wait another day to make her his wife. They'd gone to the courthouse after crossing over the Illinois border. There was a day to wait, no matter what. One day was long enough. He had trouble keeping his hands off her after being deprived of her presence for two years, but he'd managed to rein it in until their wedding night.

Man, he was glad he didn't have to hold back anymore.

"What's she like? Give me some intel. How can I win her over?" Janell pursed her lips like she always did when formulating a plan.

Oh, he wanted to kiss them. He leaned over.

She slapped him away. "Stop it! I'm driving." Her laugh bubbled out, flirtatious and tantalizing.

There were benefits to his driver's license expiring while he was in prison. He could keep his eyes on her instead of on the road. He took her right hand and planted a trail of kisses on her arm.

"DeAndre! Seriously. Stop. I'm going to crash if you keep that up." Her voice danced around, playful. Inviting.

He dropped her arm. "Fine. But I'll make it up to you later."

"You'd better."

How did she do that? Seduce him with just a look? He melted in her hands. He blew out a breath and turned his gaze to the window, trying to cool himself from the fire she lit in him.

His mama. She'd asked about his mama.

"Mama loves to cook. She can make most anything, but her specialty is soul food. The kind that fills you up so good you don't think you'll be able to eat again for two days."

"Soul food?" She squinted at him. "Like comfort food? Chicken potpie?" With her eyebrows lifted and forehead crinkled, she looked proud of herself.

Why burst her bubble?

"Sort of. She can make a good chicken potpie, but that's not what she's known for. Black-eyed peas, candied yams, smothered pork chops, okra, gumbo, hush puppies. Soul food."

Janell scrunched her nose. "I don't know what any of that is. You're going to have to find something else. Another way for me to get on her good side."

"She likes gospel music."

Raised eyebrows.

"BeBe and CeCe Winans?"

She shook her head. "I got nothing."

"Okay, then. Stick to the Bible. Mama loves her Bible."

Finally, a smile. "Bible. I can do that."

"But she only reads the King James Version. Anything else is heretical."

Her shoulders slumped. "Uhhh …"

"Don't worry, babe. You'll win her over. You win everyone over." Hopefully, he was telling the truth. That Janell would charm Mama with her wit and kindness so much so that Mama wouldn't even notice she was white.

Because, yeah, he'd forgotten to mention that.

Perhaps, on purpose.

But her parents hadn't had a problem with him being black, so surely his mama wouldn't mind him being married to a white girl, right? Or that the marriage had happened days after being released from prison.

Janell's parents *did* have a problem with that one—or maybe with her marrying a felon, in general. They weren't on speaking terms with her at the moment. His stomach sank at the reminder. He was supposed to be her golden ticket, not a ticket out of her parents' lives. But maybe—*maybe*—Janell would find new family in his mama. Accepting. Embracing. He could hope, at least.

Of course, he hadn't told Mama he was coming or that he was bringing someone with him. She never liked surprises. But he found asking for forgiveness was easier than asking for permission, and he couldn't risk her saying no—a very real possibility.

Janell settled her hand on his knee. He must have been bobbing it up and down. His tension eased at her calming touch.

"It's going to be okay." She blinked, her eyes serious.

"I know." But he didn't. What if Mama threw them out? What if she just couldn't reconcile having a felon as a son? What if she wouldn't accept Janell? What if she didn't want to see either of them? They hadn't exactly left things in a happy place with their letters.

Okay, so there'd only been three letters in two years. The last one ended with *I hope you learned your lesson.*

He'd learned a number of lessons during his time in prison. About God's mercy and grace and love. The question was, had she?

Janell slowed the car as they came to a line of traffic snaking in front of them.

"We're getting close." DeAndre drummed his fingers on the armrest.

"It's not even rush hour." Janell released a breath that sent wisps of hair flying from around her face.

"Welcome to Chicago."

An hour later, they arrived in the correct neighborhood. Janell nibbled her lip as she turned onto Ashland. Was she as nervous as he was? He opened his mouth to reassure her, but could he speak without his voice shaking? Because he couldn't seem to stop his hands from trembling. He took a deep breath, then blew it out, long and slow. He could do this. They could do this, together.

"This doesn't look like the best neighborhood." Nervousness leaked from her voice as she leaned over the steering wheel, peering at the mailboxes. Many of the addresses were faded, hard to read, even in the bright afternoon sunshine.

DeAndre shrugged, scanning the numbers along with her. "It's better than the apartment she lived in when I was here before. That 'hood was rough. This is a step up, for sure." He glanced down again at the gray envelope with Mama's elegant script and spied the numbers that matched the return address on her last letter to him. "That one." He pointed.

They pulled in front of a beige brick one-and-a-half-story. A set of concrete stairs led to a cement porch where a lone folding chair sat under the overhang. The large bush under the front window was neat and trimmed, the yard freshly mowed and well kept. Definitely a step-up.

Breathe in. Breathe out.

Janell squeezed his hand. "Here goes nothing." Her smile wobbled, and he worked to keep his from doing the same.

They walked hand in hand up the walkway, their steps slow and purposeful.

DeAndre held up his hand to knock but paused. "Why don't you have a seat, babe. I want her to see me first. Then I can introduce you."

Janell nodded and sank into the folding chair. It groaned in protest. DeAndre eyed it to make sure it would hold her thin frame. Seemed steady.

He knocked.

Waited.

Were those voices? Or just a TV?

Knocked again.

Mama flung open the door, blocking her view of Janell entirely. Her initial expression of annoyance transformed. Her mouth hung open.

He managed a smile. "Hi, Mama."

"DeAndre! What are you doing here?" She searched him up and down, as if trying to decipher if he were real.

"I'm out." *Obviously.* "I came to see you." Also completely obvious.

She stood frozen in place for a moment, and he debated his next move. Should he apologize again for his wretched behavior? Promise her that he was a changed man? Tell her he loved her? Thrust Janell in front of him as a peace offering?

"What's wrong with me? Come here and give your mama a hug." She stepped toward him and wrapped her arms around him, tight and secure. He squeezed back, surprised at how quickly tears sprang to his eyes. For so long, all they'd had was each other. Well, he'd had Reg. Always Reg. But she'd been his breath. Until she left, stealing the air from his lungs.

"I missed you." Tears choked his voice.

"I missed you too. I'm so glad you're okay."

"I'm good, Mama. Real good."

She pulled away, searching his face, brushing her palm against his cheek. "You look good."

"How you been?" She looked good too. Younger than the last time he'd seen her, even. Fresh and crisp in her business suit. Mama never did know how to let her hair down. No one would ever catch her in sweats.

"Good, baby. But you caught me by surprise." She pressed her hands to her cheeks. "I wasn't expecting company, and I don't think I've got enough on hand to make a decent meal for you."

"Don't worry about that. After the sorry excuse for food I've been eating, anything you touch will taste like heaven."

Her face fell. He shouldn't have mentioned prison.

Out of the corner of his eye, he saw Janell lean forward in the chair. He probably should—

"There's something I need to tell you, Dre." Mama clasped her hands together. "I don't know how you're gonna feel about it."

Mama's statement caught him off guard, and he shook his head to try and knock his thoughts into place. What was she talking about? Something she needed to tell him? But he had something he needed to tell her. Now.

"I need to introduce you to someone, Mama."

She cocked her head, confusion spreading across her face. "What?"

"I got married." There. He'd said it. That wasn't so hard.

"Married? You just got out of prison. What are you talking about?" Mama put her hand on the doorframe, steadying herself.

"Do you need to sit down?" She looked like she might pass out on her front porch.

"What I need is for you to tell me what you're talking about." There it was. Her no-nonsense Mama voice he'd heard so often when he was younger.

"I told you before, uh, everything that I met a girl. She stuck by me through it all. We got married as soon as I got out."

Janell cleared her throat, and Mama took a step over the threshold, peeking around the door. Janell smiled and waved.

Mama's head snapped back in DeAndre's direction, her eyes bugging out, her face taut. She grabbed his arm and yanked him inside, letting the screen door slam shut behind them with a thud, a bounce, and a thump.

"A white girl? You done married a white girl?" Mama's whisper shouted.

"Her name is Janell." DeAndre kept his voice calm and even.

"Boy, what were you thinking?"

"That I love her." Deep breath.

"Couldn't you find a nice girl of your kind? What about Henrietta from the church you went to out here? She was sweet on you."

He couldn't hold in the laugh that escaped. Henrietta with her short skirts and tight tops. Henrietta running her fake fingernails down his arm during service. Why would Mama prefer her to Janell?

"Mama, give her a chance. You're going to love her."

Mama huffed. "What choice did you give me? You already put a ring on her finger. I got myself a white daughter-in-law. You bring a complete stranger over to my home unannounced. I guess you're both expecting dinner?"

He winced. "And we were hoping to stay the night?"

"Stay the—Boy, you're grown now. You best not be expecting to mooch off me. You gotta make your own way in this world, and it ain't going to be easy."

"Just one night."

"Just one night? Lord have mercy. That's how it always starts, and then people have forty-year-old grown children living in their basements."

"You have a basement?" He cracked a smile.

Mama slapped his arm. "No, we don't. We got two bedrooms. Our room and a guest room. *Guest* room. You can be a guest for one night, but that room ain't going to have your name on it, you hear? Not yours. Not Jane's."

"Janell." He put his hand on Mama's arm to stop her rant. "What do you mean *we*?"

"Huh?"

"You said *we* and *ours*."

Mama sighed, lifting her eyes up to the ceiling. "That's what I was trying to tell you." She brought her gaze down to his, sober. "You know I loved your pa. I still do."

"Pa? What are you talking about?" A sinking feeling seeped into his gut.

"I met someone a few years ago. He plays sax at the jazz club I work at. I didn't want to upset you, but we got married last year."

"You got married?" DeAndre stumbled backward, bumping into the wall.

"Do you need to sit down?"

He shook his head.

"Just because I married Harlem doesn't mean I didn't love your pa. Or that I don't still. But life moves on, and," she said with a flicker of a smile, "I found a new love."

"Harlem?"

"Yes, Harlem."

"What kind of name is Harlem?" DeAndre spit the words out, woozy. Mama had married? He'd suspected she was seeing someone back when he went to art school, but married? He had a stepfather he'd never met?

Memories swirled of Mama and Pa together, laughing, dancing, kissing with his arm around her. She'd wept at his funeral, shoulders shaking as they lowered his casket into the ground. Hadn't she taken the job at the jazz club so she could feel closer to Pa? But now she'd married someone else?

"Come on. Why don't you meet him?" She put her arm around DeAndre to guide him toward the living room.

He stopped. "Janell is sitting on your porch."

She closed her eyes and nodded. "Okay." When she opened them, her dark eyes held resolve. "First things first. Let me meet that wife of yours."

He popped his head out the door. "Come on in."

Her smile looked forced, and when she grabbed his hand, it shook in his. "It's going to be okay," he whispered in her ear.

She nodded, but her shoulders remained stiff.

"Janell, this is my mama."

Mama squared her shoulders. "You can call me Margie."

Janell rocked back and forth from the balls of her feet to her heels. "Nice to meet you."

"You'll have to forgive me." Mama's voice oozed thick like honey. "DeAndre caught me by surprise. I wasn't expecting him, much less a wife. It's good to meet you. Welcome to the family." Mama stepped forward and patted Janell's shoulder in an awkward half hug.

Something in between a laugh and a cry escaped from Janell's mouth. She wiped the corner of her eye with her sleeve.

"Let me introduce you to my husband." Mama spun and headed down the hallway, her heels clacking on the tile.

Janell's eyebrows shot up.

He mouthed *I had no idea* as they followed her through a short hallway to the living room where a man lounged in a recliner watching television, sweaty glass soda bottle in hand.

"Harlem, we have guests." Mama stood between husband and son with her hands clasped in front of her.

Harlem set his drink on the coffee table and sat up, flipping the wooden knob of his chair. The footrest slammed closed with a thud. He picked up the remote, flicked the television off, and rose to face them. He matched DeAndre's height almost exactly, meeting him eye to eye, though Harlem didn't have DeAndre's muscular build. His wiry frame didn't intimidate DeAndre, but the way Harlem carried himself called for respect.

Mama's voice came out as crisp as an ironed sheet. "This is my son, DeAndre, and his new wife, Janell."

Harlem grasped DeAndre's hand, giving it a hearty shake. His eyes flickered over Janell with a gaze doused in suspicion. Gray flecked his mustache and beard. Deep lines creased his eyes. His skin looked leathery and worn, like a lot of life had been lived in it, but there was a kindness to the corners of his mouth. At least when he looked at DeAndre.

"Harlem. Nice to meet you." Janell smiled at him, undeterred. "I hope you don't mind me asking, but what's the story behind your name? It's so interesting."

"My parents named me after where they first met." Though he answered Janell, he continued staring at DeAndre.

"That's a great idea." Janell leaned into DeAndre, laying her head on his shoulder as if trying to sway into Harlem's line of sight. "Hey, babe." She turned her gaze to him. "Maybe we should name our first kid Java."

"Or Joe." They chuckled for a moment. When DeAndre looked back, Mama and Harlem were staring at them blankly.

"Because we met at Java Joe's." Janell's smile faltered. "The coffee shop we both worked at. Never mind."

Harlem glanced at her, the slightest smile tugging at his lips.

She'd win the man over. For sure.

"Let me show you to your room." Mama pointed to a door behind the kitchen. "The *guest* room where you are welcome to stay for *one* night."

"We got it, Mama." He hooked his arm around Janell's shoulder.

"I guess I could make some mac and cheese for dinner. And some sweet potato pie." Mama led the way.

"Soul food," he whispered to Janell.

~

DeAndre crept into the kitchen and pried a cabinet open, searching for a glass.

"To your right." Mama's voice sounded from behind him.

He startled and spun around to see Mama sitting at the kitchen table. "Mama! Jeez. You 'bout scared me to death. What are you doing here?"

"It's my house."

"I mean, why are you awake?" DeAndre peered at the numbers softly glowing on the oven. "It's two a.m."

"Hard to sleep with a stranger in the house."

"I'm not a stranger."

"Wasn't talking 'bout you."

DeAndre grabbed orange juice from the fridge and poured himself a glass. "You like her, don't you? Or at least you will."

"I suppose so." She wrapped her hands around a steamy mug but didn't drink from it. The only light in the room shone from the streetlamp outside. It cast a hazy rectangle of illumination on her nose and mouth. Her eyes remained shaded.

He sat across from her. Took a drink. "You will."

His eyes roamed the room, adjusting to the dimness and taking in details he'd been too nervous to notice earlier. A few praying angel knickknacks on a shelf, a cross-stitch of the Lord's Prayer, and a Bulls banner. Did that belong to Harlem?

"Hey, you still have those travel magazines." There had to be two dozen of them on the bookshelf.

She angled herself toward the collection and smiled. "Of course I do."

"I never could figure out why you collected pictures of places you'd never been. Places you could never afford to go." But they'd given him plenty of material to paint.

"I've got to know there's more out there than what's right in front of me, Dre. Those pictures helped me get through some very tough times."

"What's in front of you right now?" What was her life like? How might he fit into it?

"My son, I don't know what else lies ahead, but I know I got you."

2

February 2020
Renada, Nebraska

Mercy swiped a line of orange paint on her canvas above the horizon line, overlapping the pink.

She used her knuckle to increase the volume on her iPod. Mandisa. Her mom let her listen to Mandisa. That proved her friends wrong, didn't it?

She raised the volume a few more notches to drown out the hum of buzzing voices in the living room below. But she didn't want to hear "Good Morning." Skipping ahead to "He is with You," Mercy grumbled when she smeared a dab of paint on the iPod. She tried to rub it off with the corner of her apron but just ended up smudging it across the screen.

A knock sounded at the door, and she huffed. Why couldn't everyone leave her alone? Let her paint in her walk-in closet, away from the party downstairs. Her closet was her safe place, and right now, she needed her brush to make everything feel all right inside her.

Another knock.

Mercy peeked outside the closet, glaring at the closed bedroom door. But she put on her polite voice in case it was her mom or grandma or an aunt. "Who is it?"

"It's Bethany, baby. Mind if I come in?"

Well, Grandma Bethany was okay. She wasn't annoying like everyone else. She wasn't really her grandma, just a nice old lady that Mom had been friends with since before Mercy was born. She punched down the volume and exited the closet. "Okay."

Bethany ambled in and plopped on the bed, ruffling the purple quilt. "Whoo-wee, young Mercy. I sure do love your room. Makes me feel like a princess just being up here."

Why did Bethany always call her young, like she was some little kid? She'd turned nine in December. Not so little anymore. But Bethany had called her that for as long as she could remember. Mercy *did* have the best room. Their house looked like a princess's castle, and she got to sleep in the princess's tower. Mom called it a turret.

Mercy lowered into her desk chair and found a smile.

"You want me to go to the front yard and yell, 'Rapunzel, let down your hair'?" Mercy asked, giggling because Bethany's hair looked nothing like Rapunzel's long straight hair in the movie.

Bethany bounced a short silver curl with her hand. "Would you now?" Her grin drew a wider one out of Mercy. It felt good to smile for a minute, to forget that she was mad at everybody and everything.

But then she remembered.

"Why did you come up here?" Mercy leaned forward, voice low so Mom couldn't overhear and scold her for being disrespectful.

"To see you." Bethany's eyes were honest, but Mercy wasn't dumb.

"To get me to go downstairs?" She crossed her arms.

"Baby, everyone wants to see you. They're asking about you. Don't you want to at least say hi to Aunt Laura and Tia? What about your grandma?

Mercy shook her head. "I'm not going. You can't make me."

"Okay, okay. You're right. I can't make you. I mean, I could drag you by your hair—"

Her hands flew to her hips. "Grandma Bethany!"

Bethany smiled, but her eyes drooped in a sad way.

A wave of guilt crashed into Mercy. She was being difficult. That's what Hope would say. *Why do you always have to be so difficult?* But her insides were a storm—all thunder and lightning and hail—and she couldn't simply walk downstairs and grin, pretending everything was fine and happy.

"Just know that you are loved and wanted and missed." Bethany looked at her as if it were all true, and the storm got quiet for a moment. "Here, help an old woman up." She held out her hand, and Mercy grasped onto it and pulled.

"Now look at that. You painted me orange." Bethany held out her hand to show an orange streak of tempera on her palm.

Mercy cringed. "Sorry."

"No problem, baby. Something to remember you by." She winked as she left.

Mercy grabbed a wipe from her closet and scrubbed her hands.

Back to work.

Time for the sky. She dipped her brush in the blue paint. The color of Mom's tears.

Mom had been crying for years. Mercy hadn't understood why at first, didn't get what was going on. Mom and Dad wanted another baby, but their babies kept on dying. First Ava, then Asa, both dying before they grew big enough for anyone to know they'd ever been in Mom's belly. Mom had named the second baby Asa, saying it meant *healer*. She said God would use Asa to heal all their hearts from the first baby that died. When Asa went to be with Jesus too, Mom cried for a long time. It seemed like Asa just broke their hearts more is all.

But then Mom stopped crying and started smiling and laughing again. She seemed all glowy and bright. Her and Dad didn't say anything, but Hope and Faith and Mercy whispered among themselves, wondering if there was another baby. Mom's belly got rounder, and she started wearing different pants and shirts. Finally, Mom and Dad told them that Havilah was going to be their new sister. The name Havilah means *to dance*. Mom said God was turning their sadness into dancing.

Mom's belly grew and grew, but then one day, she went to the doctor and found out Havilah's heart had stopped beating. For no reason. Just stopped. So, Mom went to the hospital and Havilah came out, only she was dead.

When Mercy saw Havilah, it clicked. Why Mom had been so sad; why she'd been crying for years. Havilah didn't look like a normal baby. She was so tiny, and her face looked squished and strange under the little blue and pink hat. But one thing was clear.

Havilah was white.

Mom had been crying because she wanted a white baby.

It was what she'd wanted when Mercy had been put inside her. She wanted a white baby, but she got Mercy instead.

All the babies after Mercy kept dying. And Mom kept crying, kept wanting her white baby.

Now everyone was downstairs celebrating a new baby that had grown big enough and made Mom's stomach gigantic. This baby would live for sure. Mom would finally get the white baby she'd wanted all along. Everyone came over for a party. They called it a shower, but it was really a party for the baby. For baby Charity.

Mercy sniffed, and the blue streak blurred.

Charity means *love*. That's what Mom said. In Mercy's Sunday school class, they memorized a verse about faith, hope, and love remaining. That means staying. But the Bible says the greatest of everything is love. Mercy didn't know how her sisters Faith and Hope felt to know that their sister Love would always be better than them. Mercy's stomach dropped. She hadn't even made the list. Charity would be the greatest. The best in the family. Where would that leave Mercy?

Great. She had smeared the blue into the orange. That's what she got for painting while crying again. She'd have to wait until it dried to fix it.

Another knock.

"What?" Mercy shouted, swiping away tears with the back of her hand. Then she pictured how Mom would frown if she heard Mercy's rude words. She sneaked some politeness into her tone and tried again. "Who is it?"

"It's me."

David. Her only sibling that wasn't annoying. At least he'd come home from college for the party.

She sighed. "Come in."

He appeared, holding a cup and plate, his blonde hair slicked back. "Hey, Sis. Whoa! You got paint all over your face."

She growled and snatched a wipe, scrubbing her face raw while David kicked the door shut with his foot and sauntered over to her desk. He set down the goodies.

"I smuggled you some orange soda and a cookie."

"Soda?" She squealed. Mom never let them drink soda.

"I think Aunt Breanna brought it. Shh. Don't say anything." He winked.

Mercy giggled.

Breanna wasn't their aunt, just Mom's friend, but they called her that because she liked it.

Mercy tossed the blue wipe into the trash can and then bounded over to the desk, snatched the cup, and took a gulp. *Mmm.* Soda. Mom's stupid rules. No sugar. Only a little candy sometimes. No Twinkies ever.

Mom didn't even let her listen to the same music as her friends at school.

Mercy told her friend Tayna that Mom didn't let her listen to Drake. Tayna said that's because Mom is racist and doesn't like black people. But Mom wasn't racist, was she? They went as a family to black church sometimes with Grandma Bethany and Tia. Mercy even had three black Barbies. But maybe Mom *was* racist because she wanted that white baby.

"Why don't you bring some of your paintings down to show everyone?" David wandered to her closet and looked at the canvases lining the walls, then shuffled through the ones stacked in the corner. "What about this one?" He held up one of an elephant spraying a rainbow out of its trunk. "Or this one?" He pointed to one where a dozen brightly colored starfish lay on a glittering shore.

"You're just trying to get me to go downstairs." She scarfed a huge bite of her cookie. Crumbs sprayed all over her desk and carpet.

"This stuff is too beautiful to be stuck in your closet." David leaned against her doorframe, crossing his ankles. His navy button-down shirt had creases in it like he'd just gotten it out of the package or maybe Mom had ironed it for him. And were those jeans new?

"Mom doesn't like it." Mercy stuffed the rest of the cookie into her mouth, crumpled her napkin, and tossed it into the trash can.

"What do you mean? Doesn't like what?"

"My art." Her voice was muffled by the cookie.

"That's ridiculous. Of course, she does."

"Does not."

"Does so."

"Then why does she get so quiet whenever anyone talks about it? Mrs. Lamert went on and on at conferences." Mercy snatched a pair of sunglasses from her dresser and perched them on the edge of her nose, then made her voice sound all nasally like Mrs. Lamert's. "Mercy has amazing talent for her age. She shows outstanding promise." Mercy waved her arms around until the glasses slid off her face.

She dropped the act. "Mom didn't even smile. She just sat there and looked sad." Like Mercy had disappointed her. Again.

David winced and made a sour-candy pucker with his lips. He sank onto her bed. "It's not because she doesn't like your art, Mercy."

"Then why isn't she happy for me?" Mercy slumped in her desk chair.

His voice was little more than a whisper. "It's because it reminds her of your father."

"Dad?" Mercy scrunched her nose. "What does Dad have to do with anything? He can't even draw a stick figure."

"No, not Dad. Your … Oh man. I probably shouldn't say anything."

She snapped her head up. "What? My what?"

"Y-your biological father." David met her gaze.

"My… wait, you know about my father?" She jumped up and came to kneel in front of him.

"Not much. But I know that he's an artist. He painted the mural on St. Anthony Street."

She closed her eyes to keep the room from spinning. Her father? The one she made up stories and dreamed about? She'd always wondered who he was. She knew nothing. Nothing other than that he was a bad man. If only she could pretend that he didn't matter because he was a bad man. But he mattered to her. Especially since he was a secret that Mom and Dad had kept hidden from her all her life. An artist? How could a bad man be an artist?

"Tell me everything you know! What's his name? Where is he?" She grabbed David's hand and yanked on it, trying to pull information from him.

He looked uneasy. "Maybe—"

"Knock, knock." Aunt Breanna cracked open the door, the yellow sundress underneath her leather jacket like a flashlight probing into their private conversation.

David leaned over and whispered, "We'll finish talking later." Then he stood and walked out with all of Mercy's questions chasing after him, unanswered.

3

______

1868,
Just outside of New Orleans, Louisiana

My breath hitches as I peer around the tree trunk to see Mingo's feet dangling in midair. I shove my fist into my mouth, cramming back the wail that threatens to burst forth. As much as a snap of a twig and I'll be swinging from that tree next to my brother.

Mingo's strangled choking assaults my ears as I press my back onto the rough bark of my hiding place. I wince as it rubs against my scars through the fabric of my thin cotton dress. I'm eighteen now and haven't been whipped for seven years, but the lash marks on my back remind me that I grew up as a slave.

"Where's your sister?" One of the men's voices echoes through the woods, bouncing off each tree. "Did she tuck tail and run like all the others? Don't worry. Next time we see her, we'll take care of her. And we won't waste good rope. A well-placed bullet will do just fine."

My stomach lurches as the men's laughter ricochets through my chest. When will they leave? I don't pray much anymore, but I venture a prayer now. *God, make them go.* There isn't much time.

I turn my head to peek at the scene once more. I've read of night riders in other states wearing white hoods to disguise their identities, but this group of a dozen men gathered in front of Mingo's church don't bother hiding. Their wide-brimmed hats do little to conceal their features. I don't know who they are. Someone surely will. Yet no one will care.

After so much fighting, freedom didn't necessarily mean liberty. *Liberty.* Mama named me that believing that God would answer her prayers for the end of slavery. *I named you in faith, child. I knew the day would come when you would walk out your name.*

Is this what you prayed for, Mama? Three years after the war between the states ended, and freedom doesn't look at all how I imagined it would. I dig my fingernails into the bark, and splinters pierce my fingertips. I hold my breath, anger burning.

The sound of spittle dropping into dirt causes me to risk another glance. The men kick up dust with their boots, sending it swirling like a cloud. Then they turn to leave.

But not before tossing several of their burning torches into the church.

Crackles and hisses mix with the sound of Mingo's desperate choking as smoke fills the air. Laughter and the clomp of horses' hooves die in the distance. I search the horizon once more, just to be safe.

I emerge from my hiding place, damp with sweat, pulse beating wildly. My brother's eyes bulge as he sees me. His hands grasp at the rope encircling his neck.

"Hold on," I say, already hitching up my skirt and tying it in a knot between my legs. With my muscles screaming, I scale the tree and pull out my pocketknife. Gritting my teeth, I saw at the rope. Harder and harder. Threads spring free, but the core holds tight. *Please, God.* I press all my weight onto the knife, grunting.

There.

With a snap, the rope breaks, and Mingo collapses on the ground with a thud. My balance falters. The space around me swirls. I grab onto a branch to steady myself. Beneath me, Mingo lies in a heap. He sputters and coughs. Heaves in a breath. Coughs some more.

I shimmy down and snatch the rope from his neck, pulling it free.

Mingo sits up and cranes his head to see his church in flames. "Ole Faithful." His voice sounds like gravel.

"Forget your wretched church. You nearly met your Maker." I stoop over and plant my hands on my knees to slow my breath.

"I was prepared to." He raises himself up, one shaky leg and then the other, stumbling a bit before bracing himself on the tree trunk. "But I was not prepared to be the reason you got yourself in a fix. What are you doing here? Trying to get yourself killed?"

"A thank you would be nice." I untie my dress and shake out the skirt.

He hammers his chest with his fist, expelling a rattling wheeze. "Mama's gonna have my hide when she hears of this."

I take his hand. "Come back to the farm. Stay with us tonight. It's too dangerous here for you."

Mingo shakes his head. "I can't. My flock needs me. They scattered at the sight of them riders. Now our church is gone. I have to stay. To pick up the pieces."

His flock? The man just had a noose around his neck for those people. "When are you gonna look out for yourself?"

"It's my calling, Sis." His gaze caresses the flames lapping up the white wooden beams of his first love. "You wouldn't understand."

Of course, I wouldn't. I don't have a calling or a mission. Some big reason for existing. I work for white men, and I always will.

"I'll stay too." I cross my arms.

"You crazy? Those men want to put a bullet in you. Go back to Mama. Let her know that I'm all right. She's liable to hear something."

There he goes again. My big brother bossing me around. I eye him, but he seems to be sure-footed now, and his voice pours forth smooth and normal. He'll be all right.

"Fine." I storm off through the woods, twigs and leaves crackling under my feet.

A cool breeze whips around me as I tromp through my worn path in between Mingo's church and the borders of my farm. I scoff. *My farm.* It will never be mine. If the federal government would have made good on what they said they were going to do, I—along with my brothers and sisters and Mama—would have had our own forty acres, free and clear. But no. The Freedmen's Bureau gave us a plot of land only to snatch it away months later. That's what we all get for trusting a white man.

How is being free that much different from being a slave? Mama still toils in the cane field from dawn 'til dusk day in and day out. Instead of receiving her rations, she works for her food.

How long has it been since I joined my mother in the fields? Nearly a season, surely. The work's far too strenuous for the measly amount the planters pay me. I make more money by jobbing and can work my own hours, traveling from farm to farm. Plus, the look on the men's faces when they see me show up and split wood nearly as good as any man! Surprising them like that is worth more than the wages I earn.

But Mama? What's the difference between how she's living now and how she lived before the war?

I asked Mama as much, late at night in the same cabin we lived in during slavery.

"You're still living like you're a slave. Breaking your back for the master, sunup 'til sundown. Living without any luxuries. Why?" I paced through the small space, five steps to the bed, five steps back to the table.

Mama sat still and steady in her chair. "I did it then because I had to. I do it now because I choose to. There's a difference."

"From the outside you can't tell a lick of difference."

"Oh, child, everything important happens on the inside."

I squinted down at her, trying to twist the meaning out of what she said, but not being able to wring a bit of sense from it. Most things she says drip with importance, which is why all the freedmen and freedwomen call her "Mama Mercy" and "The Mother of Israel." Scores of people look up to Mama, but I can't seem to wrap my mind around her.

I slow as I come to the clearing and scan the road in the distance. My eyes roam my surroundings, all senses tingling, ready to flee at the first sign of danger. Are the riders out looking for me? What if they find me here? What if I put Mama or my brothers and sisters in danger? But I have nowhere else to go.

The rustle of leaves and the song of crickets and toads meet my ears, but no horses' hooves. No men's voices. No crackle of fire. I take a deep breath and emerge into the vast space, vulnerable as a deer to a hunter.

I swallow, hitch up my skirt, and run for home.

4

———

April 2020
Renada, Nebraska

The doorbell rang, and Natassa wiped the counter one last time before shuffling to the front door. She peeked through the peephole to ensure the delivery personnel had left, then opened the door. She almost reached for the package on her front porch before remembering. Doubling back to the kitchen, she grabbed her all-natural disinfectant spray and a pair of disposable gloves.

She disinfected the package and brought it inside with the relieved air of someone who had just come through a decontamination chamber.

"Gosh, Mom. Paranoid much?" Daniel smirked from behind his laptop where he sat cross-legged on the sofa next to his brother.

"Just being safe." She said it so much lately it had become her mantra. Brandon even accused her of mumbling it in her sleep.

"Sure thing. Hey, do you want me to go take a bath in hand sanitizer?" Daniel chortled, and David snorted.

She squirted the disinfectant spray toward them, dispersing a fine mist in their direction. "No, I think that'll do."

"Hey!" Both boys swatted the air in unison.

"What? It's made of botanical ingredients. It won't hurt you. I didn't get it in your eyes, did I?"

David groaned. The side of Daniel's mouth twitched. Though Daniel was in high school and David in college, both boys had a full day of online school to complete.

"Get back to work." She scrunched up her face and threw the boys a sassy smile over her shoulder as she walked to the kitchen.

"Mom, I need help with math." Hope thrust a packet of papers toward her. "The whole packet is due tomorrow. It's like a zillion pages."

"Mom." Faith careened into the kitchen. "I can't find the right link for my Zoom meeting, and it starts in three minutes."

"It's on Class Dojo," Natassa said, then reconsidered. "Wait, no. Google Classrooms." Or was that Hope's information?

"Well, that's just great." Daniel slammed his laptop shut.

"What's the matter with you?" Natassa turned to him, tension knotting in her shoulders.

"They officially canceled my high school graduation. I won't get to walk across the stage."

Her heart sank. She wouldn't be able to see her second-born son receive his diploma in his cap and gown. "Oh, honey. I'm so sorry."

Daniel huffed.

"We'll still throw you a party," she offered without thinking. "Well, maybe a Zoom party. I'll bake you a cake?"

"Whatever." Daniel stood and stormed off, tripping over a throw pillow on his way. He growled and threw it toward the couch.

She turned back to Hope, who still held the papers out as if they, too, needed disinfecting. A quick glance at the first page caused Natassa's pulse to quicken. She'd be useless in helping with this *new* kind of math.

"Mom, Daniel's videobombing my English class." Faith's quiet whine grated on Natassa's nerves.

"I am not. I was just grabbing a glass of water."

"He did bunny ears."

Natassa scurried toward the kitchen table, where Faith sat in front of her computer. "Daniel, come on. You are seventeen years old," Natassa whispered to keep the entire eighth-grade English class from hearing her.

"Oh, is that how old I am? Thanks for letting me know."

"Daniel, cool it." Brandon came down the steps. His tone and stare shut Daniel up, sending relief coursing through Natassa. He walked straight toward her and kissed the top of her head. "How's it going?"

She chuckled. If she didn't laugh, she'd cry.

Brandon put his hands on her shoulders and began to knead. "Whoa, babe. If your muscles get any more tense, you'll turn into a statue. I might need to go to night school to get licensed in massage therapy."

"Mmm." She rolled her neck from side to side. "Sounds good."

"Yeah, you could pick up a second job and get me a beamer for graduation." Daniel scoured the pantry.

"There are pretzels you can have. Or apples in the fridge." Natassa turned, putting her arms around Brandon's shoulders. "If you become a massage therapist, I have to be your only client. I don't want you touching other women."

"There goes my beamer."

She laughed, then squeezed Brandon's shoulder. "You remember I have my OB appointment at one, right? You got off work? You can run things on the home front?"

Brandon's brow furrowed. "Don't you want me to come with you? The boys can handle things here."

She bit her lip. "I'm not so sure."

"Babe, lower your standards. This is crisis schooling. It's not going to be perfect. The stress level around here is through the roof, and that's not healthy for anyone."

She threw her hands up in exasperation. "Their teachers expect—"

"Their teachers will understand. Everyone is doing the best they can, and we all have to adjust. No one is flunking this year, babe."

If only she could believe him. But he didn't understand the pressure of corralling five kids into online schoolwork. This wasn't herding cats—this was dressing cats in tutus and expecting a ballet performance. Even so, she had to keep trying. She wouldn't be the reason her children fell behind.

He looked around, lips pressed together as if deep in thought. "Okay, this is what we're going to do. Everyone, drop what you're doing. We're going for a walk."

Faith's mouth fell open. "I'm in the middle of a Zoom class."

Brandon hunched over her computer screen and typed in the chat box. *Faith has to leave to take care of a health thing.*

"A health thing?" Natassa tilted her head.

"Vitamin D. I've read it's one of the best ways to protect yourself from this virus."

"Do we need our masks?" Faith asked.

"No. We'll stay six feet away from all other humans. I promise. No masks. Just vitamin D and fresh air. All of you. Out. Now." Brandon tossed a confused look to Natassa. "Where's Mercy?"

"In her room again. She hardly ever comes out anymore. She does her schoolwork up there by herself all day."

"Go get her, will you?"

She nodded, steeling herself as she climbed the stairs. Not another battle. Please, no. Lately, any conversation with Mercy turned into a fight. Her nine-year-old was surly and short-tempered. Moody. *Isn't she too young to be a brooding teenager?* Mercy didn't budge when Natassa tried to pry her open for a heart-to-heart. *Lord, what's going on? How can I reach her?*

She knocked on the door.

When Mercy didn't answer, she went in. Mercy sat at her desk with her computer open and a teacher speaking on Zoom. A notebook lay on the desk, full of doodling. Natassa took a step toward it, and Mercy's eyes bulged.

She snapped the notebook shut. "What?" Mercy asked with panic laced in her voice.

"We're all going on a family walk. Right now. Daddy's orders."

Mercy pursed her lips. "David too?"

Natassa nodded. "Yep. Everyone."

"Okay." Mercy shut her laptop and bounded out of the room and down the steps.

Natassa cast a long look at the notebook lying closed on the desk. Why hadn't Mercy wanted her to see it? Maybe she could find a way to peek inside when Mercy wasn't there. Children didn't have a right to privacy, did they? Especially not when something was wrong, and they wouldn't talk about it. Natassa had to figure out what was going on with her little girl, and soon.

~

"You worry too much. She's fine." How did Brandon do that? Slough off all the concerns that hung on to her like clinging vines. His shoulders were relaxed, his hands loose on the steering wheel. He looked so confident and at ease. As if the world hadn't gone absolutely crazy around him. As if his family wasn't swimming in stress and his youngest daughter wasn't wading through some invisible internal crisis.

"She certainly doesn't seem fine." Natassa adjusted her seat belt around her blossoming midsection. Maybe she did worry too much, but could he blame her? Disappointment and devastation had followed her around for the past few years like her shadow, always lurking just behind her. Three babies. She'd lost three babies. After having such an easy time getting pregnant the first five times, she'd never dreamed of such heartache.

They'd been blissfully unaware of the tragedy that awaited them before the first miscarriage. She had no premonition, not even a singular thought that her pregnancy could end in anything other than a newborn cooing in her arms. Different people had miscarriages, not her. Everyone had their story of pain. She had hers, for sure, but it didn't include that specific loss.

Until it did.

They hadn't yet come up with a name for the baby when she started bleeding. Why would they? She was only twelve weeks along. They had plenty of time to settle on a name. After she'd miscarried the oh-so-small-but-very-distinct female child in their bathroom, she'd clung to the child and wept over the loss. Their baby girl needed a name.

A week later, she sat on the steps of St. Anthony's Baptist and wept into Bethany's arms. Old Ezra sat on the bottom step, hat on the ground in front of him, just as he had the first day that she'd met him. The man she once thought to be a beggar had turned out to be one of the wisest men she knew. She asked him to help her think of a name that meant life. A name to help remind her that her baby girl lived, even if not on earth. She lived in the arms of Jesus. Ava, he'd offered. Ava means *breath of life*. She'd named her baby a week after burying her under the weeping willow tree in her backyard.

When she got pregnant again the next year, she needed to choose a name right away. She would never again bury a nameless child. Once again, she consulted Old Ezra. They settled on Asa, which means *healer*. This baby would be a healing balm to their hearts. What were the odds it would happen a second time? Yet, it did. She started bleeding at ten weeks.

Were they crazy to try again? But how could they let that heartache be the end of their story? Their family couldn't end that way. Except nothing could compare to the devastation of losing Havilah at twenty-four weeks. Not that Ava and Asa weren't every bit as much her children and as much a part of her heart. But the third time took the wind out of her, the breath, the life. As the weeks went on without problems, she had opened her heart and allowed herself to hope again. When the twelve-week milestone passed, then fifteen, then twenty, hope grew as her stomach did—stretching out its arms to embrace new life. She went to the next doctor's appointment full of excitement. Then dread dropped like lead into her body as the ultrasound technician searched for a heartbeat that was not there. She walked numb and unbelieving into the hospital to deliver a baby who would never take her first breath.

She worried too much?

Surely, she was justified.

Her phone gave a soft ding. A text message sent by Breanna: *Have a great appointment. Get a pretty picture of Charity for me.*

Charity somersaulted inside her belly, almost as if she knew Breanna was thinking about her. She was thirty weeks along now. If Charity decided to make her entrance today, she'd have a ninety-nine percent chance of survival. They were almost in the clear. Peace washed over her. Everything was going to be okay this time. This baby would breathe her first breath, wail loud and strong in the delivery room. This baby would have first words and first foods and first steps. Charity would live. A supernatural assurance inside bolstered Natassa, though fear came often to challenge it.

But Mercy. What was going on with her sweet Mercy?

"She drew something in her notebook that she didn't want me to see. I feel like I need to look at it, Brandon. It might give me a clue as to what's up with her."

"Okay. Go for it." He shrugged. No big deal.

"How can I get it from her without her noticing? I don't know if you realize this, but no one leaves the house. Like, ever."

"Easy. We'll stop on the way home and pick up ice cream. I'll dish some up for her. While we eat, you go and play spy." He threw her a lopsided smile.

"Yeah, okay." She nodded. "As long as you save me some ice cream."

5

April 2020
Chicago, Illinois

DeAndre jaunted down the last five steps of his apartment building and threw open the door to welcome the sunshine. A fresh breeze sent an abandoned 7-Eleven cup skidding across the sidewalk. The promise of rain in the air penetrated his mask. He'd bought Janell a hot pink mask that said, "Hot Mama," and in return, she'd bought him one that said, "Who's Your Daddy?" He wore it around her and the boys, but not today. When he was on his own, a plain black mask would do.

Turning right onto State Street, he began the two-block walk. The pandemic had shaken Chicago to the core. Months ago, the streets had been full of hundreds of people—businessmen, shoppers, tourists. Now, the Loop resembled a ghost town. He spotted maybe fifteen people walking the streets, including Harold, the friendly Loop Ambassador who strode the sidewalks picking up discarded masks and gloves.

Ralph, one of the homeless men who frequented their city block, was still out to his left, sitting on the fire hydrant, feeding the birds bread crumbs. Dozens of pigeons flocked around him, one sitting on his knee, all eager for a bite. A sliver of normalcy in a world gone crazy.

"Hey, Ralph. How are you, man?" DeAndre said with a nod.

Ralph waved. "Fine. You?"

"Fine."

Who was he kidding? Was anyone really fine?

Groggy, DeAndre stumbled over his own feet as he passed on top of a metal grate. He wouldn't normally even register the dull, hollow thud, but without the noises of traffic, construction, and chatter, it sounded overly loud to his tired ears. He'd slept a total of six hours in two days. Prior to that, he hadn't gotten more than a two-hour stretch of sleep in three weeks. He brought his hand up to rub his eyes but then dropped it. *Don't touch your face.* He stuffed his hands in his pockets.

Three weeks? Had it really been three weeks since Janell gave birth to Joe? Days and nights blurred together in a fuzzy mess of crying, shushing, rocking, and diapers. He didn't remember their son Java being so difficult. Then again, after three years, his memory of that newborn phase could be a little hazy.

DeAndre waited at the crosswalk as a car and truck zipped past. So strange to see the streets not teeming with vehicles. And no buses either. Mayor Lightfoot had paused public transit. Most businesses had closed—anything nonessential. That included his. Of course, when had art ever been considered essential? But many people suffered during the economic shutdown. He didn't have the right to complain. They'd saved a bit. Enough to carry them through for nearly a year, hopefully. And even though galleries weren't open, and the majority of people didn't want to spend what money they had on such luxuries, some people found they had extra time to redecorate. Online sales trickled in.

His fingers itched for a brush. He hadn't left the apartment for three weeks. Mama had kept them stocked with groceries, meals, and necessities. She'd even procured toilet paper somehow. As thankful as he was for her care, he might have jumped out of his skin if he hadn't gotten out of the house. He'd asked the couple across the hall if they would watch Java for a few hours while he checked on his studio. Janell planned to nap when Joe did. *If* Joe did.

A sweet satisfaction enveloped him at the sight of Scott Studios. His haven. His small corner of everything good and right in the world. He turned the key in the lock and stepped inside, relishing the sound of the bell jingling. The heady mix of tempera oils and solvents wafted to his nostrils. Heaven.

He hung his mask on the coatrack, then stepped past the half dozen easels displaying an assortment of his work at different angles and price ranges. Several more pieces hung on the wall above two emerald-green accent chairs. He stepped through the folding dividers separating the gallery area from his studio, his sanctuary.

Graffiti art splashed the walls in bright, bold colors. St. Anthony's Baptist Church in the far-right corner and his pa driving a blue convertible on the left wall. Janell's painted figure stood dead center, her hair whipping around her face as if he'd left the window open, her hands on her hips and mouth tipped in a teasing smile. He'd painted Java clinging to her leg. Of course, that was a year ago, and his boy looked much bigger now. On the right wall, cardinals perched in the branches of an oak with a river running beneath them. The rest of the space he'd filled with geometric shapes and lines, covering every inch of brick. Only then had he set up shop, filling the space with easels and canvases, mason jars, brushes, and palettes.

Janell's desk sat in the far corner, their wedding picture perched on one side, and on the other, a family picture minus the newcomer Joe. Papers typically lay splayed across the top, along with three or four coffee cups. Now she worked from home, stuffing their miniscule den space with budgets, bills, inventories, and orders.

Because as much as he wanted to claim this space as his, it wasn't. Not legally. Not on paper.

It belonged to Janell.

When they'd first arrived in Chicago, he'd been so naive. Thinking his past wouldn't matter. Thinking his talent could make up for a criminal record. Janell had saved every penny of profit from his artwork during his time in prison. What didn't go into a fund to help Tia get on her feet went into savings for a down payment on a studio. She'd scrimped and saved for their future home. He'd painted in prison for the opportunity to paint in freedom in the future. They arrived in the Windy City with cash in hand, ready to make offers.

But no one would rent to a felon.

Finally, a sweet spot on State Street opened up. Prime property at a reasonable price. Janell wisely suggested DeAndre hang low. She'd be the one to meet with the agent. She'd be the one to fill out the paperwork. She'd rent the property, own the business. DeAndre would merely be her employee.

What a way to trample a man's pride.

But it worked. So, what did it matter?

And after a year of renting a studio apartment in Mama's neighborhood, a two-bedroom condo opened up just two blocks away from the art studio. Good thing because Janell was eight months pregnant with Java. Even though Mama and Harlem had warmed up to her, she wanted a bit more space in between her and her in-laws. If forced to admit it, living farther away would give him a sense of freedom as well. Harlem was a decent man, but he and his friends at the jazz club were constantly trying to drag DeAndre into their political debates.

DeAndre stretched, scanning the tubes of acrylic paint on the shelf in front of him. What did he want to create? Only vague ideas surfaced, but his hands buzzed, needing to move, to breathe life. Sometimes, he brainstormed ahead of time, sketching his plans out first using graph paper. But today, he just plunked a canvas onto an easel, confident that after three weeks of idleness, something of tempered genius would rush out.

On sunny days, the wall-to-wall windows in front filled the studio with natural light that shone over the six-foot dividers with no problem. But today, the sun played indecisive, peeking out for a few minutes only to sulk away behind a cloud tinged with gray. He flipped on the floor lamp and angled it toward the easel. He grabbed an apron off the wall hook and wrapped it around himself, then snatched a palette. Squeezing a rainbow of colors into the indentations, he inhaled. How he'd missed that smell. Janell thought him crazy, but she was the only thing that smelled better to him.

Sometimes, he'd stick his earbuds in and listen to Lecrae or Bryann Trejo while he worked. Or maybe Marvin Sapp, depending on what he painted. But today, he basked in the quiet. No screaming or crying. Just blissful silence.

Before he became conscious of the blurring colors, he'd fashioned a face. The subtle lines he swept under the eyes, creasing the temples, and the forehead placed the mocha-colored man at around forty years. The goatee looked solid, with only the slightest touches of gray sneaking in to steal his youth. The eyes shown tawny brown, shades brighter than his skin. DeAndre painted a navy bucket hat covering all but a few of his twisted curls. The lines of his mouth betrayed him as serious and steady.

A father.

He had painted another father.

His trademark as of late.

He washed his brush, clinking it against the mason jar of water, then dried it on the rag half hanging out of the front pocket of his apron. He surveyed his work while he wiped his hands on the other side of the rag.

He could paint breathtaking landscapes. His paintings of the sights along Lake Shore Drive had been a hit. But he kept coming back to this face of a father.

Maybe it was the pressure of raising black boys to be black men in a society where their value would be constantly questioned. Maybe it was because he'd lost his own father when he was only a boy, saw his crumpled body in the street after hearing gunshots. Maybe it was because his status as a felon buzzed in his ears, forever challenging his ability to be a good father.

Java idolized cops, God love him. He was hooked on Paw Patrol. His toy police car had to be right next to his bed for him to fall asleep. He'd asked for handcuffs for Christmas and Janell had bought him a whole officer's kit with the cuffs, a walkie-talkie, and a badge. DeAndre just stared at those flimsy plastic cuffs, remembering the metal ones around his wrists and ankles and how they had rubbed his skin raw.

How could he be a good father to his boy? To both his boys?

Oh, Lord! Why'd you give me boys?

And even though they had just as much of Janell's genes as his, society would see them as black boys. And then they'd see them as black men.

Janell didn't get it.

A year ago, he'd been driving when a cop pulled them over. Janell in the passenger's seat, Java strapped in his car seat in back. DeAndre couldn't stop shaking as he put his hands on the dash. But Janell? She'd been furious.

"Ma'am, are you okay?" the officer asked her when he stooped to peer through DeAndre's open window.

"Am I okay? Of course, I'm okay. What's that supposed to mean? This is my *husband*. That little boy back there"—she pointed—"is our *son*. What did *my husband* do wrong? Why did you pull us over?" She leaned forward, arms flailing.

"Janell, stop," he whispered through clenched teeth. What was she trying to do? Get them killed? Didn't anyone ever teach her not to talk to a cop like that?

"Speeding. Ten miles over the limit. Forty-five in a thirty-five."

DeAndre's brow furrowed as he studied the GPS on the screen in front of him with a clearly marked forty-five mph sign in the corner. But he bit his lip and said nothing.

"I'm sorry, officer, but our GPS clearly says the speed limit's forty-five, and the sign just a half-mile back said the same. If it changed, it had to be very recently because we missed it, and so did our GPS." Janell tilted her head and offered a sweet smile, trying another approach.

Beads of perspiration broke out on DeAndre's brow. His hands grew sweaty on the dash. Why wouldn't she shut up?

The officer pointed behind him, and DeAndre turned to see a speed limit sign about a yard behind the police car. "It *clearly* says thirty-five." He smacked his gum and pulled out a notepad. "License and registration."

"Wait. You're seriously not going to give us a ticket, are you?"

"License and registration." He shifted his weight and leveled his gaze.

DeAndre coughed, hoping she would get the point. He held his hands in the air. "I'm going to reach for my wallet to get my license and insurance card."

"Is this really necessary?" Janell's voice dripped with sweetness, and he raised his eyebrows, willing her to shut her mouth.

The cop took DeAndre's info without answering and walked back to his car, promising to return with a ticket.

As soon as he was out of earshot, DeAndre laid into her. "What do you think you're doing? You don't argue with a cop. Ever. You just shut your mouth and do what he says."

"But he's being completely unreasonable!"

"Yeah. And?"

"It's not fair. He shouldn't be allowed to get away with it."

"Guess what. He does. Because he's got the badge."

They'd driven home in silence, and it'd taken them nearly twenty-four hours to kiss and make up. He'd forgiven her. She hadn't known better. Why would she? But if they were going to partner together to raise black boys, she'd have to get a clue. Teach your boy to do anything other than one hundred percent comply with a cop and he may not come home to you one day.

Or maybe Java would be the one with the badge. Maybe he could be a part of bringing justice to his people instead of wringing it from them. But how could DeAndre raise him right? With his past, his background, he was entirely unqualified.

He ripped off the apron, hung it on the hook, and spun toward the door. Grabbing his mask from the coatrack, he thrust the door open, sending the bell jangling, and stepped into the chilly drizzle.

~

Something was off. That was obvious as soon as Brenda cracked open the door. DeAndre's across-the-hall neighbor eyed him suspiciously, only opening the door wide enough for him to see her frowning face and the form of her husband, Kent, hovering behind her. Where was Java?

"I hope he behaved himself." DeAndre tried to push a smile past his concern.

"Your son's not the problem." She clutched the doorknob with one hand and braced the doorframe with the other. Was she barring his entrance? Did she think he'd force his way inside?

"Excuse me?" His brow furrowed.

"I did a search on the sex offender website. You're on it." Kent widened his stance and crossed his arms. Was he bracing for a challenge? Brenda's eyes bored into him.

DeAndre's breath left him, and his heart seized. He lowered his eyes. What could he say? "I see." His voice dripped with defeat.

"You stay away from us, you hear? We don't want nothing to do with you."

"I understand." He briefly lifted his gaze in acknowledgement, but the accusation in their eyes stung too much to continue holding his head up. He didn't even see them gather his son, only felt them thrusting him out the door. "Hey, buddy." He tried to turn the corners of his mouth upward for his boy, but they felt weighted down.

"You be a good boy now, Java." Brenda bent low to make eye contact. "You grow up and be good. Not like your daddy. He's a bad man. You be a good one, you hear?"

Java looked back and forth between Brenda and DeAndre. DeAndre glared at her, then snatched Java's hand and led him into their condo, pushing quick, hot breaths out of his mouth. He hung his mask and keys on the hooks by the door and kicked off his shoes. One went soaring into the coffee table with a thud.

"What in the world?" Janell craned her neck to look at him from her spot on the couch. Little Joe was scrunched over her shoulder, his face squished against a burp rag.

"Sorry," DeAndre mumbled.

"Daddy, are you a bad man?" Java bit his lip, eyes glistening.

He closed his eyes. Pressed his lips together. How in the world could he answer his boy? He didn't want to lie. But his gut plummeted at the thought of telling the truth. He opened his mouth, about to say, "Not anymore," but Janell's voice sounded like a bullhorn directly in front of him. His eyes sprang open.

"No." She squatted in front of Java, her hands squarely on his shoulders. He hadn't heard her walk over or even lay the baby on a blanket on the floor. "No, your daddy is not a bad man. He is a good man. A great man." The firm lines on her face shouted her fierce determination. Her eyes lit with indignation. She met his gaze. "Don't let anyone ever tell you that your daddy is a bad man."

6

———

May 2020
Renada, Nebraska

Mercy closed her laptop, filled her cheeks with air, then popped them with her palms. She'd just finished her last Zoom meeting of the year. School was over. Freedom! If only she had a twirly chair at her desk like her mom. She would spin and spin until the dizziness made her head float away.

David had finished his college semester the week before, but she still hadn't had any time to talk to him. Libby stuck to him like a leech. Mercy had watched a video about leeches in science class. She always pictured those ugly sucky things when Libby walked through the door. Why did Mom even allow David's girlfriend to be here? She wasn't family. She should be quarantining away from David. Six feet away. Mom followed all the rules for how to keep the coronavirus away. Why didn't she care that Libby brought her germs into their house and kissed them all over David's mouth?

Gross.

Mercy stood and stretched. Should she go into her closet and finish working on her painting of the bridge against the night sky? Her stomach rumbled. No. She wanted a snack first, and she should probably tell Mom she'd finished with school.

She grabbed her sketchbook off her desk and stuffed it in her pillowcase. No snooping eyes. The last time she'd gone downstairs to have ice cream with dad, she came back to find her stuff all turned around, as if someone had gotten into it. She closed the door behind her and then tried to scoot her bottom onto the banister to slide down like her sisters. Hope made it look so easy, but Mercy could never make it past a few inches before stumbling onto the stairs. She jogged down the rest of the steps to find her family hunched around the kitchen island, a carton of ice cream between them. Ice cream? Mom hardly ever let them eat ice cream. Only on really special occasions.

She stopped for a moment and stared at this group of people who looked alike, sounded alike, even laughed alike. They all fit together as they passed a bottle of chocolate syrup back and forth, chuckling about something she didn't understand. And were those maraschino cherries? Mercy loved maraschino cherries.

"Mercy, come on over." Dad finally noticed her and waved her over. "We're celebrating the last day of school."

She angled herself in David's direction, her steps small and slow.

"Where's Libby?" Her lip stuck out in a pout as she grabbed a bowl from the center of the island.

"She left on vacation with her family." He brought a heaping spoonful of ice cream to his mouth. Drips oozed over the sides of his spoon and splattered on the granite surface.

"I still think it's entirely too dangerous." Mom shook her head, eyes flying up to the ceiling in that way that said she was better than everyone.

David shrugged. "Flights are cheap right now."

"Is that worth their lives?" Mom wagged her head, then scoffed. "Cheap flights."

"Stop being so dramatic. They'll be fine." David spoke with his mouth full. It sounded like he'd just gotten back from the dentist.

"When she gets back, you're not allowed to see her for two weeks." Mom turned and dumped her bowl and spoon in the sink with a clatter.

"Oh, come on!"

"Two weeks." Mom pointed a finger at him.

David turned to Dad. "Seriously? She's being unreasonable."

"She's being safe." Dad clamped a hand on David's shoulder.

Mom's phone made a noise, and she snatched it from the counter. She tapped Dad on the shoulder. "Honey, the Denvers want to put an offer on the house on Hollaway."

Dad swallowed his spoonful before he spoke. "That's great."

"Yes, it is. Business has been so slow. I've got to get working on this." She climbed the stairs, texting as she went.

Dad dropped his bowl and spoon in the sink and followed Mom to their office.

"Let's go ride bikes," Hope said. She and Faith bounded out the front door, leaving their dishes sitting on the island, surrounded by drops of melted ice cream.

"Minecraft time." Daniel spun toward the living room, also leaving a mess behind.

David collected the discarded bowls and spoons, took them to the sink, squirted them off, and placed them in the dishwasher. As Mercy finished the last few bites of her ice cream, he put the syrup and cherries in the fridge, threw out the empty ice cream carton, and wet a rag.

They were alone together?

"I'll do it." She took the rag from David and wiped down the island as he cleaned off her bowl and put it away. Hopefully, she'd gotten on his good side by cleaning. "So," she said, "can we talk now."

"Hmm?"

"You told me we'd finish our conversation later. That's what you said at the baby shower. Can we talk now? Please?"

She turned to him and clasped her hands together. She stuck out her bottom lip for good measure.

David sighed. "Okay, kid. Let's go upstairs."

She took the steps two at a time, then crashed into her room and slid onto her bed. She patted the spot next to her, but David hadn't even gotten in there yet. When he appeared, his shoulders slumped. He closed the door behind him so quietly that she didn't hear it click.

She patted the bed again, and he sat cross-legged.

"Tell me everything." She stared him down, trying not to blink.

The slightest smile traced his lips, but it looked sad. His eyes looked sad too. "What have Mom and Dad told you? About your biological father?"

Mercy tilted her head. "Not much. Hardly anything really. They said a bad man put a baby in Mom's tummy, but that they both loved the baby so much they were happy to welcome it into their family. Happy to welcome me."

"You … uh … know about the birds and the bees, right?" He scrunched his nose.

She raised an eyebrow. What did animals and insects have to do with anything?

"You know where babies come from?"

She scoffed but averted her eyes. "Well, yeah. I'm not a dummy."

He cleared his throat. "Then, you know how … the man put the baby inside of Mom."

Mercy squirmed. She'd never thought about it. David took her hand, but she let it lay limp inside his.

"Look, that man hurt Mom. He forced himself on her. And made a baby. You. And he went to jail." David blew out a loud breath. "When your birth father was in jail, we found out that another guy put drugs into his drink that made him act different. Different from how he normally would act. Do you understand?"

Mercy shook her head. All the words he'd said swirled around her until nausea swirled in her gut. If only she could slow the words down so she could study them, force them to make sense, but they zipped past.

"I mean that the bad man—your biological father—maybe he isn't really a bad man. Maybe he is a good man who made a really bad choice. Maybe if his friend hadn't put drugs in his drink, he would have chosen differently."

She pressed her lips together. What were these feelings bubbling inside her? Was she sad or relieved? Did she feel mad or empty or thankful? She couldn't tell. Everything felt jumbled. The brew of emotions in her belly weren't all bad, were they? A sliver of light poked through the clouds.

"Do you remember Janell? She used to babysit for us, well, for the girls." David looked up at the ceiling for a moment. "I guess she never babysat you. You probably never met her. That was before you were born."

Janell? A spark of recognition lit within her. "I think I remember a Janell. Mom and I met her at the coffee shop. She likes brown people."

"Janell married your biological father." David shifted and sat with his knees together, hands pressed between them. "Janell is a good person. I don't think she'd marry a bad man." He looked Mercy in the eye. "So, I think that maybe your dad is …"

"A good man?" Mercy leaned forward, hope springing up within her.

"Maybe."

She stared straight ahead, eyes focusing on nothing much at all, her mind a blur. Her father. A good man. It could be true. What if it was? What would it change inside her? But what if David was wrong?

"How do you know all this?" She turned her attention back to David, eyes narrowing.

His face turned sheepish. "I follow him on Instagram."

She sat back, stunned. He followed her father on Instagram? Knew all about him all this time while she knew nothing? How could he keep her own father from her?

"What if …" David closed his eyes for a moment before opening them and staring straight at her. "What if I took you to meet him."

She jumped up. "Meet him? Meet my father? You'd do that?"

He nodded without a smile.

"Where is he?"

"Chicago."

"How would we go to Chicago?" She paced. "Mom would never let us go to Chicago. Not now. You heard what she said about Libby going on vacation." Plus, her mom hadn't shared anything about her birth father. Mom must not have wanted her to know about him." She faced David. "If Mom knew why we wanted to go to Chicago, she'd never ever let us go."

He dropped his shoulders and put out his hands in an offering. "I could tell her I'm taking you camping."

"Camping? It will never work. Mom wouldn't let you take me camping in a zillion years. Not with the coronavirus."

He smirked. "Don't underestimate me, Mercy Girl. I've always been able to sweet-talk Mom."

"There's no way." Mercy crossed her arms around herself.

"We'll see."

~

Two days later, Mercy waved back to her mother as David's fancy gray car glided out of the driveway.

"Be safe!" Mom shouted loud enough to be heard through the rolled-up windows.

David gave her two thumbs-up, and Mom threw her arms up like she always did when she was exasperated. Mom hated when he took his hands off the steering wheel, even for a second.

As soon as they turned the corner, leaving their mother as a fading blip in the rearview mirror, David let out a whoop. "Freedom!"

Mercy giggled. "I can't believe she let us go."

They'd shoved the trunk full of camping gear: a tent and sleeping bags, even a Coleman stove. Mom insisted Mercy pack two bottles of DEET-free bug spray along with four bottles of hand sanitizer "just in case." Plus, two extra masks.

David's car smelled like food, and she tried to figure out what kind. They played that game sometimes since he'd started working for DoorDash.

"Did you deliver Five Guys last night?"

"No. I had two orders from that Chinese place and a pizza order." He drummed his fingers on the steering wheel.

She sniffed. "Smells like burgers."

"Oh yeah. I did have a delivery from a burger joint. But not Five Guys."

She shrugged. "I was close."

He took a gulp of his water. Oh no. Hand off the wheel. Mom would flip.

"You're a pretty good liar." Mercy shifted in the back seat, adjusting her seat belt. Mom still forced her to ride in a booster seat even though none of her friends had to. Embarrassing.

"Yeah, well, I don't like lying. And I don't make a habit of it." He turned to glance at her. Mom would freak about him taking his eyes off the road. "But these are special circumstances. The end justifies the means."

The end of what? She rolled her eyes. "Whatever."

"How did you get her to agree?" Mercy's mouth twisted just like her insides. At least she would get the chance to see her father. But what did it mean that Mom had said yes? Didn't she think going anywhere outside their house was dangerous? Didn't she care about keeping them safe?

"She's been worried about you lately. I overheard her and Dad talking about it once. She's asked me a few times if I knew why you were so quiet and sulky."

"I'm not sulky." She crossed her arms over her chest.

"You spend most of your time holed up in your closet. You hardly talk to Mom."

Mercy tossed her shoulder up as if flipping away his concern.

"Anyway, I told her I wanted to spend some quality time with you, see if you'd open up and talk about what was bothering you. Since most everything is shut down, we can't hang out anywhere in public. But some campgrounds are open."

"So, basically, she wanted you to spy on me." Mercy's eyes narrowed.

David laughed.

"She probably wouldn't care if I got eaten by a bear."

David's laugher died. In the rearview mirror, she could see his brow furrow. "That's not true."

"It feels true." She looked at her hands. Dark hands that moved in a light world. Would she ever fit anywhere? She blew out a breath, eager to change the subject. "Where are we going? How are we going to find him? Do you know where he lives?"

"No. But I have a plan."

She shrugged. Okay. Good enough for her. She laid her head back and closed her eyes. "Can you turn some music on?"

"Sure. What do you want to hear?"

Her face scrunched up. "What about Drake?"

David chuckled. "Yeah, right. I'll already be ticking Mom off enough with all this. How about Mandisa?"

Mercy groaned and settled in for the ride.

7

———

1868,
Just Outside of New Orleans, Louisiana

I spot Mama's form in the distance, still and serene in her chair on our cabin's front porch. Moonlight casts a soft glow on the right side of her face. She isn't smiling, but neither is she frowning. Just sitting. Waiting. Waiting for me, again.

The grass swishes as I run toward the cabin. The place makes my stomach turn with all the memories it dredges up of my years as a slave. Mama stands as I approach. I take the steps two at a time, then press my hand to my middle, gasping air.

"Where were you this time, child?" Mama's voice remains even, her face untelling save for the slight dimpling of her forehead.

Why does Mama always call me child? I'm a grown woman, free to make my own choices, live my own life. But this isn't about me. "It's Mingo."

Mama's mouth twitches at the mention of her oldest son.

"He's okay." I gulp in another breath.

Mama closes her eyes and sighs deep, relief pooling out of her.

"But they tried to lynch him."

Mama startles. Her lips part. "No."

"When they left, I cut him down. He's alive. They burned his church, but he's alive."

Mama falls into her chair with a thud. "They didn't shoot him?"

"No. They hung him and left. Could have burned him but didn't. We're lucky."

"It ain't luck." Mama snaps her eyes closed again and lifts her hands high. "Hallelujah! Thank You, Lord for savin' my son."

I roll my eyes and fall to my knees in front of Mama. "*I* cut him down. You can be thankin' me."

Mama cups my face in her calloused hands. "Thank you, child. You're a brave one." She drops her hands and narrows her eyes. "But what were you doin' out there that late at night? I keep tellin' you to stay on the plantation after sundown."

"And I keep tellin' you that I'll not be bossed by any white man's rules."

Mama's voice shakes with conviction. "You gotta do what you gotta do to stay alive."

A sad smile graces my lips as my eyes plead for my mother to understand. "Your way of life ain't livin'."

With a huff, Mama stands and marches into the cabin.

I sigh and follow, closing the door quietly behind me. A solitary candle flickers on the table, causing shadows to shift across Kolle and Ayda sleeping in one bed and Omey and Mirsa in another. A johnnycake sits on a tin plate in my place.

Mama's gaze flicks to it. "Did you eat?" We keep our voices low.

"No." I plop onto a ladder-back chair and take a cold bite.

"I'm guessin' Mingo's pretty upset about Ole Faithful."

I groan. "That wretched church. He cares more for it than he does his own life."

Mama lowers herself into the chair across from me and levels her gaze. "Mingo would die for what he believes in. You would die just for being reckless."

"Mama—"

Mama holds up a hand. "No. You need to listen to what I'm sayin'. It's not safe for you here anymore. The same men that are out for your brother are after you too. You've got to get away from here."

The clink of metal on metal echoes as I drop my fork. "Away from here? Where? What are you saying?"

"You've got to leave, child. Go where it's safe."

I shake my head, willing my jumbled thoughts to come together. Leave? Mama wants me to leave? "You want me to be a squatter on the neighbor's land like Summer? Is that what you're sayin'?" I could do that. Construct a shelter and forage for food. Work only when I want to. Might be nice, actually.

Mama tilts her head like she does when I say something foolish. "For how long until they run you off? There's a fire in you that's liable to burn down everything around you. Thirsty flames lickin' all you set your eyes on. Fire is good and useful, but you've got to learn to contain it, love."

Love. Much better than child. I soften at the name and let the rebuke slide off.

"There's only one person I know who can encircle those flames and direct them without snuffing them out."

"Who?"

"Mama. My mama. Your grandmother. You've got to go to her. Go to my friend Susan Renald in Georgetown. She took your grandmother in to be her house slave when the master and missus sold me away from Hopecrest. She'll know where Mama is. There's no life for you here. Only bitterness like poison." Mama's voice radiates confidence. She nods once as if it's settled.

I scoot my chair back, my mouth gaping open. "You'd send me away?"

Mama props her elbows on the table and leans forward. "Away? Child! I'm sendin' you forward. Into a world of new beginnings and fresh possibilities. Into a place where you can thrive."

I stand and pace. "Well then, if it's so great, come with me."

Mama grows quiet, her gaze probing beyond the walls of the cabin. Into the past, maybe. Into a world I know nothing about. "My roots dug deep into this here soil. Your brothers and sisters. I can't just leave them. What's left for me in Georgetown? Only whispers of the past. A past that pains. My future is here."

"B-but," I stutter, "h-how will I get all the way to Georgetown?"

Mama's gaze drops to the table as she traces patterns on the wood with her finger. "Did I ever tell you how I traveled from Kentucky to South Carolina? By myself? When I was lookin' for my mother."

I go as still as a statue. Mama has never mentioned Kentucky or South Carolina, never mentioned life before marrying my father. "No."

Mama shakes her head and meets my gaze. "Well, if I did it when I was your age, you can do it too. You're smart as a whip. I know you'll figure it out."

I stare at my mother. How could this woman who has claimed to love me send me away? Alone, without a guide or an escort? Without family? I swallow. My throat burns. "I'll ask Mingo and Mayme to come with me."

~

In the morning, Mama kisses my hair through tears, then heads to the fields. I retrace my steps across the clearing and through the woods to the Lemonts' plantation where Mingo and Mayme live and work. I pass the charred remains of his church and keep walking for another half mile. My feet are familiar with this path. I job, sometimes, for the Lemonts— mostly chopping wood—but today, work is far from my mind.

I find Mingo's cabin empty and take off to the fields to find him. The Lemonts, like many planters, have switched from cane to cotton in hopes of salvaging their plantations. Let Mingo and Mayme mess with the prickly plants. I won't touch that unfamiliar crop.

I spot Mingo in the distance, Mayme in the row beside him. Their straw hats shade their faces from the sun, and though it's early, Mingo has already rolled up his sleeves. I rush to their side, swishing through the stalks.

Mayme sees me first and waves.

Mingo glances up from where his hand picks soft white balls and drops them into a sack. "What you doin' here, Sis?"

"I need to talk to you."

His gaze dips back to his work. "So, talk."

"Mama's sendin' me away." The sun beats down on my back, and I sweep my hair off my sweaty neck.

"Away where?" Mingo's fingers continue moving, quick and skilled. He doesn't look up.

"To Georgetown. Did you know that's where she's from?"

Mingo shakes his head and grunts.

"She's got a friend there. Our grandmother lives there. She wants me to go to them. Says it'll be safer for me." My head still spins with the revelation that Mama has a white friend who owned slaves.

Mingo shrugs. "Probably will be."

"Are you even hearin' me?" I put my hand on his shoulder.

He pauses, looks up at me, and wipes his forehead with his sleeve. The sun shines on the ugly welt on his neck and the bruise on his cheek.

"She wants me to go to Georgetown. Alone."

"Better than stayin' here and gettin' shot."

I stomp my foot, stirring up a circle of dust. "You're in greater danger than me."

Mingo lifts a shoulder and resumes his work.

"Go with me. You and Mayme. We can all go together. None of us is safe here," I plead with him, but he doesn't look up.

"My duty is to my flock."

I sigh. "To lead them to the Lord, not to a Republican president." If he hadn't tried to educate the freedmen about their voting rights, none of us would be in this mess.

"To guide them in truth and freedom."

"At the risk of your life?"

"Yes."

I throw up my hands. "Let someone else guide them."

Mingo stops and puts his hands on my shoulders. "You go. Find Mama's friend. Find our grandmother." He pats my cheek. "Find yourself along the way."

8

———

May 2020
Chicago, Illinois

DeAndre stumbled through the front door of his studio, sending the bell jangling over his head. He fumbled with his keys. Meant to shove them in his pocket, but they tumbled toward the floor. He snatched them from midair and dropped them on the desk. Slipping behind the dividers, he threw on an apron. The tips of his fingers sizzled with anticipation.

He'd awoken that morning with an idea, a crack of light—of inspiration—that gradually broadened throughout the morning until he couldn't hold it in anymore. Creative energy threatened to burst from him. His knee had shaken the breakfast table with such force that milk had sloshed out of Java's cereal bowl. He'd paced around like a caged bear, his imagination going wild with possibilities.

Janell had finally banished him. "Go on! Get out of here. Go paint, you big buffoon." She'd waved him off. Her expression conveyed exasperation, but her eyes twinkled, betraying the ruse.

He'd almost sprinted to the studio.

Faces. He'd painted faces for months. Faces of fathers. Some serious. Others who sported laugh lines and bemused expressions. Some had wisdom to pass on. Others seemed like they were treasuring each moment with their children. A few looked as if they bore immeasurable weight. He told stories through their eyes, through their eyebrows, and the creases around their mouths. Through the tilt of their chins. These paintings sold because the buyers could see their own fathers in the faces. Grandfathers or uncles. Mentors. Perhaps even a piece of themselves.

But a face only told where that man had been.

What if DeAndre could paint a picture of where that man could go?

He squirted paint into the palette so fast an array of it splattered onto his gray T-shirt. He blew out a breath. Janell would love that. But he didn't have time to do anything about it. He swished his brush into the brown and started swiping it across the waiting canvas.

Arms. Instead of a face, he painted open arms.

He bent and crouched, contorting his body as he painted angles and curves. And then, inside those open arms, what did he want to paint? What did this father have to give his children? What could he offer? DeAndre cocked his head, studying the arms, imagining the man behind them. Not money. Not position nor prestige. But he did have history, roots that went down deep and thick. Ancient. He had tears that had watered the ground, creating luscious vegetation for the generation after him to feast on.

The man had a resilience to pass on. How could DeAndre paint resilience? Strength? He rattled his brush around in the mason jar of water, washing it clean, then swiped the bristles against the sides of the jar. He picked up a new brush and dipped it into the gray. A steel cord. Strong enough to lift weight. Resilient enough to weather the elements. DeAndre wove it around the tree roots.

What else?

He had a story, a testimony. DeAndre started to paint an open book, the pages on the left filled in with illegible script.

The pages on the right, blank. He wanted to paint colors exploding from the book, dark and light, tragedy and triumph. He dipped his brush into the forest green.

The door creaked open, and the bell clanged.

DeAndre paused, brush held in midair. His brow furrowed. He must have forgotten to lock the door in his haste. Probably someone window shopping.

Should he tell them the gallery was closed? But what if they wanted to make a purchase? He shouldn't turn down a sale.

"Be right with you." He sighed and slid his palette and brush onto the shelf. He wiped his hands on the rag in his apron and stepped out from behind the divider.

A boy stood by the front door with his hands shoved in his pockets. A young man, really. He shifted his weight from one foot to the other, his mouth twitching back and forth from a forced smile to a deer-in-the-headlights expression. DeAndre flicked his gaze from the boy to the young girl beside him. She looked familiar. Where had he seen her before?

"Sorry. Do we need masks?" The boy pointed toward DeAndre's face. "We left ours in the car. We can go get them."

DeAndre's hand flew up to his mouth. His mask. He'd forgotten to take it off when he came in. He'd been so eager to get started, so consumed by his imagination.

He snapped it off and held it in his hand.

Who's Your Daddy?

Janell had washed his plain black mask, and it wasn't dry yet, so he'd worn the one she'd given him.

The girl stared at him with wide eyes, her mouth clamped shut. She looked like she'd seen a ghost.

Man, she looked familiar. His mouth twisted as he racked his brain trying to place her.

"You're DeAndre Scott?" The boy's voice cracked with the question.

"The one and only." DeAndre tilted his head, eyeing the two visitors. Definitely not serious buyers. Who were they? Why were they here? "How can I help you?"

"You're my dad." The girl spoke in a rush, her words tumbling out and sweeping toward him, cascading around him. Echoing in his ears.

"Mercy?" He stumbled back and gripped the desk behind him, steadying himself.

She nodded. Could her eyes get any wider? Questions flew out of them. Questions and hopes and dreams. They shot out of her big brown eyes and hit him square in the chest. He pressed his hand over his heart, applying pressure to keep it from beating out of his rib cage. To keep from unraveling.

"Why are you here? How did you find me?" He shook his head. Did he sound callous? Hopefully not. Confusion buzzed around his head. Would answers silence it?

"She wanted to meet you." The boy tilted his head toward the girl.

She bit her lip and nodded.

"I need to sit." DeAndre whirled around and ran his hands through his hair. He took a few deep breaths and pulled Janell's chair out from behind the desk. He gestured to the accent chairs. "Sit." Then he plopped down, the chair bouncing with his weight.

"Does your mom know you're here?"

Mercy opened her mouth, but the boy spoke before she got a word out. "Yeah. She's cool with it. She told me to take Mercy here. I'm David, her brother." He extended his hand, and DeAndre leaned forward and shook it. It was probably the first time he'd shaken someone's hand since COVID started.

David pulled his hand away, a streak of green on his palm.

DeAndre cringed. "Sorry." He handed David the rag.

"No problem." David scrubbed the paint off.

Mercy blinked. Stared.

"She's cool with it?" DeAndre eyed David, not convinced, but David held his gaze. Steady. Confident. Maybe he told the truth.

"How old are you?" His eyes explored Mercy's face. There were definite traces of the little girl who sat in the booth next to Natassa all those years ago. He'd recognized her, all right. But were there traces of his face in hers? He couldn't tell.

"I'm nine." Her mouth wobbled into a smile that dissipated as she bit her lip. Her little legs bounced up and down, making the leather of the chair squeak.

"Nine." He sighed. It'd been nine years since he'd screwed up his life. And nine years since God redeemed it. Now, his daughter sat in front of him, wanting to know him. He swallowed.

Who was he kidding?

Mercy wasn't his daughter. She wasn't his anything. She didn't belong to him.

He should send her back. Back to her real mother and father. Her true family.

He was a rapist. Not a father. Not to her.

But she looked at him with her big solemn eyes like she needed something from him, like he could fill a hole inside of her. He had no right to open his heart to her, his arms to her. And yet her eyes beckoned him with questions.

Nine.

He had been nine when someone gunned his pa down, leaving the man dying in the street. The shooter stole his father from him and left him with so many questions that no one could answer.

Mercy had questions.

Questions he *could* answer.

How could he fail her? No. Not now.

He fiddled with the mask in his lap, a dab of green on the edge from where he had wiped it off. *Who's Your Daddy?* He wasn't, was he? She already had a daddy. A good one. But Natassa's husband couldn't teach Mercy what it meant to move as a black person in a white world. He couldn't speak to that place inside her identity and call it forth into something she could be proud of. Confident in. He didn't have black blood in his roots, black ink in his story, black strength in his steel.

DeAndre did.

He had open arms that she could step into.

He shouldn't, yet how could he resist? "Do you want to come over for dinner?"

Both of them smiled as their shoulders dropped, relief etching their features.

"Yes." David grinned at Mercy, who returned the gesture.

"Let me call my wife."

~

DeAndre passed the Caesar salad to Mercy on his left while eyeing David who sat at the end of the table. The boy had just heaped his plate with thirds of spaghetti and garlic bread. Is that how teenagers ate? DeAndre had better be selling a whole lot more art by the time his boys reached that age. Their grocery bill would skyrocket.

"So, David." Janell put down her knife and fork and directed her attention to the boy. "What are your plans for the night? Do you have reservations at a hotel?"

He shook his head and shrugged her question away. "Nah. We've got a tent in the trunk. I just need to find a place to pitch it."

DeAndre coughed. "Pitch a tent? In Chicago?"

"Yeah. You got any ideas?"

Ideas? What did Mama always tell him when he was a teen? *Your upstairs brain is still under construction, Dre.* She'd read it in some book.

"I can search for campgrounds nearby, but I'm not aware of any that are close." Janell's brow knit in concern. "And I'm not sure what's open right now."

David shoved a forkful of spaghetti into his mouth. "Don't worry. I'm sure we'll find some place."

Janell pushed her chair back. Her eyes darted to him. "DeAndre, can you help me with something in our room?"

"Uh, sure." He tossed his napkin on his plate and followed her to their bedroom, closing the door behind him.

"There is no way I can let them pitch a tent in some park in the middle of Chicago, DeAndre." Janell flung her arms out, her whisper panicked.

"I know."

"What was Natassa thinking? Sending them out here like this in the middle of a pandemic with only a tent for accommodations?" Her voice came out as a hiss.

He only shook his head, not trusting his voice. Did Natassa even know the two of them were in Chicago, much less send them here? He didn't know the woman that well, but this kind of idea didn't seem to be in her wheelhouse. But if he told Janell his suspicions, she'd make him call Natassa. And no. Not yet. Tomorrow, sure. But tonight, he would get to know Mercy a little.

Lord, forgive me.

"They can stay here." He said it as if the idea had just occurred to him, as if it had materialized out of thin air and not like he'd been hashing over it ever since he'd called Janell earlier.

"Yeah." Janell ran a hand through her hair. "I guess I could put the blow-up mattress in the den for Mercy."

"And David can have the couch."

"That could work. We don't have a lot of extra space here." Janell glanced around at their small bedroom.

"We have enough."

~

The den was little more than a closet, and with Janell's desk at the far end, there was hardly enough room to walk around the inflatable twin mattress to get to it. If Janell needed anything from there, she'd have to step on top of the bed to get it.

What their condo lacked in space, it made up for in light. Wall-to-wall windows stretched six feet high, displaying the city. They could even see glimpses of the lake from their balcony and more from the building's rooftop patio. The view from his window made the world seem big and him small in it. And yet, he was anchored in a city that always moved around him.

He couldn't tell what Mercy thought as she sat on the edge of the bed, knees to her chest, staring out into the city lights. Did she feel big or small? Anchored or spinning? She wore *Frozen II* pajama pants and a button-up pajama shirt.

"Are you going to be warm enough?" He stood at the edge of the room, leaning against the doorframe, afraid to come any closer. He didn't have a right to draw near to this little girl. His little girl, and yet not his. Not at all.

"This is good." She clutched the fluffy white fleece blanket Janell had brought her.

"Do you need anything else?"

"A story?" There they were again, those wide eyes that pulled at him.

"The only story books we have around here are probably too babyish for you. Java can't get enough of Paw Patrol and Daniel Tiger, and I don't think you'd like me to read you any of those."

"Do you know any stories by heart?"

He chuckled. She was definitely persistent. "I'm not sure, kiddo."

"Didn't your mom tell you stories when you were little?"

He closed his eyes for a moment, considering. "Yeah. I guess she did. 'Br'er Rabbit and the Tar Baby'. 'Anansi the Spider'." He smiled as he remembered Mama's animated voice and solemn warnings.

Mercy raised to her knees and leaned forward. "Tell me!"

He chuckled. "Alright, then." He knelt in the hallway outside of the door, not wanting to overstep by sitting on her bed. He racked his memory, trying to get all the details straight. "I'll tell you the story of 'Br'er Rabbit and the Tar Baby'."

As he related the classic African folktale about the little person made of tar that Br'er Fox concocted to trick Br'er Rabbit, Mercy sat forward, enraptured. She laughed when DeAndre told how Br'er Rabbit punched the tar baby and got stuck inside, and then she sucked in a breath when he told her how Br'er Rabbit tricked Br'er Fox into setting him free by throwing him into a briar patch. Watching her reactions filled him with wonder.

"Mommy only tells me Bible stories." She sat back and draped the blanket over herself.

"Those are the best kind." Would Natassa be okay with him telling an African folktale instead of a Bible story? Who was he kidding? Natassa probably wouldn't want him speaking to her daughter at all. He cleared his throat. "Well, good night."

"Aren't you going to pray for me?" Mercy yawned and laid her head on her pillow.

"Sure." He pressed his lips together, emotion rushing over him. His girl wanted him to pray for her. No. Not his girl. Not his. But still… "God, thank You for bringing Mercy here safe and sound. I pray that You will give her a good night's sleep and surround her with Your peace. And I pray that she would find whatever she's looking for. Amen."

A beat of silence. Then, a soft voice. "Amen."

9

—————

May 2020
Chicago, Illinois

It must have rained, a least a little, because Mercy heard a car skid on the street below, its tires making sploshy sounds. What time was it anyway? The apartment lay still and silent. And dark. She wasn't used to sleeping in unfamiliar places. She'd stayed over at Bethany's once, but whenever she'd asked to go to a sleepover at a friend's house, Mom always said, "Why don't you have them over here instead?" She probably didn't trust their rules and thought they'd feed her Twinkies and let her listen to Drake.

Mercy brought the fluffy blanket to her face and inhaled. It smelled like Janell. Like vanilla, maybe, and something else. Something most likely artificial, not one of the essential oils Mom used. Janell probably used scented detergent and dryer sheets and all the other things Mom said caused cancer. Mercy took another big whiff, like a rebel.

"I laugh in the face of danger," she whispered, mimicking Daniel. Maybe it would rub off on her clothes so she could smell like Janell too.

Mercy turned on her side, and the mattress squeaked with her movement. The door was cracked open, and a sliver of dim light cast a skinny triangle over her. She bit her lip. Would they mind if she explored a little? Would she get in trouble? She wiggled out from under the blanket. If they caught her, she'd tell them she couldn't sleep.

Mercy crept through the hall and into the living room, careful not to wake David on the couch. The living room, dining room, and kitchen were one big rectangle with no walls separating them. Light shone through the giant windows from streetlamps and buildings.

A shelf, crammed with toys, filled the corner by the windows. She counted five big police cars and a bin full of Hot Wheels. Superhero figurines, Paw Patrol toys, and Mega Blocks filled the shelf. And there was a bin full of baby toys for Joe. Mercy smiled. Janell had let her hold baby Joe. He'd grabbed onto her finger tight as if he'd never let go.

Her brother. She had a baby brother.

A black baby brother.

And another three-year-old black brother.

Well, half black, but then again, she was only half black too. The half of her that was black just called out louder than the white half of her.

She ran her hand along the dining room table, then yanked it away when she touched something sticky. Jelly? Maybe the sticky from a sucker since Janell let Java have candy. And it wasn't even Christmastime. Lucky brother.

She walked to the kitchen and washed her hands with a generous squirt of lemon-scented soap. The sink filled with suds. She clapped them away before drying her hands on a yellow towel. She glanced over to make sure she hadn't woken David, but he remained draped over the edge of the couch, mouth gaping open.

The refrigerator beckoned her, and she peeked inside. Her jaw dropped as the little light illuminated the space around her. Chocolate milk? A whole gallon of real brown chocolate milk? She ran her finger down the cold jug.

"You want some?" DeAndre's soft voice came from behind her.

She jumped, then spun around. Oh no. She'd been caught snooping. Would he kick her out? Send her back?

"It's okay." He smiled.

She let out a relieved breath.

"Do you want a glass of milk?"

"Yes, please. A glass of milk would be great." She spoke fast, her words nearly tripping over each other.

He chuckled. "Have a seat."

She sat at the table and watched him pour two glasses of chocolate milk and carry them to the table.

"Couldn't sleep, huh?"

She shook her head.

"Me either." He nodded toward David. "Looks like your brother can sleep through anything."

"Mom says he could sleep through a tornado."

He snickered.

Her mouth twisted. Why had she brought Mom into it? Mom should stay far away from the two of them.

"I'm an artist. Like you." Where did that come from? She hadn't planned to say it.

DeAndre sat back, his eyes suddenly looking less sleepy than they had a moment before. "You are?"

"Yes. I paint. All the time. In my closet because I don't have a studio. Not yet." She put both hands around the glass in front of her for something to do with them.

"What do you paint?" He tilted his head. Was that a gleam of pride in his eyes?

"Lots of things. Animals and flowers and rainbows. Fairy-tale things. Not many things that are real. Things I make up in my imagination."

"Those are the best kinds." Why did his smile look sad? Had she disappointed him somehow?

She twisted her mouth, then took a gulp of her milk to wash the worry away. "What do you paint?"

"All kinds of things. But maybe not enough fairy tales. Maybe too much real stuff and not enough dreams."

"You're really good. I saw your mural on St. Anthony Street."

His smile dropped, and he nodded. "Yeah?"

How could she make him smile again? "I'm really good too. At least my art teacher says so. She says I have 'great promise.'"

"Does she now?" The corners of his mouth tipped up, but what was going on inside of him? It looked like happy and sad all twisted together. Was he going to cry?

She took another drink, and he did too. A long one, nearly finishing his entire glass in one gulp.

"I painted that." He pointed to a canvas hanging above the couch. She stood and walked toward it, squinting to make out the details in the dim lighting. Her breath caught. In the painting, DeAndre stood on one side of a bridge, and Janell stood on another. Their arms stretched toward each other, and water crashed below them.

"It's beautiful." She glanced over her shoulder.

"Thanks." He stood a few feet behind her, arms wrapped around himself.

"Can you teach me how to paint like that?"

He shrugged her off. "I bet you have natural talent."

"If I do, I get it from you."

She turned. They stood staring at each other in the dimness. She tried to reach out to him with her eyes, to plead with him to give her a piece of himself.

He sighed. "Mercy, I'll do what I can, but I don't know how long you'll be here. I'm going to call your mom in the morning."

Panic rose within her. "What? No!" Tears welled.

David let out a snore behind her and shifted on the couch, then drifted into quiet slumber again.

"She doesn't know you guys are here, does she?"

Mercy lowered her head, scuffing her bare toe on the floor. "No."

"I didn't think so."

She raised her eyes to see him shift his jaw. "Are you mad?"

"No." But he sounded a world away.

"Please don't tell her. I want more time with you. She'll come and take me away. Or she'll make David take me right home."

"I have to tell her, Mercy. She's your mother."

"But…" Mercy looked around the big rectangle room full of cozy touches: splashes of yellow and gray, cute and cluttered, sticky and sweet. "I've never fit anywhere before. Until here. Until now." Tears began to trickle down her cheeks. "I don't look like anybody back home, but Java looks like me, and Joe looks like me. And you can teach me how to paint, and I can help Janell with the baby. Let me stay. Please!"

DeAndre rubbed his arms as if warding off a chill and closed his eyes. He shook his head, and a sound came from his throat, like a moan. A sound like the kind Mercy made when her stomach hurt. "I'm not trying…" He took a shaky breath. "I don't mean to turn you away, Mercy. I want you to have a place here with me. But I have a feeling that's not what your mom would want."

"Because you're a bad man?" Mercy shook her head. She couldn't believe it. Her mom had to be wrong. Had to be. "That's what my mom says, but I don't believe her."

He leaned over as if someone had punched him. "Your mom has every right to say that."

"It's not true." Mercy stomped her foot. She didn't care if she woke David or the baby or all of Chicago. She needed him to tell her that her mom was wrong, that he was a good man, and that she could trust him. Could love him.

DeAndre crouched and held out his hands. She stepped forward and placed her hands in his.

They matched.

She met his gaze.

"I did a very bad thing. Made a horrible, terrible mistake. An awful sin. So, yes, I was a bad man. But then, Jesus took that sin away and changed me into a new man. When some people look at me, they still see the old man. When other people look at me, they see the new man. It just depends on what eyes you're looking through."

Mercy nodded. That made sense. She'd memorized 2 Corinthians 5:17 for Sunday school. *Therefore, if anyone is in Christ, he is a new creation; the old has passed away, and see, the new has come!* DeAndre's old, bad man had gone. The new, good man had come.

"I see the new." Her lip trembled.

His eyes shimmered with tears. "Not everyone does, and that's okay. I don't blame them."

"Do you have to call Mom? Can't you just wait a few days?" Mercy used her best puppy dog face.

DeAndre stood. "We need to call her tomorrow."

Mercy's shoulders slumped.

"But tell you what. How about you and I go to my studio first thing in the morning while Janell makes the call. We can at least get a bit of painting in before your mom issues a verdict."

Mercy beamed. "Yes."

"Okay, kiddo. Go get some sleep." He tilted his head in the direction of the den.

"Wait." She looked up at him, weighing whether to ask. How to ask— "Can I hug you?"

DeAndre sucked in a breath. "Sure." He bent down and opened his arms to her. She crashed into him. As he enclosed her in an embrace, the broken pieces of her heart seemed to fit back into place.

"Can I call you Dad?" She spoke against his shirt, her voice muffled.

He stilled. Had she gone too far? She should have kept her mouth shut.

"Okay." His whisper sounded hoarse.

"Thanks…Dad." The word dropped between them like a basketball and bounced a few times. She pulled back, wondering if he would pick it up—accept the name she'd given him.

He wiped his moist eyes with the back of his hand. "Alright, kiddo. To bed."

Did he like her calling him that or not? As she snuggled under her vanilla-scented fluffy blanket, she thanked God for her dad and begged Him not to let her mom snatch him away.

~

DeAndre shuffled into his room to find Janell vacantly staring at the ceiling. "You're up?"

"Can't sleep." She sighed.

"That makes three of us." He nestled under the covers and took Janell into his arms.

"Mercy's up? Or David?"

"Mercy was."

"Go figure. The one night that Joe sleeps well, and my mind won't quit racing and let me rest."

He propped himself on his elbow and peeked at the bassinet in the corner. The baby didn't so much as stir. His little fists rested above his head, and his mouth settled in a perfect *O*, slightly sucking in his sleep. "How long has he been out?"

"Four and a half hours." Janell yawned and turned toward DeAndre.

"She wants to call me Dad." He kissed Janell's temple.

"Hmm?" She buried her head in his shoulder.

"Mercy asked to call me Dad."

Janell shook her head as if jostling herself awake. "Uh oh."

"I know."

"What did you say?" She cranked one eye open to look at him.

"What was I supposed to say?" His voice dripped with defeat. "No, you can't call me Dad. You can't hug me. Actually, why don't you go away and never come back." He groaned. "How can I look at that sweet little girl and turn her away?" He ran his hand through her hair, letting it cascade gracefully onto the pillow.

"You hugged her?" She cringed.

"She asked me to."

Her face twisted. "She's got you wrapped around her finger."

"Yep."

"I wonder what Natassa is going to say about that."

He exhaled long and slow. "Natassa doesn't know they're here."

Janell bolted upright. "What?"

"That's what Mercy said."

"Oh my gosh, DeAndre. We've got to call her! Now." Janell's hand flew to the side table as she searched for her phone. Joe shifted in his bassinet.

DeAndre put a hand on her arm. "It's two a.m., babe. It can wait until the morning."

She threw herself back against her pillow. "She's going to freak."

"Yep."

Joe started to fuss, his arms flailing. Janell leaned over and swept him up. She cradled him in a side-lying position to nurse.

"We shouldn't have had them over, Dre. When you called me, I thought it was odd, but I shrugged it off. Why didn't I insist on calling to confirm?"

He spooned next to her, wrapping his arm around her, and rubbing Joe's little foot through his pajamas. "Both of our brain cells are fried from lack of sleep. Neither of us are thinking clearly."

"I was so concerned with the house being a mess and that I had to cook dinner."

"Shh." He planted a kiss on the back of her head. "This isn't your fault."

"Natassa's going to kill me. She's going to kill you first, and then she'll kill me."

"At least we'll both be together."

She spit out a laugh, which rumbled into another and another, causing him to crack up too.

"It's not funny," she said, but her body continued to convulse with laughter she couldn't seem to suppress.

Joe let out a howl as her giggles jostled him.

She shushed the infant gently, her merriment gradually dissipating like retreating waves.

DeAndre wiped the corners of his eyes and took a deep breath, trying to calm himself. "I'm so tired."

"Me too."

They sighed simultaneously.

"I'm taking her to the studio in the morning to paint." He rubbed his eyes. "You'll call Natassa, right? I'm sure she'd rather hear from you than me."

Janell groaned. "You're getting attached."

"I don't know how not to."

She settled Joe back into his bassinet. "DeAndre." She rolled onto her back and looked at him.

"I know." He bit his lower lip.

"I'll make the call."

"Thanks."

"Be careful. With your heart and with hers."

He nodded, but how was he supposed to handle either? If he turned Mercy away, he would wound her. If he welcomed her only to have Natassa rip her away, it would be worse. How could he possibly escape unscathed?

And his boys. How could he explain this to them? What would they think of him when they grew old enough to understand the situation? When he'd left prison, he'd hoped to leave his past there in the parking lot. Instead, it followed him here, mingling with his new life, blurring any lines of distinction.

Lord, show me what to do. What's best for Mercy? Give me wisdom. And strength to do what's right. He fell asleep and dreamed of fairy-tale things.

10

May 2020
Renada, Nebraska

Natassa nestled Mercy's shirts inside her dresser and slid the drawer closed. The room seemed lifeless without Mercy. She peeked inside the desk. No notebook. Mercy must have taken it with her camping. She pulled her phone out of her back pocket and scrolled through her photo gallery until she came to the pictures she'd taken of those notebook pages.

When she'd first seen them, her breath had caught at the discovery of what Mercy had been hiding. Not a diary full of written secrets but a sketchbook full of drawings.

What snatched her attention was the stunning replica of the St. Anthony Street mural.

The colors. The shapes. Her daughter had done a remarkable job imitating the professional artwork gracing the brick building on the street by their church. She certainly had a gift. Could Mercy simply be admiring random art that she saw? Perhaps it had nothing to do with the artist and her connection to him.

Worry nagged at Natassa. What did Mercy know?

What did she want to know?

A ripple of tightening spread across Natassa's midsection. She sucked in a breath, dropping her phone and planting her hands on the square of her back.

Braxton Hicks contractions? At thirty-three weeks? She forced herself to breathe out slowly, and the false contraction eased.

Okay. Everything was okay. Braxton Hicks were completely normal. A good sign that her body was gearing up to have the baby. She rubbed her belly, and Charity rewarded her with a kick. "It's alright, sweet girl."

Now, she did need to slog her way upstairs. Business had slowed with the pandemic, but people were still selling and buying homes, and she had work to do.

She sat on Mercy's bed and bent over her large belly to retrieve her phone. It vibrated in her hand and belted out the standard ringtone.

She stared at the caller ID.

Janell?

Why would Janell be calling her? She hadn't talked to her in years. Not since DeAndre had gone to prison.

She shuddered and pushed the answer icon. "Hello?"

"Natassa. Hi. It's Janell." She sounded nervous. Hesitant. What was going on? "I know it's probably a surprise to hear from me, but…um…David and Mercy are here."

She pulled the phone away from her ear and looked at it, confused. Janell. It said she was talking to Janell. "What? Where?"

"They're in Chicago. They're safe. Here with me…and DeAndre and our boys."

Natassa swallowed, then gripped her stomach as another contraction cascaded across her middle. She stifled a grunt. "Chicago? No. They're camping. David took Mercy camping." She puffed out a breath.

"I know that's what they told you, but it was all a ploy. David brought Mercy here. To meet DeAndre."

The room tilted. She clamped a hand on Mercy's bed to keep from falling over. Her stomach tightened again, this time with a thread of pain accompanying it. "I don't...I don't understand."

But she did. Mercy knew who drew that mural. She'd been drawn toward him. Her sullenness, moodiness, and irritability—it all made sense. She wanted to meet her birth father. The man who'd attacked Natassa. Who violated her. Who...asked for and received her forgiveness. But not her permission to enter their lives, to access her daughter.

"Natassa, they're here with us right now, but I need to know what you want to do. Do you want us to tell David to take Mercy back home? Do you want to come here and get them?"

David? She could ring his neck.

"We'll come get them. We'll come right now."

"Okay." Janell exhaled. "I'll text you our address."

"Can I talk to Mercy?" Another contraction, and she doubled over, biting her lip to keep from crying out.

Breathe, Natassa. It's just Braxton Hicks. You're fine. Relax. But her heart galloped, and she failed to keep her breathing slow and even.

"She's at the studio with DeAndre right now. Can I have her call you when she gets back?" An apology filled her tone, and Natassa winced. At the studio with DeAndre? Having what? Father-daughter time? *This cannot be happening.*

She groaned, part frustration, part pain.

"Are you okay?"

"I've got to go. I'll text."

She hung up and screamed for Brandon. By the third time, she'd crumpled from the bed onto the floor.

Brandon dashed into Mercy's room and slid to her side. "Natassa! What's wrong?"

"Contractions." She focused on breathing slowly in and out.

He rubbed her back. "Okay. I'll call the doctor. We'll go straight to the hospital." He stood and pulled his phone out of his pocket.

She gripped the leg of his pants. "No. Mercy's in Chicago."

"What?"

"David took Mercy to Chicago to meet DeAndre. We have to go get them."

"You've got to be kidding me."

She shook her head.

Brandon crouched and took her face in his hands. "Babe, we'll take care of that, I promise. But right now, we've got to get you to the hospital. This is a high-risk pregnancy. We've got to take care of you and the baby."

Tears pooled, but she nodded. She blew out short, quick breaths as another contraction pummeled her. Brandon took her hand, and she squeezed. He dialed the doctor with his other hand. While he talked, she concentrated on trying to relax. And she prayed.

Please God, don't let anything happen to this baby. Keep her safe. Keep me safe. Keep Mercy and David safe.

"They want us to go straight in." Brandon bent down and put his arm under her arm, supporting her to stand and then walk. "I've got you, honey. I'm right here. You and me together. We've got this."

His confidence tugged at her, but a smothering blanket of fear kept the words from giving her comfort.

~

Natassa closed her eyes against the florescent lighting. The heart rate monitor beat a steady rhythm. "How long did they say we have to stay here?" She wiggled her toes in her bright yellow hospital socks.

"They didn't." Brandon sat in the chair next to her hospital bed, holding her hand.

"What does that mean?" she whined, frustration gnawing at her. She needed to be driving to Chicago, not stuck in a hospital bed.

"It means you're not going anywhere. At least not today." He kissed the back of her hand.

"But the contractions stopped."

"Yes, the medicine they gave you worked to stop the contractions, but your blood pressure is high, babe. They need to keep an eye on both you and the baby for a while." He swept a stray hair from her face.

It was for the best. Natassa couldn't lose another baby, so of course, she'd do whatever it took to keep Charity safe. But Mercy...

"You need to go to Chicago, Brandon. I'll be fine here by myself." She pried open one eye.

He shook his head. "Absolutely not. I'm not leaving you."

She groaned. "Brandon, come on! Our little girl is all by herself in a strange city with a criminal. You've got to go get her." She flung her hands up, and the IV inside her right wrist stung. She flinched.

"She's not alone. She's with David."

Natassa scoffed. "David. Oh yes, our star son. So responsible. Forgive me for not feeling reassured right now after he lied to me and dragged her to Chicago to see my rapist."

"She's with Janell." He kept his tone calm and even. "You trusted Janell with our other girls. You can trust Janell with Mercy." He took her hand again and brushed his lips to her knuckles.

Her heart rate monitor beeped faster. "How are you not through the roof right now?"

"Because you need to stay calm for the baby, and you need me to stay calm for you."

She stared at him. As if it were that easy.

Brandon's phone rang. He dropped her hand to answer it. "Okay, slow down. Can't Daniel help you? Alright, unplug the router, then wait a minute and plug it back in. See if that works. If not let me know." He hung up his phone and shoved it in his pocket. "That was Hope. The internet went out, and she's missing her online summer club."

"Daniel can't help her?"

"He's at work."

Natassa sighed. While David did DoorDash, Daniel stuck to delivering for a local pizza joint. Both boys were considered essential and had a flood of work to fill the summer hours. "Someone needs to stay with the girls if I'm going to be here awhile."

"What about Breanna?" Brandon sat back and rubbed the arms of the chair.

"I can call her." She held out her hand for her phone.

He handed it to her.

Breanna answered after the second ring. "Hey, Chicka. What's up?"

"Hey, Bre. I'm in the hospital right now."

A gasp.

"I'm okay. The baby's okay. I just started having contractions, and they had to give me medicine to stop them. Now, my blood pressure's high. They're keeping me overnight."

"Oh my goodness." Natassa pictured Breanna putting her hand over her heart.

She wouldn't even go into what was going on with Mercy.

"I'm just wondering if you could possibly stay with the girls. Or bring them to your house?"

Silence, then a loud exhale. "You know I would in a heartbeat, but I'm quarantining right now. My sister tested positive for COVID, and I was at her house this past weekend. I have to stay home and away from people for two weeks."

"What? Why didn't you tell me?"

"I didn't want to worry you."

Her head throbbed. Charity twisted and turned in her abdomen. "Are you okay? Any symptoms?"

"So far, so good."

She fiddled with the button to her right side, inclining the head of her bed. "How's your sister?"

"Kate's alright, I guess. She feels like a dog, but she's weathering it out okay at home."

"This whole thing stinks." She'd had it in the back of her mind that if Plan A failed, maybe she could convince Brandon to go to Chicago and get Mercy if Breanna stayed with her at the hospital. But Breanna had her own set of concerns.

"Tell me about it."

They hung up after promising to keep each other updated.

"Breanna's a no." She shifted to her right side and explained the situation. Her hospital gown kept slipping off her shoulder. She adjusted it before settling her head back on the pillow. The alarm dinged, indicating that her IV bag had finished.

"We could try your mother." Brandon's voice carried above the annoying sound.

She moaned.

His face scrunched, showing that he was just as displeased with the suggestion as she. "She's more than likely available."

Natassa buried her head in her pillow. "Fine."

Brandon stood. "I'll go to the lobby and call her. And I'll grab a nurse on my way to see if she can shut off that wretched noise."

Natassa wrapped the pillow around her ears to stifle the sound as tears welled. How had it come to this? In a hospital bed, her daughter in Chicago, Brandon calling her mom to watch the girls. None of this was in her carefully crafted plans for her third trimester.

Why did Mercy leave, Lord? Am I not enough for her? Is there something wrong with me?

The tears pooled and then released, trailing down her cheeks, dampening her pillow. She pressed her mouth into the soft stuffing to muffle her cries.

Shouldn't my love be enough?

A hum sounded near the door as hand sanitizer dispensed. She hurried to wipe her face with the back of her hand.

"Sorry about that. Let me get this switched off for you." A nurse with a mass of bleached blonde curls stood at her IV stand. Her eyes crinkled at the sides of the stiff blue mask covering her face. She was smiling. She pressed some buttons, eliciting several beeps of different tones. "You're all set."

"Thank you." Natassa's voice wobbled.

"You okay, sweetheart?" The nurse tilted her head to the side, her eyes soft and kind.

Natassa began to nod, then shook her head, blinking her eyes against the tears.

"Your baby is going to be okay. Her vitals are good." She put her hand out, touching the space between them.

Natassa released hot breath into her mask. "It's just I have five other babies too. Five other children. And I want all of them to be okay. And I can't" —she sniffed— "seem to make it all okay for everyone."

"Oh, sweetheart." The nurse's curls bounced as she leaned in Natassa's direction. "That's too big of a job for one person. That's why there's such a big God."

A cross dangled from the woman's neck. She fixed her eyes on it and managed a small smile.

"Let me know if you need anything." The nurse nearly spun into Brandon as she turned to leave.

"Your mom is headed over right now." His wore a grim expression, but he stood tall and solid, her wall of strength.

"Should we warn Daniel?"

"I texted him. Texted Janell too to let her know we're going to be delayed and that we'll call her later with details." He slid back into the chair and picked up the remote. "Let's see what there is to distract us from this mess, shall we?"

He flipped through the channels at a rapid pace, never landing on anything long enough to generate interest. Finally settling on the news, they watched the latest reports on coronavirus numbers. She closed her eyes and began to drift off.

"Oh no. Not again." Brandon's voice jostled her awake.

"Huh? What?" She opened her eyes to find him hunched forward, staring intently at the television.

"Another black man killed by a police officer."

She shook herself awake, then lifted herself to a sitting position. The headline read "Hundreds Demand Justice in Minneapolis After Police Killing of George Floyd." She looked at Brandon. "Protests?"

"Protests. Riots." He shifted in his chair but didn't take his eyes from the screen. "This is bad, Natassa. The officer knelt on the guy's neck."

She watched as a video played of a black man crying, "I can't breathe," while an officer held his knee on the man's neck. A sinking feeling dropped in her stomach, and tears stung her eyes yet again. Had the world gone mad?

Brandon had been so calm and collected earlier, but now his knee bounced with nervous energy, unraveling her nerves. He flipped the TV off, but the words *I can't breathe* continued to reverberate.

11

1868,
Just outside of New Orleans, Louisiana

Morning dawns with streaks of brilliant light, painting the bed where I lie. The cabin bustles with voices and footsteps. A spoon clangs against a pot.

"Finally, child. You're up." Mama dusts her hands on the front of her dress and shuffles over to the bed, pulling the blanket down from my chin. "Your brother and sisters want to say goodbye to you, but you know they've got to get out to that cane. I wanted to let you sleep as long as I could. You've got a long journey ahead of you."

I press my lips together and yank the blanket back up.

"Come on, now. Get up and say your goodbyes."

Omey, Mirsa, Kolle, and Ayda hover around the bed, eyes solemn, brows furrowed. Beyond them, Daffney stands with her babe on her hip.

I sigh and throw the covers off. I rise to clamp my arms around my siblings' shoulders.

I go to Daffney first. She's not my sister by blood, but Mama and Papa raised her since she was a young'n, so she's family in all the ways that matter. Though she's married now with a family of her own, she lives only a few cabins down.

"You take care now." Daffney kisses the top of my head. "Be brave."

The baby yanks at my dress, pulling one sleeve off my shoulder. I kiss her chubby cheek, then lean farther into Daffney's embrace. "I will. Love you."

I move on to Omey, who towers over me. I stand on my tiptoes to kiss her cheek. "Bye, big sis. Love you."

She crushes my shoulders with a tight hug. "You take care now, you hear? Make it there safe."

"I will."

Though two years older, Mirsa stands eye to eye with me. Her gaze pierces, and she opens her mouth to speak, but only a strangled squeak comes out. Mirsa collapses into my arms, her tears dampening my dress. "What am I gonna do without you?"

I force a chuckle. "Have your pick of all the handsome men without me around to turn their eye."

Mirsa wipes her cheeks with the back of her hand. "I'm gonna miss you something fierce."

"I'll miss you too."

Tears prick at the edges of my eyes, but I blink them back. Squaring my shoulders, I turn to Kolle.

At sixteen, my brother stands perhaps an inch shorter than me, broad-shouldered and muscular. Looking less like a boy and more like a man every day. Glimpses of Mingo shine through him. And shadows of Papa. My throat burns as I wrap my arms around his neck. "Love you, little brother."

"Love you too." He pulls back and looks me in the eye. "If anyone gives you trouble, you sock them good like I showed you."

A laugh bubbles forth. "You showed me that, did you?"

A sheepish grin crosses his face.

I step in front of Ayda and take her hands, swinging them between us like a church bell. Ayda keeps her head down but lifts her eyes to meet mine. Her bottom lip trembles.

I'll never get to see my little sister blossom into a woman. This truth hits me square in the chest. I suck in a breath. What words should I leave Ayda with? Be good? Listen to Mama? My baby sister will do this and more without prompting, and such advice coming from me would be laughable. "Don't let anyone talk down to you," I finally choke out. But these words, too, aren't the right ones. They're impossible in this world of white folk peering down their noses at negroes. Am I setting up my sister to be lynched like Mingo?

Ayda crashes into my chest, squeezing tight around my ribs.

I rub my sister's back and kiss the top of her kerchiefed head. "Love you."

Ayda pulls back. Nods. Then flees out the cabin door.

Mama waves her hands in front of her eyes then shoos at my siblings. "Get on now. You're late."

They cast last misty-eyed looks at me and retreat. The patter of their feet matches that of my heart.

After I eat, Mama reaches up in the rafters and pulls out a canvas bag. Old and dusty, yet fine.

"Where'd you get that? Looks expensive."

"It's mine. Used it on a long trip a long time ago."

Was it the trip from Kentucky to Georgetown? I don't ask, just take it from Mama's outstretched hands and brush off the dust.

"You got any money saved up?" Mama turns her back, rustling around the kitchen.

"No."

Mama's head snaps around. "None?"

I shake my head and shrug.

"You get paid more than I do, but you ain't got a thing to show for it?"

"I wouldn't say that." I sweep my hand under my bed and pull out a fancy hat with a peacock feather. I twirl it on my finger before setting it on my head.

Mama scoffs. "A hat. What good is a hat gonna do you when you've got to get clear to another state?"

I crouch and scoot the basket out from underneath my bed. I place a necklace, a bracelet, and three handkerchiefs in the canvas bag. "These might help." I yank out my extra pair of shoes and hold them high, triumphant.

Mama sighs. "At least you have a couple extra dresses."

I grin and toss the shoes in the bag, then move to the trunk at the end of the bed. I take out my calico dresses and, after changing into one, stuff them in the bag next to my shoes.

"Here." Mama pushes a wad of money into my hand. "You spend your money as fast as you get it. You gotta learn not to be so reckless, child."

I roll my eyes. "I enjoy buying things at the commissary that make me feel like less of a slave."

Mama's eyes peer deep. "It ain't the things you buy that show who you are."

I turn away from Mama's intense gaze and tuck the money into the bag, trying to count it as I do so. I can't make out the sum, being all discreet like that, but it's significant. Was this the money Mama had been saving up to purchase land?

"Thank you." My voice is hoarse as I speak.

"You're welcome, child." Something clanks—maybe the lid to a jar—and Mama's feet shuffle closer.

I inhale sharply and turn.

"Here. Take this." Mama's arms are full of a sack of cornmeal and some rice, crackers, bread, and a wedge of cheese.

Surely this will clear out the family's rations for the week, plus the extras Mama purchased at the commissary. "But Mama—"

"Take it." She nods toward the bag.

I swallow and unburden Mama of the weight, tucking the provisions into the canvas bag.

Mama pulls a bundle out from her apron pocket. "And take this with you. Give it to Susan when you see her." She points to the fine script on the front. "There's the address of where you're goin'."

"What is this?" I inspect the stack of folded paper tied with a string.

"Letters for Susan. And for Mama. I sent her letters for years after I came here. Right up until the war, I reckon. Then I had no one to post the letters for me. After the war, the postal system was in disarray. It would have been impossible to get word to her. I still wrote from time to time but never sent them. So much time had passed, and it seemed like a different life…"

Is Mama remembering her life before she came to New Orleans? Before she married Papa? Does she miss it? Long to return?

Mama shakes herself, and her countenance clears. "Anyway, they're for her eyes only." Mama's brow furrows. She means to look stern, but she can't possibly expect me not to peek. She knows me better than that, doesn't she?

I stare, not about to agree.

"Come here. Give your Mama a big bear hug." She holds out her arms.

I rush into them, allowing her warmth to seep into me. We rock back and forth, our arms entwined, our shuddering breaths proving that we each fight back tears we refuse to shed.

Mama pulls back. "You're my coffee, love."

I raise an eyebrow. What a strange thing to say.

"Go and make a big, beautiful life for yourself." Mama pats my cheek. "I know you can."

With a stiff nod, I say, "I love you," then grab my canvas bag and head out the door.

~

The canvas bag weighs heavy on my shoulder as I trudge through the woods. I can't leave without saying goodbye to my older brother, my best friend. The lace hem of my pale blue calico dress darkens with dust, and I hitch up my skirt to keep from dirtying it further.

When I come to the Lemonts', Mayme is in the distance, shoulders hunched and head bowed in the field of white. A light breeze spurs me along. My sister-in-law faces me, and though a straw hat shields Mayme's face, the bright red scarf tied around her neck gives her away—the scarf I gave her last

Christmas. My shoulder strains as I run to Mayme, bag thumping my side with each step.

When I reach her row, I drop the bag at my feet and press a hand to my side, rubbing away the ache. "I've come to say goodbye."

Mayme's head snaps up, and she gasps. "What are you doin' here?"

I cock an eyebrow. Didn't I just explain?

Mayme crouches low until the stalks rise above her head. I follow suit.

"They're lookin' for you. For you and Mingo both."

I drop my voice to a whisper. "The riders?"

"Yeah. The Knights of the White Camelia. They heard what you did and vowed to take you out."

A tremble climbs up my spine, but I firm my jaw. "I'm not leaving until I say goodbye to my brother. Where is he?"

"Hiding out in the swamp. I don't even know where."

My throat burns. "But I've got to say goodbye. To tell him I love him."

Mayme's hand cups my cheek, the touch soothing despite the cuts on her fingers. "He knows."

I wrap my sister-in-law in a hug and press my eyes together against the threat of tears. I will not begin my journey crying. I must be strong. As we embrace, a protrusion presses into me. I pull back and drop a hand to Mayme's belly. My wide eyes search her gaze.

Mayme nods.

I suck in a breath. "Why didn't you tell me?"

Her mouth twitches. "It's so new. Much could go wrong."

"But a baby? I'll be an auntie." I press my palms to my smiling cheeks, then drop them as my face droops. Will I even meet my niece or nephew? Will I ever see Mingo and Mayme again?

I take a step back. "Tell Mingo I came and that I love him."

"I will."

"I love you too, Mayme."

Her eyes fill, tears shimmering in the morning sun. "I love you, Liberty. You're the sister I never had. Take care of yourself."

I nod, heave the bag to my shoulder, and head for the woods.

An hour later, I tromp through the forested area toward New Orleans always keeping the road in distant view. I have no solid plans for getting to Georgetown. A steamer? A train? Were all the trains destroyed in the war? I might even get to ride a stagecoach. Excitement courses through me at the thought. Do they allow negroes on stagecoaches? How much will travel cost? Hopefully, I have enough.

I switch the bag to my other shoulder, muttering to myself. If only I could toss out the rice and cornmeal to lighten the load. But who knows when I might need it?

The clomp of horses' hooves draws my gaze to the road on my far right. A Union soldier rides at a slow pace. I let out a breath. Not a night rider. Not a threat. I plod forward.

"What are you doing stomping around the woods like that?" His slow, steady speech barrels through the trees surrounding me.

I stare straight ahead as I walk. "I'm hiding away from the night riders."

He chuckles. Waits a beat. "If that's hiding away, I'd like to see what you do to garner attention."

My jaw clenches, and the leaves and twigs crunch louder beneath my steps.

"T-tell me, where are you going?"

The stutter in his words gives me pause. I've heard that voice somewhere. I stop and cast a narrow-eyed gaze at the man. "Georgetown."

He opens his mouth but stills again before he speaks. "By yourself?"

I nod. Where do I know this man from? Or did I imagine the spark of recognition? The shadow from his blue cap along with his neatly trimmed moustache and beard make it hard to discern his age. Midtwenties?

"The riders are out to kill me." My eyes travel from his blue eyes to his matching uniform. "Y'all are supposed to protect us from them. Some job you're doin'. They 'bout lynched my brother."

His forehead dimples as he frowns. "My d-deepest apologies."

There it is again. The stutter. I tilt my head, sifting through recent memories.

When he speaks again, it is slow and purposeful. "I've just been released from service. You shouldn't be t-traveling alone. I…I could escort you."

I scoff. "They hate you 'bout as much as they hate me."

The corner of his mouth lifts in a smile. "Yes, but I have a gun."

My mouth twists, my eyes mere slits as I take in the man before me. Why should I trust him? Since when did a white man ever keep a promise? "Why would you do that for me? What's in it for you?"

He shrugs. "To make up for what we d-didn't do well in the past. I'm going th-that way anyway." He swings down from his horse and takes a step toward me, extending his hand. "The name's Th-Thaddeus Wyndom."

Thaddeus.

I take a step back. "You're the Freedmen's Bureau agent."

He lowers his head. "Yes."

"The one who gave us land only to snatch it away."

He takes off his hat and twists it in his hands. "My apologies 'bout th-that, miss. I was just f-following orders."

I drop my bag and throw my hands up. "Following orders? All you white folk do is lie and cheat."

"I did negotiate your f-family's contracts to get your mother and siblings higher wages th-this year." He holds his hat in front of him as if offering a truce.

"At Mingo's insistence, not Mama's." I bristle. "You knew who I was all this time?"

He dips his head, sheepish. The nerve!

"I'm not goin' anywhere with you." I fling my bag over my shoulder, spin around, and stomp in the direction of the city. I ignore the presence of Thaddeus on the road as he rides his horse beside me. I no longer care if my dress's lace trim soils.

He doesn't leave but simply keeps pace with me, whistling as if he doesn't have a care in the world. The sound grates on me. Maybe I should dig my extra shoes out of the bag and hurl them at his head.

My arms ache, and my pace slows.

"Want me to carry th-that bag for you? I got a spot f-for it right here." Thaddeus pats the backside of his horse.

"And have you ride off with my things?" I strengthen my resolve and plod on, veering deeper into the woods.

The pounding of hooves sounds in the distance, and the rumble of men's voices ascends. "Here, little colored wench," they catcall.

I freeze. *The riders!* I duck behind a large oak and hold my breath. *Lord, make me invisible.*

"What are you boys looking for?" Thaddeus's voice rings confident, the slowness of it only serving to bolster his authority.

"We're just looking for a negro girl. She owes us something."

Thaddeus puts his hand on his gun, his face like steel. "I've been on this road all morning, gentlemen," he says as he looks each man in the eye, "and I assure you I haven't seen a negro girl." He spits on the ground. "If this girl owes you something, take it up with the bureau."

The men stare hard, then sweep their gazes over the woods. "Alright then. But we'll find her." They turn their horses around.

I heave a breath at the sound of the galloping hooves. My mouth is dry. How could I have thought to bring food but not water? I cough.

"Need a d-drink?" Thaddeus holds a canteen out to me.

Should I take it from the hands of a white man? One who betrayed my family by taking away our land? He did just save my life. My tongue sticks to the roof of my mouth.

I drag my feet toward the outstretched canteen and mutter, "Thank you."

"You're welcome."

I take a long, cool drink, feeling Thaddeus's gaze on me the entire time.

"Better?" he asks with a smirk.

I frown. "Why didn't you stutter just then when you talked to those men?"

Red creeps up his cheeks. He opens his mouth, and his lips move, but no sound comes.

I cross my arms. "You stutter sometimes, but sometimes you don't. Why?"

When he speaks again, it's with a pause between each word. "I've learned that if I speak slowly enough, I can," he enunciates as his face contorts, "control it. It's when I speak too fast that it gets the best of me."

I tilt my head to the side. "I guess that makes sense. But I'd rather hear you stutter than have it take a year for you to get out what you'se tryin' to say."

A ghost of a smile forms on his lips. "Are you ready t-to let me help you now?"

I toe my shoe in the dirt. I can make it by myself, can't I? Mama has always said I'm strong and brave.

And reckless. And impulsive.

Can I trust this man—this white man—to escort me? What if he takes advantage of me? Robs me or…worse? But if he hadn't been there on the road, I might be hanging from a tree. Or laced with bullets. I can use his help to escape from New Orleans and then find my way on my own. Once away from the riders, I'll have little to fear.

I press my lips together. "Fine."

In a flash, he dismounts from his horse, retrieves my bag, and settles it on the animal. He mounts again and extends a hand toward me. "You know how t-to ride?"

"Ride? With you?" Is he crazy? A white man riding the same horse with a negro?

He hesitates. "When we get closer to the city, you can get off and w-walk. I'm selling the horse anyway. But for now, we'll get there much faster if you ride."

I take his hand.

12

—————

1868,
New Orleans, Louisiana

The rhythmic jostling of the horse slows as we near New Orleans. My clenched grip on the back of his jacket loosens. I can breathe more easily now, my fear of being thrown from the horse abating. I would have rather fallen to my death than put my arms around the waist of a white man, but I am glad to have made it alive and well, though shaken by his nearness.

"T-time to hop off." Thaddeus brings the mare to a halt. His blue jacket is wrinkled from where I clutched it. "Now you can be a servant t-toting my bag." He dismounts and extends a hand to me.

I ignore it and slide off the animal on my own, stumbling only a bit and brushing off my skirt to cover my missteps. My eyes spark at his suggestion. If that man thinks I'm about to carry some white man's pack for him, he's got another think coming. My teeth clench and heat creeps up my ears.

His back is to me as he unloads the horse. He turns and places a coin in my hand. "I believe th-this is th-the going rate."

I almost spit out, "I don't need your money," but my hand welcomes the weight of the coin. I might indeed need this for the journey. Who knows what lies ahead? I clamp my fingers around the cool metal.

He places my canvas bag on the ground next to me. "That," he says and points to my clenched fist with the coin nestled inside, "is for carrying this for me." He winks.

He doesn't expect me to carry his pack but to shoulder my own? A ruse to justify traveling together. My blood cools. I flip the coin in the air and catch it with my other hand.

"I'm likely to strike for higher wages." I work to keep the corners of my mouth from turning upward.

He laughs. "I wouldn't put it past you."

He gestures to the bag. "Carry it up on your shoulders and keep your head d-down. Less of a chance anyone will recognize you th-that way."

I want to bristle at another white man telling me to keep my head down, but he makes sense. Anyone looking for me wouldn't be keeping his eye out for a cowering servant.

Thaddeus mounts and grins down at me. "Ready?"

I nod and lug the bag to my shoulders.

As we enter the city, the scent of roses wafts. The white flowers climb high and proud on trellises and verandas, adorning house after house. Orange trees stretch toward balconies, and banana leaves larger than me sway in the breeze. Moss swings heavy from magnolias and oaks, guarding yards. We pass vegetable gardens with rows of lettuce, carrots, beets, and peas in neat rows.

We enter the French quarter and walk by streets named Good Children, Piety, and Apollo. French phrases fill the air around us, tickling my ears. Many shop signs are written in French as well.

I take in the bustling city from the corner of my eye. A mesh of white and black and those with near-white skin, like Mama, prance through the street. Creoles. Many wear silk and enter streetcars, their French tongue peppered with laughter. If Mama learned French, could she pass as a Creole? Melt into this class of respected people? Have a servant instead of being one?

We near the wharves, busy streets on one side and merchants on the other. Masts of sailboats and smoke pipes of steamers fill the horizon. Some arriving, others departing. Some loading, others unloading. Boatmen and laborers bustle about, their voices rising above the slosh of water and clank of vessels. All around us, vendors haggle with customers over flour and corn, hides and furs, cattle and hogs, whiskey and tobacco. Shouts from mates at the docks wrestle with the bleating of animals and chatter of buyers for prominence in my ears.

"Stay here." Thaddeus motions with his hand, then adjusts the brim of his blue cap to block out the sun's glare.

I plant my feet in front of a drugstore.

People swarm around me as he rides across the street and speaks to a man at the wharf. I shrug the bag off my shoulders. The sun beats down on me, causing sweat to pool at the nape of my neck. I keep my head down, but my eyes dart around. I buzz with energy at the lively city surrounding me.

A crowd forms a few feet from me—men, women, and children, all hovering around a glass.

"Remarkable!" one man shouts.

Children clap their hands.

I take a step closer, rising on my tiptoes to see what the fuss is about.

The glass is full of champagne and something else. A clear, solid chunk floats inside.

"It's melting as we watch." The woman sounds breathless.

I take another step. "What is it?" I ask, all thought of keeping my head down forgotten.

"Why, it's ice," another woman answers without looking at me.

Ice? In New Orleans? I've heard of the magic of frozen water but never thought such a thing possible in this place of oppressive heat.

"It's from the Louisiana Ice Manufacturing Company, right there on Tchoupitoulas Street." A mustached man points behind us. "Only three-quarters of a cent per pound."

I nod my thanks even though the group is too fascinated with the ice to notice. I peer across the street. Thaddeus is standing by his horse, still talking with the merchant. I bite my lip. He won't even know I'm gone, will he? I snatch my bag and head in the direction the man pointed.

Only two streets farther and I find the ice company by the throng of people outside. After a modest wait, I emerge from the crowd with a cold sheet of ice. Two and a half feet long, twelve inches wide, and two and a half inches thick, according to the advertisement. What am I to do with this? My fingers numb as I carry the sheet back toward the riverfront.

I turn the corner and collide into Thaddeus. The ice tumbles from my hand and crashes to the ground, shattering into pieces. Now it is the size that will fit into a glass of champagne, but dust coats each piece. I stare at my broken prize.

Thaddeus plants his hands on my shoulders and shakes. "Where were you?" He speaks through his teeth, his eyes narrow.

"I went to get ice." My eyes spark back at him. He doesn't own me. He can't tell me where to go or what to do. I'm not his slave.

His voice hisses out. "I'm t-trying to keep you alive."

My shoulders slump. What if the riders had cornered me on my errand? Was a sheet of ice worth my life? "Sorry," I mumble. I kick a piece of frozen water and watch it slide. "You broke my ice."

His tone cools. "We can wash it."

"Can we?"

His mouth curves up, and when he speaks again, it's slow and sure. "Certainly. Wash it and put it in th-the canteen. It'll cool our water d-down real good."

"But I can't see it melt that way."

He chuckles. "We'll leave a piece out, and you can watch it melt."

As if suddenly realizing we are in public, his gaze darts around. He squares his shoulders and raises his voice. "F-foolish girl! I told you to get me ice. I didn't t-tell you to break it."

I bite my lip to keep from retorting. He's playing a role, and so must I if I want to make it to Georgetown in one piece.

He bends down and gathers the ice in his hands, then rinses the pieces with water from the canteen. He shoves the oddly shaped scraps into the container only after discreetly pressing one into my palm.

"Come now. We have a t-train to catch. We need to make it to th-the steamer by sunset."

We board the train at half past four o'clock and my stomach tumbles as New Orleans flies by me. We reach Lake Ponchartrain in time to set off into the good-night kiss of evening.

~

I awaken to the sound of gulls and waves. The fresh sea breeze lies just out of grasp from my stale, stuffy cabin. The sign outside of the steamer boasted "black facilities altogether separate and distinct from the main cabin." The clerk walked me all the way around the area for the white ladies' cabins and the white gentlemen's cabins, past where the waiters and cooks stay, until we came right behind the hot, noisy engines. The white ladies get to stay as far away from these wretched moaning monsters as possible, but us colored folk have to cozy up right next to them in our smaller, shabbier staterooms.

I stretch out my legs on the hard bed and shift the cornhusk pillow underneath me. Thaddeus is probably in a comfortable room on the other side of the ship, the difference in the color of our skin determining our accommodations even though I paid the same amount as he. The steward yesterday told me to be grateful the boat wasn't overcrowded. When it is, passengers must double and triple up in cabins. I dig down deep to find gratitude.

I eat my breakfast of waffles and coffee amongst other negroes. The roar of the engines makes it hard to converse with any of them. Surely, Thaddeus doesn't have this problem.

On the train yesterday, I plopped down right next to Thaddeus. A woman nearby nearly fanned herself into a tizzy.

"Let's find another seat in more respectable company." The gentleman next to her extended his arm.

The woman huffed as she stomped away.

Thaddeus and I had the front of the train to ourselves. Is that what the future will be like as transportation continues to integrate? Streetcars in New Orleans have only been integrated for a year, and I've heard that some whites refuse to ride when negroes are on board. Will whites always think themselves better?

I stand and step out of my cabin onto the deck to view the waters lapping like silk. Porpoises tumble through the Gulf, and pelicans dive all around. A cook on the other end of the deck dumps a scrap of food overboard. It tumbles into the water, and a swarm of perhaps a hundred gulls swoop down and fight for the morsel. They flap low and close. If I reach my arm out, could I touch one?

I inhale the salty air as the sea breeze billows my dress. When was the last time I felt this free?

Suddenly, I remember Mama's letters. I scamper back to my bag and pull out the bundle. Returning to the deck, I prop my back against the railing and read the first one.

July 10, 1862
My dearest Susan,
Our world here has been flipped upside down. In April, a naval fleet came to New Orleans, and federal troops took over. We watched Union gunboats pass by for days, the twittering of gossip passing amongst us over what it all might mean. Then, all of a sudden, my fellow slaves began to flee for federal lines, bolting for freedom like a stampede.

Oh, the churning in my heart to join them! To rush toward the summation of all those kettle prayers. But I stayed and urged Mingo and the rest of my children to stay as well. If we leave, how will Odel find us when the battle is over? We must remain here if we ever hope to be reunited as a family.

Very few of us remain here now, and the growing season slips away from under us with far too much work for the few hands left to tend the cane. We labor even longer hours, and still, it stretches seemingly without end. What can we do? We shall do what we can and leave the rest in the Good Lord's hands.

Mingo and Mayme have married! I performed the small ceremony in the clearing, and they jumped the broom. They moved into a vacated cabin and have the entire space to themselves. They married on the cusp of freedom, just down the river from Union troops. They chose each other, and for that, I am grateful. No white man made the choice for them, yoking them together by force. There was no master to ask for permission, only a mother to give blessing.

Watching them together awakens a yearning for my Odel. I did not choose him then, but I am choosing him now. Choosing to wait and to hope he'll return to us. Choosing to remain chained to the same land that's drawn blood and tears from this old body. I long for his quiet strength to speak peace over the storm that brews around us. My throat closes at the thought that he might never return. We created a life together, a family. My hand tingles with want for his.

I hope you are safe and well and that Mama is in good health. I trust that you have been good to her and she to you as she's helped to raise your baby. The years have flown by— must not be a baby anymore. I don't know how the war has touched you there. I don't even know when I'll be able to send this letter, as it seems we are all alone in this field of cane, and I have no one to post it for me. Please take care. I wish you all the best.

Yours truly,
Mercy

I remember watching people flee to federal lines. My feet desiring to fly along with them. Mama's insistence that we stay and wait for Papa. Endless hours and days and weeks of waiting for a father who never came.

We worked the land without the help of our fellow man, overwhelmed and burdened. Mama, melancholy and longing. I, bitter and seething. The war waged wasn't only between Federals and Confederates. My very heart drew its own battle lines.

What did Mama mean that she didn't choose Papa then but is choosing him now? Did Master force Mama and Papa to marry? Did he strip them of their choice to pick a mate? I shake my head. Such things were not uncommon, but I'm unable to fathom a point in time when Mama and Papa did not love each other deeply. How can this be?

Footsteps interrupt my thoughts. A chambermaid peers down at me, hands clasped in front of her.

"Are you Liberty, ma'am?" The maid looks no older than me, her ebony skin shining in a beam of sunlight. Her pressed white apron flutters with a breeze.

"Yes."

"A gentleman has need of you. He'd like you to meet him in the rear stairwell."

A gentleman? "Thaddeus?"

"He didn't say."

"A Union soldier?"

"Yes, ma'am."

"Thank you." I hasten to fold the letter and tuck it into the hidden pocket sewn into my skirt. I rush toward the back stairwell.

Thaddeus stands a floor above me. Worry lines crease his face as he looks down at me.

I take the steps two at a time to reach him. "What's wrong?"

He leans toward me, speaking low and keeping his gaze on the door beside us. "I heard t-two men talking. Th-they're after you. Saw you get on and know you're bound f-for Georgetown. Th-they said they'll follow you all the way to New York if they have to. They've pledged to put a bullet in you if it's the last th-thing they do."

I try to swallow, but my mouth has gone dry. My lip trembles. "What do I do?"

"We need t-to get off at Mobile."

"Mobile? But that's hardly any closer to Georgetown."

"We'll find another way to get you th-there. Alive." His eyes probe mine, and I find a tenderness there I did not expect.

I push back the wave of emotion that threatens to crash over me and nod.

"When the ship d-docks in Mobile, you need to sneak out and melt into the crowd. Find a butcher shop. I'll meet you th-there."

"Do they know we're traveling together?"

"I don't know." He pulls off his cap and wipes his brow, then scrunches it back on his head. "Th-they might. To be safe, I'll wait until the last minute to d-disembark. See if you can t-trade bags with someone."

I step back. "But Mama gave me that bag. She said she used it on a trip a long time ago."

He crosses his arms, his jaw firm. "This is no t-time for sentiment. Th-they've seen you with the canvas bag. You need to d-ditch it or trade it."

My brow furrows, but I make no further argument. Thaddeus does not have to go out of his way for me. He does not need to disembark the steamer and find an alternative route. But he's choosing to look after me, and I'm grateful. I spin around and return to my cabin to retrieve the canvas bag and make a trade.

I find a woman with a shabby brown suitcase who nearly squeals at the possibility of trading for the much-finer canvas bag. I grumble as I pack my clothes and food into the inferior case and lug it out on deck.

The steamer passes a strange line with yellowish river water on one side and pure blue ocean water on the other. The two colors dance awkwardly together as if afraid to touch. On the left, white waves burst upon rocks with a clap. On the right, the sand gleams as white as snow. As we draw closer to the city, the ship passes piles of sunken wrecks. I blink. Is this what war looks like up close?

As soon as the boat docks, I slip off with my head down, suitcase in hand.

13

———

May 2020
Chicago, Illinois

DeAndre's arm brushed Janell's shoulders as he stretched it over the back of the couch. He propped his feet on the coffee table and watched Mercy play with Java. She pushed a line of matchbox cars through the makeshift car wash they'd created from a cardboard box and streamers. Java made swishing sounds as each car entered. He scrubbed them with a toothbrush, then grabbed them and pulled them through.

Joe lay across Janell's knees, sucking on a pacifier, content for the time being. DeAndre sighed. Could life get any more perfect?

Janell laid her head on his shoulder.

The front door creaked open. DeAndre and Janell cranked their heads in that direction. David shoved his keys in his pocket and closed the door behind him.

"Back so soon?" DeAndre kept his tone light. David was a good kid, and he didn't mind having him around, but it'd been nice to have Mercy to himself for a bit while David went to do some DoorDashing.

"I only got one order, and they didn't tip well. What a waste of time." He dropped onto the other couch. "Did you hear from my mom?"

Janell sat straighter. "Your dad sent a text hours ago saying they were delayed and would call later. I haven't heard anything else."

"I should call them." But David didn't reach for his phone. "What's for dinner?"

"I need to figure that out." Janell transferred Joe into his bouncy seat and went to the kitchen where she opened and closed cabinets. "I guess you guys will be staying here another night?"

"Looks like it." David picked up the remote and flipped on the television.

DeAndre chuckled. "Make yourself at home."

Java abandoned the car wash and bounded over to the toy bin. "Let's play superheroes." He dumped out the bin, and an assortment of figurines toppled onto the floor.

Mercy picked up Black Panther and turned it around in her hands. Her brow furrowed.

"You be Black Panther. I'll be Captain America." Java picked up his figurine and held it toward the sky. "Wait. We need someone to be the bad guy." He stuck out his tongue in concentration, then his eyes lit as he looked to DeAndre. "Daddy, will you be the bad guy?"

DeAndre laughed. "Why do I always have to be the bad guy? What about Joe?" He nodded in the baby's direction.

"Daddy! Joe can't play. He's too little." Java ran to DeAndre and thrust a Darth Vader toy into his hands. So much for story continuity.

DeAndre propped the toy on Joe's bouncy seat. "Sure, Joe can play. Look at him." Drool dripped from the baby's mouth, down his chin, and onto his onesie. "He looks like he has an evil plan to invade Wakanda and steal all the vibranium."

"Invade Waka-what?" Mercy stood with her hands on her hips, her face registering utter confusion.

"Wakanda forever!" Java shouted. He crossed his arms over his chest in the Wakanda salute.

Mercy raised her eyebrows. "Huh?"

"Don't tell me you've never seen *Black Panther*?" DeAndre eyed her.

"No." Mercy shook her head. "My mom—" She stopped and looked at David. They communicated something with their gazes that he couldn't decipher. "No. I haven't seen it. Can we watch it?" There she went again with those pleading eyes.

"How about you?" He shifted his attention to David, who had finally settled on *Sports Center*. "Have you seen it?"

He shook his head but kept his eyes on the screen. "No. I've seen a few Marvel movies with my girlfriend, but not that one."

"Okay." DeAndre nodded. "Let's watch it tonight."

Mercy grinned. She ran over to David and wrapped him in a hug, whispering something in his ear. He smiled. Then she bounced over to DeAndre and flung her arms around his neck. "Thanks, Dad."

David coughed.

"Is mac and cheese okay?" Janell called from the kitchen. "We don't have much here. I really need to place a grocery pick-up order."

"I love mac and cheese!" Mercy skipped over to where Janell stood peering into the fridge.

"Good." Janell tousled her hair and opened the freezer. "It looks like we do have ice cream for dessert."

Mercy squealed.

"Mac and cheese and ice cream? She's never going to want to leave. You know that, right?" David glanced at DeAndre.

He tried to smile at the joke, but he couldn't make his face cooperate. His heart twisted. If only she didn't have to leave. Ever. He took a deep breath. *At least I have tonight.*

Janell's phone sang out its disco ringtone. She pulled it out of her back pocket and looked at the screen. "It's Brandon." She pressed the phone against her right ear and plugged her left with her finger.

David muted the TV.

Mercy and DeAndre froze and stared at Janell. Only Java remained in motion, flying Captain America above his head with a whishing sound.

"Okay. Oh my goodness."

David sat forward.

"Is she okay?" Janell's brow furrowed.

"What? What's wrong?" David stood.

Janell turned toward the wall. "What about the baby?"

"Something's wrong with the baby?" David crossed the room in three giant steps. "Let me talk to him."

Janell held up a finger to David and nodded into the phone. "Okay, yeah. That's fine. I understand. They're fine here. Everyone's safe and sound. Just keep us updated."

David stepped right in front of Janell, blocking DeAndre's view of her. "What's going on?"

"David wants to talk to you."

David turned, phone in hand, and walked onto the balcony. Janell came over and sat next to DeAndre. Mercy stared at her, lip trembling.

"Come here, sweetie. It's okay." Janell patted the spot next to her.

Mercy perched on the edge of the couch. Her eyes darted from Janell to the balcony door.

Janell grabbed Mercy's hand. "Your mom and the baby are fine. But your mom is in the hospital right now because she started having contractions this morning. They had to give her some medicine, and they need to keep her there a little while just to make sure she and the baby and healthy and strong. She can't come and get you right now. You can stay with us until the doctors say it's okay for her to leave."

A smile spread slowly across Mercy's face. "Okay. We still get to watch the movie, right?"

Janell nodded, and Mercy jumped up to join Java.

DeAndre sighed in relief and felt a twinge of guilt. But he was just thankful Natassa and the baby were all right, wasn't he? It had nothing to do with keeping Mercy longer. Should he insist on sending the two of them back in David's car? Nah.

He'd leave those decisions to Brandon and Natassa. And hope they'd opt to avoid that plan.

David stormed in and banged the door shut behind him. He handed Janell her phone. "Here."

"Everything okay?" DeAndre's voice held a modicum of warning.

"Sorry." He ran his hand through his hair and paced in front of the television. "He said I'm grounded for a year or something, which is ridiculous. I'm nineteen. I live in the dorms. They can't ground me."

"I understand why they're upset. Don't you?" Janell crossed her legs and tilted her head up at him.

"Yeah, I get it." He slouched on the couch and dropped his head in his hands. "He said they'll take my car away. They're paying for it, so I guess they can do that. But they won't, will they?" He looked at DeAndre, his eyes begging for understanding. "I need it for work. It was a birthday present."

DeAndre shrugged. "I don't know what they'll do."

"Dad told me to bring Mercy home, and I told him no."

DeAndre sucked in a breath.

"I mean, look at her." He tilted his head in Mercy's direction. She and Java ran in circles around the dining table, flying their superheroes around. "I'm not going to be the one to take this away from her. If they're going to break her heart, they're going to have to do it themselves."

He grabbed the remote and threw himself back against the cushion, turning the volume on. His show ended, and he flipped the channel. A news report filled the screen. "Video Shows Minneapolis Police Officer Kneeling on Black Man's Neck."

DeAndre leaned forward.

Janell cleared her throat. "Let's start the movie now, shall we?" She reached over and took the remote from David.

"Yeah!" Java shouted as he ran and tumbled onto the couch next to them. "Wakanda forever!"

~

DeAndre sat on the couch with Mercy curled next to him, her eyes glued to the screen. It was far more entertaining for him to watch Mercy than the movie, but his phone distracted him. He kept stealing glances at news stories, careful to keep them shielded from Mercy's view. He had a Bluetooth earbud in his left ear, allowing him to hear the coverage. And, yes, he'd watched the sickening video.

On the television before him, powerful black men and women fought a valiant battle for justice. Mercy leaned in as if lured by the message of strength. *This is what it means to be black.*

On the small phone screen in his hand, an ordinary black man crumpled under the weight of a white oppressor. His stomach turned sour at the sight of it. *This is what it means to be black.*

What message would his boys carry through this world? What message would Mercy carry?

The butterfly she had painted in his studio this morning had been full of hope. Its bright magenta and teal wings sparkled as it released a trail of hearts in its wake.

Would she always paint fairy-tale things?

~

Four days later, DeAndre checked his Amazon notifications. The package was only ten stops away. He smiled, anticipating the look on Mercy's face.

"Any word from my mom?" David asked as he passed by DeAndre and opened the fridge.

"She texted Janell about an hour ago. Still no word on when they're discharging her." During the time Natassa had been in the hospital, DeAndre had helped Mercy with blending colors and adding depth and dimension. Her art teacher was right; she showed great promise. His chest puffed out a little at the thought. *That's my girl.* He shook himself from the delusion.

No. He couldn't let himself go there.

She wasn't his girl.

She wasn't his.

Mercy sat on the living room floor, cradling Joe in her lap. She exaggerated her expression as she cooed at him, and he rewarded her with gurgling sounds. Java sat next to them, thumbing through a pile of picture books.

DeAndre and Mercy had left the studio early yesterday when DeAndre heard a crowd of people shouting, "George Floyd!" He hadn't wanted to alarm Mercy. He wasn't opposed in the least to a peaceful march, but a flicker of anger could quickly burst into flames. He'd ushered her out the door and down the street under the pretense of hunger that only Janell's cooking could satisfy.

They were safely inside and watching out the windows when the crowd marched past, waving signs and chanting. He'd heard later that the demonstrators had shut down streets and blocked traffic. Down the street from them, some threw bottles and climbed on top of cars.

"You going to the studio today?" David emerged from behind the refrigerator door with a slice of leftover pizza in his hand.

"I'm not sure if we should." DeAndre crossed his arms, debating. Mercy was nearly finished with her unicorn painting, and he wanted to show her how to use the stippling technique to make the horn look three-dimensional. But after yesterday, was it wise to be out?

Janell came up behind him, putting her hand on the small of his back. "Stay here. We can play Monopoly."

He groaned. "That's almost as bad as Scrabble."

Her laugh resounded. "Would you rather play Candy Land?"

"I'd rather paint."

"Then, bust out the watercolors and let Java paint with you. You know he loves it." She stretched on her tiptoes and kissed his cheek before retreating to the office.

He sighed. "Yeah, okay." Children's plastic watercolor sets. But better than nothing.

"That's cool with me. Art is my life." Mercy beamed at him.

David grinned and pointed to DeAndre. "Don't let her fool you. She's not just good at art. She's also super smart. She's in the gifted program at school. Won the state science fair last year."

"You must get that from your mom. I never did get good grades." The moment the words were out of his mouth, regret chased them. If only he could snatch them back. He hadn't meant for it to sound like the white part of Mercy was smart and the black part of her wasn't. Mercy shrugged. "But I'm an artist. I don't care about science."

Shoot.

The girl felt like she had to choose.

He went to the bookshelf and pulled out a picture book. "Come here and read with me, Mercy." He sat down on the couch and patted the spot next to him.

She slid onto the cushion, bringing Joe with her, who was happily babbling in her lap.

"This book is about five great black scientists."

"But I don't—"

"I know. I know. You don't like science. Humor me, will you? I know it's a little below your reading level, but it's interesting. Do you know about Susan McKinney Steward?"

She shook her head.

"What about George Washington Carver? Shirley Ann Jackson?"

Raised eyebrows.

"Well, let's learn."

For someone who didn't like science, she sure seemed engrossed in the pages. Leaning forward, hungry and eager. Joe swiped at the pages, and Mercy tugged him back.

DeAndre closed the book. "You don't have to choose between being great at art and being smart at other things. You can paint like me and be a computer whiz like your dad. You can love oil pastels *and* chemistry kits. The whole world is yours."

She bit her lip. Nodded. A smile cracked through. "The world is mine."

From the bookshelf, Alexa's voice sounded a notification, and the device flashed green. "Your package must be here, babe." Janell breezed in and grabbed Joe from Mercy's arms.

DeAndre dashed to open the front door and snatched the package from on top of the welcome mat. "Hey, Mercy, come here. I got something for you." He should wrap it. At least put it in a gift bag, but they didn't have any, and he couldn't wait to give it to her.

Mercy bounced up and over to him, her shoulders raised and hands out in expectation. "What is it?"

"Open it." He tossed her the white bag.

When she had trouble tearing it open, he pulled out his keys and punctured the bag. She put her fingers in the hole and stretched. "A costume?" She pulled the red and blue fabric out and held it up, the packaging falling to the floor. "A Wakanda costume!" She jumped up and down.

"Now you can be one of Black Panther's warriors." He beamed.

"Can I try it on?"

"Go for it."

She raced into her bedroom, the door slamming with a thud behind her. Minutes later, she emerged as a Wakandan princess.

He crossed his arms in salute.

She did the same. "Wakanda forever!" Then she crashed into him with a fierce hug. "Thank you! Thank you so much."

He rubbed her back, his voice choked with emotion. "You're welcome." He swiped at the corners of his eyes with the back of his hand and cleared his throat. "Now, who wants to paint with watercolors?"

~

Two dozen watercolor pictures covered the dining room table, bookshelf, and kitchen island. Their little patchwork family had huddled around the coffee table to eat their hot dog lunch, not wanting to disturb the artwork. Janell had put Java down for a nap and retreated to the bedroom to nurse Joe and, hopefully, get him to sleep as well. David slept on one couch, phone on his chest, while Mercy snuggled against DeAndre on the other. *Frozen II* played on the TV, but no one seemed to be paying much attention. He itched to turn on the news, but Janell had insisted they keep it off around their guests. She argued that since they didn't know what Natassa allowed her children to watch, they should avoid anything controversial.

Mercy yawned, and it triggered a yawn from him.

"What's that noise?" Mercy bolted upright, her head inclined toward the window.

Shouting.

He stood and walked over to the window. A crowd of protestors barreled down the street, their shouts reverberating.

"Black lives matter!"

"I can't breathe!"

Most wore masks or bandanas and carried signs: Defund the Police.

Mercy came beside him. "What's going on?"

He worried his lip, considering how to answer. What would Natassa want him to say? Could he just tell her what they'd told Java a few days ago? "People are mad."

"Why?" She looked up at him with solemn eyes.

He crouched down and took her hands in his own. "Because a police officer killed a black man."

She cocked her head. "A bad man?"

"A man…a man that didn't deserve to die."

"Why did the officer kill him?"

DeAndre shrugged. "Maybe because he was afraid, because people are taught to be afraid of black people."

Mercy frowned. Her brow pinched as if in thought. She stood silent for a moment. "What was his name? The man who died."

DeAndre wrapped his arms around her. His shoulders shook with the weight of unshed tears. She got it. His girl understood. "George Floyd."

"Are you sad?" Her voice leaked out small and soft.

A tear fell. "Very."

"I'm sad too."

He rubbed her back, then stood and turned to watch the scene unfolding on the street. A man with a bottle of spray paint tagged the building across from them with BLM, then proceeded to tag a bus shelter. A group of people surrounded a police car that attempted to turn onto their street, blocking its path.

Mercy gasped. "What are they doing?" She pointed to a cellular store down the street.

He moaned. "Looting." Shattered glass splayed all over the sidewalk, and a dozen people shoved their way inside. Mercy raised her eyebrows. "Stealing. They broke into that store and stole the stuff inside."

She scoffed in disgust. "That's not nice. It's…against the law."

"You're right. It is against the law, and it's not nice. Some people do things that are not nice when they're mad."

A sharp inhale, and Mercy's hand flew to her mouth. "They won't steal my unicorn painting, will they?"

He swallowed. "My studio. I should board it up." He nudged David awake.

"Huh? What?" David jostled awake and rubbed his eyes.

"You guys stay here. I've got to check on my studio."

~

DeAndre wove his way through the sea of people. Every now and then, a sign hit his shoulder, or an elbow jostled him, but he remained focused on his mission.

"I can't breathe! I can't breathe!" The chants rose around DeAndre as he pushed through the crowd.

The closer he came to the studio, the more dread pooled in his gut. Business after business with busted windows. Shattered glass glistening from the sidewalk, crunching under shoes.

When his studio came into view, he stopped, mouth agape.

Someone slammed into him from behind. "Move it."

But he couldn't move.

He was too late.

Triangles of glass poked inward like knife blades, exposing a large hole where a window used to be. The easels in the front stood bare, stripped of their canvases.

People swarmed, bumping and jostling him. He snatched in a breath and walked forward, crouching through the shards, shuddering at the clinking sound under his feet.

All the canvases that had been displayed up front were gone save one that had been broken in half. The black man's face was split in two, the father's smile torn haphazardly. His shoulders drooped. Thousands of dollars, gone. Countless hours of labor, gone.

He slipped behind the dividers and found Mercy's unicorn painting intact on the easel and her butterfly painting safe and sound, propped in the corner. His painting of the father's arms stood unharmed as well. He sighed, relief washing over him. At least he had these.

By the time DeAndre grabbed plywood from the back and nailed it over the broken windows, the crowd had moved on and then circled back around, nearly doubling in size. He tucked the three canvases under his arm and wove his way back toward his apartment, dodging signs and a few bottles aimed at police officers who were guarding businesses. Down the street, demonstrators flipped a police car. He hurried his pace.

When he finally ducked inside the building, a car alarm blared out behind him. Punching the button for the elevator, he thanked God for his family's safety. The damages to his studio and artwork felt insurmountable, but he would pull through. The people inside were what really mattered. His wife. His children. Mercy.

He pushed open the door, and Java ran to greet him.

"Daddy! Daddy! There are policemen out there!" He pointed to the window.

"Yeah, buddy. I know."

Janell came up to him, wrapping her arms around him. "Thank God. I was worried sick about you. You forgot your phone here." She pushed his phone into his hand.

He set down the canvases and held her tight. "I'm fine. But they busted into the studio and stole several paintings."

Janell's hand flew to cover her heart. "Oh no."

"I saved these." He nodded. "Mercy's. And my newest."

"They didn't steal my unicorn?" Mercy came up and shuffled through the canvases, taking out her latest painting.

"Nope."

"Thank you for saving it." She gave him a one-armed hug.

"You're welcome."

Janell walked over to the window and peered out. "Looks like it's getting crazy out there."

DeAndre, Mercy, and David followed.

"Oh no! That's my car!" David pointed below where a man jammed a crowbar through the window of a gray Camaro. The scream of breaking glass and then the blare of the alarm rose above the shouting crowd.

Janell bit her lip.

David dashed out the door. His shoes pounded down the steps.

Janell leaned over and hissed in DeAndre's ear, "Natassa's going to kill us."

He bared his teeth and scrunched up his face before following David down the steps and outside.

14

———

May 2020
Renada, Nebraska

Natassa clamped her eyes shut against the threat of tears. In the distance, monitors beeped, alarms dinged, and a doctor barked orders. Shoes squeaked on linoleum. The elevator pinged, and a soft voice asked for a loved one. The wheels of a cart rolled by. Lunch? It passed her room. Not yet. When would Brandon get back from making his work calls?

She blew out a long, steady breath. She could not give in to the torrent of fear and helplessness that swept over her. That would only cause her blood pressure to skyrocket even higher, and then who knew how long she'd be stuck here. She had to exercise self-control. Restraint. She had to push the waves of emotion down, down, down, beneath the surface. For the sake of her baby. She had to remain strong.

She couldn't think about Mercy spending four days—four whole days—with a man Natassa had hoped to never see again, never think about again. She couldn't torture herself with scenarios of them bonding like two peas in a pod, laughing and joking, cuddling on the couch and reading stories together. Because if she allowed her mind to wander down that path, her stomach turned sour, and tension built in her body. No. She had to put all thoughts of what was going on in Chicago out of her mind.

How could David have refused—outright refused—to bring Mercy home, even when threatened with losing his car? Her sweet golden boy had taken a stand against her. It pierced her heart, nearly causing her to double over in pain. After all she'd done for him.

She'd sat by his bedside in this very hospital when he was sick with RSV as a baby, her tears splashing on his blanket as she cried out to God to heal him. As a new mother, she'd never been so scared in her life. Never felt so helpless. When he'd recovered, and they'd brought him home, she didn't want to put him down. She held him in her arms, kissing his fuzzy head over and over, thanking God for sparing his life.

And now, that same child she'd poured her heart out for time and time again had planted his feet in enemy territory and refused to budge.

She felt her pulse rise.

No. She couldn't think about David. Not now.

Deep, cleansing breaths. She breathed in antiseptic-tinged air and blew it out.

She needed to do whatever she had to do to get out of this place. Even if it meant shutting everything out of her mind.

She opened her eyes and grabbed the remote, switching the television on to a rerun of *Everybody Loves Raymond*. She kept the volume low. The characters argued on the screen while a laugh track played in the background, but she couldn't focus on the plot. Maybe just the sound of laughter would cheer her.

No. It only annoyed her.

She flipped the television off.

She shifted in her bed, antsy and bored. *I'm going to jump out of my skin.* Bethany. She needed to talk to her mama.

She grabbed her phone and dialed.

Natassa heard a laugh track and bent over to grab her remote to turn her television off again. Wait, that sound came from Bethany's end. "Bethany? Are you watching *Everybody Loves Raymond*?"

"Hey, sugar. You caught me." Her voice sounded labored.

What was that beeping sound in the background? "Are you oka—"

"How are you doing…" She took a shaky breath. "Natassa with a *T*?"

Her brow furrowed, but she answered, "Not great, actually. I'm in the hospital." She told Bethany what had happened and how the doctors were having trouble getting her blood pressure stabilized. Then, without even meaning to, she spilled her heart about Mercy. Tears trailed down her cheeks. She sniffed and wiped them away with the back of her hands.

"Oh, sugar. I'm so sorry."

Was that an intercom paging someone in the background? "Bethany, where are you?"

A pause. "Now, don't you worry none."

"What's going on?" A wave of panic rose inside her.

"I'm in the hospital too."

Natassa gasped. "What's wrong?" Please don't let it be…

She coughed, and Natassa cringed.

"I tested positive for COVID."

Her heart dropped. "Oh no."

"They might have to…" Another shuddering breath. "Put me on a ventilator here…" Another cough. "Soon."

Natassa put her fist to her mouth to keep herself from crying out. *Oh God, no. Not Bethany.* "No."

"Now, sugar. If the Good Lord…wants to take me…who's gonna…stop Him?" Her voice came out strained.

Natassa's chest constricted.

"Please." She had to clear her throat to speak past the emotions welling. "Don't tell me you're giving up."

"I've lived…a good life. I'm tired now." She sounded tired. Weary. Like she could drift away from this world.

Natassa strengthened her resolve. "I know you're tired. I know you're ready. But I'm not. I'm not ready to lose you. I need you. If that's selfish of me, then fine. I'll be selfish. But you need to grab hold of whatever strength you've got and stand on the promises of God. And you need to come back to me." Her voice cracked. "You hear me, Mama? You *need* to come back to me."

An alarm beeped loudly in her ear.

"Bethany?"

The phone went silent, the line dead.

~

"What's the matter, babe?" Brandon bent over her hospital bed and touched her shoulder, deep lines etching his face.

Natassa sniffed. "Bethany…has…COVID." She heaved in shaky breaths.

"What?"

She nodded, tears splashing onto her pillow.

He handed her a tissue.

"She doesn't know if she's going to make it."

"She will." He spoke too fast, too assured of something he had no knowledge of. No guarantee.

She shook her head, unable to speak.

"We'll pray." His eyes bored into hers, daring her to believe that God heard and answered when it really mattered. "Let's pray now."

She swallowed. Nodded. But she couldn't force any words past her throat.

Brandon grasped her hands and closed his eyes. His voice echoed with authority. He didn't even ask God to spare Bethany's life. He thanked the Lord for doing so. Natassa squeezed his hand, clinging to the strength in his words like a ladder that she climbed rung by rung heavenward. But she wasn't where Brandon was. Wave after wave had pummeled her, and she could only muster the strength to plead in her heart for the Lord to save her friend, her spiritual mama.

Brandon gave her hands one last squeeze. "Amen." He smiled as if he'd already gotten a call that Bethany was well on her way to recovery. Must be nice to be so confident. How did he do that?

He sat back and sighed. "Is there anything you need before I dig in? I've got to do some more work. I feel bad, but this project is due on Monday, and the team needs me to pull my weight."

She shook her head.

He pulled his laptop from his bag on the side table.

"It's fine. I understand." She twisted the thin hospital blanket in her hands.

He flipped open his laptop and began to type. "I hate to sit here and work while you have nothing to do."

She swallowed. If only she could have him all to herself. But she couldn't be selfish. Needy. She forced a smile. "You gotta do what you gotta do."

She picked up the remote and flipped the television on again.

"What about *House Hunters*?" Brandon didn't even glance up.

"What do you care? You're not even watching." She thumbed through the channels.

"I'll listen. You know I love that show."

"Okay." She turned on HGTV and set the remote in her lap.

The squeak of a cart rolled closer, almost drowning out the clink of computer keys. *Please, let it be lunch.* Her stomach rumbled.

A round woman, who looked a bit like Mrs. Claus, stepped into the room. "Well, hello, sugar. I've got your meal here for you."

At the sound of the nickname Bethany always used, her eyes welled with tears. "Thank you." She brushed her cheeks with the sleeve of her hospital gown.

"Oh dear!" The woman set the tray on her side table, pushing the box of tissues off to the side. "I know the food here isn't that good, but I've never seen it make anyone cry before."

Natassa let out a mix between a laugh and a sob. "Hard day is all."

Brandon's gaze flitted in their direction, but he didn't stop typing.

"Well, I hope it will look up with some food in your stomach." The woman's rosy cheeks brought a warmth into the room.

"Thank you."

"You're welcome, dear. Anything else I can get for you?"

Healing for Bethany? Contentment for Mercy? Could you knock some sense into my thick-headed son? She lifted the cover from the tray. "Salt?"

The woman tsked. "No can do, I'm afraid. You're on a low sodium diet. Doctor's orders."

She exhaled. "Then no."

When the squeak of the cart faded in the distance, she brought a bite of the mashed potatoes to her mouth. She recoiled at the bland mush. The peas weren't any better. She barely forced down a bite of meat loaf.

Y'all's food is bland as heck. She remembered Tia's assessment of her cooking—of white people's cooking— when she lived with them.

A wave of nostalgia washed over Natassa. She missed Tia, missed seeing everybody since the pandemic started but especially Tia. She hadn't even called her in…had it been months? How had she let this much time pass without checking in?

Natassa picked up her phone and punched out a text: *Thinking about you. How are you?*

She forced herself to eat another bite of potatoes while waiting for a reply. Her phone pinged.

I'm OK. You?

She frowned. She wasn't after polite conversation, but digging into the tsunami that was her life? Not today. She ignored Tia's question. *How's the new job?*

Tia had gotten hired on at a daycare after years of watching children out of her apartment.

I got furloughed. No job right now. Money's tight. Need a necklace?

Her jewelry-making side job with Laura must be her only income.

No, she didn't but…

As a matter of fact…let me check your Etsy page again.

A thumbs-up emoji as a reply, and the end of their conversation.

She hopped onto Tia's Etsy page and added three necklaces to the cart. She could give them as Christmas presents.

Brandon eyed her. "You're not eating."

"It's disgusting."

"You need to eat."

She rolled her eyes but took a bite of meat loaf, chewing slowly and swallowing it down with a swig of water.

Her phone pinged again. Tia? She grabbed it and groaned.

"What?" Brandon finally stopped typing.

"The Robertsons want to put an offer on that four bedroom."

He wrinkled his forehead. "That's great, isn't it?"

She sighed. "I'm going to have to give it to Martha. I can't…I don't even have my laptop."

Brandon shook his head. "No, babe. You worked for this. You should be the one getting the sale. You can use my laptop."

"You need it."

"I can run home and get yours."

"Brandon." Her voice came out sharp. Shoot. Not what she meant. She rubbed her temples. "I don't have the mental capacity for this right now. I'm dealing with a lot, and I just can't."

"Okay. Okay." He closed his computer and set it aside, taking her hands in his.

"I'll ask for a referral fee."

"Sure." He kissed her knuckles.

"I'm sorry." Her voice wavered.

"Nothing to be sorry about."

"I wish I were strong like you." His image shimmered under her watery gaze.

"You're stronger."

She laughed.

"It's true."

She shook her head.

He leaned his forehead against hers. "You are so much stronger than you know." Another shake and a tear slid down her cheek. "Hey, let the weak say…"

The Bible reference brought a small smile to her face. "I am strong."

15

———

May 2020
Chicago, Illinois

Mercy pushed the toy car back and forth, back and forth, but really, she was listening to DeAndre's phone conversation with his mom. Her grandmother.

"It got pretty ugly here yesterday. The National Guard is here now." He paced the tiled floor in the kitchen. Step, step, step, turn. Step, step, step, turn. "No, no. We're all safe. It's not like anyone's storming apartment buildings." He ran his hand over his face as if trying to wipe off a nightmare. "They got my studio pretty bad."

The murmur of a female voice sounded from the phone. Mercy tilted her head toward the sound. Who was this grandmother? What was she like? Did she give stiff, awkward hugs like Grandma back home? Would her mouth sag in disapproval if Mercy chewed with her mouth open or spilled some of her dinner on her lap? Would her lips say, "That's nice, dear," while her eyes said, "Would you leave me alone?"

DeAndre sighed. "Looted. I haven't added up the damages. Enough to hurt."

Mercy hadn't noticed the creases under his eyes before.

"Yeah, okay. That sounds like a good idea." He met her gaze, and his mouth twitched. "But Mama, we've got some company here. We'd have to bring them with us."

From where she sat, it sounded like Charlie Brown's mom answered.

"It's a long story. I'll explain when we get there." He nodded into the phone. "Love you too, Mama." He clicked his phone off and slid it onto the kitchen counter.

"We're going somewhere?" Would they go to her grandma's house? Could she call the woman her grandma?

DeAndre leaned over the kitchen island and craned his neck in Janell's direction. She nursed Joe on the couch, a blanket tossed over her shoulder. "Is it okay if we go to my mom's, babe? She's worried about us. Thinks it'll be safer there."

"Yeah, okay." Janell pulled Joe out from under the blanket like a magician yanking a rabbit out of a hat. She held him up and smiled at him and then brought him to her shoulder, patting his back.

"Yay! MeeMaw's house!" Java abandoned his pile of cars and jumped up and down.

David only looked up from his phone for a second before continuing to scroll. "Cool. Whatever."

Butterflies had invaded Mercy's belly. "I'd better go change. I want to look nice for gra—for your mom."

~

They emerged from the apartment building into a quiet garage stuffed with cars. Mercy strained to listen but couldn't hear any chanting or shouting coming from the street. DeAndre pushed a button on his keys, and a blue sedan beeped, its lights flashing. They walked in that direction.

Janell stopped abruptly. "We didn't think this through. There are only three spots in the back seat."

Mercy looked from David, to Java, and then Joe in Janell's arms. She bit her lip.

"I can follow in my car." David closed his eyes and exhaled. "Wait, no, I can't. My car got busted last night."

Janell shook her head as if shooing off a fly. "It's okay. It's not a big deal. David and Mercy can just share a seat belt. They can squeeze together, or she can sit in his lap."

DeAndre dipped his head. "Are you crazy, woman?"

Janell rolled her eyes. "It's not far. It's fine." She opened the back door and buckled Joe in his car seat.

DeAndre went around to the other side and opened the door so Java could climb in, then he reached in and buckled him. "Do you think you two could fit?"

David ducked down and surveyed the remaining space. "Sure. We'll make it work, right, Sis?"

Mercy's stomach rumbled, and her heart raced with excitement. Mom would never, ever in a million years let Mercy and David share a seat belt. She still made Mercy sit in a booster seat. Mercy grinned up at David and nodded.

DeAndre tossed the keys to Janell. "You're driving. There is no way I'm going to risk getting pulled over right now."

Janell shrugged. "Fair enough."

David slid into the back seat, then Mercy squeezed beside him and pulled the door closed. She sat tilted sideways with half of her bottom wedged against the door, but David managed to get the seat belt buckled around them both.

Janell looked over her shoulder from the driver's seat. "Everyone okay?"

"Yep." Mercy's whole head buzzed as if she'd drunk an entire Mountain Dew.

The car pulled onto the street. Her mouth went dry as she surveyed the damage from the day before. Glass. So much broken glass. Broken bottles and bricks. Shattered windows. Trash littered the streets. Spray-painted words covered brick and concrete. She swallowed and turned her gaze inside the car.

No one talked.

Joe fussed, and Mercy stretched her arm over David and Java to try to grab his hand, but she couldn't reach.

"Here." DeAndre handed David a pacifier. "Try this."

David popped it in Joe's mouth, and he quieted.

After a long stretch of silence, Mercy let out a rush of boldness. "Do you think Grandma's going to like me?" She bit her lip. Why had she said that? Why did she call her Grandma?

DeAndre turned to look at her. He smiled. "Of course. She's going to love you."

Mercy's shoulders relaxed.

"Do you think she's going to like me?" David asked.

Janell and DeAndre exchanged a look. "Well…"

"Grandpa doesn't like white people. Grandma neither." Java kicked his legs.

DeAndre cleared his throat.

"They like me." Janell's smile looked strange. Bigger than normal.

"Took years." DeAndre spoke low like he didn't expect Mercy to hear him.

"Yeah, well," Janell mumbled. Then she tossed a glance over her shoulder. "Just talk about the Bulls, and you'll be fine."

"Bulls?" Mercy asked. Why would they want to talk about some big, stinky animals?

"You'll be fine, Mercy." Janell's voice was kind and soft like a pillow. "David, you might have to work a bit."

David flashed a cocky grin. "Don't worry. Moms love me."

Mercy rolled her eyes.

~

When they pulled up in front of Grandma's house, Mercy froze. The brick house stood neat and orderly. Everything in its place. DeAndre opened his car door, and Mercy caught a whiff of grass, confirming the lawn had just been mowed.

David reached around her and released the buckle. "Come on. Get out."

But she couldn't move. Her body was stiff with fear.

What if she wasn't wanted here? What if this grandma didn't like her? Sent her away? She sucked in her breath. What if Grandma convinced DeAndre to send her back and never see her again?

David nudged her. "Sis, let's go."

DeAndre stood at her door, his head tilted toward her, concern written on his face. He reached his hand out, and she took it. He pulled her to standing. "Don't worry, kid. She's going to love you. They both are."

Oh yeah, Grandpa. She'd never had a grandpa before.

DeAndre started to pull his hand away, but she squeezed it tight. They walked together toward the front door. David followed right behind them. Janell unbuckled Java, then trailed behind with Joe in her arms. Java raced in front of everyone, making it to the door first and pounding it with his fist.

The door swung open, and a solid woman with curls that reached her shoulders stood in the threshold. She wore a warm smile. Bethany had curly hair too, only shorter with gray streaks. And Bethany was softer, like a cushion you could snuggle up to. The woman who stood before Mercy didn't look soft but strong, like her arms could squeeze tight enough to hold you together but maybe to hurt a little too. She wore a light purple business suit and white dress shoes with a little heel. All of a sudden, a pang hit Mercy right in the chest. She knew nothing about this woman. Not what she did for a job, or what she liked to do for fun, or what she wanted from almost granddaughters.

The woman cupped DeAndre's face in her hands, then her gaze darted to Mercy, and she stilled. She looked Mercy up and down. *Please let her like me. Please let her like me.*

DeAndre cleared his throat. "Mama, this is—"

"I know who this is."

Mercy's breath caught.

"I could tell my son's daughter anywhere." She bent over and ran a finger along Mercy's cheek. "What's your name, child?"

"Mercy."

Her smile spread. "Well now. Isn't that a precious name for a precious girl? You can call me MeeMaw. That's what Java calls me."

David shifted his weight beside her. "I'm David. I'm her brother." He smiled and stuck out his hand.

Her smile faded, and she stared at his hand, then glanced back at DeAndre, question marks in her eyes.

DeAndre lifted one shoulder. "He drove Mercy here to meet me."

She turned her attention back to David and shook his hand. Her smile was stiff. "Well, thank you for bringing Mercy here to us."

Java crashed into her legs, and she wrapped him in a hug. "How's my Java Bean?" She waved everyone inside. "Come in, come in. I've got sweet potato casserole in the oven."

16

1868,
Mobile, Alabama

I duck through the crowd, keeping my head low and eyes high, then skirt around a building still in ruins. A deep pit yawns in the middle, water filling its open mouth. Fragments of iron and bricks surround it.

The riverfront bustles with activity. I pass stores packed with liquor, soap, and flour. In the cadence of voices, I listen for the catcall of the riders but don't hear it. My eyes dart all around but don't rest upon anyone familiar. I come upon a butcher shop, its racks laden with meat. Customers wait in line to choose their cuts. Red blotchy stains mar the butcher's apron.

Seeing the delicacies inside awakens my hunger. I haven't eaten since breakfast, having been too preoccupied with my escape to join the other negroes for the noon meal. Now it's late afternoon. Plopping the suitcase down at my feet, I extract a hunk of hardened bread and chomp into it. Crumbs spray onto the dirt by my feet.

"I killed me three darkies just the other day." A voice to my left startles me, and I snap my head around to see who is speaking.

The man wears dusty trousers, and his hat is pulled low over his eyes. He puffs smoke out of a pipe, exhaling a laugh that sends the scent of tobacco wafting in my direction. He rocks back and forth on his heels as he speaks to a man in a Confederate uniform.

I turn my back to the men but incline my ear to their conversation.

"You don't say?"

"A heap of the planters want 'em all done away with. Can't stand their haughty attitudes now. I told one I'd do him a favor, for compensation, of course." The man snorts, then coughs.

A chill tingles up my spine. I duck my head lower. Where is Thaddeus?

"Such a shame." The other man's voice sneaks up on me from behind. "The country's been ruined. Our prosperity died with the death of slavery. Now the negro doesn't know his place."

I feel the man's eyes boring into the back of my head. Am I just imagining it?

Suddenly, Thaddeus is by my side. Relief washes over his face as his eyes take me in and find me unharmed.

One of the men behind me scoffs. "Another Yankee. Just what we need."

Thaddeus casts a glance their way but says nothing to them. Instead, he leans in toward me and, in a low voice, asks, "Any sign of the r-riders?"

I shake my head.

The Confederate raises his voice. "I don't know how y'all do things where you come from, but here in Alabama, white men don't mix 'round with negroes."

I turn and narrow my eyes at the man, emboldened with Thaddeus at my side.

"I've hired her to carry my suitcase, gentleman. Nothing more." Thaddeus keeps his voice slow and even, and I hear nothing of the tenderness I sensed in the stairwell of the steamer. This act of his, he plays it well. Or is it truly an act? Does he think nothing more of me than a common servant?

"That there is your suitcase?" The Confederate dips his head toward the brown case resting at my feet.

"Yes, it is."

"You'd better watch that darkie of yours. She rifled through there just moments ago and ate some of your bread."

"No." Thaddeus narrows his eyes at me.

"I swear she did. We both saw her."

"Is that right, girl?" Thaddeus's brow furrows as he glares at me.

I nod, unable to force my mouth to play along.

"I shall dock your wages for this."

"What she needs is a good lashing." The man with the straw in his mouth smiles as he says this. "But then again, we ain't supposed to be lashing darkies no more, is we, Yankee?"

Ignoring the comment, Thaddeus focuses his attention on me. "Come now, girl. We must secure passage for the remainder of our trip."

I follow, stomping a little. Must he call me girl? Look down his nose at me with such disdain? I've had enough of being looked at that way, talked to that way. If not for the negro-killing man just steps behind, I'd take the rest of that hard bread and whack Thaddeus on the head with it.

Instead of heading toward the dock, he turns toward the central section of the city. I follow with the suitcase. We pass stores, hotels, and restaurants.

"What was that?" I mumble to him when we reach a break in the crowd.

He tosses a smile at me. "Just playing th-the part."

"A bit too well. You seem mighty comfortable talkin' down to me."

He chuckles. "Never had much practice t-talking down to anyone. It's amusing to play at, I guess."

I arch an eyebrow at him.

He tilts his head toward me as he explains. "All my life, I've been talked d-down to. Ridiculed. Must be why I know the part. I've had a f-front row seat to it."

"Ridiculed? You mean, for the way you talk?"

He nods.

A horse whinnies as it clomps past pulling a stagecoach.

"Got many spankings as a child."

"Your parents spanked you for stuttering?" Much of the fight drains out of me at the thought of a little boy getting a whooping for something he can't help. The tension in my jaw eases.

"Yes. Wanted to beat it out of me, I r-reckon. Didn't work."

"I reckon not."

A group of men pass on our right, and I duck my head.

At the corner of Royal and St. Anthony Streets, Thaddeus stops. I nearly bump into him.

"A slave market used to stand th-there." He gestures ahead. "R-right in between St. Louis and St. Anthony Streets. That over th-there," he says and points to a three-story barracks, "housed slaves between auctions. This was the slave t-trading center of the state until the fifties. Until r-rail made Montgomery a competition."

I swallow. Why is he telling me this?

"Your mother was sold, wasn't she?"

My shoulders slump. "Yes. I guess she was." Another part of Mama's life I've never given much consideration. I stare at the spot where my people were once auctioned off, gut burning.

"My dad took me here when I was young." His eyes glaze over as if he's seeing into the past. "Such a shame. Selling human beings. A blight on our nation." He shakes his head, his jaw tense. When he starts walking again, his boots thud against the dirt. Once we pass the market area and barracks, he turns to me. "We'll take a r-river steamer up toward Atlanta. From there, I think we can r-ride a train."

My spirits sink at the thought of once again traveling in a separate space from the man next to me. What is going on? I set out to take this journey alone. Why should it matter? But it does. I want to hear him talk more, whether he stutters or takes forever to get out what he means to say. Where is he from? Where is he going? What did he see during the war? These questions ricochet around in my mind, and I want space to ask them. He might know a little about my family, but I know next to nothing about him.

~

The Alabama River steamer is far smaller and shabbier than the vessel we took from New Orleans. The negro cabins are located up high on the hurricane deck, behind the pilot house. I thought the ocean steamer's cabins cramped, but these cabins are scarcely large enough for the bed they contain. The mattress is so lumpy it's like sleeping on a bag full of sticks. The grimy carpeting complements the tobacco-stained walls. Once again, there are no windows, but the walls are thin enough for me to hear the river lapping in between the bells and whistles and boilers hissing.

In the morning, after a breakfast of eggs and toast, I open a newspaper Thaddeus gave me and read. A headline catches my eye: "Steamboat Explosion." I gulp.

The beautiful boat *Xavier* has succumbed to an untimely death, shattering upon the waters and leaving great carnage behind. The number of lives lost by the accident could never be ascertained. Many passengers writhed in agony as others plummeted to their death by drowning.

Throat tight, I snap the paper shut and stuff it into the back of my suitcase. The hiss of escaping steam makes me jump, and the smell of scorching oil turns my stomach. *Relax. Mama once took a steamboat and made it in one piece. So will you.*

Mama. I pull out her letters.

February 17, 1863
Dearest Susan,
I am sure you have heard of President Abraham Lincoln's Emancipation Proclamation issued on January 1st. I pray that it means that Mama is free. We, down here in the sugar region, however, are exempt from the edict, being that this area is already under federal control, and they've taken steps to create a loyal government here. We are somewhere in the in-

between. Not rightly slaves any longer, but not fully free either. The process of cultivating cane is such that many say the industry will collapse without forced labor as no one would break their backs to make sugar if they didn't have to.

We are not opposed to the work, only to the way we've been forced to do it—the way we've been treated. If they will give us our dignity, we will work diligently. But for many, that seems too high a price to pay.

The stretches of unharvested cane mock the planters. The fields should not only be harvested by now but prepared for the next planting. Many would cooperate if the planters will but swallow their pride and seek to negotiate.

Most workers have returned to the plantation now that labor guidelines are in place. We are expected to provide faithful labor and exhibit "perfect subordination," and they've placed armed military guards to ensure we do so. At the end of the year, we shall receive one-twentieth share of the proceeds of the crop, which we must divide between all the workers. If both parties would agree, we could receive monthly wages instead: $2 for men, $1 for women. Simon, the overseer left to manage the plantation, doesn't want to pay us monthly, afraid that we won't have incentive to stay until the cane is fully harvested.

Military orders prohibit using the whip on us any longer, and without the threat of physical discipline, no master or overseer can seem to keep his plantation in order. Workers come and go as they please, even with the military patrols. If they don't want to work, they don't. If there's bad weather, they break. They've decided to take Saturdays off and to refuse night watches as well. They say planters have no right to boss us around any longer, and we'll work when we want to, as is our right. When Simon keeps to his own business, we tend to ours, operating the plantation with greater returns than when he stood over us with a whip, barking orders.

Each day I watch over the fields, hoping for a glimpse of Odel trudging over the hill, hat low on his head. Every day that passes without him tears him away from me a bit more. My memories grow hazy, and my dreams for our future together pinched as fine as mist.

My children surround me, speaking strength into me. Mingo and Omey and Mirsa. And Liberty. Oh, sweet Liberty. She came out kick'n and scream'n, and she hasn't rightly stopped. That girl has such spunk in her, such fire in her veins. She's a force to be reckoned with. Kolle and Ayda are sweet and soft like petals. Daffney has found herself a good man and moved into a nearby cabin. She's my daughter too, in all ways that count. I love them all so much my heart feels full to bursting. I wish you could meet them, and that Mama could meet her legacy.

I pray you all are safe and well.

Much love,

Mercy

I note Mama's choice of words in her letter, how Mama, even here, places herself separate from the other workers. *If they don't want to work, they don't.* But Mama? She will work whether she wants to or not, in bad weather and on Saturdays. She will do what is asked of her for the scraps they give her. Why? Why won't she stand up for herself? Demand fair treatment? Maybe we are just too different to understand each other.

~

When we dock at Selma, the captain announces that we are free to disembark and explore the town as the boat won't be moving on until sunset. I stuff a few coins into a small reticule and dash toward the pier. A bluff rises from the river, and we all must climb arduous steps from the landing to the heart of the town. I hoist up my skirt for the ascent.

"Without th-the excuse of carrying my pack, we must r-remain separate."

Thaddeus's hushed voice comes from behind me, but I do not turn. Still, my skin prickles with awareness of his presence.

"I'll stay f-far enough away to avoid suspicion, but r-rest assured, I won't let you out of my sight."

I duck my head, a ghost of a smile forming. Days ago, the same sentiment would have sent me fuming, but now I relish his protectiveness.

By the time I reach the top of the stairs, I have to stop to catch my breath. When I gather my bearings and look up, I blink at the sight before me.

A chain gang of negroes stands chained together at the ankles, repairing the street while people look on. My mouth gapes as I step closer toward the watching crowd. Weariness lines the men's faces as their shovels and shackles clank. Men? Can I call them that? At least four of them look younger than my little brother—mere children.

"What did they do to find themselves with such a punishment?" Thaddeus's voice rises above the onlookers' hushed whispers. He's standing down the road, a group of five men and women in between us.

"Vagrancy," one man supplies.

"Not just that." A woman puts her hand on the gentleman's arm. "That one" —she points to a thin young man with gaunt features— "is accused of using abusive language toward a white man. And that one" —she points to a boy with large, frightened eyes— "sold farm produce within the town limits. Everyone around here knows that's a violation." She notches up her chin. "Several of them are here on account of disorderly conduct."

My teeth clench. I glare at the woman. "Some of them are just children."

The woman levels her gaze. "They broke the law."

"That they did." The gentleman nods. "This is what freedom is like for negroes. Pay attention girl. You must toe the line."

I clench my fists at my side and step toward the couple. How dare they speak to me that way!

Thaddeus's voice breaks through my haze of rage. "I hear there's good salt pork right down the road a ways. Is that true?"

My gaze darts to him. His eyes plead with me.

The man and woman spin toward him, their backs now toward me. "Why, yes, just down a block on the left."

Thaddeus tips his hat and motions to me with a slight nod of his head.

I huff off in that direction.

His plodding steps follow my stomping ones, but I refuse to turn. That fire Mama talked about could burn all of Selma to the ground 'bout now if I could breathe it out of my nostrils. *Salt pork.* He thought to pacify me with salt pork? When mere boys are chained for doing no more than selling fruit?

"I know it's infuriating, but you have to keep your cool." Thaddeus's low voice pounces upon me from behind.

I spin around. Sparks could nearly fly from my fingertips. "Keep my cool? Are you daft?"

He stops in his tracks a couple feet behind me, his brow creased. "Pardon me?"

"Don't you see? You fought a war—killed people, I reckon—to put an end to slavery. But it ain't gone." I cast my arm in the direction of the chain gang. "Not for them. It just looks different."

"But not for you. You're f-free."

"Am I? Free to what? Run for my life? Live fearful that if I make one little mistake, like selling fruit in the wrong place, some white man will clank a chain on my ankle? That ain't the same kind of freedom you enjoy." I swipe my nose with my sleeve. "Now, if you'll excuse me, I've got to go eat some salt pork."

I swing around and march off, my skirt swishing. The breath comes out of my flared nostrils so hard I barely hear his hushed reply.

"Liberty."

I stop. Put my hands on my hips.

"I'm sorry."

His tone is laced with a gentleness I wish I could collapse into. I turn my head to meet his gaze and find a watery sheen there. Unshed tears? I've never seen a man cry. Not Papa when he was whipped. Not Mingo when Ole Faithful burned to the ground. My heart leaps in my chest.

A woman passes by on my left, jostling the connection between us.

I nod my forgiveness and walk forward.

~

May 12, 1864

Banks passed a new labor policy in February. In this one, we are no longer called slaves but laborers. Think of it! Laborers! The power in that change of name. Our share of the crop was raised to one-fourteenth, and we are allowed garden plots of up to an acre. And for the first time, we are free to choose our employers. Of course, I cannot leave this place, not when Odel might still return. I must be here if and when he does. So, I stayed in Simon's employ and signed a labor contract with him.

But last month, Simon disappeared, leaving the plantation abandoned. No master. No overseer. Only us laborers to tend the cane. For nearly four weeks, we worked the plantation on our own, without any white oversight. I cannot even describe the feeling. Like owning our own land! The dirt smelled different, the air was fresher, the cane cooperated more. I woke up dearly anticipating each day as the master of my own fate.

Some fellow laborers petitioned the Treasury Department for official permission to work the plantation on our own, but the government officials informed them that the planation would be leased to a Northerner. Apparently, many Yankees are coming to the South looking for such an opportunity. Our time as landowners was short-lived, but it lit a spark in me I doubt will easily be quenched. I must own my own land someday.

Yankee Gabe paraded onto our property last week with a puffed-out chest and a head far too big for his britches. He don't know a thing about cane. Not a thing about farming at all. He don't have a lick of money or sense, and he thinks this is the way he's gonna strike it rich. Fool. We thought maybe being a Yankee, he might have goodwill in his heart toward us, but he don't rightly care one way or another. He wants to work us hard to make him a quick fortune so that he can go back to New York and find himself a pretty little wife. If he expects these workers to pile all their energy into making him rich, he's got another think coming.

I hope all is well there with you.

Give Mama my love.

Mercy

Guilt gnaws at me as I reread Mama's words. *I must own my own land someday.* The money Mama had been saving up to buy her own land now sits in my suitcase, what I haven't already spent on fare. Will Mama never have her dream? Will she resent me for it?

The boat lurches, and I bump my head against the wall. Blasted snags. That one must have been hidden for no warning bell sounded. I stand and stumble at another rough patch, then walk onto the deck to welcome the breeze.

Bits of conversation waft from the deck below.

"I can't stand them Yankees. Got one boarding right next to me."

"The nerve of them coming down here, prancing all over our South."

"This one's a soldier."

Thaddeus.

Spittle drips from the deck into the river below.

"I'll tell you what them Yanks did to me. They came in on Sunday night, robbed my house. Stole my gold, my silver, my watch."

"Scoundrels."

"Didn't leave one bit of food. Not even for the negroes they're supposed to love. Ransacked their cabins too."

I frown and strain to hear more, but the men must have moved. Is what they said true? Did the Yankees pillage homes? Steal food from slave cabins? I can't picture Thaddeus doing so. Then again, how well do I really know him?

~

When the steamer docks in Montgomery, I don't get off. My stomach sours at the thought of seeing another chain gang in the streets. I watch passengers stream from the boat, Thaddeus among them.

He catches my eye and winks.

I smile and lift two fingers in a subtle wave.

When will I get to spend some time with him? I want to ask him about what I overheard.

As his form disappears in the distance, I turn my attention to the roustabouts unloading the boat. Some carry boxes and crates, others hoist bags of cottonseed onto the bare backs of other men. Dark-skinned workers with mud clinging to their boots coax mules, horses, and oxen across a gangplank that looks to be about five feet wide. A few roustabouts sling stubborn hogs over their shoulders. One roustabout bites a cow's tail to get it to move forward. Chickens cluck.

When they finish unloading, the loading begins. Men with cotton hooks wrestle bales of cotton onto the steamer. I chuckle as the fleecy stuff clings to their clothes and hair. They look like giant sheep.

As the commotion dies down, I sigh and turn back to my quarters where I read another letter.

June 12, 1865
Dearest Susan,
The Freedmen's Bureau began to parcel out abandoned properties to freed families. Mingo sent in our application as I waited anxiously for Odel to return. We got word that they're going to give us forty acres from a plantation just a few miles from here. The thought of owning my own piece of land sent a thrill of excitement buzzing through me, making this forty-something-year-old body feel like I's twenty again. I told Mingo and Mayme to take the rest of the children with them to stake our claim on the new property—our little slice of freedom. 'Course Omey, Mirsa, and Liberty aren't children anymore. They're grown enough to be findin' suitors of their own, though none of them have. It's hard for me to see them

that way, and I dare say they'll be my babies forever. Kolle and Ayda are stretching out of childhood themselves, but they're still small enough to nestle under my wing. For a while at least. Daffney wanted to stay here with me.

Then, a few days ago, the master returned. He hobbled up the path, leaning heavy on a walking stick. I squinted. Who was this man? His shoulders slumped forward. Any trace of the confident man who bought me and married me off was lost in the weary and worn and defeated soldier clobbering up the way. When he got close enough for me to see he was Master, I scanned the horizon for Odel. Where was my husband?

Master lifted his eyes to take in the Big House, fallen into a dreadful state of disrepair, then scanned the surroundin' fields, still tall with unharvested cane. He stooped over his stick and put a hand down to brace himself on the bottom step. I ran to him and asked if he be alright.

He slumped down on the step and stretched out his right leg, rubbing it at the knee. A grimace filled his face. Then, as if just noticing me standing there, his head snapped in my direction. He called me You There, then said, "Odel's wife."

I asked him where my husband was, clutching fistfuls of my skirt at my sides, knuckles stiff.

He patted the spot next to him on the step and told me to sit down.

I craned my head back. Sit? Next to him? Had he lost his mind in the war? I lowered myself down with caution, my pulse skittering like a rabbit.

He said Odel was a good man, his right-hand man the past few years. And that Odel had saved his life.

My hand flew to cover my heart.

He told me he would have been blown to smithereens by cannon fire if Odel hadn't dragged him away from the battle. He came away with only minor injury to his knee. But Odel didn't walk away from the blast. He laid down his life for Master's.

Master put his hand over mine as he told me this, eyes mistin' and shoulders shakin'. I flinched and yanked my hand away.

"I'm so sorry, You There," he said.

I spoke through clenched teeth. "My name is Mercy."

He startled. "Mercy?"

"Yes. Mercy."

We sat next to each other on that bottom step in the moist heat—former master and former slave—now on equal ground, according to ideals if not reality. I did not know how to navigate this status of free but clearly beneath him. I doubted he did either. It was as if we were seeing this new world through a fog and nothing was crisp and clear. All I knew then was that I'd been waiting for a dead man. I let my tears run freely, cooling my face.

He dabbed his sweaty forehead with a handkerchief and asked if his farm was ruined.

I told him I thought perhaps it could be saved.

He lifted himself up, slow and steady, then plodded up the stairs. "We shall see, Mercy. We shall see." He disappeared inside, leaving me to mourn my husband alone.

Now I am left to decide whether to join my family on their piece of land—our land—or whether to stay here. Odel will not be coming to me, so it seems there is nothing left for me here. And yet, if Odel laid down his life for this man, I should be willing to do the same. To serve him. To help him bring his farm back from the brink of ruin. His brokenness and battle-weariness show in the creases on his face and the stoop of his shoulders. He cannot work the land alone, and he has no overseer. Since Gabe packed his bags and headed back north, he is utterly without aid. I feel sorry for the man, this planter who purchased me and put me to work in such deplorable conditions. I've prayed for him day in and day out for years, and what if I'm to be the answer to my own prayers? Can I leave him now?

My family works the land—their own land—but miles away, and I should go to them, shouldn't I? Oh, Susan. I wish I could talk with you and ask for your advice. Or ask Mama what she would do. What is right in the Lord's eyes? It is His opinion I treasure.

I know I said I would come to you at the end of the war, but I am now so firmly planted in Louisiana soil. I don't know how that would ever be possible.

That doesn't mean you are far from my thoughts and prayers.

Yours truly,

Mercy

I grip the letter in trembling hands. The tears I worked so hard to restrain now freely flow down my cheeks. The memory of Mama stumbling into the cabin on our new land, eyes puffy and red, haunts me. The scratchiness of Mama's voice when she said, "Your papa's dead," grates. We all sank then, together. Doubled over in piles of grief. Our sobs melted into each other, indistinguishable.

Still, in the midst of her suffering, Mama exuded strength for all of us. Cupping our faces in her hands, stroking our hair in her lap. Speaking of Papa's love for each of us. Recounting the Wolof stories Papa used to tell. She stayed that night, pushing life back into us, but the next day, she went back. No one knew why.

Now, I know. How do I feel about this? How should I feel?

Everything burns. My throat. My eyes. My chest.

Maybe that's where love has rubbed me raw.

~

I startle at the rap on my door. I'd fallen asleep sitting up, letter cradled in my lap. Now I return it to the suitcase and hurry to the door.

A chambermaid stands there with her knuckles poised to knock again. The woman freezes in place, then drops her hand to her side. "Excuse me, miss. A gentleman requested I fetch you straight away. He would like you to meet him—"

"Rear stairwell?" I quirk an eyebrow.

The woman tilts her head to the side. "Yes, ma'am."

"Thank you." I scoot around the maid, barely remembering to close the door behind me. Why does

Thaddeus want to see me now? Are the riders back? Have they found me again? My pulse kicks up a notch as I dash toward the back of the boat.

I open the door and scan the steps below me. I blink. Stare. *Thaddeus?*

He is free of his uniform. With brown trousers and a white shirt, I hardly recognize him. Or maybe it's because he's clean shaven. The difference is remarkable.

"Oh, close your mouth." His lips curve upward for only a moment as he meets my gaze.

I'd been gaping at him? I press my lips together and scramble for something witty to say. "Forgive me, I thought I was meeting Thaddeus Wyndom here, not a gentleman."

He rolls his eyes, and I try not to smile as he jogs up the steps toward me. I press a hand to my stomach to calm the jittery feeling springing up there.

"We have to get off. T-take the train f-from here."

The fishy river smell wafts to my nostrils. "But why?"

He closes his eyes, his words coming out on a sigh. "Because a man f-from here boarded, and he's after me."

I rear my head back. "After you?"

"Yes. A Reb. Says I killed his best f-friend in the war. He remembers me. I guess f-from the way I speak. Vowed justice f-for his buddy."

"Did you? Did you kill him?"

He presses his palms to his eyes. "I d-don't know. It was war. I killed a lot of men."

I swallow. I can't imagine such a tenderhearted man pulling a trigger, watching other men bleed on the battlefield. Do the memories haunt him?

He shakes his head as if to wipe away whatever thoughts were lodged there.

"You shucked the uniform so they wouldn't recognize you."

He nods, his eyes weary.

"Then we take the train. I'll grab my suitcase." I take a step, then turn around with a wink. "*Your* suitcase."

17

1868,
Montgomery, Alabama

I watch Thaddeus duck into the gentlemen's train car, and then I board the negro car. My knee bounces as I wait for the whistle to blow again and the engine to move. What if the Reb realizes Thaddeus has left and comes after him? What if he boards the train as well? Will there be a shootout? I've read in newspapers about gun fights at train depots. I bite my lip. *Hurry!*

As I look out the window, someone slides into the seat beside me. Normally, I would relish a lively conversation, but right now, my thoughts distract me. Why won't everyone leave me alone? I don't turn my head.

"Liberty." Thaddeus's whisper sends a tingle up my spine.

My head snaps in his direction. "What are you doin' here? This is the negro car." As if he doesn't know.

"I saw th-the Reb get off the steamer. He won't f-find me in here."

"That's 'cause you're not supposed to be here." My eyes dart frantically around the car.

He shrugs. "They d-don't much care if I sit here. Not like if you'd sit in th-there." He angles his head forward. "Besides,

I didn't th-think you put much stock into white men's rules." He winks.

I shift in my seat. A white man sitting next to a colored woman on a negro car in Alabama?

"Thaddeus Wyndom, you surprise me."

He extends a hand to me. "You can call me Thad."

"Oh, can I now?" My smile broadens. "Well then, you can call me Libs."

He scoffs. "No can do. I like your name. Liberty. It's what I f-fought for. What I'll still f-fight for." He holds my gaze, and I forget to breathe.

The train whistle sounds and snaps our connection. As the engine puffs and the attendant comes to punch our tickets, I ignore the curious stares of those around us.

The train squeaks and screams along the tracks as we pick up speed.

"Might be rough going," Thaddeus says. "Th-these railroads have been patched up but were badly d-damaged during the war."

I open my mouth to ask him about the war, about what he did and what he saw, but I bite back my questions. Instead, I ask, "How was Montgomery?"

A shoulder rises and falls. "Wasn't impressed. Saw the capitol. Looked cheap and shabby up close."

I snicker. Spoken like a true Yankee.

"What'd you do while I was gone?"

I chance another look at him, hoping not to get drawn in by the pull of his gaze. "I read one of my mama's letters. She wrote to an old friend in Georgetown 'bout what happened in Louisiana during and after the war. It's strange reading her words."

"How so?" His green eyes probe.

"I guess I don't really know her like I thought I did. There's a side of her I've never seen. So much of her story I don't have a clue about."

"Isn't th-that always the case with our parents?"

"Maybe." I study my hands in my lap. My dark skin such a contrast to Mama's. What had it been like for Mama to grow up with light skin? Was she treated better for it?

I yawn, weariness pulling at me. I lean my head against the glass and attempt to rest despite the constant jostling.

~

I startle awake to find my head resting on Thaddeus's shoulder. I gasp and straighten.

"I'm sorry." I shake myself from slumber.

"It's all right. My shoulder must certainly make a better pillow th-than the window." His mouth curves upward.

I press my palms to my warm cheeks. The train has stopped, and commotion ensues as new passengers board. He leans close. "We're at West Point."

"Which means?"

"Only seven more hours to Atlanta."

I groan, sitting forward and arching my back to release tension.

When the train starts moving again, we pass blackened ruins.

"What's that?" I point to the mass.

"When the Yankees came here, we were going to burn the railroad d-depot, but a lady told us that we'd burn her house if we d-did that. So, we ran the t-train cars down the t-track and fired them there."

I search his face. "So, you had mercy."

He frowns. "That t-time we did."

A shower of sparks blows through the passenger car.

I tremble. "I've heard stories."

"Many of them are likely t-true, I'm afraid. Some of our soldiers t-took more than what was needed. Enacted revenge."

"Left people without food? Even my people?"

He sighs. "Some did."

"But you? What did you do?"

He angles himself toward me, his brow dimpled. "I never t-took an article of clothing or a piece of jewelry, I swear. And I left f-food for the people to live on. Would never t-take a person's livelihood and leave them to starve."

"And did you stand up to the men who were stealing food away from the very slaves they were there to free? Did you stop them?"

Thaddeus dips his head. "No one listens to me. I'm not a leader. I'm not a person people f-follow."

"That's a foolish excuse." I spit out my words. "I followed you, didn't I? And I ain't likely to follow anybody. Don't you dare tell me you can't stand up for what's right." I turn to face the window as darkness settles across the horizon.

~

Sunlight streams through the window as the train screeches to a halt. I rub my eyes. "We here?" I mumble, my voice heavy with sleep.

"Yes. In Atlanta." Thaddeus sits forward, holding his pack between his knees, gaze fixed out the window.

I begin to stand, but he places a gentle hand on my arm. "Wait."

I pause. Did he change his mind? Will we travel farther on this train?

He squints out the window. "See that burned d-down building?" He points. In between a new building and a shanty that appears to be a bakery is the charred remains of a store. A broken wall stands waist-high, surrounded by a heap of rubbish. "When you get off and retrieve your suitcase, meet me th-there."

I narrow my eyes. "In that pile of trash?"

"Behind the wall."

I stand and cross my arms. "You want me to crouch back there?" I toss a glance over my shoulder.

"Yes." The single word comes out as a hiss. "Now go."

The train has nearly emptied around us. I don't have time to argue. I huff and stomp off and out into the blazing sunshine. After claiming my case from the attendant, I shield my eyes and survey the surroundings. Our planned hideaway isn't the only burned-out ruins on the street. Other pitiful piles of rubble dot the horizon in between both new buildings and temporary shacks. Mud cakes the streets, and rubbish lies in haphazard piles here and there. A swift breeze stirs up a wretched smell.

I amble among the storefronts as if I mean to shop, but after casting a furtive glance in all directions, I crouch behind the blackened half wall Thaddeus had pointed to.

"You f-finally made it."

His voice startles me. I place a hand over my racing heart. "I didn't know you were already here."

"Of course. D-dashed over straight away. Had to keep out of sight of th-that Reb." He pats a place on the ground next to him.

I sit. "Did he spot you?"

"Don't think so." He hands me a piece of jerky.

"Where do we go from here?" I take a bite, and my hunger awakens.

"We can stay here for the night and in the morning t-take a train to Augusta. From there, it gets a bit tricky with the railroads still not being serviceable in places, but I'll get you th-there." He turns and meets my gaze. "I promise."

I flick my attention away and focus on the shadow cast by my shoes. When I move my foot, the shadow moves. This is something I can control, unlike what happens in my chest when Thaddeus looks into my eyes. "Where are you headed anyway? You said you were going toward Georgetown, but you never said where."

He dips his head. "Charleston."

"Charleston?" My eyebrows lift. "Why?"

He sighs deep and long. "That's where I'm f-from."

My mouth drops open. "I thought you were a Yankee!"

He gives a small, sheepish smile. "I lived in Nebraska before the war. But I was born and raised in Charleston."

"No."

"'Fraid so."

"Why'd you move away?"

His fingers fiddle in his lap while his eyes stare into the distance. "Never did f-fit there, I reckon. Couldn't seem to see eye to eye with my f-folks. No one there th-thought much of me."

I place a tentative hand on his shoulder. When his gaze fixes upon it, I drop my hand to my side again, heat creeping into my cheeks. I must keep talking. Distract.

"But you still care for them. Your family."

"Of course. I d-didn't want to sign up for the Union army." He raises a hand, touching the space between us. "Not because I d-didn't believe in the cause. I just couldn't stomach the th-thought of fighting my kin. Took me a bit to come around to it, to gather the courage."

"Must have been hard." My voice hitches, but I train my gaze on a rusty nail, not wanting to risk linking eyes again.

"Yes." That one word is laced thick with weighty emotion.

We sit in silence for a while. Train whistles blare. Footsteps and voices pass by. Hammering and shouts ring in the distance. The heat of the day barrels down on us, the wall blocking any breeze. Pinpricks creep up my legs. Still, I don't move, relishing sitting next to this man who has become so dear.

When we emerge from our hiding place, we keep separate but always close enough to see each other. He has said he will keep me always in his sight, but it is I who won't let him out of mine.

When dusk begins to settle, Thaddeus tilts his head away from the heart of town, and I follow a few yards behind him to what looks like a gypsy camp. Here, jagged pieces of tin roofing cover huts made of old, blackened boards. Stones on the top keep the warped shreds of tin from blowing away. Dark-skinned children swarm around the shacks while women and the elderly stand and sit at the entrances.

Thaddeus dips his head toward the ebony woman standing just a few feet away, sloshing clothes in a basin.

I cock my head. Does he want me to ask this woman if I can stay with her?

As if reading my mind, he nods.

I turn to her. "Excuse me, miss."

She looks up, curiosity in her features.

"Would you have room for me to bunk here for the night?"

Dropping the shirt into the basin, she eyes me up and down. "You payin'?"

"Sure."

With a long glance at the sky, the woman says, "Yeah, we got room. Seeing as it don't look like rain, it's as fine a place to stay as anywhere. It leaks right bad when it rains." She frowns. "We ain't got much food though."

I bring my suitcase to my chest, wrapping my arms around it. "I've got rice and cornmeal to share."

"You don't say?" She smiles, revealing a gap in her bottom teeth. "My name's Dandy." She stretches out a wet hand for me to shake.

~

In the morning, I hear Thaddeus whistling as I finish my johnnycake. I step out of the hut to find him leaning against an oak a stone's throw away. I rush to him.

"Good mornin'." I keep my voice to a whisper.

"Good morning to you." He tips his head. "We've got to catch the t-train to Gordon in less than an hour. You ready?"

"Gordon? I thought we were going to Augusta?"

"The Reb went that way. It's safer to take another route. He might be watching out for me along that one."

I frown. For a soldier, Thaddeus sure seems afraid of confrontation. "I'll grab my things and meet you there."

"I'll get my ticket, then. Get passage to Gordon, and we'll figure it out from there."

I tip a smile up at him and then spin around to say goodbye to Dandy's family and grab my suitcase.

I arrive at the train platform just in time to see Thaddeus board the first-class car. I still, my shoulders slumping. What did I think? That he would ride in the negro car with me again? He's only done so to save his own hide. Did I think it was because he enjoyed my company? My throat burns.

Pressing my lips together, I make a decision. I straighten the fancy hat on my head, shake out my skirt, and square my shoulders. I hold my worn suitcase low as I approach the platform.

"One first-class ticket, please." I notch my chin higher.

The attendant narrows his eyes but takes my money and issues me a ticket. I board the same car as Thaddeus and—ignoring every stare as I walk up the aisle—sit next to him.

"Hello, Thad." I grin at my first use of the nickname.

"Liberty." His voice hitches on a whisper as he scans the area around us. "What are you d-doing here?"

I giggle. "I think that's just what I said last time we took the train."

"But—"

I put my hand up. "I purchased a first-class ticket, so I'm sitting in the first-class car."

He drops his head in his hands but says nothing further. I stare out the train window as rain begins to fall. Groups of freedmen and freedwomen huddle around a few fires. A family of negroes sleeps on the platform, covered in old rags. A young child awakens, and an older child gives the little girl a drink from a tin cup. Bent railroad iron lies in a tangled mess by the track along with a pile of bricks. A few yards away lies a mound of what looks like old bones. From the battlefield? I scrunch up my nose. A whistle blares, and the train hisses, inching us forward down the tracks, then pushing us with a jolt.

"How was your night?" Thaddeus asks.

"Just fine." I wrap my arms around myself. "Dandy's got six children to raise all by herself. Her husband got killed in the war, fighting with your army. Feeds all them little mouths with her washing." Green trees swish by out the window. "Guess it made me feel mighty grateful for what I have." I shrug. "Had. I don't rightly know what I have now." I bite my lip on the emotion that threatens to crest. "How 'bout you? How was your night?"

He chuckles. "Hotels were f-full, but I ended up finding lodging in a tavern room with a clergyman."

"Doesn't sound half bad."

"It was infested with rats. They scampered across the f-floor and our beds all night long. I could hear them rustling through newspapers. This morning, the clergyman f-found they'd eaten holes through his stockings."

I shudder.

"But 'twas a place to sleep. I've been th-through worse." His forehead creases as his eyes cloud over for a moment. Then he shakes himself from the fog. "I gather we both have."

"Yes." If only I could take his hand and ask what he's seen that haunts him so. The way he stared at my hand on his shoulder flashes in my mind. I finger my reticule instead. "I brought my mother's letters with me so I could read on the train. Want me to read one to you?"

"Sure." His smile does not reach his eyes.

I retrieve the next letter and read aloud.

September 20, 1865

Dearest Susan,

Sometimes when we cannot discern the Lord's will, we are simply to wait upon Him. My family is now back here with me, though the circumstance of their return is sad indeed. You probably heard that President Johnson ordered bureau-controlled property to be returned to its former owners once they received presidential pardons. They gave land to my family and then snatched it back right quick. We owned it but for a breath of time before an apology and promise of cooperation grabbed it from us and handed it back to the Confederate planters. We are once again laborers on someone else's land.

There are rumblings of discontent all around us, with some freedmen refusing to leave the land they claimed as theirs and others squatting on any land they can find. So many have placed their hope in the government's promise to give us land that being forced to return to former masters feels like a blow that some cannot bear. Liberty, in particular, is taking it especially hard. She fusses and frets, bucking at every order. She cannot stand to humble herself into submission, instead intent on standing her ground and asserting her rights. She refuses to work on Saturdays or Sundays and will not work a night shift.

Master Man—as we call him now—has changed quite a bit and treats us now like ladies and gentlemen, making polite requests instead of demanding orders. Food is scarce, and he is forever apologizing for that, but we have our own gardens now. We will not starve.

I hope you and Mama are safe and well.

Yours truly,

Mercy

Thaddeus shifts beside me and brings his fist to his mouth. "I'm sorry again about the land."

"I know." I trace Mama's signature with my finger, heart stinging at her assessment of me. *She fusses and frets. Cannot stand to humble herself.* Is that how Mama sees me? As a spoiled child forever demanding my way? The letter makes Master Man seem like the reasonable one and I entirely unreasonable.

"Will you read another?" Thaddeus softly prods.

I sort through the letters just to be sure. "There is no more." Disappointment drips from my voice. "That's the last one."

"Oh." The simple word dips down and mingles with my sorrow.

Neither of us talks as the train clacks forward, engine puffing. We pass log huts crowded with the poor—some black, some white. I can tell their status by the gaunt faces that stare back at me. Thin, barefoot girls with long tangled hair stand on slanted porches and watch the train pass by. We ride on a sandy ridge by a river, passing oaks and pines.

A water boy steps through with a long spout can and glasses. Thaddeus hands him a couple coins, and we both take a drink. The cool water eases the lump in my throat.

Hushed conversations whip around me. The men in front of us talk of Sherman's destruction, their voices embittered. The couple across the aisle speaks of the new tracks being laid across the state.

A woman interjects from behind. "I'd rather walk than share a train car with a *slave*."

The word punches me in the gut, and I spin around. Face hot, I hiss out, "I am not a slave. I'm a free woman, same as you."

Thaddeus touches my shoulder, but I don't turn.

The woman sticks her nose in the air. "You people will always be slaves. You'll never make it as freedmen. You don't know how to care for yourselves."

I rise, shaking off the pressure of Thaddeus's hand. "I can take care of myself just fine, thank you."

The conductor comes rushing down the aisle. "Is there a problem here, miss?" He directs the question toward the white woman, ignoring me entirely.

"Yes. That negro is acting disorderly."

He casts a dark look over his shoulder. "I see. I'll get this taken care of, ma'am."

He turns to me. "You will need to get off at the next stop."

My mouth parts. "But I purchased passage to Gordon."

"Nevertheless, you must disembark. And if you wish to ride our line again" —his eyes narrow— "you must use the negro car."

I huff and open my mouth to object, but he is already halfway down the aisle. I plop back down into my seat, teeth clenched.

Thaddeus sighs. "Looks like we're getting off at Macon."

18

———

June 2020
Chicago, Illinois

DeAndre peeked out the kitchen window. Mercy swung so high the legs of the rusted metal swing set lifted off the ground slightly each time she kicked her legs back. Java rode his Little Tykes police car around on the patio while Janell sat and watched. Joe sucked contentedly on his fingers from his spot on a blanket in the grass.

"You gonna tell me what's going on now?" Mama leaned her hip against the kitchen counter.

DeAndre looked over her shoulder to where Harlem lounged in his recliner, engrossed in a rerun of a basketball game. David sat on the couch, his eyes glazed over.

"Don't worry about him. Spill it." Her eyes bored into him.

"I don't know what you want me to say. David drove Mercy here to meet me. They walked into my studio, and I invited them for dinner." He crossed his arms. "We found out they had no solid plans for the night, so we told them they could stay over. Turns out their mom didn't know they were in Chicago. She's in the hospital right now."

Mama gasped and put her hand over her heart. "Does she got the corona?"

"No, Mama. Complications with her pregnancy."

"She's having another baby? How many children does she have?"

"This will be her sixth."

Mama tossed her gaze heavenward. "Lord, have mercy."

DeAndre's gaze drifted out the back window again. Mercy's face filled with light and joy with each pump of her legs. She looked as if she might break free of the confines of the swing—of gravity even—and fly.

"Mama, I didn't ask for this. Didn't pray for it. Didn't ever think to dream of something—someone—so beautiful. She's only been here a few days, and she's woven her way into my heart." He cleared his throat. "I don't know how I'm going to let her go."

Mama sighed. "You sure got yourself into a big mess now, didn't you, Dre?"

He blew a breath out of his nostrils and nodded.

She lowered her voice and spoke out of the corner of her mouth. "Any chance you can get rid of the brother?"

He chuckled. "He's a good kid."

"He's a punk."

DeAndre's mouth tipped up in a smile. "Nah. He's growing on me."

"He's cocky."

DeAndre tilted his head. "I'll give you that. But he sure does love his sister."

Mama scoffed.

"Give him a chance."

She waved a hand in front of her. "Oh, he won't be around here long enough for all that."

DeAndre's stomach sank. She was probably right. But if David left, Mercy would leave too. His throat constricted at the thought of losing her.

"What are you doing standing here in my kitchen anyway? You can't leave us alone with him. Get yourself back in there." She pointed her thumb over her shoulder.

They were intimidated by David? He held back a laugh. "I just came in here for something to drink."

"Then, grab it and go."

He opened the fridge, grabbed a Coke and meandered back into the living room. David lounged on the couch, his thumb caressing his phone in his lap. The boy must be itching to scroll social media rather than watch a rerun of a basketball game. Football and baseball were David's jam. Basketball? Not so much.

DeAndre settled next to him and slapped a hand on the boy's back. Harlem's eyes didn't drift from the screen. Mama sat in her rocker, pulling out her blue yarn and crochet hook.

David cleared his throat. "How about them Bulls?"

Mama lifted her eyes but didn't crack a smile. Harlem ignored him completely.

David drummed his hands on his knees. "So, are you guys Cubs or White Sox fans?"

Harlem groaned, and Mama shook her head. Neither made a move to answer his question or alleviate the awkwardness.

DeAndre closed his eyes. Why did they have to make things so difficult? He should carry the conversation, but if he did, they surely never would. The seconds ticked by to the squeak of tennis shoes and the whistle from the referees.

David sat forward, resting his forearms on his knees. "So, you two just don't like white people, is that it?"

DeAndre coughed.

Mama dropped her crochet needle in her lap and swiveled around to face him. "Don't like white people, huh? You think we just woke up one day and decided, you know what, I think I'm going to not like white people from now on?"

David shrugged.

Harlem turned the game on mute and hit the button to lower his footrest and propel himself forward. "The white man has been out to get our people from the beginning of our time in this country."

"You can't be serious." David rolled his eyes.

DeAndre nudged him with his knee.

"You're darn right I'm serious. The white man has only wanted to keep us down."

"But not all white men. You can't lump us all together like that." David's face registered disgust.

Mama nodded. "You're right. There are some gems out there. Our Janell is one of them. A true ally. But forgive us if we don't trust easily. You got to earn our trust. We don't give it out for free."

"What about innocent until proven guilty?" David spread his arms out.

Mama shifted to the edge of her rocker. "Oh, you talking about the legal system, honey? The legal system that works just fine and dandy for people who look like you and not a bit for people who look like us?"

David threw his hands up. "Hey, I know. I saw what happened to George Floyd, and it's terrible, right? Black people should never get killed needlessly by cops. But my uncle was a cop who got killed by a black man, and no one marched through the streets for him." David's brow pinched. "No one carried a sign. And certainly no one burned a building or smashed a car window because they were mad about it."

Harlem leaned over the armrest of his chair. "And tell me, where is the man who murdered your uncle now?"

"In jail." David dipped his head.

Harlem pointed at David. "That's the difference." His finger hung in midair like a gavel waiting to fall.

DeAndre rubbed his hands together. "Great conversation. You want some air, David?"

David nodded, and they rose and exited the back sliding door into the piercing sun.

"So much for getting them to like me." David scuffed his shoe on the patio.

DeAndre shrugged. "They like to debate. At least Harlem does. Mama never used to. Never used to be much for politics either. Harlem's rubbed off on her a lot. I feel like I'm getting reacquainted with her still, after all this time."

"What's his problem?" David huffed.

DeAndre stuffed his hands in his pockets. "He witnessed the Harlem riots when he was four years old. Saw bricks and bottles falling from rooftops like rain. Bullets. Hoses. It does something to you, seeing all that. Don't be too quick to judge."

David crossed his arms. "Tell him that."

DeAndre shielded his eyes from the sun and peered at David. "It goes both ways. You can't imagine what his life has been like. A little compassion goes a long way."

"Go ahead. Take his side." His voice rang defensive.

"This isn't about sides."

But David marched off toward the sandbox where Mercy and Java sat building sandcastles.

Janell stood and walked toward him. "Is that steam coming out of his ears?"

He chuckled but couldn't hold a smile.

"What happened?" She squinted up at him.

"He tried to win them over but ended up getting in an argument about race."

She winced. "Ouch."

"Yep."

"Looks like he may need some pointers from me."

"Pretty boy with a sports car is having a hard time relating to these black hustlers from the hood." DeAndre's hands found his pockets again. "He's been handed everything he's ever wanted in life."

David sat on the edge of the sandbox and raked his fingers through the sand.

Janell tilted her head in David's direction, her expression thoughtful. "I bet they can find some common ground."

DeAndre kissed the top of her head. "My ever-optimistic queen."

She lifted her head to meet his mouth with hers for a brief kiss. "We are all human, after all. We're all made from the same stuff."

"More alike than different?" He laid his head on top of hers.

"More alike than different."

~

Mercy jolted awake. What was that noise? She turned in her sleeping bag on the living room floor of MeeMaw and Papa's house. She patted the sleeping bag next to her, but her hand didn't run over the expected bump. Java wasn't there. She sat up and rubbed her eyes, allowing them to adjust to the dimness.

Light shone in from the front window. Not the steady light from a streetlamp. This light flickered and danced. She shifted to her knees.

"Java?" She didn't want to wake David, who slept on the couch, so she kept her voice soft. "Java, where are you?" And what was that noise outside? Shouting again? And what else?

She stood and stumbled to the window, her legs heavy with pinpricks. To get the feeling back into her feet, she stomped them a few times. She squinted out in the darkness and gasped. Was that fire down the street? Firefighters sprayed the blaze.

In the other direction, protestors swarmed the street, but police officers tried to block their path. People ducked into a drugstore with a big hole where a door used to be. Others paraded out, arms loaded with boxes. Papers blew all over the sidewalk.

Mercy's breath caught. In the midst of all those big people was a small one. *Java?*

She raced to the front door and swung it open, but glass glistened on the street. She needed shoes. She rushed back to the living room and crammed her feet into her pink Nikes, scrunching the tongue up. She didn't stop to fix it but flew out the door and into the street, not bothering to shut the door behind her.

She cupped her hands around her mouth. "Java!"

How would he hear her above all the noise?

People chanted, "Justice for Floyd! Justice for Floyd!"

She tried again. "Java!"

He didn't acknowledge her. He stood on the sidelines, a few feet from the line of police. His mouth opened, and he rocked forward, shouting something. She couldn't tell what. People shoved past him.

She ran toward him.

A brick flew just inches from his head and hit an officer in the chest.

A bottle cascaded through the air and shattered by another officer's feet.

She was close enough to hear him now.

"Stop! Stop! Don't hurt the policemen!"

The crowd pressed up against the officers, and a man got in one cop's face. The cop used his baton to push him back, and when the man wouldn't budge, the officer began to hit the guy with his baton. Mercy froze and cringed with each blow. *Whap. Whap. Whap.*

She swallowed.

Java.

She had to get to Java.

A few people pushed past her, knocking into her. One turned and scoffed. "Go home, little girl."

She pressed her lips together and kept walking. Smoke itched her nose as heat clawed at her back. Glass crunched under her feet.

A gunshot rang out, and someone screamed. A dozen people huddled around someone in the street, shouting.

Fear coursed through her. What if she died? What if Java died? What if a brick or a bullet hit them in the head? Tears pricked at the edges of her eyes.

"Java!"

Finally, he turned.

"Mercy!" He ran to her and threw himself in her arms. "They're hurting the police officers. Tell them to stop! Tell them to stop!"

She rubbed his back and kissed the side of his head. "They won't listen, Java. We need to go home where it's safe." The air smelled like sweat and tasted dirty.

An officer came and crouched by them, back to the crowd while another officer covered him. "Are you okay? Where are your parents?"

Mercy pointed to MeeMaw and Papa's house down the street.

"Hurry on back there. It's not safe here."

Mercy gave Java an I-told-you-so look.

"I don't want them to hurt you." Java bit his lip, looking up at the officer.

The cop smiled sadly and reached into his breast pocket. He pulled out a blue and white ribbon bar and placed it into Java's hand. "This is the Chicago Police Leadership Award. I got it for leading my team well. I'd like you to hold on to it for me. I can tell you're a good leader too."

Java beamed. "Really?"

"Really, buddy. Now, go on home. The best way you can keep us safe is to pray."

Java nodded. "I know how to do that."

The officer tousled Java's hair. "I bet you do."

Mercy tugged on Java's hand. "Come on. Let's go."

They raced back toward the house.

Just as they reached the gate, David emerged onto the front porch. "What's going on?" His voice climbed above the crackling and shouting. Had she ever heard him sound scared before?

"I went to get Java." Mercy bounded up the stairs and wrapped her arms around David's waist before breezing inside. She slipped off her shoes and nestled into her sleeping bag.

Next to her, Java turned the ribbon over in his hands.

Mercy tried to keep her eyes open as she waited for David to come back to the couch, but they drifted shut without a trace of him.

19

June 2020
Renada, Nebraska

Morning sunlight streamed through the hospital window.

"Sign here, and you'll be all set." The nurse pointed to a highlighted line, and Natassa slapped her signature across it as quickly as possible. "Don't forget to take your medications as prescribed, stay hydrated, and limit your sodium intake."

"Got it. Thanks." Natassa strung her purse on her arm.

Brandon threaded his arm through hers, and they trekked down the hallway. "You sure you don't want a wheelchair, babe?"

"No way. I've been confined to that bed for six days. I need to move." Even if it was slow going. "You're sure my mom's fine with staying with the girls and Daniel a couple more days?"

Brandon pushed the button for the elevator. "Oh yeah. I mean, after she lectured me about not having a handle on David, she said she'd be fine. She did the whole dramatic sigh thing like a martyr but agreed."

Natassa groaned. "Sorry."

"Hey, you don't choose your family."

Natassa shifted her weight. Mercy certainly had. She chose her "family" in Chicago over the family who had loved and cared for her for nine years.

The elevator pinged, the door opened, and they stepped on. When it dropped, so did her stomach. As eager as she had been to jet to Chicago to rescue Mercy from the clutches of DeAndre, she dreaded the confrontation. *Grab her and go. Grab her and go.*

Another ding, and the door slid open. They shuffled to the lobby past a trickle of nurses, including one guarding the entrance with a thermometer in hand.

"Wait here." Brandon pointed to a hard plastic chair. "I'll get the car."

She'd just settled into the chair when her phone rang. Her mom. She winced. Should she answer it or let it go to voice mail? She took a deep breath. "Hey, Mom. What's up?"

"Hi, dear. I don't want to alarm you, but—"

Her hand flew to cover her mask. "Oh my gosh. What's wrong?"

"It's just that Hope has a fever."

She sucked in a breath. "How high?"

"A hundred and two."

Natassa dropped her head in her hands.

"She's been coughing and says her throat hurts. I'm going to get her tested."

Tears pricked her eyes. Before COVID, a fever, sore throat, and cough would have been nothing to panic about, but now… "We'll come home. I just got discharged. We'll come home and take care of her."

"Nonsense. I've got everything under control." How did her mother do that? Keep her voice void of all emotion.

"But Mom, you shouldn't be exposed."

"I'm exposed already, Natassa. You're the one who's pregnant. If anything, you need to stay away for two weeks."

"Stay away?" Her voice cracked.

"You've got to think about that baby. It's already a high-risk pregnancy. You've got to take precautions, Natassa. Don't be a fool. Stay in a hotel for a couple weeks if you have to."

"I can't stay away from my own home. My own children."

"I swear, you can be so unreasonable and stubborn. I am handling everything just fine here without you. I cooked the girls chicken noodle soup from scratch—made my own noodles, mind you. They are in good hands. You take care of yourself and that baby and my grandson."

"And Mercy?"

A sigh. "Yes, and Mercy."

Natassa shook her head. "I don't know. I'll talk to Brandon about it." His car pulled up in front of the building.

"You married a smart man. He'll see the reason in what I'm saying."

She sighed and hoisted herself up. "I'll call you later."

"Fine, dear."

~

Natassa maneuvered her seat belt under her protruding belly. She shifted her weight and crossed her ankles, trying to get comfortable for the nine-hour drive ahead.

"Could you turn the air down? Please? It feels like Antarctica in here." The edge in her tone grated on ever her nerves. She tried to soften it with a "Thanks, babe" when Brandon switched the AC dial.

"Just breathe." His voice radiated a calm that she envied. "Everything's going to be fine."

She pouted. "I need chocolate."

"There's an apple in back." He pointed over his shoulder.

"A candy apple?"

He cracked a smile. "Healthy mama, healthy baby."

She glared at him. "I hate you."

His mouth twitched, and he held back a laugh. "No, you don't. You love me. Even when you're stressed."

She rolled her neck from side by side, willing the tension in her shoulders to ease. "You're right. I love you. Almost as much as I love M&M'S."

He chuckled and placed a hand on her knee. "That's my girl."

"Ugh. I really want sugar right now. It's the stress, right? It's gotta be the stress."

"You—Mrs. Crunchy Granola Mom—have always indulged in ice cream and M&M'S."

"True. I just don't remember being so hangry." She looked out the window at the rolling farmland. "So, what's the plan?" *Grab her and go, right? Please say grab her and go.*

"I thought we'd stay one night in a hotel there in Chicago, then drive back closer to home and wait out the rest of the quarantine, if Hope's test comes back positive."

She balked. "Stay in Chicago a night? Why? I can rest on the drive there and be ready to drive home."

Brandon stared straight ahead at the road before him. His jaw shifted.

"Brandon? What are you not telling me?" She turned to study his expression. Too bad he could always keep a great poker face.

"I didn't want to worry you."

Her breath caught and concern began to bubble up in her gut. "Worry me about what?"

"I purposely kept you from watching the news."

She frowned. "I thought you loved *Everybody Loves Raymond.* And *House Hunters.*"

"I do." He met her gaze for a brief second, then returned his attention to the highway. Both hands gripped the wheel. "Natassa, there have been protests." He shook his head. "No, protests isn't the right word. Riots. There have been riots."

A sour taste invaded her mouth, and her stomach lurched. "Where?"

"A lot of places, actually. But Chicago."

She slammed her eyes shut, but it did little to block out the worst-case scenarios that flew into her mind's eye. She'd been in the middle of the frenzy in her city when Ferguson erupted. Was her daughter in the midst of fire and boiling anger, helpless and alone?

"Is Mercy okay?" Her voice came out small, unable to sustain the weight of her question.

"She's fine. They're safe. But David's car got busted into. I've been dealing with the insurance company about it, but I need to get it to a repair shop to get it fixed before he attempts to drive it back."

A wave of anger swarmed over her fear. "Why hasn't DeAndre taken care of that? It's his fault, isn't it? For not…not protecting David's property?"

Brandon rolled his eyes in her direction. "Really, Natassa? You're blaming DeAndre for a riot?" He sobered, and his knuckles tightened on the steering wheel. "He may be to blame for a lot of things…" Tension filled the car like static electricity. Brandon pressed his lips together. "But not the car. I told them I'd take care of it."

She frowned. "Are you going to be okay? Seeing him in person?" She hadn't considered this, the impact on her husband. Brandon in the same room as the man who had raped her. Her mind flashed back to the memory of Brandon drunk in the den, searching for evidence, his quest for justice eating him alive.

Brandon shook himself as if shooing off a fly. "Don't worry about me. I forgave the guy years ago. It's you I'm concerned about. You and your blood pressure."

She bit her lip. Should she pursue the conversation further? He didn't seem okay.

He flashed her a smile. Maybe he was.

She crossed her arms around herself. "Okay, so one night. And then we're out of there." Far away. Never to return.

Did she even have to go in? Could she wait in the car while Brandon ran into DeAndre's apartment, swooped up Mercy, and brought her to the car? Would he have to carry her over his shoulder kicking and screaming? Natassa shuddered. Whatever. They'd do whatever they had to do to keep their daughter safe. To protect her. That's what good parents did.

"What are you thinking about?" Brandon tossed a glance in her direction.

"The hotel," she lied. But now that she thought about it… "I really wish we didn't have to stay in one. They are notoriously germy."

"Nah. They sanitize everything everywhere now."

She scrunched up her face. "I don't know. Do you remember that documentary we watched about the number of bacteria on the water glasses in hotel rooms?"

He cringed. "Ew. Yeah."

"Just think. The same people who 'clean' those glasses are sanitizing the rooms from COVID. The person who stayed in that same room the night before could have been hacking his lungs out on the sheets." She shook her hands in the air. "It gives me the willies."

"Would you rather go home and cozy up to someone who has a known case of the virus?"

She shifted in her seat again, her back aching. "No. I guess not."

"Then, we don't have tons of options."

They rode in silence for a few minutes, and her thoughts ventured to David. He'd always been such a good boy. So considerate and polite. An A student, a baseball star. He'd stood up for her when his siblings complained about the house rules or chores, doing what he was told without complaint. What had happened?

Her head felt too heavy to hold up. She pressed her palm to her forehead. "I'm so mad at David. I don't think I'll even be able to talk to him."

Brandon mumbled his assent.

"Where did we go wrong?" She bit her lip, tears threatening the corners of her eyes.

"I'm not sure we did, babe."

She scoffed. "Of course, we did. He turned on us."

Brandon kept his voice even. "He's an adult now. He makes his own choices."

"But didn't we raise him to make good ones?" She rubbed her belly.

Brandon shrugged. "I mean, you do kind of let him get away with things you'd never let slide with the other children. If we're scrutinizing our parenting."

"What are you talking about?" she balked. "That's not true."

"C'mon. You let Libby hang out at our house during a global pandemic. You wouldn't even let the girls play with the neighbors outside in the yard."

She sighed. "That's because if I didn't, he'd just go over to her house. I wouldn't be able to stop him. He's an adult, like you said. I'd rather have them where I know the environment is safe than have them over at Libby's. David said her mom goes to the store without a mask."

Brandon tilted his head and nodded. "I get that. But from the outside, it looks a whole lot like favoritism. And maybe to him, it seems like he can get away with whatever he wants if he slaps on a charming smile."

Her mouth twisted upward. "He does have a great smile."

"Award-winning."

"I feel like slapping it off his face about now."

Brandon laughed. "You know, part of me is proud of him. For standing up for what he believes in."

Her mouth fell open. "Oh, you did *not* just say that."

"The other part of me wants to strangle him."

"There's the husband I know and love."

"More than M&M'S?" He smirked.

She pursed her lips, considering. "Yes, more than M&M'S."

~

Natassa startled awake when the car slowed. She rubbed her eyes. "Are we here?"

"Just entered the Chicago city limits." Brandon covered a yawn. Dark bags hung under his eyes. How much sleep had he gotten in the past week? That hospital couch couldn't have been comfortable, but he'd refused to leave her side.

Hopefully, he'd sleep well in the hotel. They had to have a better thread count.

She took a long sip of water, trying to release the tightness in her throat. No such luck. "How much longer?"

"Twenty minutes or so." Brandon raised his eyebrows at her. "Don't tell me you need another bathroom break."

She rolled her eyes. *Give me a break. I'm pregnant.* "No. I can make it twenty minutes." Time to incline her seat. *Get your head in the game, Natassa.* She pressed her lips together and stared out the window.

They passed a boarded-up building, and a tingle crept up the back of her spine. The closer they drove to DeAndre's apartment, the more her stomach rolled, and a sour taste filled her mouth. Shattered glass on the concrete. Litter covering the sidewalks. Graffiti on walls. Was there a business that hadn't been broken into?

"It looks like a war zone." She swallowed, throat burning.

"It's messed up." Brandon squinted at the building to his left. "This is it." He looked over his shoulder and parallel parked on the street.

"This?" She craned her neck upward. "It's huge."

"They live on the seventh floor." He turned off the ignition and slapped his hands on his thighs. "You ready?"

She fiddled with her sleeve. "Why don't you go in. I'll wait here."

"Babe." He reached out a finger and tipped her face toward him. "I know this is hard, and I don't want to retraumatize you or anything, but I look at you, and I think of all you've been through and all you've accomplished in the face of your pain." His eyes searched hers. "You are the bravest woman I know. You can do hard things."

She took his hand and placed his palm against her cheek. "That sounds like a Bethany pep talk." She sniffed. This was no time to think about Bethany, who was fighting for her life in the hospital. She could not lose it moments before rescuing her daughter. She had to be strong.

"It's the truth." He dipped his face toward hers, and he met her with a gentle kiss that pushed strength into her and siphoned out the fear.

"Okay." She took a deep breath and then put her hand on the door handle. "Let's do this."

They stepped out into the late afternoon breeze, and Brandon hit the button on his key fob, receiving a resounding beep. Glass crunched under her feet, and a stray paper fluttered by. Brandon met her on the sidewalk, and they marched hand in hand toward the entrance.

She sucked in a breath. "Is that David's car?"

Up ahead, a gray sports car was parked on the cross street. They picked up their pace. At the car, Natassa let out a gasp. The window was busted, the door was dented up, and the CD player had been stolen. Someone had slashed the leather upholstery in front.

Brandon muttered under his breath.

She freed her hand from his and hugged herself.

"It's worse than he let on." Brandon ran a hand through his hair.

"I'm sure he didn't want to worry you."

He eyed her. "You've got to be honest when dealing with the insurance company. I hope this doesn't cause any problems."

She frowned. Why did she always jump to defend David? She always had. As if her firstborn could do no wrong. Maybe she had thought he couldn't. Until now.

"I'll deal with this later." He waved his hand toward the car. "Let's go see Mercy."

Her pulse kicked up a notch, but she nodded. Through the door, up the elevator, and into the hallway. Her heart galloped in her ears. She nibbled on her lip.

They stood before DeAndre's door, and Brandon grabbed her hand and gave it a squeeze before he knocked.

Janell opened the door. Soft lines edged her face as she smiled. The shadows under her eyes were not entirely concealed with makeup. This spunky teen who had babysat

Natassa's girls had grown into a woman, a mother. "Come in." She gestured inside.

"Thank you." Brandon stepped across the threshold.

Natassa followed, clutching his hand. They hovered near the entrance.

"Welcome to our humble abode." Janell's chuckle reeked of nerves. "It's small. Much smaller than your place. Your old place, I mean. Mercy said you moved?"

Natassa opened her mouth but couldn't seem to force any words out.

Brandon nodded. "Yes. To the city."

"That's great. She talked all about her princess room. Anyway, what this place lacks in space, it makes up for in ambiance. Am I right?" She pointed to the wall-to-wall windows. Her smile faltered.

"Uh. Very nice." Brandon cleared his throat. "Where's Mercy?"

A little boy ran into the room, Paw Patrol action figure in hand. He stopped in his tracks and stared.

Janell smiled down at him and then made eye contact with Natassa. "This is Java."

Natassa nodded toward him, still unable to muster even a small greeting.

Janell didn't seem to notice. "Java, can you tell Mercy her parents are here?"

The boy bit his bottom lip before replying. "She knows. She's hiding in her closet."

Natassa frowned. Her closet? She'd been here long enough to claim a closet? One they'd have to drag her from? Kicking and screaming no doubt.

Janell wrinkled her forehead. "I'm so sorry. She's been having…a hard time with the transition. I'll talk to her." She spun around and took a few steps toward the hallway.

"Where's David?" Natassa's voice sounded hoarse and foreign to her ears.

Janell stopped and turned. "I think he's still on the rooftop. There's a patio up there with tables and grills. He said he needed some air. I think…" A flash of an apology crossed her face. "I think he might be hiding too. In his own way."

Once Janell disappeared into a room to the right of the hallway, Natassa sent a panicked look to Brandon. "What are we going to do?" she whispered. "I don't want to cause a scene."

He shrugged. "We'll do whatever we need to do, babe. Scene or no scene."

She shifted her weight from foot to foot. "Shouldn't we be the ones to talk to her?"

Brandon released his hand from her grasp and sank onto the couch. She hesitated only a moment before settling beside him. A baby stirred from a bouncy seat next to them.

"Oh my gosh!" Her hand flew to her heart. "I didn't know he was there."

Brandon chuckled.

The baby wiggled and started to fuss.

She glanced in the direction Janell had gone. Could she hear the baby? Was she going to come and get him? Natassa reached over and gently bounced the seat. "It's okay. Your mommy'll be back soon."

The fuss escalated to an all-out cry, and still, Janell did not emerge. His little face twisted as he writhed. "I can't take it." Natassa reached over and unbuckled him from the seat. She swooped him up and laid him over her shoulder, then bounced him and patted his back. "You're okay, sweetie."

Her lips brushed the top of his head. His soft curls reminded her of Mercy's baby hair. She inhaled his baby scent.

Brandon grinned at her.

"What?"

"Nothing. I just love watching you be who you are."

She tossed a glance to the ceiling. "I couldn't just sit there and listen to him cry."

"I know. That's why I love you."

She peered down the hallway. "What's taking them so long?"

Brandon leaned toward her, his voice low. "I think Janell got reinforcements."

"What?"

"While you were grabbing the baby, Janell left, went down the hall, and came back with DeAndre."

Natassa spoke through gritted teeth. "We should be the reinforcements. We should be the ones talking to Mercy right now. Us."

"Mercy doesn't want to talk to us right now."

Tears burned the corners of her eyes. "Why, Brandon? Why did she choose them over us? Haven't we been good to her? Haven't we given her everything a little girl could ever want?" She squeezed her eyes shut to prevent an onslaught. "Aren't we good enough?" She perched on the edge of the couch, bouncing the baby gently.

Brandon wrapped his arm around her shoulder and drew her close. "We've done the best we knew how to do." He kissed the top of her head. "We've loved that girl with all our heart and soul."

"Then, why isn't it enough?"

~

Mercy's lip trembled, but she took DeAndre's outstretched hand and allowed him to pull her to her feet.

"Come on, sweetheart." He gave her arm a soft tug.

She gripped his hand tight, then enfolded herself under the crook of his arm. She wasn't leaving his side. She could feel his heart beating in his wrist, quick and hard. He breathed funny too. Maybe he was as nervous as she was. Mercy had overheard DeAndre tell Janell he would stay in their bedroom when Mom and Dad came to get Mercy. He wanted to hide too, but why? He was bigger, and her mom couldn't make him do anything he didn't want to do.

But Mercy? She could make Mercy go home and never come back.

Janell stepped back out of the doorway and let them go first. Java hugged her leg, unusually calm and quiet.

When Mercy saw Mom and Dad, she pressed closer to DeAndre. She wouldn't let him hide from her. He nudged her forward. Mom paced with Joe, patting his back and talking baby talk in his ear. When she saw Mercy, she stopped and stared.

Janell brushed past them. "Oh, I'm sorry. Was he fussing?"

"Just a bit." Mom handed Joe to Janell, who swooped him over her shoulder. Mom took a couple steps toward Mercy and squatted, her belly sticking out between them like a giant beach ball. "Oh, sweetie, I missed you so much." Her eyes were all watery.

Something inside of Mercy shifted. She broke free of DeAndre and fell into her mother's arms. "I'm sorry." She clung to her mom's neck, her throat and eyes hot and scratchy.

Dad pressed his leg against Mom's back to steady her.

"It's okay, baby. I forgive you."

"I love you." And she did. Mercy loved her mom and her dad and her brothers and sisters and her life back home. She didn't hate everyone and everything like she thought she did. Her love was just torn in two was all.

Mercy glanced at Dad, her hand gripping the back of his leg around her mom's back. Then she cringed. "Am I gonna be grounded for a million years?"

Mom laughed. "No, baby. Your brother might, though."

DeAndre chuckled. He took a step back, and already her back felt cold. She missed his nearness from one step away.

She turned and looked up at him. His smile and eyes looked sad again like they had the first day she came. A lump rose in her throat.

Dad held his hand out to Mom and pulled her up.

"What's this you're wearing?" Mom fingered the blue lace on Mercy's skirt.

"It's my Black Panther costume. DeAndre bought it for me." Mercy smiled up at him.

"Oh." Mom's voice sounded strange—high and like it came out of her nose. She locked eyes with DeAndre. "She doesn't really know about any of those superheroes."

"We watched the movie." Mercy stepped over and grabbed DeAndre's hand. "Watched it twice, actually."

Mom's smile was tight. "I see."

Janell cleared her throat and motioned toward the couches. "Won't you sit down?"

Mom gripped her purse as if someone was going to steal it. "I don't know."

Dad's throat looked strange as he swallowed. "Just for a minute." He sat slowly and stiffly.

Mercy tugged DeAndre toward the couch that David normally occupied, then settled next to him. Janell sat on the other side of her with both Joe and Java in her lap. Mom and Dad sat on the opposite couch, looking uncomfortable.

Dad and Janell both started to talk at the same time, but Dad stopped asking his question about auto body shops and gestured to Janell to go ahead.

"So, what's your plan for the night?" Janell must always be thinking about plans. She'd asked Mercy and David the same thing the first night they were there.

Dad had his business face on. No smile, but not unfriendly. "We're going to get a hotel here in Chicago tonight and get David's car fixed. We'll head home tomorrow, hopefully."

Mercy's breathing quickened. *No. No. No.* Leaving. They were leaving? Going to a hotel today. Going home tomorrow. She let out a soft whimper.

"Can we stay for dinner?" Mercy's eyes went wide as they darted between Mom and Dad.

Janell stammered. "Y-yes. Please do. I'm making lasagna. They'll be plenty."

Mom and Dad looked at each other.

Mom bit her lip. "That's not necessary."

Janell leaned forward, and her eyes zeroed in on Mercy. "I don't know how it is where you live, but right now, restaurants are still closed for dine in. You could place a pickup order, but around here, a lot of places got broken in to, so it's hit and miss."

Mom wiggled. Looked at Mercy, then back at Dad. She nodded so little that if Mercy had blinked, she would've missed it.

"Okay. Thank you." Dad put his hand on Mom's knee. "We'll stay for dinner."

DeAndre gave Mercy's hand a little squeeze.

She covered her smile with her other hand.

20

———

June 2020
Chicago, Illinois

Natassa left the awkwardness of the apartment and punched the up arrow on the elevator. She tried to shake off the picture of Mercy sitting wedged between DeAndre and Janell and their boys. One big happy family with Natassa and Brandon left to skirt around the edges like outsiders. The way Mercy tucked her hand into DeAndre's as if it belonged there made her shoulders slump.

The elevator pinged, and she stepped on, alone. The building sat as quiet as the eye of a hurricane. She didn't trust the appearance of peace.

Why had she consented to dinner? It was sure to be torture. She'd have to watch Mercy interact with her "new family," have to sit across from the man who wrought such destruction in her life. And what? Make polite conversation? What had she been thinking?

Mercy's grip on this place, on these people, was knuckle-white tight. It would take a fight to pry her fingers free and pull her away. And all of a sudden, the fight had fled Natassa. She didn't have the strength it would take. She leaned into the easier road of delaying the inevitable. Maybe after dinner, she could summon the courage. Or maybe Brandon could gather strength enough for both of them instead of wavering.

When the elevator door slid open and revealed the rooftop patio, wind gusted around her. She shivered despite the lingering warmth. She needed to find her golden boy to know that his heart remained as true as ever, even with his betrayal.

She stepped out, and her breath caught at the view. On one side, the city stretched below her, expansive and impressive. On the other side, in between towering buildings, sunlight glistened over the lake. A soft breeze tousled her hair, and she tucked a stray strand behind her ear.

David reclined in a patio chair, silhouetted by the sun. His T-shirt rustled with a gust of wind. "You found me."

She pulled out the seat next to him and sat, propping her swollen feet up on another chair. "Hiding from me?" The wind tossed her words toward him.

He squinted, shading his eyes from the sun. "I didn't think you'd want to see me."

Her gaze probed his. "You know I love you, right? More than anything. No matter what."

"I know." His gaze drifted back toward the restless waters.

"Why'd you do it?" She kept her voice soft, prodding with the raw places of her heart instead of the anger that had bubbled forth before.

"Because I saw her, Mom. You used to see her." He brought his gaze to meet hers, then abruptly looked away. "And then...I don't know when it happened. I don't know if it was when you lost the first baby or the second or the third, but somewhere in there, fear crept in and clouded your vision. You stopped seeing what was right in front of you."

She swallowed, her throat tight, chest hot. "That man has no right to my daughter."

David shrugged. "Maybe not." He sat forward, propped his elbows on his knees, and laced his fingers together. "But your daughter, what are her rights? She hungers for him. You can see the longing in her eyes. If you look, I mean." He angled his gaze at her, his blue eyes piercing.

She shifted her weight in the chair and wrapped her arms around herself, defensive.

David didn't break eye contact. "She's been so happy this past week. Happier than I've seen her in years."

Natassa huffed. "What can he give her that we can't?"

"A lot, I think. A lot that I don't understand because I'm not black." He talked to her as if he were the parent and she the child.

The nerve! She didn't have to listen to this. She slid her feet off the chair and leaned forward. "I'm going downstairs."

David put a hand on her arm. "Just look, Mom. Look at her face when she looks at him. See how her eyes light up. If you really love her, don't you want to do what's best for her?"

Natassa's jaw dropped, and she shook her arm free from David's touch. "*If* I really love her? Are you kidding me right now?"

David rolled his eyes and opened his mouth to speak, but she cut him off.

She stood, towering over him. "You have no right to lecture me about love or parenting. You are nineteen years old. Nineteen."

"I know how old I am."

She waved him off and started toward the elevator, then spun around. "When you have a couple of kids of your own, then maybe—just maybe—you will have earned the right to talk to me about what it's like to love a child, to have a piece of your heart walking around outside your body. Until then, you'd better keep your mouth shut." She stormed off, punching the elevator button while muttering to herself.

But wait. She still had unanswered questions. A dull pain throbbed in her lower back, and she shifted her weight. Here she was again, running from her problems instead of facing them. The old Natassa had resurfaced. She grimaced. With a ding, the elevator door opened. She stared at the gaping space. Leaning against the wall, she watched the door slide closed and then walked back toward David.

He tilted his chair back, the front two legs suspended in the air. She hated when he did that as a kid; it always freaked her out. Now, a sad smile tugged at her lips. He'd grown into an adult. She could no longer admonish him to keep the feet of his chair firmly planted on the ground. As an adult, he was free to take risks and suffer the consequences of his choices.

She lowered herself back down, propping her elbows on the table in front of her. "When did you come up with this whole crazy scheme?"

He regarded her, looking, at that moment, every bit like his father. "Mercy's last day of school. The day we all had ice cream to celebrate."

She tilted her head, remembering.

"Why did we have ice cream without her, Mom?" The front legs of his chair hit the concrete with a scrape as he sat forward and pressed his palms on the table.

"What?" She shook her head. "We didn't have ice cream without her. She was right there with us."

"Not at first. She came down the steps, and all of us were huddled around, already eating. Did you see her face, Mom? It was like somebody slapped her. She had to feel completely left out."

Natassa scoffed. "No. We would never leave her out."

"You did, Mom."

"No. I told Alexa to announce it. I figured she'd be down in just a minute."

David's eyes fluttered closed. "Her Echo would have been unplugged."

"What do you mean? Unplugged?"

"Her lamp is on her desk. If she needs to plug her laptop in, she has to unplug the Echo There are no other outlets that reach."

Natassa frowned. "How do you know this?"

"I pay attention."

His words stung, and she squirmed. "I guess I have been distracted…but I never meant to leave her out."

"I know that. I'm just not sure if she does. You and Dad rushed off to do work, Hope and Faith went to ride bikes without even inviting her—"

"She doesn't like to ride her bike."

"Maybe she'd like to be invited. I'm just saying that everyone else scattered, and we talked. She begged me to meet DeAndre, Mom. I couldn't tell her no."

She sighed, taking in her little boy turned man. "I know what that's like."

A grin as her golden boy must have sensed himself sliding back into her good graces. And then, "Is Dad seriously going to take away my car?"

"We'll see." She found a smile and offered it as a truce.

~

Mercy took a piece of garlic bread from the platter her mom handed her, then passed the tray to DeAndre on her left. Her old family sat on the right side of her, her new family on the left. She'd wedged herself in the middle.

"Would you like any green beans?" Janell held the dish out to her.

"No, thank you." Mercy stuffed a bite of lasagna in her mouth.

Mom made a little sound in her throat. "Mercy, take a scoop of vegetables."

Mercy eyed Janell, but Janell's eyes roamed her own plate. "Janell doesn't make me eat my vegetables." A little tomato sauce splattered onto Mercy's lap, and she wiped it with her napkin.

Mom spoke low and firm, scooping a big pile of green beans onto Mercy's plate. "Eat your vegetables."

She sighed. "Fine." She poked her fork into a green bean and took a small bite. She liked Janell's rules better.

Forks and knives clattered on plates without interruption from people talking.

Mom kept studying Mercy like she had changed in the past week and Mom was trying to figure out what was different. Mercy squirmed under her gaze.

Dad cleared his throat. "So, the rioting, is it over?"

DeAndre and Janell shrugged at the same time. "Who knows?"

"It's been primarily in this area, right?"

DeAndre shook his head, then swallowed and wiped his mouth with his napkin. "No, it started here but then spread all over. We can never tell where it's going to break out next."

Mom fiddled with her napkin and looked at Dad. "We're just trying to figure out the best place to get a hotel room for the night."

A burning feeling spread around Mercy's heart. Would this be the last meal she had with her new family? Would Mom and Dad let her stay the night? Or never let her stay again? She pressed her lips together, but a whimper escaped just the same. Her eyes misted over, and the food on her plate looked cloudy.

Mom stared at her.

"You could all stay here tonight." Janell brought her gaze up to meet Mom's and then Dad's before returning it to her plate. "I mean, if you want to."

DeAndre looked at Janell, and they talked with their eyes like a secret code.

A bubble of hope rose in Mercy's belly.

Dad glanced around the small apartment, a deep wrinkle on his forehead.

"It's small, but we could make room." Janell took a drink of her soda. "Java could sleep with us, and you could have his bed. Not sure if both of you would fit. Or David could sleep in Java's room, and you two could take the couches."

Mom stared at the sofa. "I don't know."

Mercy pushed her chair back from the table. "Please, Mommy." She knelt on the floor, laying her head on Mom's knee, tears pooling. "Please, can we stay? I don't want to go to a hotel. I want to stay here."

"Mercy—" Dad spoke in his bad news voice, the soft but firm one he always used when he told bad news.

She tilted her head up at him, cheeks wet, lip trembling. "Daddy, please!"

Dad bent over and whispered something in Mom's ear, and she whispered something back. Seconds ticked by. If they didn't answer soon, she might jump out of her skin.

Mom nodded. "Okay."

Mercy stood and maneuvered around Mom's large belly onto her lap. The table pressed into Mercy's back, but she didn't care. She wrapped her arms around Mom's neck. "Thank you."

Mom kissed the top of her head. "I love you."

"I love you, too."

Mercy turned and grinned at DeAndre, who ducked his head to try to hide his smile.

"I'll sleep with Mercy." Mom put a protective arm around her shoulder.

Janell frowned. "But she sleeps on an air mattress on the floor. And it's only a twin."

"It'll be fine."

"Okay." Janell's smile looked funny.

"I guess I'll take the other couch." Dad nodded at David like they were partners or something.

"Thank you for the offer." Mom tilted her head toward Janell.

DeAndre exchanged a look with his wife. "No problem."

Mercy wiggled off Mom's lap and crammed the last bite of lasagna into her mouth.

"Anyone want dessert?" Janell went to the kitchen and retrieved brownies.

Java stuck both sauce-covered arms in the air. "Meeeeee."

Janell scooped a brownie onto his plate.

"Me! Me!" Mercy raised her hand, bouncing in her chair.

Mom pointed to her plate. "Not until you eat your vegetables."

Mercy groaned.

~

At bedtime, Natassa tucked the covers over Mercy and kissed the top of her head. "Good night, sweetheart. I'll be to bed in a bit."

"Okay. Night." Mercy turned on her side.

Natassa hoisted herself up and slipped out of the room, leaving the door cracked open. How wonderful to tuck her little girl in again, to tell her a Bible story and pray over her, and to sing their songs. Oh, how she'd missed this.

Mommy. Mercy had called her Mommy for the first time in maybe a year. No wonder she'd melted. She blew Mercy a kiss through the small opening before joining the others in front of the TV.

In the living room, David and Brandon sat on one couch, DeAndre and Janell on another. An old football game played on the television. Neutral territory. A safe topic of conversation. Natassa nestled next to Brandon.

If only she didn't have to disturb the peaceful scene, but she had to get something off her chest.

She angled herself in DeAndre's direction and tented her hands under her chin. "I don't allow Mercy to watch the Marvel movies."

"We're sorry." Janell's hand flew to cover her heart. "We didn't know."

"It's just that…they contain a lot of violence, and I don't think it's healthy for children to be exposed to that." Frankly, she couldn't believe they were not only okay with her nine-year-old watching the films but also their three-year-old.

"We're sorry." Janell's face scrunched.

DeAndre put a fist to his mouth and stared at her. Then he sat forward. "I think it's important for Mercy to see people who look like her playing heroic roles."

Natassa scoffed.

Brandon rubbed her back. He was trying to calm her so she'd drop the subject, but DeAndre had no right to interject the way he did.

"*Black Panther* is not Dove approved."

David chuckled.

She glared at him.

DeAndre's face registered confusion, then a flicker of self-righteousness. "Natassa, you are raising a black child. Mercy may be mixed, but she moves in this world as a black child. She needs to grow up with an understanding of what that means."

Natassa rolled her eyes. "I don't know what you're talking about."

He pointed in her direction. "That's what scares me."

Janell nibbled her lip.

Brandon dug his thumbs harder. "Honey—"

"Look, Mercy has people of color in her life. We moved from the white suburbs to the city so that she wouldn't feel out of place all the time. We go to St. Anthony's once a month. She has an understanding of what it means to be black."

"But do you ever talk to her about it? Do you talk to her about race? About racism?"

Natassa huffed. "She's nine years old! She too young—too innocent—for those conversations. In time, I'm sure we will—"

"Do you know how old I was when my dad sat me down and talked to me about what it means to be black? Four years old. Black families don't avoid the subject, Natassa. She's experiencing a whole host of things in this world, and if you're not talking about them, she's not going to know how to process them."

Natassa shook her head. "She's too young."

Brandon took her hand and squeezed. "Your blood pressure."

"Does she know the names of any of the black people who were murdered unjustly? What about Breanna Taylor? Does Mercy know about her? Tamir Rice? Alton Sterling? Philando Castile? Does she know their names?" DeAndre's questions pummeled her.

"I don't know."

"Well, she knows George Floyd's name." DeAndre sat back and flung his arm over the couch cushion. "Because I told her. I talked to her about what happened."

Heat spread through her veins as she spoke through clenched teeth. "You had no right."

"The world blew up outside our window. She deserved to know why." His eyes bored into her.

Brandon kneaded her shoulders. "Look, the circumstances have been crazy. We can't blame you for not knowing how to navigate life with *our* daughter." He leveled his gaze at DeAndre. "And you can't blame us for the way we are choosing to raise her."

DeAndre pressed his lips together and nodded.

"So." David flashed a smile. "How about them Bulls?"

21

_1868,_
Gordon, Georgia

We eventually make it to Gordon. I ride in the negro car the rest of the way. Thaddeus's absence looms large next to my own smallness in the journey. I wrap my arms tightly around myself when a man in my car speaks about a sportsman in Macon shooting a negro for the fun of it. "He just be walking along the street and bam! Shot and killed."

If only Thaddeus could be beside me.

When we get off in Gordon, we find that Thaddeus was correct. Bent rails and burned bridges make traveling farther by train impossible.

As we stand behind a grove of trees, he rakes his hand through his hair. "We need to get to Savannah so we can t-take a steamer to Charleston. This would be more or less a straight shot if everything was operational."

"What now?"

He scrubs the back of his neck. "We start walking to Scarborough to catch another train."

I lift an eyebrow. "How far is it?"

"About a hundred miles." He takes a few steps, motioning for me to follow.

I don't. "You expect me to be your servant carrying this case for a hundred miles?"

He turns his head and winks at me, not altering his pace. "Maybe we'll get lucky."

Groaning, I hoist the suitcase to my shoulders and follow. The case is much lighter without the rice and cornmeal I shared with Dandy's family. Humidity presses down upon me, and dust coats the inside of my mouth as it puffs up with our steps.

As it turns out, we do get lucky. A wagon of freedmen stops and offers a ride. We take this to a station that's still in operation, if only for half the distance of the trip. We end up having to walk merely thirty miles out of the hundred. Thaddeus's whistling has made the time pass quickly. His very presence lightens my burden. We laugh as we walk. Thaddeus recounts pranks his brothers used to play on each other. I tell of leaving spiders on my sisters' pillows just to see the girls jump.

When the Scarborough Station comes into view, a pit forms in my stomach. Once again, we will part ways. I glance up at him. He has not stuttered during the entire walk. The ease with which his words have flowed causes a pang in my chest. He is as comfortable with me as I am with him.

The ride from Scarborough to Savannah is rough. Workers have straightened many old rails, putting them down again. My car contains plain board seats where negroes cram together and bump into each other with each jostle of the ragged tracks. My teeth chatter. We pass ruins of old railroad tracks that are wrapped around tree trunks, twisting and curving every which way. When we arrive at Savannah, Thaddeus reports that his car had wooden dining chairs in place of seats. They slid and bumped into each other along the way.

"Did you enjoy Sherman's hairpins?" Thaddeus asks, grinning. "That's what they call the straightened-out tracks."

I stretch my aching back. "I think I'll enjoy me a nice steamer ride."

One more ride to Charleston. Then just another to Georgetown. I'm almost there. Why does the thought of reaching the end of my journey cause my chest to ache? I feel loss like water falling through my fingers. Mama. My brothers and sisters. Mayme and Mingo. My new niece or nephew. I may never see any of them again. And what of Thaddeus? Once he delivers me safely to Georgetown, will he disappear from my life forever?

~

The air in Savannah hangs heavy and moist. As evening descends, a fog comes with it, lowering like a thick curtain. I shuffle down its sandy streets, ducking under the canopy of moss-draped live oaks that line them. Thaddeus has gone to purchase our passage to Charleston. Whether he's paying my fare to be a gentleman or to avoid a scene like the one on the Macon train, I can't be sure. He's taken my suitcase to the porter, and my steps are lighter without it. Freer. I pause to inhale the fragrance of magnolias. I need to wash up, change my dusty dress. My toes curl at the welcome thought of a steamer cabin and three complete meals.

"Whoo-wee, Liberty. Do I have good news for you!" Thaddeus takes large steps to meet me, his grin stretching across his face.

I look around warily. He's addressing me in public without playing the role of master and servant. My forehead puckers. "What is it?"

"The steamer's newly integrated. I got both you and me first-class fare. You get to bunk first-class same as us white folk."

My mouth parts. "What?"

His head tilts back as he laughs. "Yes, ma'am. You can sit at the same table, sit in the same ladies' cabin, and sleep in a first-class cabin for the night."

I clap my hands together, my smile broad. But then I still. "You sure? I'm not gonna get kicked off again, am I?"

"Not this time. They're boasting of their big ole welcome to all races." His eyes shine.

I allow myself jubilation.

Posters hang upon the steamer's entrance stating the rules, which include no gambling, smoking, or swearing. I can only assume, from what Thaddeus has told me of his experience of steamboats thus far, that those rules will be promptly ignored. My stomach tumbles with excitement.

At mealtime, waiters stretch tables out. They place plates, utensils, bread, and vegetables, then cake and candies. Then they bring out the chairs, and finally the meats. My mouth waters as the tantalizing scents of roast beef and chicken waft through the cabin. I choose the best seat for myself at the table. I stand behind my chair as the barkeeper bows to the ladies. Once the gong sounds, we can finally sit and eat. The clink of knives and forks drowns out the growling of my stomach. When the first bite of beef hits my tongue, I can't help but moan a little. I ain't never tasted anything like it. If only we were traveling a much farther distance so I could eat more of it.

Gas lamps light crystal chandeliers above me, creating sparkling glitters of light on the walnut-paneled walls. The gilt-painted columns and arches also reflect golden light. I stuff myself full of pie, and I am one of the last to leave the table.

In the evening, I sit on one of the velvet sofas with two other freedwomen in the ladies' cabin, swapping stories and laughing loud, until the white women and their children take their leave, and the black women have the sitting area all to ourselves. I kick off my shoes and dig my toes into the plush, floral-patterned carpet.

The huge mirror makes this space seem twice as large as it truly is. There's a sizeable silver watercooler with silver drinking cups chained to its side. My lips have never before touched anything so fine, and I relish delicate sips. Music from the orchestra weaves its way to us, and we tap our feet to the beat. When a lively reel begins, I stand and extend my hands to one of my new friends. We dance around as the other woman keeps time by slapping her knee. Finally, we retire to our rooms.

They've furnished my stateroom with a sofa, mirror, lamp, and two chairs, along with a marble washstand, which I make use of. That night, I sink onto the luxurious horsehair mattress with soft covers and bury my face in the feather pillow. Bells and whistles sound, but they don't bother me now. I'm full and happy and free.

~

I awaken to a misty morning. After breakfast, I saunter onto the veranda. Thaddeus stands with his elbows resting on the rail, eyes searching through the fog to the horizon. Towels and linen sheets hang out to dry beside him, flapping in the breeze. The scent of cigar smoke from the gentlemen's cabin clings to him.

We drift past a huge bulge. I point. "What's that?"

"F-fort Sumter." He says nothing else, and I don't prod. I haven't a clue what he means, but it must have to do with the war. Thaddeus grows pensive at the mention of the battle between the states, his expression clouding like the air around us.

As we stand together in silence, buildings slowly take shape before us, edging through the mist. Warehouses and church steeples. Large black birds circle overhead. Buzzards?

"Welcome home," Thaddeus whispers to himself.

As the boat prepares to land, one long whistle sounds, followed by two short, then another long whistle and two more short ones. Thaddeus cringes.

Before I can think better of it, my hand is once again on his shoulder. He squeezes his eyes shut, and his face twists. His body trembles with each breath. I open my mouth to speak comfort but stop. I have no words. If only I could wrap my arms around this man, but the touch of my hand has already crossed a line. I let it fall and instead rest my fingers next to his on the railing. Near, but not touching. The space between our different colored skin so slight yet so broad.

Thaddeus says little as we disembark. He doesn't whistle, joke, or grin. His steps plod past the markets and gardens of shrubs and trees. I follow at a short distance, suitcase on my shoulders. We pass heaps of ashes where homes must have once stood. Broken down walls and flights of marble steps that lead nowhere. The rest of the structure is crushed and charred. A broken pillar in a pile of rubble. The stone tower of a cathedral, its roof gone. A burned-out shell of another church. A post-office full of holes. I swallow past the lump in my throat as I watch Thaddeus's shoulders slump further with each step.

He turns down a side street and sulks up to what once must have been a stately house. Now it droops, like it is weary from what it has seen. The porch that wraps around the length of it has boards sinking in places, and the white paint is peeling. Brown tufts of grass sprinkle the yard.

Thaddeus stops and heaves a sigh. "Stay here."

My forehead pinches, but I obey.

He drags himself up the crooked steps and knocks. As he waits, he rubs the back of his neck, his head down.

The door opens.

A middle-aged woman in a pale blue day dress appears. Her hair is pulled back into a severe bun, and thick lines crease her forehead. She gasps. "Thad? Is that you?"

"Hi, Mama."

She cries out and covers her mouth, then wraps him in a stiff hug.

His arm comes around her back, and he pats. His shoulders do not relax.

"Ronald! Jim! It's your brother." Her shouts radiate joy, and yet the emotion doesn't seem to penetrate the man in front of her. She pulls back and holds on to his shoulders. "Let me look at you." She shakes her head, her eyes shimmering with pride. Then her gaze flickers to me. "Who's that?"

My eyes meet hers, and I prepare an introduction. *Nice to meet you, ma'am. Your son is helping me get to my family in Georgetown.*

But before I have a chance to speak, Thaddeus's words cut through. "Just a servant I hired to carry my case."

I suck in a breath, eyes threatening to mist. *Just a servant.* Nothing more? I dip my head as my stomach tenses.

"Oh, okay. Well, come inside dear." His mother ushers him in the house, and I am left standing on the street alone.

22

————

June 2020
Chicago, Illinois

DeAndre stepped onto the moonlit balcony and slid the door shut behind him. "I thought I'd find you out here."

Janell's cheeks shimmered. She wiped them with the bottom of her T-shirt. "Couldn't sleep." She sniffed.

"Me either." He dropped into the other plastic chair beside her.

The story of their lives. At least recently.

"Is everyone else asleep?" Her gaze remained fixed on the lake. Her voice trembled.

"Yeah. Natassa and Brandon are guarding their children like security dogs." Natassa was sleeping with her arm slung around Mercy, protecting her even while dreaming. Brandon was sleeping on his back with his arms crossed as if challenging anyone who might mess with his son on the opposite couch.

Janell's shoulders shook. "I love her, DeAndre. I don't know how I could fall in love with a little girl so quickly and completely, but I did. Head over heels." She planted her palms over her eyes. "She doesn't have a speck of my DNA, and yet she's woven her way into my heart. I don't—" Her voice cracked. "I don't know how I can bear to see her go."

His heart plummeted. Down, down, down until he despaired of ever feeling a shred of joy again. "I know." His voice came out thick, far too thick for two little words. And yet, if he said everything that tumbled through his mind, he'd break down right there on his balcony.

"When I tucked Java in tonight, his big brown eyes filled with tears as he asked why Mercy had to leave and if he'd ever see her again. I didn't know what to say."

DeAndre scrubbed his hand over his face. "Oh man."

"Did you see the way she begged to stay?"

He nodded.

In the distance, a car horn blared, and someone shouted an obscenity.

Janell turned to him, tears shining her eyes like stars. "She loves us as much as we love her."

"She's not ours to keep." Defeat dripped from his voice.

Janell flicked her gaze up to the night sky. "I used to think that love was enough. Always. That it could overcome any obstacle. But this?" She spread her arms out. "We love her. She loves us. But all of our hearts are about to be shattered."

DeAndre slammed his eyes shut to block out the tears that threatened. "If only I could paint a bridge."

A small squeak of a sound escaped Janell's lips. "If only you could."

~

Mercy woke up squished by the weight of Mom's arm. Half of her body hung off the mattress where Mom's belly had pushed her. Mom breathed in slow and deep. If Mercy could wiggle away without waking her mother, she could grab a bowl of Cocoa Puffs before Mom had time to stop her.

Mercy carefully slid the rest of her body off the mattress while lifting Mom's arm up and gently setting it down. She tiptoed from the room and into the kitchen.

Mercy scowled. Dad was awake already. He sat at the dining room table, laptop open, drinking coffee. Maybe he wouldn't notice.

She pulled up the stool to reach the cereal from the top cabinet.

"Good morning." Dad's voice boomed in the quiet.

She put a finger to her lips, then pointed to the couch where David snored away.

"He could sleep through a tornado." Dad took another sip of his coffee, then turned his attention back to his computer screen.

Mercy snatched a bowl and poured cereal into it, her back to her father. She reached up to put the cereal away in case Mom came out.

"I have an appointment to get David's car fixed at the auto body shop a block from here right when they open. We should be able to leave by three or four."

She didn't turn to look at him, not about to make dragging her away from DeAndre easy for him. She grabbed the milk from the fridge and sloshed it in her bowl, then ate hunched over the kitchen counter, back still toward the dining room.

Mom stepped from their bedroom, yawning.

Mercy shoveled the cereal into her mouth.

"Good morning." Mom walked into the kitchen and stretched.

"Good morning." A cocoa puff popped out of her full mouth as she answered. Her eyes went wide, and she turned to dump her bowl in the sink and wash out the evidence.

Mom didn't seem to notice. She meandered to the table and looked over Dad's shoulder.

He repeated what he had told Mercy moments earlier.

"Good. I'm glad we'll be able to start back before dark." She put a hand on Dad's shoulder, and he put his own on top of hers. Mom slid into the chair next to him.

"Does that mean we'll get home tonight?" Mercy hadn't been paying attention to how long the drive took on the way here, but it seemed too long to make it home before bedtime if they didn't leave until late in the afternoon.

Mom and Dad exchanged a look. Mom locked eyes with Mercy, her expression serious. "We won't be able to go home tonight. Hope has COVID. Or she might. We won't know for sure until tomorrow, probably. But if she does, we need to stay away until she is cleared from quarantine."

David stirred, rubbed his eyes, and sat up. His hair stuck up in all directions. "What?"

Mom repeated herself in the same bad-news voice.

"Is she okay?" David asked.

"Yeah. Seems mild. But with my pregnancy, I can't take the chance of catching it. We'll stay in a hotel close to home."

"Are you kidding me?" David ran a hand through his hair but only made it stick up at different angles. "There's no way I'm spending two weeks in a hotel. I'll crash at Libby's. They're coming back tonight."

Mom stared him down. "No way. You're not allowed to see her for two weeks, remember? And even if you were, there will never be any 'crashing' at your girlfriend's place."

Dad threw David a quick glance. "Listen to your mother."

"I'm an adult." David tossed the blanket off of him and onto the other couch.

Dad continued typing. "And when you make enough money to fully support yourself, you can consider making your own choices."

David jumped to his feet. "Ridiculous." He stalked to the kitchen and rummaged through the cabinets, emerging with a handful of mini white powdered donuts. Those were in there? He sat across from Mom.

Mom frowned. "I can't believe you're eating that."

He crammed a donut into his mouth, powdered sugar falling onto the table like snow. "Mmm. So good." He angled his face toward Mercy and smiled, mouth still full. "Want one?"

She'd be crazy to agree. She shook her head.

DeAndre stumbled into the kitchen and headed straight toward the coffee maker. Mercy scooted out of his way.

"Hey, pumpkin." He tousled her hair.

"Hey" She wanted to say Dad but couldn't. Not with Mom and Dad right there. How could she call two people Dad anyway? But if they left today, she might not ever be able to say it to DeAndre again. "We're leaving at three."

She searched his face for a sign of disappointment. A sign that he would argue. Would fight to keep her here. But there were only dark bags under his eyes.

"Okay." He filled his mug to the brim and brought it to his lips.

Okay? It was okay with him if she left? If he never saw her again?

She narrowed her eyes at him. "Hope has COVID. Maybe. We might have to stay in a hotel for two weeks." He had to say something about that. He didn't want her to catch the coronavirus, did he? What if she caught the virus from her sister and died? How would he feel then? And didn't he think it was the stupidest thing ever for her to stay in a hotel for two weeks when she could just stay here?

His mouth twisted. "Is she okay?"

Mercy shrugged. She wasn't about to say, *Yes, Hope is fine. No need to worry.* Let him worry. Not about her sister. About her. Let him show he cared.

"She'll be fine." Dad lifted his gaze from the laptop screen.

"Good." DeAndre took another drink.

"There is something else I need to tell you." Mom patted the chair next to her.

Mercy eyed her mother. What was going on?

Mom tilted her head toward the open chair. "Come on."

She crept over and lowered herself, feeling like a gray cloud followed overhead.

Mom took her hand. "Bethany has COVID too." Her eyes bored into Mercy's. "She's in the hospital. She's…not doing well." Sadness touched the edges of her voice.

Mercy sucked in a breath. "Bethany?"

The last time she'd seen Bethany had been at Mom's shower. Bethany had sat on the bed and joked about Rapunzel. Mercy had been rude, refusing to go downstairs with her.

"She's not doing well," Mom repeated.

Heat spread through Mercy's chest. The hospital? Bethany was in the hospital? "Is she on one of those breathing things?"

Mom nodded. "I think she's on a ventilator."

DeAndre's voice dropped like a bowling ball behind her. "Oh no."

David put his head in his hands.

"I want to see her." Mercy brought her eyes up to plead with Mom. "I wasn't nice to her the last time she was over. I need to see her. To tell her I'm sorry."

Mom squeezed her hand. "You can't, baby."

Mercy snatched her hand away. "What do you mean? Yes, I can. I need to."

Dad sighed and closed his laptop.

Mom shook her head. "You can't. I'm sorry. Those are the rules."

Mercy shot out of her chair. "You and your stupid rules. I hate your rules!" She crossed her arms. "I don't want to go home with you and your dumb rules. I'm staying here with DeAndre." In two steps, her arms were around his waist. She clung on.

DeAndre took a deep, shaky breath and rubbed her back. "Honey, you can't stay here with me. You have to go back with your mom and dad."

"What?" She looked up at him, unbelieving. He couldn't be saying this. He couldn't mean it.

She clutched the front of his shirt. "You're my dad. You are."

He shook his head and pried her hands off. "No, Mercy. You have to go. They're your family." His voice sounded rough and scratchy. It rubbed her heart raw.

She looked back and forth between her fathers. They both looked pained, like Mercy was a bee who'd stung them. Did they want to squash her like a bee?

Mom winced, and her hand flew to her stomach. She groaned.

"What? What's wrong?" Dad shifted to her side.

"Contraction." Her mouth formed an *O* as she breathed out.

"I don't want to go!" Mercy stomped her foot.

"Mercy, stop!" David stood. "Can't you see what you're doing to Mom? You don't want to make her sick again. You're going to hurt the baby."

Tears spilled forth. "Good! I don't care about the stupid baby anyway." She spun around, but not before seeing the shock on Mom's face and the disappointment on Dad's. She ran straight into Janell, who frowned at her. After looking one last time at DeAndre, whose sad eyes haunted her, she ran into her room and collapsed on her bed, then pounded the mattress with her fist.

Bad, bad, bad. They all thought she was bad. Her Mom and Dad and David. Janell and DeAndre. They all looked at her like she was a bad person. Maybe this baby would die too, and it would be all her fault. Her mom would cry forever and ever, and Mercy would always feel bad inside because of it. She shoved her face into her pillow to cover her sobs. Now neither side of her family wanted her.

~

Natassa grasped onto the dining room table and pushed herself to standing. She inhaled nice and slow. In through her nose. Out through her mouth. Again. The pain that had gripped her eased. "Let me go talk to her."

DeAndre inched toward the bedroom door. He obviously wanted to go to Mercy. His gaze stretched toward her bedroom, and his arms clamped around himself as if it took all of his self-control to hold himself back from running to her.

Natassa straightened and took a minute to breathe before stepping forward.

Janell stood, legs spread slightly apart, one foot planted in the hallway outside of Mercy's room, one foot in the dining area. She looked pulled in both directions, torn as to what to do. Her eyes darted from the bedroom door to Natassa and back again until Java banged into her leg and held on, snatching her attention.

Brandon's and David's sole focus remained on Natassa, their foreheads lined with concern. Brandon crouched next to her, ready to pounce at her next muffled groan of pain and whisk her back to the hospital.

But no. She was not going back there. Not today.

Her daughter needed her, and she would be there for Mercy.

"Are you okay?" Brandon and David asked in unison.

She waved them off and waddled with deep, steady breaths into the room where Mercy writhed under the blanket and sobbed into her pillow.

Her heart dropped at the sight of her little girl, racked with heart pain so deep it had nowhere to go.

"Mercy, baby." With a soft grunt, she lowered herself, one knee at a time, beside the mattress and put a calming hand on her daughter's shoulder.

"Go away." Mercy's voice was choked by tears, snot, and anger.

"Nope. You're not getting rid of me that easy." She rubbed her girl's back.

Mercy balled the blanket in her fists and twisted and pulled.

"Honey, the rule about not visiting Bethany—that's the hospital's rule, not mine. They want to keep people safe. They don't want the virus to spread."

Mercy turned on her side, keeping her back to Natassa. "It's a stupid rule."

"I wish I could see her too. But rules are there to keep people safe." She kept her voice soft, hoping to spread a gentle balm over her daughter's festering wounds.

"Yeah, well, you keep me so safe that I can't breathe."

Natassa flinched.

I can't breathe.

Was her fear like a knee on Mercy's neck, suffocating her?

She lowered her eyes and studied her cuticles. "Rules are like guardrails, I guess. Guardrails are important when you're, say, in a canyon. But they're just cumbersome if you're at a playground."

Mercy flipped onto her back and squinted up at her. "What are you talking about?" Her voice was scratchy with tears.

Natassa dropped her head into her hands. "What am I trying to say?" She sighed. "Rules are supposed to keep us safe. I guess...I haven't felt safe in a very long time. Not since we lost Ava. And I think maybe I keep propping up rules to make myself feel more secure. More in control."

Natassa looked up. Mercy's brow furrowed.

"It's my problem, not yours." She smoothed the hair from Mercy's face. "It's a place inside of me that I need Jesus to come and heal."

Mercy bit her lip. "I'm sorry for saying mean things. About the baby."

Natassa nodded. "Thank you for apologizing. But I'm more concerned with why you said those things." She prodded Mercy with her gaze. "Hurt people hurt people. Something is hurting in your heart. I want to know what it is so I can help."

Mercy shook her head. "I'm fine. I didn't mean it. I'm just tired."

She eyed her daughter. How many times had she said the same thing herself? *I didn't mean that. I'm just tired.* "I think part of you did mean it, at least a little. And it's okay, Mercy. It's normal to be jealous of a new sibling."

"I'm not jealous." She wrapped her arms around her stomach, her brow pinched.

"Okay." She took Mercy's hand and gave it a squeeze. "I want you to know that I love you with all of my heart. Always and forever. No matter what. There's nothing you could ever do to change that."

Mercy tilted her head. "You can't love me with all of your heart. You've got Charity to love. And Hope and Faith and Daniel and David. And Dad."

Natassa chuckled. "Oh, you think you only get the leftovers? You must not know about a mother's superpower."

Mercy narrowed her eyes.

"Oh, yes. It's stronger than anything any of those Marvel heroes have. When you become a mother, this amazing thing happens. Your heart grows." She spread her hands out in front of her. "God gives you the ability to love more than one child with all of your heart, and it doesn't take any love away from any other child. It's miraculous." She grinned. "You'll see someday."

Mercy rolled her eyes, but a trace of a smile touched her lips.

Natassa pushed herself onto the balls of her feet. "I'll give you some time alone. But why don't you try asking Jesus what lie you're believing that's making you hurt inside? Maybe we can both go to Him for some healing." She stood, her calves begging for a stretch.

Mercy's eyes misted. "I love you, Mom."

"I love you, too."

Natassa stepped into the hallway and closed the door behind her. She took a deep breath and rolled her shoulders, trying to ease the tension. Tantalizing breakfast smells wafted from the kitchen. Peppers?

She walked into the dining area. Brandon and David were nowhere in sight. Sizzling sounds came from the kitchen. Java sat on the couch, enthralled in an episode of Paw Patrol.

"They left for the auto body shop after peeking in on you." Janell flipped an omelet on the stove.

"I didn't even notice."

"They made me promise I'd call them right away if you had even a twinge of another contraction. How are you feeling?"

A ghost of a smile. "Better."

"How's Mercy?"

"She seems better, too."

"Good." Janell slid a glass of orange juice across the kitchen island. "OJ?"

"Sure." Natassa held the cool glass. "Thanks." She took a drink.

"I hope you like ham and cheese in your omelets. Oh, and onions and green peppers?" Janell asked over her shoulder.

"You don't have to cook for me, Janell."

Janell waved her off. "It's no problem at all." She glided the omelet onto a plate and passed it to Natassa.

"Thank you." She took her plate and cup to the table.

Janell cracked a couple more eggs into the pan. DeAndre entered from the patio, phone to his ear.

At the sight of him, Natassa instinctively looked over her shoulder for Brandon. *Not here.* She inhaled slowly. *But it's okay. You're safe.*

"Okay, I'll let you know. Love you. Bye." DeAndre set his phone on the counter and then leaned over and gave Janell a peck on the cheek. "Mmm…smells good."

Natassa chewed slowly, savoring the burst of flavor. "Tastes amazing."

DeAndre rubbed his hands together and looked at Natassa. "I just talked to my mom. She asked if it would be possible to bring Mercy by her house today to say goodbye? I understand if you don't want her to go, but we could take her over there for a few hours if it's alright." He squinted like he was bracing for a blow.

She jabbed her omelet with her fork. He wanted to take Mercy to his mom's? To say goodbye? Natassa didn't like it one bit—the bond that had taken place between her daughter and a woman she had never met. But then Natassa pictured Mercy twisting and turning on the mattress, her face drenched with tears. Maybe her daughter needed the closure. Maybe Mercy needed this to be okay with leaving Chicago behind.

She let her shoulders relax as she sighed. "Okay."

"Okay?" DeAndre's brows lifted.

Natassa nodded. "She can go. You can take her." She stuffed a bite in her mouth to keep herself from saying more. Or from taking it back.

"Thank you." A smile spread as he exchanged a look with Janell. "I really appreciate it." He picked up his phone. "I'll text my mom."

23

———

June 2020
Chicago, Illinois

DeAndre opened the door to leave, only to find Brandon with his hand on the doorknob. "Oh, hey. You're back."

Brandon's face registered surprise. "Where are you going?"

"We're headed over to my mom's for a bit. Natassa said we could take Mercy over there to say goodbye." DeAndre stepped back, allowing Brandon and David to enter.

"Oh." Brandon looked past him to where Natassa sat on the couch.

She nodded.

"You wanna come?" DeAndre angled his head toward David.

He chuckled. "That's okay. I mean, I know they're going to miss me, but they'll get over it."

"Okay then." DeAndre dangled his keys from his finger. "We're out." He ushered Janell, Mercy, and Java out the door. Joe cooed from Janell's arms.

DeAndre nearly sprinted from the front door to the elevator, then shoved the down button.

Janell cocked an eyebrow. "What's the hurry, Flash?"

DeAndre leaned toward her and whispered in her ear, "Let's get outta here before they change their minds."

Janell giggled. "Aye, aye, captain."

The five of them stepped onto the gateway to freedom and dropped away from the stifling atmosphere in the apartment above.

"Don't you think it's kind of awkward?" Janell spoke low through the side of her mouth. "Leaving them there by themselves?"

His head bobbed as he matched her whisper. "Heck yeah, it's awkward. But so is sitting there with them for hours trying to make small talk. Choose your poison, babe."

"Good point."

As they exited the elevator and entered the parking garage, it was as if a weight lifted off DeAndre. Natassa seriously agreed to this? Thank God she did. He had Mercy to himself again, away from Natassa's protective guard. A grin spread across his face.

"You get your very own seat belt this time." Janell winked at Mercy.

Mercy's eyes twinkled. "Last time was fun."

DeAndre threw back his head and laughed. What was this lightness dancing between them? A burden had taken flight. Mercy bounded into the back seat, humming to herself. Why had Natassa's presence weighed her daughter down? Wasn't there something wrong with that? The change in Mercy's demeanor proved as much. She'd been injected with life, with the sparkly stuff of her paintings, shimmer and glitter and fairy-tale things. Whereas Natassa and Brandon sucked the life right out of Mercy, DeAndre seemed to breathe it into her. How could he stand by and watch his sweet girl get drained again as soon as they stepped back through that apartment door?

He shook himself from such somber thoughts. If he only had today—these next few hours—he'd treasure it.

~

"Aren't you a sight for sore eyes?" Mama swung open the door and swooped Mercy into a bear hug. "Has anyone ever told you that you are the most beautiful young black woman God ever did think to create?"

Mercy shook her head in the soft folds of Mama's button-down blouse.

"Well, come in! Come in!" Mama held the door open, and the five of them bustled into the entryway where the scent of fried okra and hush puppies swirled.

"Good to see you." DeAndre bent over and kissed his mother on the cheek.

"You too." She peeked out the front door, then nudged him with her hip. "Looks like you ditched the brother this time."

"I knew you'd miss him."

"Ha!" She sashayed toward the dining room and grabbed a box from the shelf. "I bought a new game for us to play together, Mercy. You ever heard of Exploding Kittens?"

Mercy shook her head.

"Exploding Kittens?" DeAndre mumbled under his breath. "Sounds violent. Probably not Dove approved."

Mama shot him a look. "What now?"

"Nothing."

Janell smirked and pulled out a chair.

"I did some research online, and it's one of the most popular games for children your age." Mama spread the contents of the box on the dining room table. "Come on now, DeAndre. Harlem. We're all playing today."

~

After the game ended, Mama settled Mercy in front of some show on Netflix. Would Natassa approve? DeAndre didn't much care. He still rode the high from watching his girl dissolve into fits of laughter as they brandished cards such as the Nope Ninja and Bear-O-Dactyl.

His girl? yeah. She'd entwined her way into the fabric of his heart. Maybe he had no right to claim her, but he couldn't deny they belonged to each other.

Even if they shouldn't.

He slid open the fridge. "Oooh, root beer? Don't tell me you have…" He checked the freezer. "Vanilla ice cream. Jackpot!"

Mama grabbed four tall glasses and set them on the counter. "None for me, thanks. And none for Harlem either. The doctor says he needs to cut back on them sweets."

"Hey, Mercy," he called. "You ever had a root beer float? Soda and ice cream together. Your two favorite things."

Mercy's head popped around the corner. "Really? I can try it?"

DeAndre grinned. "Sit tight. I'll bring you one." He grabbed the gallon of ice cream.

Mama handed him the ice cream scoop. "Dessert before lunch?"

"Might as well sugar her up now. Who knows when she'll taste anything sweet again." He dished out three generous scoops, packing them down into the cup. Then he added a scoop to the other glasses.

"DeAndre, I don't know how to say this, so I'm just gonna say it." Mama settled her hands on her hips and stared him down.

He paused, ice cream dripping off the scoop onto the counter.

"That girl needs you. Those people don't know a thing about raising a black child, and they're doing more harm than good."

"Mama—"

"No, you listen to me." Mama wagged her finger inches from his face. "You've got to fight for what is right for her. You hear me?"

"What are you talking about?"

"I'm talking about custody."

DeAndre balked. "You want me to…sue Natassa for custody?"

"If that's what it takes." Mama took the bottle of root beer from the counter and poured. "I know you don't like to make waves, but this isn't about you, son. This is about her, and what's best for that little girl. How is she gonna know who she is in this world without black influences guiding her?" She took spoons from the drawer and tucked one into each glass. "You said yourself that Natassa thinks it's fine and dandy to ignore the issue of race entirely. That girl is going to grow up confused and without the tools she needs to navigate through the world if you don't step in."

DeAndre frowned. He couldn't argue her point. His little girl had the joy siphoned from her the instant Natassa entered their apartment. Mercy, hiding in the closet, cloaked in fear. Mercy, begging her mother to let her stay, tears dripping from her face.

And Janell's tear-choked voice mourning the loss of Mercy from their lives. Java curled up in bed, lip trembling, asking why Mercy had to leave.

Why *did* she have to leave?

But Natassa had sent him those hymns in prison. She'd told him to marry Janell and have a big, beautiful life. She gave him mercy when he didn't deserve it.

"I don't…" He wiped the drips of ice cream from the counter with his finger. "I don't want to start anything with Natassa."

"Did you not hear a word I just said." Mama rolled her eyes. "This isn't about what you want. This is about what's best for her." Mama's eyes darted toward the living room. "You got to put that little girl's needs above your own insecurities."

His brows rose. "Insecurities?"

She tilted her head. "I call it like I see it."

He took a deep breath in and out. "We'll talk about this later." He picked up two glasses and spun around, leaving his mother and her challenge in the background.

~

"I don't know." Janell started to nibble her thumbnail, then dropped her hand to her side.

DeAndre tilted the stroller back to roll over an uneven spot in the sidewalk. They'd left Mercy and Java with Mama and Harlem in order to walk and talk.

He veered around a discarded beer bottle. "I don't like the thought of doing that to Natassa. Not after how gracious she's been with me."

"Taking a child from her mother cannot be the best thing for her." Janell squinted up at him.

"No. I agree. But what if we didn't fight for full custody, or even fifty-fifty. What if we just asked for visitation rights? Just a chance to see her, to influence her. To speak into her life."

Janell bit her lip. "But an ugly court battle?"

He sighed. "Yeah. I don't like it."

"Oh, but she's been happy here with us, DeAndre." Janell tucked her fingers into her pockets. "She bubbles with enthusiasm. It's contagious. It makes me feel like we're not in the middle of a global pandemic or racial unrest or any of the other craziness of 2020. It makes me feel like this year is full of possibilities."

The scent of fried chicken from the local fast-food joint wafted through the air, and his stomach growled. "Make up your mind, woman."

His tease pulled a smile from her lips.

"Do you think we should pursue this or not?" His gaze held hers, the weight of the decision falling heavy between them.

Janell scrunched up her nose. "Has your mom ever steered you wrong?"

DeAndre adjusted the shade on the stroller, blocking the sun from Joe's face. "Maybe. But not usually."

She stopped and turned to him. "Let's do it."

"Really?"

She nodded. "I can't stand the thought of losing her, Dre. We can do this in a civil and kind way, but we've got to give it a shot."

He grabbed her hand and squeezed. "Okay. Let's do it."

~

Natassa ambled around the cozy apartment, observing, taking in the fragments of life displayed on the walls and shelves. A family picture of DeAndre and Janell smiling at each other while Joe looked up at them and Java stared straight at the camera with a smirk. A canvas with *We Believe in Second Chances Here* displayed in beautiful calligraphy. Java's small handprint in plaster of Paris, painted in a childish splash of bright blue, yellow, and red.

"There's nothing to watch." David flipped through channels, lounging on the couch he'd claimed as his.

Brandon sat at the dining room table, bent over his laptop, looking for a hotel for the night. Turned out that more damage had been done to David's car than met the eye. It would take longer to fix. They'd have to stay in Chicago another night. "I found a place. Two double beds. Grab and go breakfast. It's about"—Brandon stroked his chin—"fifteen minutes from here."

"Can't we just stay here another night?" David plunked the remote on the couch and picked up his phone. "There's more room."

Natassa rolled her shoulders. "My body's still yelling at me from last night. I need a real bed." She rubbed the small of her back.

"Then you two go. Leave Mercy and me here." David's thumb scrolled on his phone, and his eyes didn't leave his screen.

She exchanged a glance with Brandon, whose frown mirrored her own. On one hand, that would save them from fighting with Mercy. The less drama, the better. On the other hand, was it really a good idea to relinquish more time and space to this man? To allow her daughter to get even more attached? To delay the inevitable? "I don't know."

Brandon pinched the bridge of his nose. "It's only one night."

"Let me think about it." She spun around and headed for the bathroom. She needed to be alone. To think. She shut and locked the door and splashed cool water on her face. Facing herself in the mirror, she winced. The night of tossing and turning showed up clearly in the creases and bags under her eyes. She stretched.

Curious, she peeled back the corner of the shower curtain. Coconut scented shampoo and conditioner filled a shower caddy, along with vanilla bodywash. A purple loofah hung from the hook—Janell's. A men's shampoo and conditioner combo in a woodland scent nestled next to it, along with a men's bodywash—DeAndre's. And a child's three-in-one shampoo, bodywash, and bubble bath sat in the corner with a net full of bath toys suctioned underneath. It all looked so…normal. Just an average family. Nothing about it shouted former criminal. Nothing about the scene hinted of the years DeAndre had spent behind bars.

She popped open the medicine cabinet. Tylenol. Melatonin. Benadryl. Mouthwash. Floss. Lotion. Deodorant. She could find the same things in her own cabinets in her own home.

A knock and Brandon's voice. "You okay, baby?"

"Yeah." She twisted the lock and knob, cracking open the door.

"Were you snooping?" Brandon peered around her at the open medicine cabinet.

She crinkled her nose. "Maybe."

"And?"

"And nothing. They're completely ordinary."

"Bummer." The side of his mouth curved.

"Isn't that strange?" She leaned on the doorjamb. "For so long, I thought of this man as a monster. The monster who raped me. When I thought of him like that, when I put him in that box, I didn't have to think any further." She glanced back toward the medicine cabinet. "Monsters don't floss their teeth, or shampoo their hair, or pose for family portraits. But people do."

"Is it hard, then? Seeing him as a person?"

"Yes." She rubbed her hands up and down her arms. "And no. I don't know. I forgave him and forgave him again. It's so much easier to hate people from a distance, much harder when you get close enough to see your own reflection in their eyes. I don't hate him. I don't feel animosity toward him. I just don't know where the healthy boundary lines should be drawn here. Just because I've forgiven him doesn't mean we need to be best friends."

"It doesn't mean we have to stay at his house."

"What about you? How are you holding up?" She narrowed her eyes. Could she pull the truth from him?

He blew a raspberry. "Honestly, I think it would have been easier if I could have decked him as soon as I saw his face."

She chuckled. "I thought you forgave him years ago."

"Just one good punch to the jaw." He swung his fist through the air. "Then we could move on with all that forgiveness stuff."

"Not as easy as it seems, huh?"

He tilted his head. "You've been working through it for almost a decade. I spent a good portion of that time stuffing it all down, so I've got some catching up to do."

"It's a process, for sure. Remembering to fill up my love tank with Jesus's love so I have something to give, the ability to forgive." She'd forgotten lately. No wonder she'd been struggling. She closed her eyes and breathed deep. "I still feel like I'm stumbling through it all."

"A good night's sleep might help." His voice held a touch of humor.

She rolled her head back and forth, her neck stiff. "A night at a hotel sounds nice."

"Germs and all?" He raised his eyebrows.

"Germs and all." She reached out her hand to take his. "And a night away with just the two of us actually sounds luxurious. It could be a babymoon."

"A babymoon?" He brought her hand to his mouth and kissed it. "You're sure you'd be able to sleep knowing Mercy is here?"

"I think…" She turned and closed the medicine cabinet, then shuffled out of the bathroom hand in hand with Brandon. "I think she's in good hands."

"At least we know they care about her, want to do what's best for her."

"More than that. They love her." She halted and leaned into Brandon, putting her head on his shoulder. "They love her just like we do."

~

DeAndre's heart twisted as he dialed the number Mama had given him for a lawyer. Sitting alone on the back patio, he pressed the call button, then crumpled the sticky note in his hand. What would Natassa think if she knew what he was doing at this very moment? She'd graciously allowed him to bring Mercy here, and he was going behind her back and conspiring to sue her for visitation rights for her daughter? His stomach soured.

"Regan and Sons." The man's crisp tone spoke business.

DeAndre got right to the point, spilling out his case.

"Let me get this straight. You pled guilty to rape?"

A wave of shame crested over him. "Yes, sir."

"Then I'm sorry, but you don't have a case. There are legal protections against rapists filing for custody of any kind."

DeAndre closed his eyes, the word *rapist* settling like a cloak on his shoulders. He'd almost forgotten what that label felt like.

"Thanks anyway." He hung up the phone and ripped the sticky note into tiny pieces, not caring when bits of litter blew off his lap and into the yard.

He'd failed his mom.

He's failed his wife.

He'd failed his daughter.

After trying so hard to prove himself worthy in this world that was skimpy with second chances, he'd once again let everyone he loved down. He'd have to walk in that house and tell them that Mercy would leave their lives today, never to return. They'd be left with only bittersweet memories.

Natassa would drag his sweet girl from him, and there was nothing anybody could do about it.

24

*1868, Charleston,
South Carolina*

I wait on the street outside of Thaddeus's family home, open-mouthed, for a few minutes. Surely, this is one of his jokes. He'll fling open the door in a moment, flash a grin, and wave me inside. But I count off the seconds, and the closed door stares back at me like an armed guard. My jaw clenches, and my stomach sours. I should have never trusted a white man. How could I have been so naive?

I spin around and stomp off back toward the riverfront. My narrow eyes shoot flames at every white person I see. Liars. Hypocrites. All of them. Soften your heart to them for one moment, and they'll crush you beneath their feet.

A knot forms in the back of my throat. I try to swallow it down, but it persists. My eyes sting with the threat of tears. *No. I will not give him the satisfaction.* I nod to the burned-out building to my left. *Good for you. They had it comin'.* Oh, that the war hadn't left a structure standing in this godforsaken place. The shouts of mates from the dock draw me forward.

I find a steamer bound for Georgetown and book passage. The faded paint betrays *Belle of the South* as past its prime. They have not converted the hurricane deck to segregated negro cabins, and it is not integrated. I purchase deck passage and stumble onto the crowded space stained with tobacco juice and animal excrement. Right now, this is where I belong.

I find a spot wedged up against a cotton bale and pull my knees to my chest, my suitcase nestled beside me. The pungent smell of animal waste mixes with body odor and spices from food cooking over an open fire. I bury my nose in my skirt to block out the aroma.

A decker pulls out a fiddle and plays a lively reel to my right. There's not room enough to dance, but several others tap their feet and slap their knees to the beat. One freedman sharpens his knife to my left while others pass around a bottle, laughing and telling jokes. Irish and German accents tickle my ears from the other side of the deck while the pleasant sounds of my people cozy up closer. Pipe smoke snakes throughout the space.

The shout of "Grub pile!" sounds forth, and white boatmen pop up from the front of the deck to grab food from a giant pot. They pile their fare—what looks like a mixture of everything the cabin passengers didn't eat—onto shingles and fan back out toward the front of the deck. Then the negroes come and dish out their meal. They sit on top of cotton bales and pass around one knife, using splinters of firewood for forks. When they finish, they toss their scraps and garbage overboard. Gulls dive for the discarded food, the sounds of their cries melt into the sloshing waves.

Even on this common deck, negroes and whites remain separate. Why did I have to press so close when everything around me shouts to keep my distance? Why did I have to be so reckless? My heart twists, and I pinch my lips together. *Do not cry.*

I can do this by myself. I don't need Thaddeus's help to find Susan and my grandmother. I likely never needed him at all. I could have handled myself just fine.

Georgetown appears in the distance. I stand to stretch my legs as the whistles sound. Mama lived here. I shake my head at the foreign thought. A groan crawls out of me.

I am going to inquire of a white woman.

Mama trusted Susan, but that doesn't mean I must. Who is this friend of Mama's? How does she know my mother? How could she have been a friend and a slave owner? Maybe Mama let this lady walk all over her like she lets Master Man.

When I disembark, the city of Georgetown draws me in like a tide. After seeing blackened and burned buildings throughout the South, my gaze drinks in the tidy, kempt streets and stately homes standing proudly in the afternoon sunshine. Was this city not touched by the war? I cannot find Sherman's dingy fingerprints here. Bird song fills the air. Sweet floral scents waft. I close my eyes and inhale deeply. Why would Mama not want to come back here?

I take my time ambling down Front Street and then start up the hill. The address on the envelope says Prince Street, and I find that it's the next street up. I pass under moss-draped trees and by bushes with blue bottles on them. *Odd.*

I find the house and frown. Two wrap-around porches. A stone path to the doorway trimmed neatly with bushes. My pulse skitters. This is what I came here for. I have to knock on that door. I set my suitcase down and wring my hands. Perhaps I could…What? Wait? Where else would I go? What else would I do? I swallow, pick up the case, and step forward.

A tentative knock. What will I say? I practiced on the steamer, but the words jumble together now. I knock again, a little louder.

A rustle, the clicking of a lock, and then the door cracks open. A pale face and narrow eyes peer out at me. Deep lines like trenches crease the corners of her eyes and mouth.

I was wrong. The war has touched this place as well.

"Who are you?" Suspicion laces her tone.

I cough. "Excuse me. Hello, Miss Susan?"

"Who's asking?"

"My name is Liberty, miss. My mother's name is Mercy. We're from New Orleans. Actually, my mother is from here. She—"

"Mercy? You're—" The woman's hand flies to her mouth. Her chin trembles. She opens the door an inch farther. A sob escapes her, and she hunches over, shaking.

"I'm her daughter, Liberty."

"She's alive? Please tell me she's alive." Her face twists as she cranes her head to look at me.

"Yes, ma'am."

A strangled cry escapes her as she shields her face with her arm.

"Mother? Mother, are you okay?" A young woman with loose blonde curls and bangs appears at Susan's side and hooks her arm into her mother's. The scent of rosewater billows around her bustled dress. Her presence seems to release fresh air, whereas her mother's siphons it. Her forehead dimples as she leans over to search Susan's face.

Susan nods and buries her head in her daughter's shoulder.

"Whatever is going on?" the young woman asks. She turns her attention to me.

I say the only thing that seems to matter. "I'm Mercy's daughter."

The young woman gasps. "Mercy? Mother's Mercy?"

I nod.

"Come in. Come in." She waves me inside. "I'm Minnie. Your grandmother practically raised me."

I step over the threshold and stand in front of the door, holding my suitcase in front of me, as Susan leans heavily upon Minnie. The two of them sway when Minnie moves to close the door.

"Mercy's alive. She's alive," Susan mumbles into Minnie's shoulder.

"That's splendid news, Mother. You should be delighted. And relieved." Minnie pats her mother's shoulder while taking small steps to her left. "Let's go sit down in the parlor, shall we?"

Susan grips Minnie's sleeve. "She's not a ghost, is she, Minnie? The girl?"

Minnie's voice soothes. "No, Mother. She's real. Her name is Liberty. She's Mercy's daughter."

My eyebrow lifts. A ghost? Is Mama's friend crazy? Should I run out now before I start seeing apparitions? Mama's bundle of letters weighs heavy in my pocket. And I need to find my grandmother. I follow the two as they stumble into a dimly lit room adorned with two couches. A piano stands in the far corner by the window.

Minnie settles her mother onto one of the sofas, then disappears around the corner. A moment later, she reappears with a handkerchief and hands it to Susan, who wipes her face. Minnie sits next to her mother and holds both of her hands.

I perch on the couch opposite them, resting my suitcase by my feet. Ready to bolt at the first sign of insanity.

My gaze travels the length of the room. A family portrait hangs above Susan and Minnie. In it, Minnie looks to be about five or so and able to charm just about anyone. She is straight-faced, but her eyes are light and laughing, a stark contrast to the woman sitting across from me now. The handsome gentleman next to her in the portrait has a proud tilt to his head. Is this the extent of their family? What would it be like to be an only child?

I squint to make out the painting in the far dark corner of the room. A slight intake of breath. Is that General E. Lee? And a Confederate flag? I finger the handle of my suitcase.

Minnie meets my gaze. "My father has different views than my mother and I." She bites her lip. "In fact, we should probably make sure you're not here when he gets home."

Susan squeezes Minnie's hand. "Oh no. He can't see her. Don't let him see her."

"I won't, Mother. It'll be okay. He won't be home for another couple of hours, at least."

My throat dries. What have I gotten myself into? I've come here for safety to a crazy woman with a negro-hating husband. My gaze drifts toward the door.

Minnie shifts her attention to me. "Would you like some tea?" She leans forward and picks up a bell from the table but then recoils as if bit by a snake. It slightly clinks as she sets it back down. She brushes off her skirt and stands. "I'll get some for you."

My mouth sticks as if it's full of cotton. "Water is fine," I say.

"For me too, dear." Susan smiles at her daughter, but it's the small, scared smile of a child, not the confident, assured one of a parent.

My brows furrow.

Minnie leaves and silence surrounds us for a few moments. Glasses clink in the other room. I try not to stare at the curious woman in front of me. Mama's dear friend? How could she be?

"Your mother didn't join you?" Susan asks.

My gaze skitters around like a rabbit. "No. She's still in Louisiana. With my brothers and sisters."

Minnie enters and sets three water glasses on the table.

Susan clamps her hands together. Her thumbs fidget. "But she is well?"

"Yes. Healthy. Strong."

"And your siblings? Five others, correct?"

"Yes. There's six of us in all. Seven if you count Daffney." They'd always count Daffney. "They're as well as can be expected." Best not to mention Mingo's attempted lynching.

"But Mercy sent you here alone?"

I drop my head a notch. "Yes. It wasn't safe for me there any longer. The night riders were after me."

A low rumble comes from Minnie's throat, and she exchanges a tense glance with Susan, whose Adam's apple bobs.

A shiver travels up my spine. What are they not telling me?

Minnie gives a little shake of her head, then angles herself toward me, donning a bright smile. "Your grandmother practically raised me."

"Yes, you mentioned that." I reach into my skirt pocket, fingering Mama's letters. Now that I'm here, I don't want to give them up, don't want to lose this connection to the mother I may never see again. "Truth is, I don't know hardly nothin' about Mama's life here or what she went through before she married my pa. And I never even knew about my grandmother until Mama sent me off to find her."

Minnie's mouth parts. "Do you know about the journal?"

I cock my head. "Journal?"

She pivots toward her mother, eyes pleading. "Oh, Mother, can we please give it to her? It only makes you sad, and you know Mercy would want her to have it."

Susan's trembling lips press together as she shakes her head.

A soft groan escapes Minnie's mouth. She looks at me. "Your mother kept a journal, wrote in it from the time she was a young woman. She gave it to my mother before the Millers sold her to New Orleans."

Susan's voice bursts forth like a crashing wave. "I can't part with it. It's all I have left of her."

Mama's letters warm my hand. An exchange.

I yank the stack out and hold them up. "I have letters for you from Mama."

A sharp intake of breath. "Letters? For me?"

I nod. "You can have them if you let me have the journal."

Susan bites her lip.

Minnie lays a hand on her mother's shoulder. "Come on. Think of Mercy. What she would do. What she would want."

Her assent comes out with a strangled cry. "Okay."

Minnie claps her hands and bounces up, dashing from the room. She returns holding a journal with a monogrammed *M* on the front, along with a bundle of letters. "Here are the missives your mother sent us prior to the war."

I hand over my stack. "Here are the ones she wrote after."

I trace my finger over the *M*, my knee bouncing. What will I learn in these pages? How did Mama's story unfold?

"I was your mother's dearest friend." Susan fingers the letters in her lap as she speaks, her voice as watery as her eyes. "There was no one closer to her. Except for Jonah, of course."

"Jonah?" My mouth stretches around the unfamiliar name.

Susan sighs, placing a hand over her heart.

"Of course, she wouldn't know about Jonah, Mother. Mercy married someone else. Why would she talk about her long-lost love?"

Long-lost love? I sit back, my spine pressing against the couch.

Minnie waves a hand in front of her. "Don't worry about it." She pauses, her mouth twisting. "Unless you want to meet him. To learn more about your mother, I mean. And your grandmother. He took her in after the war."

I catapult forward in my seat. Where is this Jonah? What secrets might he unveil? My senses buzz with anticipation to meet my grandmother.

Minnie continues, "And of course, you'll need a place to stay. We would be delighted to have you stay here with us, but my father wouldn't hear of it. He is," she says as she shakes her head, her chin dimpled, "not happy with the outcome of the war."

"He stirs up the ghosts," Susan says, eyes solemn.

I glance at Minnie.

She gives a tight smile. "Why don't you and I go and procure my horses from the livery stable? We can ride down to Hopecrest, and I'll introduce you to Jonah."

"And my grandmother?"

Her smile dies.

Susan coughs, then coughs again, doubling over and pressing a fist to her chest. A few hairs fall from her loose bun.

Minnie hovers over her and rubs her back. "Are you okay, Mother? Here, have some water." She holds a glass to Susan's mouth and tips it back.

When Susan's coughing fit expires, Minnie slips her arm underneath her mother's. "Come now. You need some rest. Let me help you to your room before I take Liberty to Hopecrest."

"Okay, dear." Susan sighs, her face drained of all vitality. She is Mama's age? She looks ten years older.

The two women shuffle down the hall. I watch their retreating forms, then my eyes are drawn back to the mounted

Confederate flag. What did Susan mean when she said her husband stirred up the ghosts? Mama never did abide superstitious talk, spouting it all as nonsense. But a shiver tickles the back of my neck.

Moments later, Minnie steps into the room with another bundle of papers in her hands. "Mother wanted me to give you these. They are letters she wrote to your mother but never sent. Mercy said it wasn't safe to write back."

I take the letters for Mama and tuck them and the other letters with the journal into my suitcase. What wealth I have gained for the letters I lost.

"Shall we?" Minnie gestures toward the front door.

I exit with my suitcase and fall into step beside Minnie as she walks down the street.

"I'm sorry about Mother." Her forehead creases. "These past few years have dealt her quite a blow. She's been withdrawn since I can remember, but after the war, it became so much worse. I wish I knew the cheerful, vivacious version of Mother when Mercy wrote that journal." She nods toward my case. "She sounds like she was so fun to be around back then. So full of life."

I frown. "What changed?"

"The war, maybe. Father's grown more exacting and vengeful as time has gone by. He's mad that the South lost. Hell bent on putting negroes in their place, I think." She leans close and pinches her lips together. "I think he's in the Klan." She brings a hand up to cover her mouth. "Isn't that dreadful? My own father."

I glance over my shoulder at Minnie's house and pick up my pace.

"I hate what he's done to Mother. He can be so harsh. Downright cruel at times." Her eyes narrow, and her breath comes out in little puffs. "I swear I will not marry a cruel man. I'd rather die a spinster. Eligible men are hard enough to come by after the war, and my friends tell me not to be picky. I've had several suitors. But if a man will talk down to a negro because of the color of his skin, he'll do the same to me because I'm a woman." She holds up a finger. "I will not abide it. I will marry a tender man or not marry at all."

A bit of tension seeps from my shoulders. I might like this woman. Hard to tell. Hard to trust. But maybe.

Minnie heaves a sigh. "Enough about me. You asked about my mother. I think guilt's to blame, mostly."

I shield my eyes from the sun as I peer over at her. "Guilt? Why?"

"Why indeed? I've told her countless times that it's not her fault. The Millers told Mercy they were selling her and Charity—"

"Charity?"

"Your grandmother."

My cheeks flush. I didn't even know my own grandmother's name.

"Anyway, they said they were selling both of them to a slave trader. When Mercy appealed to my mother for help, Mother offered to purchase Mercy. But, of course, Mercy asked about Charity."

We pass a white couple strolling arm in arm. Minnie smiles and waves, then continues. "My father would not agree to purchase two slaves. When he has made up his mind, no one can dissuade him. So, Mercy begged Mother to purchase Charity instead of her. Begged her. What was mother to do? Of course, she followed Mercy's wishes. She purchased Charity. Saved her from the fate of being sold south. But they shipped your mother to New Orleans." We turn toward Front Street, and the murmur of voices and clatter of carriages filter through the background of Minnie's story. She swings her arms, relaxed, seeming completely immersed in her words and not at all concerned at being seen walking next to a negro.

"When the letters started coming, my mother began retreating into herself. It was as if a weight of guilt settled on her shoulders with each one. Stories of beatings and such cruelty that it's hard to imagine. Mother began to worry that she'd be punished for allowing such awful things to happen to her friend. Always thinking it would come back to haunt her."

"The ghosts?"

"Oh, no. The ghosts have to do with the war. The Yankee's used our home for a hospital, you know. Our home and the Winyah Indigo Society building across the street. Mother fears the ghosts of Union soldiers will haunt us forever. For being on the wrong side of the war." She rolls her eyes. "Father fought for the Confederates."

"And he came back spittin' mad?"

Minnie tosses her head back and laughs. "You could say that."

We turn right and pass a hardware store on our left and a dairy on our right. Horses clomp through the streets. A boat whistles from the river.

"How do you do, Miss Renald?" An older gentleman tips his hat to Minnie.

"Just fine, thank you, Mr. Randolf." Minnie curtsies. "Lovely weather, isn't it?"

"Splendid."

"Allow me to introduce my new friend Liberty." Minnie dips her head toward me.

I curtsy toward the man.

His mustache twitches, but he says, "Pleasure to meet you."

"Likewise," I say.

He continues walking in one direction and we in the other.

Minnie begins speaking as if nothing happened. "At any rate—"

"Minnie," I whisper, "isn't it possible that your father will hear that you were associating with a negro?"

She leans in, her brows rising and eyes twinkling. "Yes. And won't it rankle him?"

I frown and take a step away from her conspiratorial grin. Is she using me to rile her father? My throat tightens. Am I to be a pawn in another white person's hand? I was right to vow to never trust one again. I wrap my arms around myself, suddenly chilled.

When we reach the livery stable, Minnie greets the keeper with a broad smile. "Good afternoon, Charles. My friend

Liberty and I will be taking Chestnut and Scamper out for a ride."

The scent of hay and manure mingle and cause my nose to itch.

Minnie bounds over to a stall where a deep brown mare stands tall and proud. He reminds me of Thaddeus's horse, and my chest pangs at the memory of taking the soldier's hand and being lifted onto the animal's back. Of grasping Thaddeus's coat as we swayed.

My eyes now itch as well, and I rub at them with my fingertips.

Minnie strokes the horse's mane, speaking to it as if it were a child. "Hello, Chestnut. How are you, baby? How's my sweet boy?"

Chestnut whinnies in response.

"That's good, baby. Real good."

My gaze shoots up to the rafters at her baby talk to an animal larger than herself.

She moves to the next stall where a black horse with a white-streaked tail looks to her for attention. "Scamper, sweetie. How are you, girl?" Minnie scratches Scamper behind the ear, then turns to me. "Which one do you want to ride?"

I shrug.

"You do know how to ride, don't you?"

I shift my jaw. "I've ridden before." Once. With Thaddeus.

She tilts her head, and the corner of her mouth lifts as if she can read my thoughts. Then she brightens. "There's nothing to it. You'll be fine. We'll go as slowly as you need."

I grunt in response. But as Minnie demonstrates how to mount and handle the reins, my confidence blooms—along with excitement. I am ready for this adventure. I choose Scamper, and we soon find ourselves at an awkward gallop behind Minnie atop Chestnut.

Leaves from majestic oaks cast dancing shadows on the ground. Birds call out to each other. Humidity dampens the nape of my neck, but the canopy of trees and moss shades us from the intensity of the sun's glare.

Minnie is silent now, and the clomp of horses' hooves and rustle of leaves from an occasional breeze are the only sounds that greet my ears. That and the pounding of my heart. I am about to meet my grandmother. This is the reason I've come, the reason I left everyone else behind. What if this meeting is not what I expect? Not what I long for? What if it does little to satisfy this ache inside me?

My throat squeezes tight, and I swallow.

We turn down a path rimmed with tall, sweet-smelling pines. A bed of needles blankets our way, softening the journey. The horses' hooves clamber over fat pine cones, sometimes sending them skittering this way and that. The trail widens enough for me to pull Scamper alongside of Minnie. Orange streaks paint the sky as the sun begins its slow curtsy of the evening.

"This is where my mama used to live?"

A trace of a smile forms on Minnie's lips. "Yes. This is Hopecrest. It used to be one of the largest rice plantations in the region. There are a dozen or so former slaves still working the land." She frowns. "The future doesn't look good for rice planters. At least not here."

I work to keep the sass out of my voice. "Hard to work the land without free labor?"

She chuckles. "Near impossible. I guess time will tell if this empire recovers or falls."

The pines give way to magnificent oaks lining both sides of the widening path, their branches wrinkled and bent.

Minnie nods to an oak. "Your mother said they look like they're worshiping. I think she's right. Don't you?"

I tilt my head, imagining the leaves as outstretched hands. Mama used to lean forward and raise her arms high in much the same way, praising the Good Lord for whatever blessing she perceived amidst our suffering. "I reckon."

The Big House that Mama described comes into view on the horizon, and in front of it, two rows of neat, white cabins. Minnie turns Chestnut down another trail and into the thicket.

I cast one last look at the sunset reflecting off the Big House's white porch and pillars before I follow. What had Mama's owners been like? What had she experienced in this place?

Minnie tosses a glance over her shoulder. "Jonah lives down here."

I want to ask if my grandmother does as well, but Minnie is several paces ahead of me now. Scamper lowers her head to snack on a berry bush. I give her side a kick and her reins a tug. We clomp forward.

We approach more cabins, these smaller and shabbier than the others. Several look to be deserted. Freedmen and freedwomen surround us now, some washing clothes in tubs of water and hanging them to dry on their porches, some working their garden plots next to their homes. The familiar scent of rice and beans wafts through open cabin doors. Barefooted children chase each other, their faces streaked with dust.

Minnie greets each person we pass with a bright smile and a "Good evening."

They answer in kind, their eyes honest and their expressions sincere. Not a shadow of wariness among them. Do they know this woman? Do they trust her?

Minnie stops in front of a cabin, her gaze searching the perimeter. Then she addresses a handsome man walking past holding a fishing pole. "We're looking for Jonah."

He swipes his hat off his head and peers up at her. "He's at the graveyard, Miss Minnie."

She nods. "Why, thank you, Solomon."

"No problem at all."

Minnie turns to me, her face shining. "This is perfect."

I raise my brows. This lady might be half as crazy as her mama. Then again, the negroes here seem comfortable with her. They know her by name. Is she using them like she's using me? Or did I judge her too harshly?

"Trust me," Minnie says as she nudges Chestnut forward.

"What about my grandmother?" I ask, keeping pace.

Minnie sighs. "She'll be there, too."

So, my grandmother sticks close to Jonah, then. What of the bond between the two of them?

We creep deeper into the thicket and finally emerge into a clearing. The sound of water tumbling and gurgling fills the background, though I can't see the river. It must be behind the thick trees. Only a few crude stones stand in the clearing. Mostly lilies bloom bright and beautiful among tufts of grass. A man with a hat pulled low over his face stands on the path in front of a purple lily, his head bowed, his mouth moving. His hands are shoved deep into his pockets, and he rocks back and forth on the balls of his feet. The sound of his voice doesn't reach my ears, but the emotion in his expression—the way his forehead crinkles as he talks—touches me down deep.

Minnie slips off Chestnut and hands me his reins. She takes small steps toward the man, then places her hand softly on his shoulder.

He startles. "Why, Miss Minnie."

"Jonah." She wraps him in a hug.

My jaw drops as he embraces her in return. What is this? A white woman embracing a black man? It's improper. Unconventional. Dangerous.

Perhaps I do like Minnie after all.

So, this is Jonah. Where is my grandmother? I scan the perimeter and see no one. A sinking feeling seeps into my gut.

"Jonah, I'd like you to meet someone." Minnie smiles at me, gesturing in my direction. "This is Liberty. She's…Mercy's daughter."

Jonah's eyes widen as he stares back at me. A gray-flecked beard covers his thin face, and if that was all there was to him, I'd think him feeble. But he's got a solid build, and his muscular arms flex as he crosses them. He must be good and strong. Just weathered a mighty strong storm is all.

I slide off Scamper and take a few steps in his direction, still holding the reins of both horses. "It's nice to meet you." I curtsy. "I understand you were a friend of my mother?"

He lets out a sharp breath. "Is she still alive? Is she well?"

I nod.

His hand flutters to cover his heart. "Thank You, Lord." His eyes moisten as he looks heavenward. "Thank You, Jesus, for keepin' her safe."

I see now how this man could have been close to my mother. They pray the same.

He swipes at the corners of his eyes with the palm of his hand. "I loved your mother dearly. This here," he says and points to the purple flower in front of his feet, "is her lily."

I cock my head. A soft breeze rustles the tree leaves above us.

"I planted it for her when she left. At this graveyard, we don't have many markers, but when someone dies, we plant a lily. Even though your mama didn't die, it felt like it to me." His voice trembles. "Just broke my heart in two. I planted this here lily to remember her by."

I open my mouth to speak, but no words come. What can I say to that? To this man who loved my mother? Loves her still? I shift from foot to foot and worry my lip.

Minnie speaks up. "I'm sure Liberty would like to learn more about her mother. She'd likely appreciate some of your stories."

I nod, then venture the question that burns in my throat. "Where's my grandmother?"

A soft smile lifts the corners of Jonah's mouth. He points farther into the clearing. "That pink one right there."

My heart seizes. "You mean…"

Minnie takes my free hand and meets my worried gaze. "She passed about six months ago."

A pinched cry escapes my mouth. "What? Why didn't you tell me?" My eyes sting.

Her brows furrow. "I'm sorry. It's just that I didn't know how you would take it. Having come all this way to find her. Mother didn't take it well at all. She went into hysterics for weeks. And I thought—"

"You should have told me." I speak through clenched teeth.

"I know." She hangs her head. "But Jonah knew her well, as did I. Between the two of us, we can tell you all about her."

I shake my head. "You don't understand. She was supposed to…" What was it Mama said? Quench my fire? No. Teach me how to burn without destroying everything around me. "Help me."

And now I'd come all this way for nothing.

25

———

June 2020
Chicago, Illinois

Natassa propped her feet up in David's lap as they sat watching *House Hunters* in DeAndre's apartment.

"Do you remember when I used to do this when you were little, and you would rub my feet?" She wiggled her toes in her fluffy pink socks.

"Yeah. Wasn't I just the sweetest?" He flashed her a cheesy grin.

"You still could be. Sweet, I mean." She nudged him with her toe.

He scoffed. "No way. I am not rubbing your feet."

She shrugged. "Worth a shot."

A rustling at the door, and she sat up, swinging her feet to the floor. *They're home.* She sucked in a breath. *Home?* Did that thought actually cross her mind? This was definitely not home. Not for Mercy.

The knob twisted, and the door burst open. Mercy skipped inside and headed straight to Java's room, tossing a "Hi, Mom. Hi, Dad" over her shoulder.

Java followed. Janell carried a sleeping Joe on her shoulder, waving as she crept past them toward the bedroom. "I'm gonna put him to bed," she whispered.

DeAndre entered, shoulders slumped, weariness radiating from him. He hung his keys on the rack and then sighed deep, pressing his palms into his eyes.

"Everything okay?" Natassa's forehead furrowed.

He harrumphed. "Can I talk to you? Alone, I mean. Or it's fine if Brandon is there. I just meant—"

"Away from smaller ears?" She glanced toward Java's bedroom. They could burst out of there at any moment.

"Yeah." He gestured upward. "We could go on the rooftop?"

"Sure." She stole a glance at Brandon. He was bent over his laptop again, earbuds in. Should she ask him to come with? She swallowed. Was she okay being alone with this man? On a public rooftop, maybe. But not on an elevator. "I'll meet you up there."

His head dipped, and he ducked into the hallway.

She pushed herself to standing and waddled over to the kitchen table where Brandon sat. "Hey, babe?" She touched his shoulder.

He pulled out an earbud and looked up at her.

"I'm going to go talk to DeAndre on the rooftop. Please keep your phone in view in case I need you, okay?"

"Do you want me to—"

"No. I've got it. Just" —she slid his phone from the middle of the table to a spot right beside his computer— "keep an eye out."

"You sure?" He quirked an eyebrow as if uncertain.

"Positive." She gave him a reassuring smile and spun around toward the door. She glanced at David, who slouched on the sofa, his fingers tapping on his phone. "Be back in a few."

"Okay." He didn't look up from his screen.

As the elevator carried her up, she rolled her neck back and forth, attempting to loosen her tight muscles. What did DeAndre want to talk to her about? A storm had brewed in his eyes. Not an angry one that threatened to trample her in its fury, though. A tortured one with lonely moans and frigid winds. *Maybe he just wants to thank me for allowing him to have Mercy for the day.* She bit her lip. *That can't be it.*

A ping and then the door slid open. A gray haze enveloped her as she stepped onto the patio, and it was as if she were walking into a cloud. Dewy moisture brushed her cheeks. The air smelled thick with rain, but none fell.

DeAndre stood with his hands in his pockets, facing the lake. A breeze whipped her hair into her face, and she flipped it back, then wrapped her arms around herself. Her slow, purposeful steps brought her next to the man who had changed her life forever.

DeAndre startled and turned to face her. "Sorry. Didn't hear you come." He wiped his eyes with the back of his hands. He'd been crying?

She frowned, nearly overcome with the impulse to take his hand. To tell him everything would be okay. She shook herself and took a step back. "What did you want to talk about?"

His gaze fluttered to the sky. "I love her. Mercy, I mean."

Natassa's mouth twisted. "I know."

"I'm all torn up inside—" His voice cracked. "About saying goodbye to her."

She swallowed. "It'll be hard on both of you, I'm sure."

DeAndre clasped his hands together and brought them up to his face. "Natassa, I know I have no right to ask this. Believe me, I know. But I'm begging you to let me see her again. For visitation rights."

Her mouth fell open. "Visitation rights?"

"She could spend summers here or spring break? Even a long weekend every once in a while."

Something seemed to lodge itself in her throat. She coughed, but it brought no relief. She banged on her chest with her fist.

"Are you okay?"

Was she okay? "Are you kidding me? No, I am not okay." She sucked in a breath. "You—after all you did—want my daughter?"

A light drizzle began to fall, and a shudder crept up her spine.

He put his hands out. "I don't want to snatch her away from you. She has an amazing family; I know that. I just want a chance to spend some time with her."

Her eyes bored into him. "You got your chance."

DeAndre dropped his arms to his sides. "Don't you want to do what's best for her?"

She let out a humorless chuckle. "Who do you think you are? You've spent a few days with her, and now *you* think you know what's best for her? Brandon and I have raised her for nine *years*."

"I know." His gaze sank to the wet pavement.

"You know. You think you know a lot, don't you?" She glared at him. "Well, do you know your place? Because it's not in her life." She brushed moisture from her forehead with her sleeve. "So, is that it, then?" She took a step toward the elevator.

"Yeah." His voice fell like the rain.

She nodded and marched away but then pivoted. DeAndre's shoulders slumped and shook. Her heart softened a little at the sight.

"Brandon and I booked a hotel for the night. We're leaving David and Mercy here with you. It'll be a nice chance for you to say your final goodbyes."

She turned and left without giving him a chance to respond.

~

Natassa nearly barreled into Brandon when she walked through the door. He shoved his phone in his pocket and put his hands on her shoulders, steadying them both.

She eyed him. "Were you pacing?"

He nodded as his eyes swept over her, as if assessing for any possible damage. "Everything okay?"

"Yeah." She sighed. "We'll talk later."

Wrapping her in a hug, Brandon kissed the top of her head. "I wanted to respect your wishes, but that was rough."

"You could have come. I thought you were busy."

"I am." He rubbed his eyes. "Overloaded at work. Feel like I'll never catch up."

She fell onto the couch and leaned her head back, closing her eyes.

"Just checked the patient portal. It's official." The cushion next to her shifted as Brandon settled in beside her. "Hope has COVID."

David groaned.

Natassa figured as much and was far less concerned about the what-ifs of that scenario after talking with her mom the night before. Virus or not, Hope appeared to be on the mend or at least progressing in that direction. Though annoyed with having to stay quarantined in her room, none of the other children showed any symptoms. Thank goodness. But her mind still swirled from her conversation with DeAndre. If only she didn't have to wait until nighttime to talk to Brandon about it.

"Where's Janell?" Natassa didn't bother opening her eyes.

"She must be napping with the baby. She hasn't come back out."

"And Mercy and Java?"

"Playing Candy Land last time I checked. She's really good with him."

They should have a few minutes uninterrupted. Should she tell Brandon what DeAndre had said? With David right there?

Her phone buzzed in her hand, but her eyes felt so heavy she didn't move to check it.

Another buzz.

Someone, probably Brandon, took her phone. A moment of silence, and then he gasped. "Oh no."

Her eyes sprang open. "What? What's wrong?" Was it Hope? Bethany? *Oh God, no.*

He brought his fist up to his mouth. "It's St. Anthony's Baptist." His eyes met hers. "It's been burned down."

She catapulted upright. "What?"

"It's a text from Old Ezra." He flashed the screen toward her.

She took the phone and read: *Riots broke out here last night and things got heated. Someone burned our church down. St. Anthony's is no more.*

The attached picture showed charred bricks and open spaces where the stained-glass windows used to be. Blackened debris lay scattered on the ground. Remnants of the frame of the roof and bell tower stood bare.

"Oh my gosh." She stared at the picture, mouth parting, head shaking.

"I know. Unbelievable." Brandon shook his head.

Her throat burned. St. Anthony's was where she'd found acceptance and belonging after immense tragedy. The first time she saw the church, it stood like a beacon in the dark night of her soul. Those stained-glass windows had beckoned her to return. And once Bethany had drawn her inside, she came to relish the hard, wooden pews and faded green hymnals, the sound of organ music, and the smell of the pine cleaner they used.

Precious memories turned to ash.

"I need a minute." She pushed herself up, dashed to the bathroom, and locked the door behind her. Pressing her back to the wall, she sank onto the floor, then buried her face in her hands and sobbed.

~

It took half an hour for Brandon to coax Natassa from the bathroom and into his arms. Her breakdown had brought Janell from her room and garnered the attention of the children.

"I'm okay," she told them in a shaky voice. But the tears would not stop flowing.

Brandon explained what had happened, and Janell's and Mercy's eyes misted over as well. At least she wasn't the only one.

DeAndre didn't return until an hour later. "What's going on?" His eyes darted around the room.

"We found out St. Anthony's Church burned down last night." Brandon's voice sounded full of gravel, but he kept his emotions in check.

"For real?"

Janell nodded.

DeAndre dipped his head and pressed his lips together. "All those memories in that place."

Everyone except for Java had memories there, but Natassa and DeAndre had deeper history than the rest. When her gaze met DeAndre's, her pain seemed to mingle with his. A shared understanding.

Her phone rang, and she reached for it. Bethany's name popped up on her screen. She sucked in a breath. Was Bethany well enough to call? Or was someone calling on her behalf? Natassa's hand trembled as she answered.

"Hello, sugar. How are you doing?"

A wave of relief crested over Natassa at the sound of her adopted mama's voice. "Bethany! You're okay?"

"Getting stronger each day." Machines beeped and whizzed in the background. "I'm still in the hospital, but I've come through the worst of it."

Her hand flew to her chest. "Thank God."

"Yes, thank God indeed. And thank you for your prayers."

Natassa's throat constricted. She couldn't speak. When she and Brandon prayed together in the hospital, her weak faith using his strong trust as a crutch. She'd read that less than five percent of people who went on ventilators came off them. God had worked a miracle.

"I'm sorry to have to tell you this, sugar, but St. Anthony's—"

"We know. Old Ezra texted us."

A heavy sigh. "Isn't it horrible?"

Natassa sniffed. Nodded. Tried to speak again but couldn't.

"It's times like these that we got to worship Him with all our hearts."

She frowned at her phone.

"Yes, sirree, we got to worship Him through the pain. But you know that by now, don't you? That we can't try to skirt around all that hurt. We gotta walk straight into it and feel it all so God can heal it all. Walk right into the eye of the storm with our arms raised high in praise to the Almighty."

Walk into the pain and worship? She wasn't so sure. But she smiled. "You sound good, Bethany. More like yourself."

"I want to thank you, baby girl. You challenged me not to give up. Helped me to believe that these old bones still have a reason for living."

Natassa wiped her cheeks with her sleeve. "Of course, you still have a reason to live. You have me."

26

June 2020
Chicago, Illinois

DeAndre scrubbed his face with his hands, fighting tears. Why did the news about St. Anthony's affect him so deeply? He hadn't been to church there since he was a boy. And yet, it was as if he'd lost a family member. A close friend.

"Sit, hon." Janell patted the spot beside her on the couch.

He took a shuddering breath and swallowed hard.

"Come on." Her eyes coaxed him near.

He slid beside her, dropping his head in his hands. At least it sounded like Bethany's situation had improved. Natassa had stepped into the other room to talk to her further, but from what little he caught of Natassa's side of the conversation, the news sounded good.

"It's a hard thing—losing a pillar in that community like St. Anthony's. When did your family start going there?" Janell ran her forefinger in small circles on his knee.

He rolled his head from side to side. "As far back as I can remember. Mama and Pa got married in that church." He sucked in his breath and held it for a beat, then released it in a sigh. "I've got to tell Mama." He reached to pull his phone from his pocket.

Janell put her hand on his arm. "That can wait. Tell us what you remember about the church."

Mercy left her spot on the other couch next to Brandon and walked over to DeAndre, snuggling beside him. He wrapped his arm around her and kissed the top of her head. She angled her watery eyes up at him, waiting.

He squinted, trying to reach back in time and pull out memories. "I remember potlucks in the basement, stuffing myself so full I couldn't button my pants without feeling like I'd pop. Mama would scold me up and down if I ate too much but even more if there was something there that I didn't want to eat at all. Bad manners, you know, not to sample everyone's dish."

"Oh no." Janell scrunched up her nose.

"Yeah, there were some doozies." He chuckled as he remembered trying to guess what was in each particular Jell-O mold. "We did outreaches to the homeless, had giant bins in the back for collecting canned food sometimes, other times for coats and gloves. And they used to decorate for Christmas by hanging a wreath at the end of every pew."

"They still do that." The edges of Mercy's mouth tipped in a smile. "It's pretty." Then her forehead puckered. "Was pretty. They won't decorate for anything anymore." Her voice trembled.

He rubbed her back. If only he could say something that would make it all okay. "Does anyone know what they plan to do? Will they rebuild? Relocate?"

Brandon shrugged. "Not sure. We haven't heard anything further."

David slapped his hands on his thighs. "Well, I, for one, am tired of all this depressing conversation. I'm going to chill on the rooftop for a while."

Brandon put his hand on David's knee. "No, son. Don't run away because you're uncomfortable. You know what your mom says. Sit in the sad."

Janell tilted her head. "Sit in the sad?"

"It's her way of saying don't ignore negative emotions. Don't push them down and try to forget about them. You have to acknowledge them and work through them." He tossed his hands up. "Something she learned from counseling, I guess."

David rolled his eyes. "She's been sitting in her sad for far too long, if you ask me."

Janell set down the mug of tea she'd been holding and wagged a finger at him. "No. You don't get to do that. You can't dictate someone else's timeline of how long it takes them to walk through grief." She sat back and crossed her arms. "It takes however long it takes."

David shrugged.

Janell tilted her head toward David. "So, what do you remember about St. Anthony's?"

He sighed. "Just the people. Bethany. Old Ezra. Mazy. Who cares about some old building? The people of God are the church, right? And they're still here."

Brandon smiled. "It's amazing how that place grew on me. Those people. I never would have thought."

DeAndre tilted his head. Brandon never would have thought what? That black people could be kind and welcoming? That they could have something to offer the world besides homicide statistics?

Brandon draped his arm around the back of the couch— DeAndre's couch. The man was a guest in *his* house. But Brandon had let his daughter cuddle up with DeAndre right before his eyes. DeAndre swallowed back his cynicism. Brandon was trying, right? They all were.

"I want to see if there's any info online." DeAndre tugged his phone from his back pocket and pulled up St. Anthony's Facebook page. Four pictures of charred remains. His throat went dry.

Janell peeked over his shoulder and gasped. "Oh my."

"Let me see." Mercy raised herself to her knees and peered at his screen. She didn't say anything, but her mouth formed a tight line.

He scrolled but couldn't find any further info. He hit the home button and scrolled, eager to see if any of his old acquaintances from that neighborhood had posted anything. Crickets. No one he knew had said anything about that old church with so much history. He paused as he came across a post from Rob. He hadn't talked to his old "friend" since he went behind bars, but they'd never unfriended each other on social media. A picture of Rob and his wife, Melanie, at a restaurant showing off their sushi. All smiles. Completely oblivious to the pile of ash down the highway from them. DeAndre's chest burned.

Underneath Rob's picture, a post from DeAndre's church caught his eye: *Come worship with us tonight.* It went on to explain that their church was joining with several other churches across the city for a night of worship just a few blocks from their apartment. *Come lift the name of Jesus high above the confusion and contention, above injustice and inequality, above pain. Come and join together as one body— made from different racial and ethnic backgrounds but all united in one purpose: to worship the King of Kings and Lord of Lords. Pursue reconciliation and restoration through praise.*

DeAndre snapped his head up.

"What is it?" Janell eyed him.

He handed her his phone. A wave of certainty crested in his chest. They needed to go, to be in that space of united praise. He needed to put to rest all thoughts of how Rob abandoned him in his time of need or Brandon's cluelessness. He needed to let his disappointment with Natassa's decision roll off him in the presence of God. He needed to breathe in the sweet fragrance of the harmony of the saints.

And he wanted to take Mercy.

"You want to go to this?" Janell flipped his phone around as if he might not know what she meant.

"Yes."

"Okay." Janell glanced at her watch. "That means I should probably make dinner so we can skedaddle." She got up and plodded to the kitchen.

"What's going on? Where are you going?" Brandon sat forward, propping his folded hands on his knees.

Natassa emerged, clasping her phone to her chest, her cheeks rosy. "Bethany is going to be alright."

DeAndre dropped his head back and smiled. "Thank God."

"Yes. Thank God." Natassa grinned.

He angled himself in her direction. Might as well ask when she was in a good mood. "Our church is having a time of worship tonight just a few blocks from here. Not just our church, actually. Several churches from the city." He cleared his throat. "We want to go. I didn't know what time you guys planned to check in to your hotel—"

"Worship Him through the pain." Natassa closed her eyes. Her voice came out as a mumble.

"What?" DeAndre cocked his head.

"We've got to walk right into the eye of the storm with our arms raised high and praise the Almighty. It's something Bethany just said." She opened her eyes and turned her attention to Brandon. "Could we all go together?"

DeAndre dipped his chin. All go together? She wanted her and Brandon to come with?

A pause as Natassa and Brandon communicated with each other through their gazes and expressions. Natassa tilted her head. *For Bethany?* she mouthed.

Brandon's brow furrowed and then relaxed.

Brandon squared his shoulders. "Sure." He ran a hand through his hair. "Janell, you really don't have to make dinner. I'll go pick up some pizza for everyone."

"Pizza!" Mercy squealed.

"Cool." David propped his feet onto the coffee table.

"Really?" Janell's voice danced in relief.

"Of course."

"That'd be amazing." She tossed down a dish towel she'd been holding and sauntered back to her spot on the sofa.

For an awkward moment, glances tangled throughout the room, some delighted, others resigned. One big, happy, dysfunctional family.

~

A thin haze still wrapped the horizon, causing the lake to blur into its surroundings. DeAndre started to sit on a chair on his back patio, but dampness seeped into his pants. Better to stand. He dialed Mama's number and waited.

"Hi, Dre." The sound of the television was muted in the background.

"Mama—" He pressed his lips together. "St. Anthony's Church burned down."

A beat of silence. "I'm sorry to hear that." The creak of her rocking chair. "Did you have a chance to talk to Natassa?"

He dropped his head. That's not what he'd called to talk about. "Did you hear what I said, Mama? St. Anthony's is gone."

"I heard you." More creaking from her chair, but not a crack of emotion in her voice.

"Don't you care? You and Pa got married in that church. You raised me there. Pa's funeral was held there."

"Sounds like you're taking this hard."

His eyes burned. "And it sounds like you're not."

"Oh, Dre." The creaking stopped, and DeAndre pictured Mama folding her hands in her lap. "You always were sentimental. You feel things so deeply. Honey, it's just a building. The memories we made there, they're a part of us. They became part of our story, and we locked them up inside of our hearts. Nobody can steal those from us, son. No one can burn those down."

He swallowed, throat dry. "You make it sound so easy."

"You make it sound so hard."

He chuckled.

"Now, did you talk to Natassa about giving you some visitation rights?"

His shoulders sank. Did they have to have this conversation? "She said no."

"And?"

"And what? I asked her. She said no. That's it." He searched the sky for a glimpse of the sun but nothing except clouds.

Mama's voice took on a no-nonsense tone. "So, what are you going to do to change her mind?"

"I don't think there's anything I can do."

"You're giving up?" Was Mama raising her eyebrows at him?

He thrust his free hand in the air. "I don't know what else to do."

Silence.

He wiped condensation off the metal railing with his finger. "We're all going to this night of worship downtown tonight. Together. Maybe God will drop some revelation or something because I honestly don't see a way forward."

"All of you are going? Together?"

"Yep."

"Sounds fun." Her voice dripped with sarcasm.

"You're welcome to join us," he joked.

"Maybe I will."

27

1868,
Georgetown, South Carolina

Minnie trots off on Chestnut into the fading light of evening. Darkness will blanket the horizon before she makes it to the main road. Solomon, a negro around my age, rides Scamper beside her. It seems Minnie didn't think this plan through, which gives me some consolation as to my own frequent blunders.

When we left the graveyard, Minnie let out a long sigh. "I wish I could stay here for the night. Wouldn't Father just love that? Me hunkering down in a former slave cabin?"

Jonah chuckled. "You know you're always welcome here, Miss Minnie."

She shook her head, a small smile creeping up on her face, then retreating. "Oh, but I can't. I wouldn't dream of putting any of you in danger."

Yet when Solomon offered to escort her home, she didn't protest. Does she realize now that Solomon will be walking home in the dark of night alone in Klan territory? That he has risked his very life to ensure she would make it back to town unharmed? She's likely not given it a thought.

I watch her honey curls bounce into the dimness before turning to Jonah. "Where am I to bunk for the night?"

He takes my suitcase and leads me down the row to an abandoned cabin furnished with a bed, small table, and rocking chair. "It's all yours." He smiles at me with eyes full of something I cannot name. It's warm and strong and a little like how Papa used to look at me, but not exactly. This gaze contains mysteries. Do I want to discover these hidden things? They might be keys to finding who I am meant to be, and yet they might be my undoing.

My eyes flitter around the neat cabin. "Does no one live here?"

One corner of his mouth twitches. "Your mother used to."

I suck in a breath. Mama lived here? Walked on this floor? Slept on that bed? Ate at this table? Breathed this air?

"I've been savin' it for her. In case she wanted to come back." His words hold a question. I swallow down the answer he surely doesn't want to hear. I asked Mama to come with me, and she said no. He is waiting in vain.

"Thank you," I say instead.

He lights the candle on the table and retreats. "See you in the mornin'."

I close the door after him and lean against it, breathing deeply of the musty air. Mama's space. Mama's world. A world I know nothing of.

I drag my suitcase over to the bed and plop down, snatching the journal and bundles of letters. Which should I read first? I trace my finger over the monogrammed *M* again, then open to the first page and read a few lines.

This is about when Mama was a child. So long ago. It makes sense that I would start at the beginning, but the letters tug at me. What happened to Mama before the letters I handed over to Susan? Since I already started at the end, perhaps I should work backward instead of forward. The dates from 1843, though before my birth, don't intimidate me as much as those decades before. I take Mama's stack of letters to the table and read by the flicker of candlelight.

I wince as I pour over Mama's recollections of being sold in New Orleans for the lowest bid of all, of my beautiful mother questioning her worth. Tears track down my cheeks when I read of the overseer ordering Manda to be drowned just because she was sick. I picture Mama trying to save that baby, nearly hear her weeping when she failed.

When I come to the letter about Master Man pairing up Mama and Papa, I sit still a minute. They started off as strangers, thrown together against their will. Yet, they ended up with a love so true I'd have never guessed how they began. I plunge deeper and read how love bloomed, how the loss of five babies tore at Mama's heart, how her faith grew hot in the fire. I come to the telling of the torture Mama went through at the overseer's hands. Anger flares within me, and while Mama reports praying for mercy for his soul, I call down hellfire. In the last letter, I see the mama I've known all my life. Strong and confident. A leader to many. One who shares her faith and wisdom to all who cross her path. One who would lay down her life for the good of someone else, even if that someone else is white, a former owner, a former oppressor.

I dry my eyes on my sleeve. I don't blame Jonah for waiting for her all these years. She is the kind of woman you thank God you had the privilege to meet. And pray that you might have just one more day with her.

Oh, Mama, I miss you. Will I ever see you again? I'm sorry for always buckin' at your ways. Will I ever get to tell you that?

I yawn. I should go to bed. The crickets sing their lullaby as the night stretches on. But Susan's bundle of letters calls to me. Maybe I'll read just one or two before I go to sleep.

July 30, 1843

Dearest Mercy,

I was so thankful to receive your letter and know, at least, that you are alive. Of course, I wish with all my heart that you are well and happy, but if you are alive, there's at least a chance that things will look up for you there, that you'll adjust to the new crop and master. That you'll settle into their way of doing things and find a portion of contentment in the cane fields of Louisiana. I pray this is so. It breaks my heart to think of you suffering.

I'm glad to hear you've found a friend in Octavia. A good companion can make the most grueling of hardships more tolerable. Though I wish I could be that friend for you, it does ease my worry to know the Good Lord has placed someone in your path to help bear your burdens.

Your mother is doing well. She's taken to my dear little Minnie as a hen to her chicks, nestling them under her wing. Charity sings to Minnie each night—the same song she sang to you as a child.

Mercy. Sweet mercy.
Good Lord, we need Your mercy.
Every morning. Every morning.
Your mercies are new.

Minnie quiets for the song, sucking on her tiny fingers, her bright blue eyes searching Charity's. What a beautiful thing to behold. It makes me feel close to you somehow.

During the day, we talk of you. Charity delights me with tales of you as a young girl getting into mischief. She's so proud of you, Mercy. She's proud of how you learned to read and write so quickly. She says she barely had to work at all to teach you. You just soaked it up like dry ground thirsty for rain. She loves hearing me talk of how we met and how you tricked the whole boat full of people into thinking you were a white woman. We've had many laughs over those memories. And quite a few tears.

Do stay safe.
We both love you dearly.
Yours forever,
Susan

December 30, 1843
Dearest Mercy,
Every day I regret allowing that boat to take you farther south. I do not know how I could have prevented it, but surely,

I could have done something. Guilt claws away at my insides. I am so very sorry. I beg you to forgive me.

After receiving your letter about the overseer drowning sweet Manda, I held Minnie tightly all night long, bathing her in my tears. How could someone be so cruel? How could a seed of callousness in a person's heart grow into such a mighty oak that killing an innocent child could be considered justified? I will never understand.

I'm so sorry. So very sorry.

Yours forever,

Susan

January 20, 1844

Dearest Mercy,

I received your letter. I'm not sure why I am shocked your master forced you to marry Odel. I've heard of masters pairing slaves off with no regard to their wishes or feelings. The practice isn't foreign. But my mind reels at the thought of you married to anyone but Jonah. I hope it is going well, that Odel is treating you kindly.

Between us, dear friend, my marriage hasn't turned out to be at all what I expected. When we were courting, Sam dazzled me with his wit and charm. Now, however, I find him to be rather domineering. In public, he exudes a sort of confidence that draws others to him. He's a natural leader, the kind of person people look up to. But at home, that confidence leans more toward arrogance, and he seems intent to squash me with it. His little barbs show that he finds me dull and stupid. I fear I made a grave mistake in marrying him, but what am I to do now? I must make the best of it. Perhaps I can yet prove to him my worth.

Oh, listen to me. Going on about my trifling troubles when your situation is so dire. I pray that you find every happiness with Odel.

Yours forever,

Susan

February 25, 1845

Dearest Mercy,

I was happy to receive your letter and know that you are alive and well. It sounds like your Odel is a good man. A kind man. For that, I am so very thankful. And you are with child! What wonderful news. I will pray that your baby makes it safely into the world.

Your mother is faring well. Minnie keeps us both quite occupied. My feisty little cherub loves to run and climb, toppling everything over in her path. Her eyes twinkle with mischief. She minds Charity better than she does me. One stern look from your mother, and Minnie ducks her head and sticks out that pretty pink lip of hers. How does your mother do it? My toughest expression only elicits giggles.

I am thankful every day to have Charity here to help with Minnie. But I also think of you daily and wish there were some way to whisk you back here as well. It only seems right that we should all be together.

Yours forever,
Susan

June 25, 1845
Dearest Mercy,

I read your last letter to Charity like you asked me to. I know she would have loved to read it herself, but her eyesight is failing now. Her face lit up with pride. She's so happy for you, so thankful.

Honestly, she must have seen something in that letter I did not see. I know you wrote of finding freedom from fear, of how you sneaked out to the prayer meetings in the cane and poured your heart out to the Lord in prayers that went deeper than your own self-preservation. I want to be happy for you because of this. I do. But my mind keeps replaying the scene of the overseer beating you. Of him digging a hole and making you lie in it while he whipped your back, and you moaned and cried. I can't get that picture out of my head, and I'm fairly sick with it.

I'm so sorry for letting you get sold down there. I'm sorry you're in a place where they treat you so cruelly. I wish I could rescue you.

Can you ever forgive me?

Can God ever forgive me?

Yours forever,

Susan

November 15, 1846

Dearest Mercy,

I was so glad to receive your letter. It had been so long since I'd heard from you last that I feared the worst. But you are alive. Thank God. And you're a mother now!

Mingo sounds delightful. Isn't motherhood the most glorious thing? I know what you mean about your heart expanding in love with his birth. I felt the same way with Minnie. And now you're expecting another. Congratulations.

Your mother is doing well. I'm attempting to press on. My marriage is difficult. I daresay your Odel treats you much better than Sam treats me. But I have Charity and Minnie to ease my burden.

Please continue to write.

Yours forever,

Susan

December 28, 1847

Dearest Mercy,

I'm sorry for the loss of your sweet baby Faja. I can only imagine how your heart must ache for her.

My stomach lurches from reading all you've been through since you wrote last. Being cast into ant piles, clawed by cats, and put in stocks. You write of baptism and nothing holding you back, but dread pulls at me. How could I have let you get sent to such a place? How could I have allowed such a fate to befall you? I am supposed to be your friend, and yet I live comfortably in my finely decorated home while you lie naked in a pile of ants with weights on your hands and feet, writhing in the hot sun as they bite you all over?

How could I not face judgment for such a sin?

Please stay safe and out of harm's way.

Yours forever,

Susan

January 3, 1850

Dearest Mercy,

I haven't heard from you in so long. Are you alive? Are you well?

Please write.

Yours forever,

Susan

April 15, 1854

Dearest Mercy,

I think about you all the time. Why haven't you written? Please tell me you are still alive. I fear that overseer has beaten you to death. I am sick with worry. Please post word to me soon.

Yours forever,

Susan

July 25, 1859

Dearest Mercy,

Have you forgotten about me? Are you angry with me for allowing you to be sold to such a wretched place? Perhaps that's it. You don't wish to write to such an awful person any longer. I understand. If I were you, I wouldn't forgive me either. But, oh, that I could have one last chance to tell you how very sorry I am for the fate I bestowed on you. With all my heart, I wish I would have done something to prevent it.

But I shall never send this letter, shall I? So, you shall never know the weight of my guilt.

I pray for you daily. I hope you are alive and well.

Yours forever,

Susan

June 17, 1861

Dearest Mercy,

A letter! We received a letter from you. Finally. We were so happy to hear that you are alive. I was terrified that you had met your death at the hands of that horrid overseer. To hear that you're alive and a mother of six thriving children does me good.

Your mother was thrilled to hear that you are teaching other children to read. She's beaming with pride over the leader you've become.

Sam has gone off to fight in the war as well. Though I hate that he's fighting for the Confederates, I'm thankful to be rid of him for the time being. I've been stifled by his presence for so long, I've almost forgotten how to breathe. But the air is lighter in the home without him. Minnie feels the difference. She skips and frolics without a care in the world now. It took Sam going to war to find a touch of liberation here.

I pray that you are right, and the North wins this war. I pray for your freedom. Do come to us. We will be waiting.

Yours forever,

Susan

June 2, 1865

Dearest Mercy,

You were right. The North has won. Slavery is no more. What does freedom feel like? I pray you are on your way to see us even now.

Here in Georgetown, we were rather fortunate to escape much of the destruction Sherman racked upon the rest of the South. The Confederate troops abandoned our city, leaving us vulnerable to federal invasion. But the Union didn't want to take a city they could not hold, so for much of the war, things here were rather quiet.

In February of this year, the gunboat *Mingoe* moved up to Georgetown, and the Federals demanded the keys to the town hall. Union soldiers raised the stars and stripes above it as a volley of six muskets resounded over town. Six companies of Marines were stationed here, using our jail for their prisoners and the Winyah Indigo Society building for their hospital. When they ran out of room there, however, they kicked us out of our home and commandeered our house to use as a hospital as well.

Minnie and I moved in with Mrs. Trusket next door. Charity and the rest of the workers stayed to help with the hospital.

Many of the troops they stationed here to keep order are negro. The air in town nearly crackles with tension because of it.

Sam came home a more sinister version of the man I used to know. He wasn't wounded in body, but the war scarred his soul. Bitterness seeps through his pores. His dear lost cause is forever on his mind. He threw all the former slaves out, including Charity. Jonah took her in, and she is safe and well, though I miss her so.

Please come and see us.

Yours forever,

Susan

February 7, 1866

Dearest Mercy,

Aren't you coming to us, dear? You said you intended to return after the North won the war. We are waiting eagerly for you.

Yours forever,

Susan

June 25, 1877

Dearest Mercy,

Have you forgotten about us? Are you alive? Are you well? Please come and see us. The ghosts of the soldiers who died in this home are not happy with me. Perhaps your presence will quiet them.

Yours forever,

Susan

I set the letters down. The candle burns low, the light dancing across the walls. Susan waited for Mama. Mama did not come. Did Grandmother die waiting to see her daughter again? Jonah waits for her still. It seems expectations here swell around my mother—around Mercy's appearing.

I sleep fitfully in Mama's old bed. Something is missing.

It's her.

It's Mercy.

~

When the first rays of sunlight touch the horizon, I amble down the row of cabins until I find Jonah standing in his doorway. He smiles and waves me over. Lighthearted banter and the scent of corn bread spills forth from his cabin.

I squeeze inside, and he introduces me to one of his sisters and her husband, one of his brothers and his wife, and two cousins. A woman passes me a tin plate, and I devour the corn bread.

Jonah scrunches his hat on his head. "I hate to leave you here with nothin' to do, but we've got to get to work."

I wave him off. "Ain't no bother. I've got readin' to do."

"You can read?" Jonah's sister gives me a playful tap on the shoulder.

Jonah's smile stretches. "Of course, she can read. This is Mercy's girl, didn't I tell ya?"

His sister leans forward, her eyes twinkling. "Maybe you can teach me. The Freedmen's Bureau set up a school, but they ain't got enough teachers or books for the heaps of people who want learnin'."

Jonah laughs. "Leave her alone, will ya? We don't even know how long Miss Liberty will be here with us. She's our guest, not our teacher."

I manage a smile but squirm under his unasked question. How long will I be here? I have no answer.

When everyone rushes to the fields, I am left to meander back to Mama's old cabin. Birds chirp their greeting. The wind rustles moss-laden trees. I change my mind. I will go for a walk first and dive into Mama's journal later. I take off my shoes and fling them onto the porch. My feet need to touch the same earth Mama's feet walked.

I wander the landscape. My dusty feet squelch into muddy terrain as I trudge deeper into the fields. I discover a trunk dock and Jonah shows me how he lifts it to let water into the fields. The workers' songs drift up around me, unearthing memories from years ago. We sang different songs in the cane fields, but the voices rise and dip in much the same way.

At some point, I end up back at the graveyard, talking to the grandmother I never knew. I ask her how to fix what's broken inside of me.

She doesn't answer.

Horses' hooves clomp in the distance.

I turn to see Minnie riding next to…Thaddeus?

For a moment, how he left me standing in front of his house gets all clouded over with the thrill of seeing him again. I smile and wave.

He waves back and prods Chestnut to a gallop. Dust puffs up with each pound of the hooves. My heart skitters in time with the beat. He pulls the horse to a stop beside me and hops off. His face flushes with relief.

"Liberty." His voice is laced with apology and regret.

I notch my chin up, the fire from his rejection kindling in my belly. "Thaddeus."

"I'm sorry." His eyes find mine.

I flick my gaze away.

Minnie pulls Scamper up beside us. "Liberty, you didn't tell me you had such a handsome escort on your journey." Her face is flushed, and her eyes sparkle as she dismounts. She threads her arm through Thaddeus's.

My insides twist.

"My father was just thrilled when a soldier came calling this morning. They had a good ole chat, didn't you, Thad?"

Thad?

Thaddeus nods and smiles down at Minnie.

"He came asking for Liberty. Father didn't know what he was talking about, of course, but I told him I'd show him the way. It wasn't until we were out of earshot that Thad told me which side of the war he fought on."

Minnie leans forward and wiggles her brows. "Wouldn't father just die if he knew I was spending time with a Union soldier?"

I manage a smile, but my stomach lurches.

"Minnie, darling," Thaddeus speaks slow and controlled, pausing between each word. "Would you mind if I speak to Liberty alone?"

My eyes narrow. He's trying to impress her. She probably doesn't even know he stutters.

She lays a hand on his arm, touching him freely like I longed to on our journey. "Not at all." She grabs the horses' reins and leads them to the grassy patch where the path opens up.

I cross my arms and scowl.

"Look, I messed up." He dips his head, all trace of a smile gone.

I stare. Wait.

"I d-didn't know how to introduce you to my f-family."

The fact that he stutters now proves to me that he is more comfortable being himself with me than he is with Minnie. This should comfort me but doesn't.

"How about 'This here is Liberty. I'm helpin' her find her family in Georgetown'? See now? That wasn't so hard, was it?"

"You d-don't know my f-father. My brothers."

"And you don't know your own strength."

He toes the ground with his boot. "How d-do you know you're not seeing something that isn't th-there?"

"I'm not the one who sees ghosts."

I stomp off toward Minnie, leaving him alone with his frown and the gurgle of the river in the background.

When I reach Minnie, her eyes are alight. She grabs my hands and squeezes. "Oh, Liberty. How could you not tell me? Thaddeus is a dream."

I swallow around the lump in my throat.

"I think he fancies me. Do you think so?" She presses her hands onto her reddened cheeks.

I shrug. I cannot force my mouth to speak.

"He's rather handsome with sort of a rugged charm, wouldn't you say? And those eyes." She brings a hand to her heart and flutters her lashes.

"His eyes are striking'," I admit. Deep. Pensive. Beautiful.

"Yes. See? I'm not the only one who thinks so. He's simply divine. The way he speaks, as if he has all the time in the world to spend with just me. I could hang on his every word."

A grunt escapes my lips before I can squelch it.

Minnie tilts her head, brows furrowed.

I wave her off. "Thaddeus is wonderful."

Her smile returns as she raises her fingers in a delicate wave. "Here he comes. Do I look alright?"

"Beautiful." I can't deny it. Minnie would be any white man's dream. My chest burns.

"Ladies." Thaddeus tips his hat as he draws near. "Would you fancy a ride around Hopecrest?" He angles his gaze toward me. "Minnie had the fine idea of giving you a tour."

I bite my lip. "There are three of us and only two horses."

Minnie links arms with Thaddeus. "Oh, no matter. You can have Scamper. Thad and I can ride Chestnut together, can't we?" Her eyes twinkle up at him.

"That'd work out mighty nice." His words pour out thick like molasses. I might gag.

Thaddeus helps me mount Scamper. The warmth lingers from where his hands touched my hand and the small of my back.

Minnie saddles up behind Thaddeus on their horse, just as cozy as can be. I follow behind them. Their lyrical laughter and conversation rushes at me in waves. I press my eyes shut against the threat of tears. How can it be so easy between them? How can they be so free? Just because of the color of their skin. My stomach turns.

Twigs snap under us. Breath puffs through the horses' nostrils. We plod up a grassy knoll toward a large barn on tall, skinny legs.

Minnie looks at me over her shoulder and raises her voice. "This here's the winnowing barn. It's where Mercy and Jonah fell in love." With that, she leans into Thaddeus as if sinking into a dream cloud.

I roll my eyes.

We pass a rice mill, a barn, the kitchen, and the dairy. We come to a chapel. Ole Faithful flashes in my mind with smoke curling up from its core. I shiver.

"They were going to get married here, Jonah and Mercy." Minnie's voice has that far away sound to it again. "If only she hadn't been sold."

This story must be in the journal. I'm nearly bursting to read it now. To be away from the gushing couple in front of me and alone with the story that came before I found my way to this earth.

When we find ourselves back in front of the cabins, we dismount, and Minnie releases a deep sigh.

"I'd best be going. Father will not be so accommodating if I arrive late again."

Thaddeus steps toward her. "Do you need me to escort you home?"

She places a hand on his chest. "You are too kind. But it's not necessary. I make this journey all the time. I wouldn't want you to think of me as another fragile female, incapable of doing a thing for myself." She winks.

He locks eyes with her and brings her hand up to his mouth as he speaks slow and smooth. "I could never think of you that way." He plants a tender kiss.

I blink long and imagine his lips brushing my hand instead of hers. A tingle dances up my spine.

"You're welcome to stay here as long as you like, I'm sure," Minnie says. "I wish you could stay with us, but if father were to find out you fought for the Union, it would not fare well for you, I'm afraid. Best to keep your distance and allow him to hold on to his ignorance."

"Understood." Thaddeus's cheeks dimple. "What about Scamper?"

She waves a hand in front of her. "I'll retrieve him tomorrow. Or another day."

Thaddeus holds out his hand and assists Minnie in mounting Chestnut again. She waves a cheery goodbye to us both before trotting away.

"What was that?" I ask Thaddeus when she is but a blur in the distance.

His forehead scrunches. "What?"

"You and Minnie. I didn't know you to be such a flirt." My tone comes out dry as dust.

A blush creeps up his cheeks. He shrugs. "She's a beautiful woman."

"Yes." My eyes avoid his.

"I can't help but notice. Does th-that bother you?" He takes a step closer, dipping his head to meet my gaze.

"No," I lie.

"Liberty?" He's frowning, those beautiful eyes flecked with concern.

I bite my lip. "Do you care for her?" I am vulnerable before him. Laid bare.

"I've only just met her." He shifts his jaw. "But I reckon the seed of such things is there."

Wrapping my arms around myself, I turn from his piercing gaze.

"What's the matter, Liberty? Is there some reason I should not have affection for Minnie?"

I shake my head, eyes misting. No. There's no reason. The two of them are perfect for each other. The touch of Thaddeus's hand warms my shoulder, and I spin back around, suddenly emboldened.

"It's just I thought you might have come to care for…for me." I lower my head, heat creeping up from the tips of my toes all the way to the crown of my head.

"I do care."

My gaze flitters up to see his confused expression.

"You're like the sister I never had."

I scoff. "Sister."

Realization dawns on his face now. Can I melt into the dust like a block of ice?

"Oh, Liberty." He takes a step back. "You know it can never be more. Not with th-the world the way it is."

I press my eyes shut against flowing tears. "I know."

I do. And yet men just fought a war to prove the color of a person's skin shouldn't keep them from freedom. How many more wars will need to be fought until we can just be equal? Until we can live our lives in peace without anyone looking down on us or telling us what we can't do?

"You're a beautiful woman." The guilt on Thaddeus's face makes me squirm. "You're brave and smart and kind. Some young man is going to get quite a catch when he wins your heart."

I press my hand to my recoiling stomach and run to Mama's cabin. The door slams behind me. Burying my face in the quilt, I weep and moan for my heart, now fully broken.

28

———

June 2020
Chicago, Illinois

Natassa fiddled with her necklace as she scanned the scene in front of her. What had she expected? Had she thought this meeting would be like the prayer meetings on the steps of St. Anthony's during the protests surrounding Mike Brown? That was a group of mostly older ladies holding hands. Of course, this time, it would be bigger, and they'd be here for worship, not intercession. But this was overwhelming.

Families, college students, elderly couples, so many people swarmed the street, moving toward the sound of drums and electric guitars.

"Everyone has their masks, right?" Her eyes darted from David to Mercy as they stepped onto the sidewalk. Dusk dimmed the scene around them.

They nodded, putting them on.

She bit her lip. Everyone would be social distancing, right?

Brandon squeezed her hand. "It'll be fine."

A few feet ahead of them, Janell pushed a stroller with Joe nestled inside. DeAndre ambled next to her. Mercy skipped up to Java and took his hand.

"I hope it doesn't rain." Janell surveyed the cloudy sky.

"I checked the forecast. Looks clear." Brandon hooked his thumbs through the belt loops of his jeans and angled toward Natassa. "It's only a four-minute walk to this park."

What Chicago boasted as a park turned out to merely be a grassy rectangle surrounded by streets and buildings. A few trees, a couple bushes, some bright blue trash cans. Not a hint of a playground or a flower, though those might have been hidden from Natassa's view by the crowd. A band played while sitting on red pavement squares near the subway entrance. Keys, guitars, drums, and a sax. Four vocalists— three black, one white. Around them, people clapped and sang in appropriately spaced groups. The muscles in her shoulders relaxed. This wasn't so scary.

They settled around the outer fringe of the gathering. Janell turned to Natassa. "We could try to get closer if you want. I'm just a bit nervous about my boys distracting other people."

"This is fine." Natassa smiled.

Janell spun back around to face the band. Mercy and Java danced together sweetly. Natassa closed her eyes and breathed in the words of the song "Waymaker." This one was familiar. She relaxed into the melody and let her voice rise and meld with this group of people. Her family in Christ. Janell's high soprano mixed with DeAndre's rich baritone. Brandon's voice, solid and strong. David's voice, deeper than she remembered it. Mercy and Java giggled as they twirled and sang. Their little group of black, white, and both was harmonizing with a community of diverse worshipers. Even at the end of a dreary day, it came like a burst of light and life.

Natassa opened her eyes and took in the crowd. Such diversity. Different shades of skin standing in the same patch of green grass. Some stood still, reverent. Some waved their arms, expressive. Some moved their bodies slightly from side to side. Some rocked back and forth, while others twisted or spun. A tambourine to the far right. A brilliant blue flag up in front. A kaleidoscope of complimentary beauty.

An unfamiliar song began. She grew silent, swaying to the music. Heavy on the drums, a vocalist began clapping, and the crowd followed suit. As they stomped and shouted through the song, a wave of peace cascaded over Natassa. She threw her arms out and received all He had to give, free. Fear and anxiety sloughed off her in His presence.

That song ended, and a softer one ensued. Natassa stood with her eyes closed, basking, full of gratitude.

"You must be Natassa."

She jumped. *Where did this woman come from?*

"Sorry to startle you. I'm Margie, DeAndre's mother."

Natassa took in a sharp breath as she studied the woman next to her. She wore a crisp navy-blue pants suit with a white dress shirt underneath. Her burgundy lipstick and gray eye shadow were conservative but pronounced.

"MeeMaw!" Mercy crashed into the woman, followed by Java.

"Well, hello, Mercy Me. My Java Bean." She smoothed Mercy's hair and then Java's, smiling warmly at them.

"I didn't know you were coming." Mercy beamed up at her.

Margie spread her hands out. "Surprise." She kissed her finger and then planted it on Mercy's nose. "Now, go back to worshiping the Good Lord with your dancing. I want to talk to your mama."

DeAndre's and Janell's eyes were closed, and they must have been lost in their time with the Lord because they didn't turn at the commotion. Brandon and David glanced over, however. Brandon's brow furrowed in a question. David grinned and waved.

Margie chuckled and waved her hand in front of her face as if to say, "Go on now."

"That's my husband, Brandon, and my son, David."

"Oh, I know David."

"That's right. I forgot you met."

Margie stood so close to Natassa that their shoulders brushed each other. Her perfume hung heavy in the air. Natassa's nose itched.

Margie leaned close to Natassa's ear. "Your son's a good kid. He can be a fool sometimes. Make a mess of things. But he's got a good heart. Am I right?"

Her mouth twisted. She wouldn't call David a fool, but taking his sister to Chicago behind her back *was* a foolish decision. So, "Yes."

"When you're a mother, you wish with all your heart you could stop your kids from doing stupid stuff, but you can't. You've just got to love them through it."

Natassa eyed her. What was she getting at?

"My boy has done some stupid stuff, too. He's messed up real bad and tangled his life up in a sticky web from those foolhardy choices. And he's mangled stuff up for you along the way. I'm sorry about that. I am. I wish I could have slapped some sense into him before he did that." She sighed. "But what's done is done. We can't go back. All I know is that he's a good man. He's got a good heart."

Natassa closed her eyes and nodded.

"Just think about what he said, will you?" Margie nudged Natassa gently with her shoulder. "Now I've got to get out of here. This music is far too loud. I don't understand why they have to blast our eardrums like that. And why they can't play some wholesome gospel music."

Natassa smiled.

Margie slunk through the crowed without DeAndre ever having opened his eyes.

~

Mercy stood on her tiptoes, peering through the crowd. Where had MeeMaw gone? The blur of colors and song whisked her away. Java snatched Mercy's hand and twirled her around, giggling, and she let her questions about her grandma float away to the clouds.

Her gaze snapped back to Mom after each turn. Mercy had never seen her mother so happy. It almost made her forget about the picture of St. Anthony's, all small and black. Her safe place all burned up. When she'd thought about that earlier, she could lock herself in her room and cry for days, like Mom had when the babies died. But here, with all the people singing and clapping …how could she feel sad here?

Maybe this could be her new safe place.

Mercy skipped and twirled, jumped and clapped. This felt like black church, only the sea of faces around her were all different colors, like a full palette of paint. She fit just fine here. How could she not? Everyone fit.

Java's steps slowed, and then he plopped in the grass. He looked like Daniel's car when it ran out of gas—going fast, slowing, then coming to a stop.

DeAndre turned around. "Getting tired, bud?"

Java yawned.

DeAndre raised his voice over the music. "We should probably be going soon." He poked his thumb over his shoulder, gesturing toward Java.

All the grown-ups turned around, their mouths curling into those smiles they use when they think something is cute.

DeAndre bent over and slung Java onto his shoulders for a piggyback ride. Janell spun the stroller around and started toward the street, everyone else following her lead. Baby Joe had slept through almost the whole thing, poor baby. He missed out on the fun. Mercy glanced over her shoulder as she walked away, trying to take a picture in her mind so she could remember the night forever.

As the music faded behind them, DeAndre and Mom continued singing. Their voices sounded nice together— DeAndre's low, Mom's high. Dad and David and Janell just listened. Mercy wove in and out of the space between them all. *This is my family.*

A spark of an idea lit inside her.

"We could move to Chicago." Mercy tugged on Mom's arm. "We can buy an apartment near DeAndre's. I can paint with him at his studio." Her eyes darted to DeAndre, then back to Mom. "Bethany can come, too." Mercy stuck her left hand in her mom's grasp and tucked her right hand in the crook of DeAndre's elbow.

Their singing faded away as their faces turned serious. Mercy's spark snuffed out. Gravel filled her stomach.

DeAndre crouched, prying Java's hands from around his neck and settling her brother on his feet. He leaned over and kissed the side of Mercy's head. "Fairy-tale things," he whispered in her ear.

Mercy's lip stuck out in a pout. They all thought she was a dumb kid. She kicked a rock, and it pinged into the sewer as they continued walking home.

Not home. Because Mom and Dad would never move here, would never let this be her home.

They stopped in front of the door to DeAndre's apartment building.

"We'll be going now." Mom pulled David into a hug.

David patted Mom's back but flashed a silly face at Mercy.

Mom turned to her. "Have a good night, sweetheart." She bent and wrapped her arms around Mercy, squeezing tight.

"I will." Mercy made her voice sound strangled so Mom would get the point that she was squashing her.

Dad slapped David on the back, then bent and kissed Mercy on the cheek. "Listen to DeAndre and Janell."

Mercy didn't know if he was talking to both of them or just her, so she said, "We will."

Mom smiled at DeAndre. "I'll text before we come over tomorrow."

"Sounds good." He smiled back.

Mercy looked between them. Something had changed. She didn't know what or why, but she liked it.

~

Up in her room, tucked snugly in bed, Mercy asked DeAndre for a story.

"How about I tell you a Bible story tonight?" He leaned his back against the wall and slid down, then hooked his arms around his knees. "Do you know the story of Hannah?"

Mercy shook her head and pulled the blanket up to her chin.

"There was this woman named Hannah who couldn't have any children. Hannah would cry and cry because she wanted a baby so badly. She went to the temple and cried and prayed to God for a child. She said, 'God, if you give me a child, I'll give him back to You.'"

Mercy leaned forward. "Did He give her one?"

"Yes. He gave her a son, and she named him Samuel. Hannah loved her son very much and kept him with her until he was about three. Then she took him to the temple and left him with Eli the priest so that Samuel could serve God there."

"What? Why?" Mercy tossed the blanket down. "Why would she just give her kid away?"

"She'd told God that if He gave her a child, she'd give the child back. So, she did. She let him go into God's hands. But that doesn't mean she didn't love him."

"This is a terrible story." Mercy crossed her arms.

DeAndre chuckled. "I see how it could seem that way. But Samuel went on to be a very important man. He changed the world."

"Changed the world?" Mercy's voice came out full of attitude. Shoot. Not what she meant. She just didn't understand.

"Yep. Just like you're going to do."

"I'm only nine."

"So?"

Mercy rolled her eyes and lay back, snuggling into her pillow. "Good night, Dad."

~

DeAndre had just stepped away from Mercy's room when a knock sounded at the front door. "Who could that be?"

"I'll get it." Janell rose from the couch, slid open the lock, and peeked out the door. "Oh, hi, Brenda."

Brenda? DeAndre tiptoed to the door, hiding himself behind it and peering through the peephole.

"This package came for you. They delivered it to our apartment by mistake."

Janell took the box from Brenda's arms. "Thank you."

"That's the third time they've confused our mail. I'm not sure why…" Her voice trailed off, and she turned as if to end the conversation but then stepped forward again and bent close to Janell. "Look, I hate to be the one to tell you this but," Brenda said in a low voice, glancing behind her shoulder, "your husband is a sex offender."

Janell's mouth parted.

Brenda put a hand out. "Lord have mercy on your soul. You didn't know what you were doing when you married that man, I'm sure. If you need out, a place to stay, my church has resources. I can connect you with one of our pastors—"

"Thank you for looking out for me, but actually, I know exactly who my husband is." Janell rocked forward onto her toes as if ready to pounce. "He's sensitive and sweet, a romantic with big dreams and a soft heart—"

"It's worse than I thought." Brenda shook her head. "He's pulled the wool over your eyes."

"No." Janell's smile tightened. "I think the Accuser of the Brethren has pulled the wool over your own eyes." Her gaze fell to the box in her hand. She ran her finger over the return address, and her breath caught. "Thank you for this." She nodded at Brenda before closing the door behind her, leaving their neighbor gaping in the hallway.

Janell's misty eyes met his. "It's from my mom." Her hands trembled.

"Your mom? How?"

She bit her lip. "I called her from the hospital after having Joe. I knew she wouldn't answer. I just wanted her to hear—" Her voice cracked. "Hear that she had a grandson. Two of them. I left our address in case she wanted to write." Janell's face contorted.

DeAndre wrapped his arms around his wife, the box, and the gaping wound her parents' abandonment had caused. They sank to the floor together, unable to support the weight of all they carried.

"Let's see what it is." He gently pried the box from her hands and ripped off the packing tape.

Janell opened the flaps and lifted out a blue blanket. And then another. She sniffed. "My mom knitted each of the boys a blanket."

A piece of green stationery fluttered to the floor. He picked it up and handed it to Janell.

"For our grandsons. We love you," Janell read, then clamped her eyes shut.

DeAndre peeked inside the box. "There's another note." He handed her a second piece of green stationery.

"Janell, we love you, and we're proud of you. Love, Mom and Dad." Janell clutched the note to her chest, folded over, and sobbed.

He scooted around to her and enfolded her in his arms. Her entire body shook as she heaved in gasping breaths of air.

"Oh, baby." His own eyes misted over at watching his beautiful wife break before him. "I'm so sorry. I'm sorry I screwed things up between you and your family. I'm sorry they haven't spoken to you in all these years because of me." He'd caused so much pain. His heart twisted.

Janell sucked in a breath and wiped her face with her sleeve. "No." She shook her head. "No, that's not what happened." She made an *O* with her mouth and exhaled slowly, then inhaled through her nose. "I made a decision, DeAndre." She touched his face, her watery eyes meeting his. "I chose you. I don't regret it."

He swallowed, cupping her hand on his cheek.

"They still love me." She thumped the note against her chest. "They still love me. That's enough."

29

---

*1868, Georgetown,
South Carolina*

When all the tears have leaked out of my eyes, I am left limp and lifeless. I should eat, but I cannot bring myself to find food. I barely have energy enough to move my limbs. My hand brushes against something under the quilt. I smooth my palm over it. Mama's journal.

Yes, this is what I need. Distraction from my wounded heart. I roll on my side, open to the first page, and read.

Mama being ripped away from my grandmother and sold to Tennessee when she was only a child. Mama rejected in Tennessee for being too white. Sold to a slave coffle. She saw little children ripped away from their mothers, heard their screams. Mama purchased and taken to Kentucky to care for a baby when she was only a little girl herself. She fell in love with baby Elizabeth. When baby Elizabeth returned the affection, the owners sold Mama again.

I am immersed in the story. When Thaddeus knocks on the door and asks if I'm okay, I ignore him. When Jonah does so, maybe an hour later, I call out that I am fine and keep reading.

Mama was a companion to another child. They changed Mama's name to Annabelle. She made friends with Emma, a fellow slave. She learned to fiddle.

Wait. Mama knows how to fiddle?

She fiddled to earn money for her freedom jar. Emma and Mama hatched plans to run north. Their master died. Emma fled. The new master beat Mama. She escaped.

I gasp.

She ran south to find my grandmother instead of fleeing north to freedom.

My stomach rumbles now, and when Jonah knocks again saying he has dinner for me, I answer. I take the tin plate he offers and give a weak smile.

"Whatcha doin'?" Jonah peers over my shoulder into the cabin.

"Readin' Mama's old journal."

"You don't say." He lets himself in and lights the candle on the table. Surely enough, the sun is sinking low. "She write anything in there 'bout me?"

I chuckle. "Haven't gotten that far, but I figure I'm about to."

"You let me know what she says 'bout me, you hear? I want to know the juicy details." He stretches, his shirt pulling tight on his muscular frame. The candlelight flickers on the flecks of gray in his beard.

I smile but make no promises. "Where's Thaddeus?" I hope he's gone away. Far away.

"In Solomon's cabin, two doors down."

I frown.

Jonah squints in my direction. "He ain't givin' you no trouble, is he?"

I shake my head.

"Alright then. You let me know if he ain't actin' the gentleman, and I'll take care of it."

I laugh. This I'd like to see.

Jonah leaves, and I read while I scarf down hoecake and fish.

Mama does write of Jonah. She writes of how he carried my grandmother up from the field when she collapsed. How he flirted with her while they threshed rice. I picture the winnowing barn and fight a smile. The way Mama tells the story makes me want to pull for her and Jonah, yet I can't betray my father. Their love story grew sweetly, though, and I can't help but be drawn in. When he asked her to marry him, my heart aches. Though it comes as no surprise, the sorrow of Mama's words as she heard she would be sold tunnels deep into me. Her heartache at the injustice finds my festering wounds from all the wrongs piled so high upon our people. I pound the table with my fist.

Susan's solution. Mama's compromise. It sounds like her, so truly sacrificial. Mama would give herself to save someone else. Every time. That's who she is. It's why I love her, even if I'll never understand her.

Why did Mama send me away? I needed her. Still need her. What could my grandmother have given me that Mama didn't possess herself? Why did she push me out of her life?

I didn't think there were tears left in me to cry, but they burst forth now. My sleeve is damp from trying to brush them away.

Suddenly, my breath catches. I flip the journal back to the beginning and read again.

Mama said it was for my good. Reckon I was too young to understand it then, but now I see she was right. The missus might have killed me if she had half a chance and another year or two. I ain't never seen hate spew from someone's eyes like it did from hers. Poison. Mama knew it was deadly and aimed right at me, so she begged Old Master to sell me to a couple from Nashville who'd come callin'. I begged Mama to keep me with her, holding on to her dusty ankles, my tears making mud as they spattered on the ground. She stood as still as stone. Just said, "I love you, Mercy. That's why I'm doing this."

I love you. That's why I'm doing this.

It's clear to me now. This is no different. Mama's great act of love was sending me away.

She didn't send me away because she didn't care, but because she did. Because she is the one who will sacrifice her happiness for the happiness of another, time and time again.

My throat is raw. I am greatly valued.

My dear mother choosing others and denying herself. When will somebody put her in the front of the line? Maybe it's time. And maybe I can do this one big, beautiful act of love for the person who constantly pours herself out for me.

I let out a low growl.

I'll need Thaddeus's help.

~

As the morning gives birth on the horizon, I awkwardly climb upon Scamper and ride off without a word. If I am to convince Thaddeus to go along with my plan, I'll need assistance from someone who holds greater sway over him than I do. Perhaps guilt over breaking my heart might motivate him, but I can't put my weight behind such a hope. Better to have Minnie at my side batting her long lashes as we plead with him to comply.

Thaddeus has yet to emerge from his cabin, and Jonah and the others are on their way to the fields. Which way is it to downtown Georgetown? I turn left at the end of the pine-lined trail. Hopefully, my keen sense of direction won't fail me now.

What time does Minnie's father head to work? My stomach somersaults at the possibility of running into that spiteful man. I slow Scamper's pace.

A few crickets still chirp as though not ready to give up the night. Birdsong rings out all around me. The crisp morning air cools my skin. The rhythmic sway of the horse calms me. I may be going to the home of a negro-hating Klansman and a crazy woman who sees ghosts, but I am going to meet Minnie. Everything within me tells me that she means no harm. I grip the reins. That doesn't mean this friendship will not hurt.

I arrive in town just as businesses are yawning and stretching, getting ready for the day. Signs in doors flip from closed to open. Hopefully, that means Minnie's father is now at work. I keep my head down as I trot past the bank.

When I knock on Minnie's door, my heart pounds in my ears. My feet are ready to flee if a man answers. But Susan's eyes peer out at me through the crack in the door, same as they did the first time. Her sharp intake of breath causes me to do the same.

"Liberty," she whispers with her forehead pressed to the door, "you can't be here. Sam is still reading his paper."

I bite my lip. "I need to see Minnie."

Susan glances over her shoulder. Her eyes dart around. "I'll tell her to meet you at the docks."

She doesn't wait for my reply before she slips the door shut. A man's voice booms through the closed door. "Who was that?"

"Oh, no one. Do you need some more coffee?"

I race from the yard and down to Front Street toward the docks. When I arrive, I wrap my arms around myself and sigh. I left Scamper tied to the post in their yard. I settle on an empty crate and watch men load flatboats and steamers with crates and bags. They're nearly all negro, and I am at home among my people. Safe.

A clomp of hooves alerts me to Minnie's arrival. She's done her hair in a simple braid slung over her shoulder instead of pinned up and fancy. Her face looks flushed as she slides off the horse and grabs my hands. "Is something the matter?" Her forehead creases.

I shake my head.

Her right hand flies to her heart. "Thank goodness. I thought maybe Thaddeus—"

"Thaddeus is fine."

She inclines her head toward me. "Then why ever are you here at such an hour?"

I squeeze her left hand. "I need your help."

We sit on the crate, and I explain my plan. "Thaddeus favors you. He told me himself. If we were to ask him together—if you were to plead with him to comply—I'm sure he'd do it." I fight to keep my voice even. "He cannot deny a beautiful woman like you."

Her eyes twinkle. "What a marvelous idea. So romantic. Yes, of course. We shall ask him together. I shall put on my best frock and use my most helpless expression."

She transforms her face into a doe-eyed, purse-lipped plea.

I clap. "Perfect."

"If you head back, I will join you as soon as I can ready myself." She stands and hands Scamper's reins to me. "Try to butter him up a bit before I arrive."

I nod, but my stomach drops at the suggestion. Minnie knows nothing of my fight with Thaddeus or my broken heart. She has no idea that my grand plan comes at great cost to me. As I ride back to Hopecrest, I dig deep and find strength. Mama's blood runs through my veins. I can do this. I can humble myself and move toward the man who hurt me. Instead of recoiling, instead of building high walls, I can choose to be vulnerable for the sake of love. Can't I?

When I arrive, Thaddeus is sitting on the steps of Mama's cabin. A look of relief washes over his face when he sees me.

He stands. Walks over to Scamper. To me. "Where were you?"

"Out for a ride."

"F-for a ride? You 'bout scared me to d-death."

I blink. I hadn't considered that he might be concerned. My brow furrows. He does care for me. Even if not in the way I've wished, it means something.

"I'm sorry about yesterday," I say as I slide off the horse.

I stumble a bit with the dismount, and he places a hand on my shoulder to steady me.

"Me too." His hand lingers.

"Don't be. I understand." I look up at him. My mouth can't quite form a smile.

"I wish—"

My hand comes up and covers his. "I know. Me too. But I'm glad to have you as a friend."

"A f-friend." The corner of his mouth twitches as he repeats this.

I drop my desire for everything more into the dust between us. He's not meant to be mine.

"Now, I'm 'bout starvin'. Have you cooked up breakfast yet?"

His grin breaks out. "Saved you an ash cake just in case."

~

Minnie arrives a couple hours later. Her hair is pinned up with a few loose curls framing her face and flowing down her back. She looks radiant in her sapphire-blue frock that pulls the blue from her eyes. I smell the rosewater emanating from her before she even gets off her horse.

"Why, Minnie. What a pleasant surprise." Thaddeus kisses her gloved hand.

"Oh, Thad. You're such a dear." Minnie's voice swoons. I hold back a laugh. She will be the perfect ally.

After exasperating small talk, Minnie and I perch on a log across from Thaddeus.

I lean forward, clasping my hands in front of me. "We have something to ask you."

"Ask me?" Thaddeus's brow rises in question.

Minnie swoops into the conversation. "Don't you think the love story between Mercy and Jonah is the most romantic thing ever?" She turns to me. "Have you told him the whole story?"

"Bits and pieces."

She proceeds to regale him with the entire tale in vivid detail, complete with hand gestures and spirited voices.

Thaddeus leans close, hat in hand, reeled in by her antics.

"And that's why," I say as she finishes, "we want you to go back to New Orleans, get my mama, and bring her here to Jonah."

He shakes his head as if waking up from a dream. "What?"

Minnie tries out the pleading face she showed me earlier. "Jonah has been waiting for Mercy all these years. Go get her, Thaddeus. Bring the two of them together."

He crosses his arms. "If she wanted to come, wouldn't she have traveled with Liberty?"

Yes, but…

"She didn't know that Jonah had been waiting for her. Didn't even know whether he was still alive or was still here." I mimic Minnie's doe-eyed gaze.

He shifts his jaw from side to side. His forehead pinches. "It's a long journey."

"You could come straight here on a steamship," I say. "No need to take multiple boats and trains to avoid the riders."

"I'm running low on money. I probably have enough for the journey but might not have much, if anything, left over."

"I'll pay you back." Maybe I can do odd jobs for the Millers. Chop wood while he travels. Will it be enough? I firm my lips. It has to be.

His gaze travels from my pleading eyes to Minnie's. He sighs. "I guess."

Minnie and I squeal and hug.

Best not to mention that Mama might not want to come. Or that she may insist on bringing the whole family. I wouldn't want him to change his mind.

"I'll leave tomorrow." He crushes his cap onto his head as if that settles it.

I run to Mama's cabin and pull out the rest of the money she gave me.

I return to see Thaddeus and Minnie entwined in an embrace, their faces inches from each other. I avert my eyes. Swallow. Toe my shoe in the dust. Curse this sting in my chest.

When I glance up to see they've parted, I walk up to Thaddeus and press the money into his hand.

~

Minnie arrives the next morning just as dawn's pink hues kiss the horizon. She's come dressed as a Southern queen to see Thaddeus off. She must have risen in inky darkness to ready herself by candlelight. The crimson gown she's chosen for the occasion is wholly inappropriate for riding and fully accentuates her curves. She stops in front of the cabins, panting for breath as if she feared missing his departure. As if he would leave without seeing her. He's planning on taking Scamper into town, but I guess they cannot have the parting they desire in the livery stable.

Thaddeus saddles his pack just as I bring him a johnnycake from Jonah's cabin. They've all left for the fields, and only the three of us remain here, keepers of this secret. Jonah knows nothing of our plans. Down the path a ways, the old woman who watches the children sits on her porch, cane in hand, the only one to witness this send off. No little ones dash to and fro this early. Perhaps she relishes this time of quiet before the rush of day.

Thaddeus extends a hand to help Minnie dismount. "Minnie, my dear. So nice to see you."

I try not to snicker at his slow, smooth speech. His stutter comforts me, perhaps even more than his lack of a stutter when we made our way to Savannah. The side of my mouth twitches upward with our shared secret.

"Oh, Thad. I'll miss you so." She bats thick eyelashes at him.

My throat itches. Tickles. I cough to clear it. I hand Thaddeus his breakfast, then walk back to Mama's cabin—my cabin—to give them a moment alone.

Inside, I pace. My hands flutter at my sides. What if this is a bad idea? What if Mama won't come? Thaddeus may go all that way for nothing. Does she even have a spark of love left for Jonah after pouring her heart out for my father? I look out the back window. The resurrection fern grows on the live oak there. Fresh and green from recent rain. Maybe the dried-up fern of affection for Jonah will spring back to life at the sight of him. But what if it doesn't? What then? *And Lord, don't let me be putting anyone in danger.* If the riders were after me, willing to follow me on a steamship, might they do the same to my family?

Perhaps this plan is reckless. Foolhardy. I should call it off right now. Burst out of the cabin and tell Thaddeus to forget it. I put my hand on the doorknob and pull it open.

The sight in front of me smacks me like a slap across the face. Thaddeus and Minnie enraptured in a deep kiss with their arms entwined around each other as if they will never let go. I stumble backward. Push the door shut. Put a hand to my tumbling stomach.

I have to let him go. Already said goodbye to my desire for deeper things between us. So why do my insides twist? Why is the picture of the two of them together branded in my mind? I close my eyes and see them. Lashes whip at my heart. I shake my head, pushing the picture away. *Pull yourself together.* I grit my teeth and open the door again, this time looking down and humming loudly as I do so. When I raise my eyes, only their hands remain clasped together.

I paste on a smile. "Ready to go?"

"I reckon." He casts a longing glance at Minnie.

"You got the letter I gave you for Mama?"

He pats his pack. "Right here."

"You take care, then. Be safe." I step forward as if to give him a hug but stop. Nod instead.

He puts a hand on my shoulder and squeezes. "I will. See you in a couple weeks." His eyes lock on to mine, and in them, I see every piece of the journey we took together. Every part of his heart he shared.

My shoulder remains warm long after he disappears in the distance. I stand and watch him go.

"Now what?" Minnie asks.

I startle. "I thought you would have ridden with him into town."

She sighs. "How many times can you say goodbye? I only care to be heartbroken once today, thank you." She wraps her arms around herself as if suddenly chilled. "So, now what?"

I mimic her gesture and wrap my arms around myself, holding myself together. "We wait."

~

Minnie departs an hour or so later, and I find Jonah in the fields. I peer up at him in the blazing sun. Sweat drips from his forehead.

"I want to job for the Millers. Do they need wood chopped, you think? They be needin' fence posts?"

Jonah wipes his sleeve across his brow and smiles at me. "You can chop wood?"

I square my shoulders. "With the best of them."

"This I gotta see."

It's nearly the lunch hour, so I wait while he finishes repairing the ditch. Then he marches me to the edge of the woods where a line of felled trees lies and hands me an ax. I hoist the ax up and bring it down with a thump. It slices down nicely. Jonah whistles. I press my lips together and wedge the ax up. My muscles pull and strain as I swing it down again.

"Well, I'll be." Jonah rocks back on his heels. "Mercy's daughter. Smart and strong."

"Yes, sir." I glow under his praise, though perhaps it's meant more for Mama than for me.

"Let's go talk to the Millers," he says.

He leads me to the Big House and up large steps to wait on the porch as he knocks. A woman answers, her face etched with weary lines, her eyes tired and sad. So, this is the woman Mama said was a kind mistress who encouraged book learning among her slaves. Mama had been so thankful to be working for the Millers instead of the spiteful master and missus she started off with down the road. In the end, though, this good mistress sold her off to pay the master's debts. What am I to think of her?

"Missus Miller, ma'am." Jonah takes off his hat and holds it in his hands.

"Yes, Jonah?"

"Do you remember Mercy, ma'am?"

Her eyes alight with recognition. "Mercy? The fiddler?"

My mind swirls. Mama's memory here is wrapped up in something that I have no knowledge of.

"Yes, ma'am." He nods. "This here is her daughter, Liberty."

The woman smiles at me, and suddenly, she doesn't look as old and worn.

"She's visitin' and wonderin' if she can earn some money choppin' wood for ya. I seen her do it, and she can split that wood near as good as I can."

The woman's eyes twinkle at me. "Can she now? I can't say that surprises me. Your mother was something special."

Yes, she was. *Is.*

I meet her gaze and give a subtle nod. I will job for the Millers. I will earn wages and not waste them, not be reckless. I will work and wait and hope that Mama comes with Thaddeus without a fuss.

~

I chop wood each day, working dawn until dusk. I must keep my hands busy, keep my mind from wandering to that picture of Thaddeus and Minnie enveloped in a kiss. But no amount of chopping pushes it away.

Each time jealousy twists her thorns into my flesh, I do my best to dig them out. Minnie said she would not marry a cruel man but a tender one. Thaddeus is nothing if not tender. But if Mama could let her dreams go due to her love for another, so can I. Her blood runs in my veins. There has to be something of goodness and mercy inside of me, something of selfless sacrifice.

In the evenings, I sit in front of my grandmother's lily, pulling up single blades of grass as I talk. "I'm tryin' to be good like Mama. Tryin' so hard. But each thorn still stings."

I am loved. I repeat this to myself with each whap of the ax as I chop wood. *I am loved. I am loved. I am loved.* It may be true, but I'm not sure Mama's love is enough to carry me through this heartache. Perhaps...perhaps I need help from Mama's God.

"Fine." I hurl the blade into a chunk of wood, ready to face off. I glare at the sky. "Mama always said You were after me." Images of night riders with torches, their faces twisted in disdain, pop into my mind. I shake them off, focusing on the puffy white clouds overhead. "You want me to love You like Mama does? You're gonna have to show me something 'cause all I can see is how You sit on that fancy throne of Yours while people who look like me get beaten, raped, and killed. Do you even care 'bout us down here?"

I search the skies. An eagle soars overhead. A flock of ducks passes. Nothing else. No rolling thunder. No booming answer from heaven. What did I expect? Mama's God has always been silent to me.

I toss and turn that night, dreaming about the man I might love in the arms of the woman whom I call a friend. And there I am alone on the side. Watching. Recoiling. Over and over again until I wake up damp with sweat. What's wrong with me? Why can't I get over this? Move on?

God, I need Your help. Tears fall onto my pillow.

I finally drift off again. God meets me, not with a booming voice proclaiming answers, but with the face of His Son. I look into the face of Jesus. On His head is a crown of thorns. I squint, peering closer. I recognize those thorns. They are the ones that have pierced me. But here they are in His brow, drawing blood. His eyes fix on me. His mouth doesn't move, but what He's saying is clear: *You are My beloved.* His eyes! He can't take them off me. And I can't look away. No one ever told me that He's so beautiful. His skin is darker than I imagined. Not dark as mine, but not light like Thaddeus's. Not like the stained-glass windows in churches. He looks nothing like their pompous depictions. He's…He's not a white man's God. He's wholly and completely beautiful. And He's mine. And now…now I am His.

30

1868,
Georgetown, South Carolina

I t's been three weeks since Thaddeus rode away and I have just pulled the covers up to my chin when I hear the clomping of hooves in the distance. I bolt upright. Minnie? This late? Or the Klan? I shudder as I shift to my knees and peek out the window. No blazing cross or hooded figures. I squint. Three horses? No, four. And several figures walking beside them, their skin as dark as night. But one man leads the charge, his light skin glowing by the light of the single lantern he holds out in front of him. My eyes strain through the dimness. Thaddeus!

I scramble from my bed and stumble out the door, down the steps, and onto the path, the evening breeze spurring me along. "Mama?" My cry pierces the night around me, silencing the hooting owl and strumming crickets for a moment. Hushed voices come from too far away, too far from my reaching arms.

I trip over a tree root and tumble onto my knees, rocks jabbing daggers into my skin. Pushing myself up, I press through the pain and toward what must be my family. The family I thought I'd never see again.

When at last I reach them—or they reach me—Mama lifts a weary smile from her place on top of Chestnut. Thaddeus extends a hand to her, and my arms engulf her before both her feet touch the ground. I bury my head in her shoulder and squeeze tight, tears brimming.

She pulls back and runs a shaky hand down my hair, over my cheek. "Oh, sweet Liberty." She chuckles. "Look what you've done."

She spreads a hand toward Mingo and Mayme, Daffney and her family, Omey, Mirsa, Kolle, and Ayda, all off their horses and swarming toward me with open arms. I spill tears onto each of them, and I clamp my arms around them, joy bubbling forth. They came. They are here. We are together.

"I can't believe you came." I shake my head and wipe my damp cheeks.

My gaze bounces through a sea of dark faces until I find Thaddeus's tired eyes. His satisfied smile prompts one of my own.

I mouth the words *Thank you.*

He nods. Winks.

In this moment, words can never be enough. But somehow the unspoken resonates. He knows the depth of my gratitude.

Mama speaks up. "I didn't feel a peace about signin' contracts for the next year. When Thaddeus showed up with your letter, I knew why. It was the Lord directin' my steps."

I fold my hands together under my chin. "Yes. The Lord."

She tips her head, and the corners of her mouth lift.

Yes, Mama. I believe.

A hum of questions buzzes through my head, drowning out crickets and the murmuring of their voices as they talk low amongst themselves. How'd she get Mingo to leave his flock? How was the journey? Any trouble from night riders? What of leaving Master Man? But Mirsa and Ayda look as tired as trees about to timber. There will be time for the story tomorrow.

"Come. Let's get y'all settled so you can get some rest." I lead the way as if Mama is my guest and not the one who knows this land better than us all.

We no more than turn and take a step before we see him. Jonah stands stock still, a mere shadow among the outline of oaks.

Mama's breath catches.

The rest of us stop. Watch. Wait.

She takes tentative steps toward him, her feet barely making a sound.

The whites of his eyes disappear and reappear as he blinks.

He does not move. Doesn't rush toward her and sweep her into his arms. The moments stretch on to match her slow steps until finally, they face each other. They are close enough to touch now but don't.

I frown. This is not the reunion I pictured. Where is the passionate embrace? The kiss of longing? I lean forward to hear Jonah's gentle voice. "Hi, Mercy Girl."

"Why hello, Jonah."

"Been a while."

"Yes, indeed."

It's too dark to see what their eyes are saying as their gazes roam each other's faces. I creep closer. Still too dark.

"Mind if I walk you home?" Jonah holds out a hand.

Mama hesitates for only a moment before taking it.

The rest of us follow behind as Jonah and Mama walk hand in hand to the cabin I've been staying in. He gives her hand a squeeze before he releases it and leaves her on the bottom step. "See you tomorrow, Mercy Girl." He dips his head toward her and walks backward a few steps, his gaze lingering. Then he turns his attention to my brothers and sisters.

"The rest of you can stay here." He leads them to the next cabin, a bit larger than ours.

My shoulders droop. Mama came all this way. Shouldn't she and Jonah have a spectacular reunion? To me, this slow and quiet whisper of meeting is a breath of disappointment.

Inside the cabin, Mama wastes not a minute before dropping into bed. She lets out a lengthy sigh. "I forgot to grab my bag."

"I'm sure Thaddeus has it."

She waves me off. "It's fine. I'm so tired."

I climb into bed next to her and tuck the covers around us both. "You can rest now."

As if hearing the questions that I haven't asked, she speaks without opening her eyes. "You gotta understand, Jonah may have been waitin' for me all these years, but I wasn't waitin' for him. I gave up on that long ago. You gotta give me some time."

I kiss her cheek. "Okay." Time. I can give her time.

As I turn onto my side, I whisper, "Thank you for coming."

"Oh, child." Her voice is already dipping into dreamland.

Child. I smile. I have never been prouder to be her child.

~

I've never been happier for a Saturday than I am today. Jonah doesn't have to work, and he knocks on our door with hot corn bread in hand just as the rooster crows. "When you're ready," he says to Mama, "why don't ya come on down to my cabin. I've got somethin' to show ya."

"Alright." There might just be a twinkle in Mama's eye.

Though I know he wasn't addressing me, I come with Mama. As we climb up his porch steps, she tilts her head at the rockers there.

Jonah appears in the doorway. "Look familiar?"

"Yes. This looks just like the one the missus—"

"It is."

She draws closer and runs her hand along the rocker's arm, then glances up at Jonah, brows furrowed.

He begins his story with a wistful half smile. "Once the Yankees came to tell us slavery was over and done with, they turned us loose on the Big House. The Millers had been gone for some time. The Yanks encouraged us to take anything we wanted, to take everything out. What we didn't take, they did.

Some took the very doors off the hinges. Some sawed off the mantle pieces and ripped up the floor." He shakes his head, eyes fogging over as if lost in the memory. "Freedmen all over was havin' a good ole time killing up goats and sheep and oxen. Takin' what was left of the lard, coffee, and tea. The Yankees grabbed all the beds and blankets that were in the house and handed them out to us."

His gaze meets Mama's. "Me? All I wanted was the two rockers from the front porch. The ones from Master and Missus." He steps closer and gives the chair a soft nudge, sending it in motion. "I wanted this for you." His eyes peer deep. "In case you ever came back. So that you could live like a queen. So that you could sit in this here rocker and feel what it's like to be the one without a care in the world."

Mama lowers herself into the chair, leans back, and pushes with the tips of her toes. She sighs.

"When the Millers came back, they went through the cabins, demanding to have their things. Their beds, blankets, lamps, pictures. But they never said a word about the rockers."

Mama rocks, eyes closed, head resting on the wood. The whisper of a smile graces her face. "So, this is what it feels like to be on top of the world."

"Mighty fine, huh?"

"Mighty fine."

Jonah sits in the other rocker, and soon, the creek of his chair matches that of hers. I back away, allowing the king and queen to reign in peace.

~

A month passes of quiet evenings with Mama and Jonah rocking on his porch, talking softly. Gentle laughter billows on cooler breezes. I give them space.

The Millers are quite pleased to have a whole crew of new workers willing to help with ditching and preparing the fields, though they haven't the money to pay outright. They give all the colored workers promissory notes that look like real money but are really just papers promising to pay later. They pay me in actual bills, though. Probably since I was the first to start working before they ran out. Thaddeus starts jobbing for the Millers as well, and we chop wood side by side. They pay him in real money, of course, since he's white. I spend a day a week helping in the field, usually next to Solomon. Our conversations weave in and out of witty banter and thirsty intellect. He's got a hunger to know more than what he's experienced on this plantation.

The sun beats down bright but not as hot as before. Leaves glimmer orange, red, and yellow. Minnie visits nearly every day and keeps us company, her chatter filling the gap between whacks of the axes. Thaddeus rarely ceases smiling when she is around. Neither do I. My appreciation for this friend of mine has swelled like a creek in heavy rain, cascading over places that were dry with hurt. I can't say she never rubs against a bruised place in me, but the waters of love are healing.

When she trots off on Scamper one afternoon, Thaddeus plops down on a stump and drags his sleeve over his forehead. His face and shoulders droop with his sigh. "I need to get back to my farm."

I rear my head back. "Your farm?"

He nods, frowning.

My eyebrow raises. "You got a farm?"

"Back in Nebraska. Moved there because of the Homestead Act. Th-they were giving away free land, so I figured, what did I have to lose? Worked it for t-two years. Joined the army. Asked my neighbor to look after th-things while I was away. T-told him he could have whatever crop the land produced." He gazes into the distance. "Who knows what shape it's in now."

I let my ax drop in the dust and settle onto my knees. He's never seemed to be in much of a hurry to get back to where he was going. Like there wasn't anything to return to. Anything to keep him from staying. My heart shrivels at the thought of losing him.

His lips twist as if he's considering his words before he speaks. "I'm th-thinking…I want to ask Minnie to come with me."

I try to swallow, but my throat won't obey. I cough instead.

Thaddeus's brows rise in concern.

"I'm okay," I manage between coughs.

He hands me his canteen, and I drink. Try to wash away the sorrow that threatens to overwhelm me. Losing both Thaddeus and Minnie?

I hand the canteen back to him. My lip trembles when I try to smile.

"Do you th-think she'll come with me?"

I shrug. I don't trust myself to speak.

"I don't want to leave her. But I've got to work th-the land for five years to own it outright. They t-take off the t-time I spent with the Union, but I can't keep d-dawdling in the Carolinas. I need to get back."

"I understand." I pinch my lips together, pushing back the tide of rising emotion.

I stand and chop harder than before. Grunt as I force the blade into the wood. Grunt because I can't scream—not here, not now.

"Liberty?" His voice slips through the chaos swarming within me.

I turn, eyes misty.

"Do you want to come?"

I go still. Travel with Thaddeus and Minnie to a farm in Nebraska? Watch them marry and have children together? I laugh without humor. "I just got here. Just got Mama here." I raise the blade again and bring it down with a whack. Where is home? Wherever Mama is.

No, child.

His voice settles within me.

Wherever I Am.

~

The next day, Minnie stays later than normal. The sun starts to dip, and she's still leaning against a tree, twirling a golden maple leaf in her fingers. Her voice dips and rises as she talks with Thaddeus. Her hair has drifted loose from her chiffon, but she pays no mind.

An angry clomp of hooves sounds in the distance. The three of us straighten. I shade my eyes to see who's coming. I don't recognize the man, but his eyes blaze with a disdain that's all too familiar.

He rears his black horse to a stop in front of us. Dust swirls, and I wave at the air in front of my face to clear it. "Minnie." Her name comes from his lips in a mix between a growl and a hiss.

"Father." Minnie's face pales as she swallows. She stuffs strands of hair back into her bonnet.

Father? I take a step back.

"Cletus told me you've been coming down here nearly every day to mingle with the darkies." He glares at me before returning his attention to Minnie. "You, a proper Southern belle, associating with slaves."

Minnie's chest inflates, and she lifts her chin, a defiant glint in her eyes. "They are not slaves, Father. They're free, same as you and me."

"Same as—" He shakes his head as his eyes narrow. "You are coming home directly." He angles toward Thaddeus. "And you, what kind of soldier are you? You're a disgrace to the cause."

Minnie scowls at her father as she takes Scamper's reins. "He's not a disgrace to *our country*. He fought for the Union, Father."

The man's neck reddens. His eyes shoot daggers at Thaddeus, then at his daughter. "You are forbidden from seeing him, do you hear? Forbidden. Now come."

Thaddeus walks over and assists Minnie onto Scamper without a word or glance in her father's direction. He gives her hand a small, discreet squeeze, and they exchange a concerned glance, as if both worried about each other.

Before the brute spins his horse around, he points at me. "You had better watch your back."

A shiver crawls up my spine as they ride off.

Should I tell Jonah and Mama about our encounter with Minnie's father? About his threat? When I approach the cabins, they are walking hand in hand, smiling. No. I'll keep it to myself. Let them enjoy their piece of happiness without the threat of an oncoming storm.

They don't seem to see me as caught up as they are in each other's gazes. I lean against an oak and watch. Listen. A few golden leaves dance down from the treetops, rustling with their final bow. The breeze blows cool and fresh against my face.

Jonah takes off his hat. "Mercy Girl, I was wonderin'…"

Her head tilts, a smile hinting at the corners of her mouth.

"I was wonderin'," he says again, twirling his hat in his hands, "if you'd want to go to a weddin' with me. In the chapel here."

Mama's face brightens. "Whose weddin' were you thinkin', Jonah?"

He dips his head all bashful-like. "I was thinkin' ours, Mercy Girl."

I gasp. Cover my mouth with a trembling hand. If only Susan could see this. Wouldn't she just swoon? A picture of my mother and father locked in an embrace floats to the top of my memory. I smile at the sweet memory, then push it back under where it belongs.

"That'd be mighty nice." Mama is full of light and life as Jonah leans down and kisses her gently.

I squeal. Clap. Parade from where I've been hiding in plain sight.

The pair startles and parts.

"We've got a wedding to plan!" I shout with a grin and uplifted hands like the worshipping trees.

~

My sisters string blue mistflowers and climbing asters around the chapel, filling the space with blues, purples, pinks, and sweet fragrance. They've swung the windows open, and happy chatter wafts with the scent. The rows of benches will soon be full of family and friends. Missus Miller has lent

Mama a veil. The mistress lost much to the war and its aftermath, her current reality only a shadow of her former abundance, but she did have netting to fashion a veil. The colored pastor is set to come at sundown.

Thaddeus has sent word to Minnie. I bite my nail as I search the horizon. She'll come, won't she? She can't miss it.

Mama paces in her cabin, fiddling with the netting in front of her face. "I feel so foolish. A woman my age gettin' married."

"Nonsense." I put a hand on her arm and gently squeeze. "Ain't no one more deservin'."

She pats my cheek, her fingers rough and worn. They've touched so much, those weathered hands. I had no idea how much before my trip here. I had to leave Mama to find her. I cup my hand over hers.

We flinch at the sound of someone approaching. The stomp of horse hooves that became familiar with Minnie's daily visits now causes me to tremble with fear of her father. I thrust my head out the door, ready to snatch Mama and run if necessary.

But it's Minnie and Susan. I release a breath and break into a grin. Though Susan's face is lined with worry, though her lip wobbles when she attempts a smile, she is here! I clap and skip up to the duo, holding out a hand for them to dismount. Minnie envelops me in a hug. Susan's eyes skitter all around. When they finally meet mine, she flashes a quick, tumultuous smile.

Minnie unloads a thick quilt from the back of Scamper. "Where's Mercy?"

I lead the two women into the cabin. Mama and Susan embrace while Minnie lays the quilt on the bed and unwraps the contents nestled inside.

"You came." Mama's voice is choked with unshed tears.

"I couldn't rightly miss your wedding." Susan looks reluctant to let go. When the women part, she keeps a protective arm around Mama's shoulder.

"I hope this fits." Minnie reveals a delicate pale blue dress, silk with lace trim.

Mama steps over to it, her intake of breath capturing the sole attention of us all. "It's beautiful."

Susan clasps her hands in front of her. "It's mine. I don't find occasion to wear it anymore."

"And I can..." Mama doesn't finish her question. Just trails nimble fingers over the bodice.

Susan steps beside her. "I'd love nothing more than for you to wear it today."

When Mama steps out of the cabin, she looks like a queen. I've never been so proud to be her daughter.

Susan walks next to Mama. Minnie and I follow, but as my feet hit the worn path to the chapel, I'm hit with a burst of inspiration.

"Wait here," I tell Minnie and rush back up to the cabin.

Last week, I showed Mama all Susan's letters, and she read them. Her face folded into a frown, then she shifted in her seat and handed them back to me, telling me I could keep them. I stuffed them into Mama's old journal, along with all her letters.

I grab the journal and bound back out the door and down the steps.

When I reach Minnie, I sift through the book to find the right pages and hand them to her. "You should have these. I learned much about Mama from reading her letters. They helped me feel closer to her. Perhaps your mother's letters can help you do the same."

She clasps the bundle over her heart. "Thank you, dear friend."

We hurry after our mothers and catch up with them just as the chapel comes into view. The sweet voices of my family swirl through the air to greet me. Thaddeus's laugh bounces among them. We draw near, up the steps, into the white building bursting with love, fragrance, and family.

Jonah stands in front in a gray suit, looking stately and fine next to the colored preacher. The moment he notices Mama, his eyes light up, and his grin shines. My heart leaps.

Mingo and Solomon start beating a slow rhythm on the drums, and a song arises. Mama walks forward to her delayed destiny.

Throughout the wedding, I do not miss how Thaddeus's gaze remains on Minnie, longing in his eyes. How when Mama and Jonah kiss, Thaddeus licks his lips as if tasting Minnie's kiss upon them. Right now, I want every happiness for them, even if it's far off in Nebraska. These two white people who have shown me love—however faulty and frail—deserve the best wishes of my heart.

As we shout in celebration of man and wife, my nose scrunches at a sickening smell. In three steps, I am outside and watching in horror at the smoke-filled horizon. The air sizzles and crackles. Heat pushes toward me. My scream brings Thaddeus to my side.

"What's wrong?" he asks, but then he looks up. "My heaven. Fire! Fire!"

Men swarm around me toward the blaze. They stream in the direction of the cabins. I clutch my stomach. *Move, feet! Move!* But they do not. Minnie grabs my hand and pulls. We reach the outskirts of the blaze just in time to hear the whinny of horses and see white-hooded figures riding off.

Minnie covers her mouth. Her voice shakes. "That's Midnight. That's Father's horse."

My eyes and throat sting as I stare at the belly of the blaze. Everyone is already making a line, passing buckets from one person to another, from the well to the fiery dragon devouring their homes. Minnie and I rush to help. Each bucket seems smaller to me, more useless in the face of this hot oppressor. But then I hear Mama's voice rising above the crackle of the fire—praying. And I take courage.

When the fire is finally stomped out, we sit covered in soot and sweat. We are weary of soul and body. Two of the cabins can be salvaged, a few more are in need of repair, and the rest have disintegrated. Susan's sniffles and sighs have not ceased as she continues to pace a few feet away, muttering her husband's name under her breath. Minnie's face is darkened and smeared. She keeps her eyes low as we slump on a log.

I touch my friend's hand. "It's not your fault."

She raises a watery gaze. "My father."

"You are not your father."

Thaddeus walks up to us. Wipes his forehead with a damp kerchief. Crouches. "Come to Nebraska with me."

My eyes dart to Minnie, then back to him. Who is he talking to? Just her? Then why does he meet my gaze?

He stands and raises his voice. "All of you. Come to Nebraska with me. The Homestead Act makes it possible f-for even f-former slaves to own their own plot of land f-free and clear. As long as you work the land for f-five years and improve it."

I flick my gaze to Minnie's face. Thaddeus has stuttered in front of her, yet she seems not to have noticed. The full moon reveals her eyes wide, not with surprise or disgust at his voice but with wonder.

Thaddeus turns his gaze to me. "Nebraska just became a state last year. You know what th-their motto is? Equality under the law. Doesn't th-that sound mighty nice?" He winks.

I lean forward and catch Mama's eye from where she sits a couple yards away, holding Jonah's hand. Her gaze drifts to her cabin, then to Jonah's where they were going to live, both cabins now piles of ash. The rockers where they were going to reign as king and queen are no more than charred rubble.

She peers up at her husband. "I am mighty fond of travelin'."

Jonah chuckles. "I ain't never left this here plantation." He bends over and kisses Mama sweet and slow. "But I could be persuaded to, I reckon."

Thaddeus kneels before Minnie, desperation edging through his voice. "Come with me."

Her forehead dimples. "Why I couldn't. It would be improper. Unless…"

He takes her hand. "Unless you were my wife."

Her eyes sparkle as she nods.

He tilts his head to his left where the preacher rests under an oak. "He's still here."

She smooths her free hand over her dress and hair. "Oh, but I must look—"

"Beautiful." He kisses her hand.

She bites her lip as a smile dawns. "Yes! Yes, Thaddeus, I will marry you."

Thaddeus whoops and jumps to his feet. "How about another wedding?" he calls.

The group, who moments before looked droopy and drained, springs to life. Rising to our feet, we clap and cheer. I yank off my kerchief and flip it inside out to where it's not soiled. A bucket sits on its side, the puddle of water inside not large enough for a crawdad to swim in, but it's enough to wet my kerchief. I dab Minnie's face with it, wiping away soot and grime, leaving the healthy glow of new love. In the process, I ask Jesus to wipe away the residue of my jealousy, of my pain. *I give it all to You, Lord. All my messy heart. Help me to love my friends with Your perfect love.* The group of my family and friends parades back toward the chapel as fireflies sparkle along the path and crickets sing to our steps.

Susan hangs back. I retrace my steps and watch.

"Go on ahead," Minnie tells Thaddeus. "I'll be right there."

She turns to her mother. "Are you okay with this?"

Susan nods. "I'm delighted you've found a good man." Her voice trembles.

Minnie grabs her mother's hands. "You're coming with us to Nebraska. Don't even try to fight it."

Susan shakes her head. "A woman doesn't just leave her husband."

"No woman should be afraid of the man she married, Mother. It's not decent. You deserve to be free, too."

Susan bites her lip.

Minnie rests her forehead on her mother's. "We live and die together."

A shaky breath. A strangled assent. They move forward arm in arm.

31

———

June 2020
Chicago, Illinois

Natassa dug her toes into the recesses of the soft comforter as she listened to Daniel finish his story of a midnight muffin-making disaster. Sunlight sneaked in through the crack between the darkening curtains, casting a beam of light onto the king-sized bed. Brandon snored softly beside her, still asleep even though the digital clock on the nightstand read half past ten.

"I found a cranberry muffin mix in the back of the pantry. I just wanted to eat something normal. She served shrimp for dinner last night. Shrimp." He sighed. "When are you coming home? Grandma is driving me crazy."

"Sorry. It'll be a while." Natassa kept her voice low. Brandon didn't stir.

Daniel groaned. "Here's Faith. She wants to talk to you."

"Okay. Bye, sweetheart. I love you."

"He's already gone, Mom." Faith's voice filled her ear.

"In that case, hello, sweetheart. I love you."

"Love you, too." Faith's exasperated teenage tone couldn't hide her affection. She filled Natassa in on how she was bearing up under her grandma's oppressive rule, then turned serious. "Why did Mercy do it, Mom? Does she not like our family? Does she like her black brothers more than her white sisters?"

Natassa crossed her ankles. *How to answer?* "No, honey." She swallowed. Was she telling the truth? "Mercy's just going through something right now. She's got to find her way is all."

"But why?" Faith's voice came out small, so vulnerable.

Natassa pursed her lips. "I guess I've thought that the color of Mercy's skin doesn't matter. That it's no different than the color of someone's eyes or hair. Some people are blonde, others brunette. I can see and acknowledge the difference, but what does it matter? It's certainly not something to sit and talk about." She picked a piece of lint from the comforter. "But it *is* different for her."

"Why? Why is it different? Mercy is my sister just like Hope. I don't care what color she is."

"Yes. But there's a shared history that comes with being black that I don't understand. And no one treats you unfairly because you have brown hair."

Faith moaned. "We learn about racism and the Civil Rights Movement in history class for a reason. Because it's in the past. No one treats Mercy any differently because of the color of her skin."

Natassa dropped her head, her stomach sinking. She'd thought by not talking about racial issues she'd been protecting Mercy. Sheltering her from a cruel world. But her children—all of them—needed to be equipped to navigate the times they lived in. *I've been so blind, Lord. I've been acting out of fear, not love. And it's affected all my children.*

"Mom? Are you still there?"

"I'm here." Natassa raised her head. "Honey, this is going to require a much longer conversation. One for the whole family to participate in. For now, just know that Mercy loves you very much."

"Yeah. Okay."

"Tell Grandma I'll call tomorrow."

As she hung up the phone, Brandon stretched beside her. He peeked open one eye.

She smiled at him. "Good morning."

"What time is it?"

"It's 10:30."

A yawn. "Man, I can't remember a time I slept that late."

"You needed it." Natassa smoothed the comforter in her lap.

"You talked to the kids?"

"Yep."

"And?"

"They're all fine. Hope feels much better."

"Good."

"Brandon," she said as she turned to face him, "DeAndre was right."

His eyes popped open. "About?"

"I didn't want Mercy to see *Black Panther* because of the violence, but she needed to see it. I didn't want her to know about any of the black men and women who've been killed because I thought she was too young. There have been protests, riots, cities burning, and all I've told her is that I don't see color." Natassa firmed her jaw. "She deserves more than that."

Brandon propped himself on his elbow. "What do you want to do?"

She slid out from beneath the covers and padded over to where her suitcase lay open on the dresser. "I don't know what it's like to be black, and I don't know what it feels like to be her. But I know someone who does." She pulled out Mercy's journal and handed it to Brandon.

He raised an eyebrow.

"I thought it was funny that you packed it for me. When I told you to grab the book from my nightstand, I meant *There's Lead in Your Lipstick*, not Mercy's journal. But now, I'm glad."

Brandon chuckled. "At your service."

She closed her eyes and drew in a deep breath, then blew it out. "I can't stay silent anymore, Brandon. I want Mercy to hear from Mercy. I want her to hear the experience of another little girl—a child born from rape, half white and half black—and see that her feelings are normal and that she can have a beautiful life."

Brandon shifted his jaw, nodding slowly.

She knelt on the bed. "I always figured I'd give it to her someday, but not until she was much older. It's hard to read. But I think she needs to hear it. Now."

Brandon pressed his lips together. "I see what you're saying, babe. But it would break my heart to see my little girl get hurt. I want to protect her just as much as you do. She's my world. My children are everything to me."

Natassa entwined her fingers in his. "I know. I've spent their whole lives trying to insulate them from anything that could possibly harm them. Bullies, toxic chemicals, UV sunrays, deadly viruses—"

"High fructose corn syrup." Brandon's mouth tipped in a smile.

"That too." She smiled back, then stretched her hands out in front of her. "My arms aren't big enough to cover them all. I've got to let them go into God's hands and trust that He loves them even more than I do."

~

Natassa and Brandon stepped into DeAndre's apartment shortly after noon, bringing sandwiches from a nearby deli. Everyone sat around the kitchen table, crunching on chips and passing the mustard and mayonnaise. Mercy sat in between Natassa and DeAndre, sulking in her chair.

"When are you guys taking off?" DeAndre wiped his face with a napkin.

Natassa shrugged. "We're in no hurry. Actually, I have something I want to read to everyone, if it's okay."

Janell paused with a chip midway to her mouth. "What is it?"

"It's called Mercy's journal. Bethany gave it to me years ago. It's a family heirloom of hers, a journal and some letters written by a mulatto enslaved girl." Natassa looked at Mercy. "Her mom was black, and her birth father was white. Her name was Mercy, like you."

Mercy straightened.

Natassa glanced around the table. "I think it's important for my daughter to hear what Good Ole Mercy has to say, and it would be nice for everyone to listen."

"Sure," Janell mumbled, mouth half full.

DeAndre nodded at her. What was that in his eyes? Respect?

Natassa read the journal from her spot on the couch with Mercy nestled beside her. Next to Mercy, Janell nursed baby Joe. Java lay on his belly at her feet, pushing a toy police car back and forth. The men occupied the other couch, eyes fixed on her.

Mama always said, "Everybody talk 'bout joy and pain like they's opposites, but they ain't really. Not to me. Not less you talkin' 'bout opposite sides of the same coin." She'd talk 'bout how if she'd have a big eraser and could 'rase every bit a sorrow in her life and in her past, people might think she'd have a right pretty picture. But she ain't. Alls she'd got would be a big white space. Empty, that's what'd be. Joy and pain—those threads are woven so tightly together ain't no one can get 'em apart. If I close my eyes, I can still hear Mama sayin' those things. I didn't know what in tarnation she was talkin' 'bout when she rambled on, but now I'm thinkin' she was talkin' 'bout me the whole time.

She continued to read about Mercy being ripped away from her mother and taken to Tennessee. About the first Missus rejecting Mercy because she looked too white, and about Mercy's long march in a slave coffle. She told about the slave auction and the man who purchased Mercy to look after baby Elizabeth. Everyone listened intently as the missus turned Mercy away out of jealousy and spite. Then Mercy ended up with Missus Rachel and Mary. She met Emma and learned to play the fiddle.

They took breaks every so often. At some point, Java lost interest, and they set him up with a movie in their bedroom. Afternoon stretched into evening. They stopped to eat dinner and then gathered around again to hear of Emma and Mercy's plans to flee and how those plans were thwarted with the master's death. Emma ran, leaving Mercy behind. Then Mercy found the courage to bolt as well, pretending to be white. When she got to the steamboat and chose to go south instead of north, Janell gasped.

"No! She chose her mama over freedom in the North?"

Mercy craned her neck up, gaping at Natassa. "She loved her mom that much?"

"She loved her that much."

Mercy's brows knit. "Did she ever find her?"

"Listen and find out."

Natassa read of the steamboat rides and meeting Susan on the second steamer. Susan helped Mercy find her way to Georgetown where she found her old plantation. But Mama's cabin was empty.

Next to Natassa, Mercy bit her nails.

"Don't worry." Natassa rubbed her back. Mercy confronted the missus and then found out that her mother was at the plantation down the road. She ran to her, and they were reunited after all those years.

Mercy's breath caught. "Mercy's mom's name was Charity? Is that why—"

"We're naming the baby after her, yes."

"I thought...it was because Charity means love, and love is the greatest of all. That the new baby would be the greatest in the whole family, and you'd love her the most out of everybody."

"You thought that?"

Mercy nodded, tears streaming down her cheeks.

"Oh, sweetheart. Do you have any idea how much I love you? You are my favorite."

"Hey, you say that about me," David chimed in.

Natassa pointed to David. "And I've never lied. It's part of that superpower moms have. We can have more than one favorite because our hearts are so big."

Mercy buried her head in her hands.

"Look at me, Mercy." She nudged her daughter's chin up. "I love you with all my heart. You are my favorite one. No one could ever take your place." She enveloped Mercy in a hug.

Janell grabbed the journal and then a tissue from the coffee table. "What a beautiful ending."

"Oh, it's not the end."

"What now?" DeAndre eyed her.

"There's more. We'll come back tomorrow. I'll read the rest."

~

As Natassa and Brandon pulled in front of DeAndre's apartment building the next morning, she smiled. That first day, she did *not* want to go in. *Grab her and go.* Yet here they were. Staying longer than planned, longer than they needed to. She was no longer in a hurry to leave.

DeAndre let them in, and the smell of syrup and powdered sugar wafted with the draft from the hall.

"Are you hungry for French toast?" Janell asked from the kitchen, spatula in hand.

Brandon smiled. "No thanks. We ate at the hotel."

Mercy skipped to them. "Hi, Dad. Hi, Mom. You ready to read the story?"

Natassa glanced around the room. Java sat at the table, his hands covered in sticky syrup. DeAndre carried his plate to the sink.

"We're almost finished here." Janell slid a piece of French toast out of the skillet and onto a plate. "I can listen and eat."

"Here." Natassa grabbed a dishcloth hanging from the faucet. "I'll help clean up." She wiped the counters, table, and Java's face and hands.

She tilted her head to her son, lounging on the couch. "David, load the dishwasher."

He did so without complaint.

When they had finished, Java ran in his room to play, and the rest of them settled in for the rest of Good Ole Mercy's story.

I guess you don't rightly realize all you'se have to be grateful for until it flies off and you'se left with nothing 'cept the air thick with memories. I've done got a good master and missus at Hopecrest, and I'm here with Mama like I's been wanting to be all my life, but I loathe to admit I sure do miss being a house slave. Harvesting rice drains the life from my body, but I's determined not to let it drain the light from my mind no more. No matter how tired I am at the end of the day, I've got to make time to write in here again.

Natassa read about Mama collapsing in the field and Jonah carrying her. Mama became a basket weaver instead of a field hand. She read of Mercy's blossoming romance with Jonah and then how Mercy saw Susan in town.

Beside Natassa, Mercy's brow knit when she heard the church scenes.

Natassa continued with Jonah's proposal and how Mercy spilled it to the missus only to find out they were selling her and Mama.

Janell's breath caught. "No!"

Natassa checked her watch. "It's about lunchtime now. Do you want us to run out and grab something to eat?"

Janell shook her head. "Not now. You can't stop reading. I have to know what happens."

So, Natassa read about Mercy placing her hope in Susan and Susan's solution. And then Mercy's response.

"Please," I whispered, tears freely flowing. "Buy Mama."

Susan's frown dipped low, and her eyes welled with regret. "I told you, I can't. Sam won't hear of it. We cannot justify purchasing two slaves. I'm sorry. I'm so sorry."

I shook my head. "No, buy Mama instead of me."

Susan sat back with a tiny gasp. "Instead of you? And allow you to get sold to New Orleans?"

I nodded. "Please." It came out a desperate whisper, and I reached out and grasped her hand, meeting my eyes with hers, pleading with my gaze.

"Mercy, I couldn't. Oh no. I couldn't watch you get shipped off ... "

"Take care of Mama. Take good care of her and treat her well, and she'll be good to you too. She'll be strong here. Let me do this for her, please." I squeezed Susan's hand, applying gentle pressure. I needed her to agree. I couldn't conceive of any other option.

We live and die together.

But if we were together, Mama would die. And I couldn't live with that.

DeAndre sniffed and pressed his wrist onto the corner of his eye. Mercy's eyes glistened. Tears streamed down Janell's face. David's frown deepened. Brandon took a shuddering breath.

And Natassa continued reading. She didn't shut the journal until Jonah had disappeared in the distance, wailing, and Mercy prepared herself for the journey farther south.

"That's the end of the journal, but there are letters. I'll read them after lunch."

Mercy crossed her arms around herself. "This is a horrible, terrible story. I wish you had stopped reading yesterday."

Natassa nodded. "I know. I felt the same way."

Janell shuffled to the kitchen and opened the refrigerator. "We have hamburger patties. Do you want to grill on the rooftop for lunch?"

A sly grin broke out on Brandon's face. "I can grill burgers."

DeAndre pointed to him. "Want some help?" He gestured to the rest of the family. "They can join us a little later."

Brandon hesitated, his smile faltering. But then he answered, "Sounds good."

The men grabbed condiments, meat, and plates from the kitchen and then headed upstairs. Natassa and Janell threw together a fruit salad. An hour later, they ate together on the rooftop, swapping stories of barbecues from their childhoods. Natassa didn't have much to contribute, save the exquisite meals her family had in lieu of traditional BBQ fare. It didn't matter. She relaxed into the patio chair, closed her eyes, and soaked up the sun.

~

After lunch, Natassa finished reading Mercy's letters to Susan. Tragic, heart-wrenching letters. She had to choke the words past the lump in her throat. And yet, as she read of Mercy's transformation, the eyes of those around her reflected what had risen in herself—the fight of endurance and a spark of determined hope. She smiled as she finished the last letter and closed the portfolio.

David sat forward, resting his hands on his knees. "That's it?"

"Yep. That's all we have."

"But that was just at the beginning of the Civil War. There's got to be more to the story. Her life couldn't have just ended out of nowhere."

Natassa shrugged.

"Where did Bethany get this, anyway?"

"I don't know. She said it was passed down in her family."

"But the letters were mailed to Susan. And the journal was left with Susan. Somehow, Mercy had to have reconnected with her friend in Georgetown, right? Otherwise, how could Bethany have gotten all of that passed on to her?"

Natassa's eyes narrowed. "I never considered that."

David pulled out his phone. "What was Susan's last name?"

"Renald, I think." Natassa flipped through the journal, searching. "Yeah. Renald."

"We just need to find the Renald family in Georgetown and see if they know anything."

Brandon scrunched his forehead. "It's a long shot, son."

"Yeah, well, so was Bethany coming off a ventilator."
Natassa met Brandon's gaze. "Then we'll pray."

~

"I've left three messages, sent one email, and contacted someone through a genealogy site. We just have to wait—" David's phone pinged. "Hold on." His fingers flew to his screen. "Oh my gosh."

"What?" Natassa leaned forward.

"It's them. Alisha Renald." He glanced up, eyes bright, then returned his focus to his screen. "She says there's a Susan Renald on her family tree, born in 1824. She had one daughter. Minnie who married a Thaddeus Wyndom. She gave me the contact info for someone in the Wyndom family who she says might have further information."

Natassa stared. Further information?

"I'll call them." David raced out the door to the balcony.

32

1868,
On the road to Nebraska

Our group of twenty has few possessions between us, as Susan and Minnie only grabbed the barest of essentials when Sam was at work. Mama's letters are among them. We put our weight behind the pride of Minnie's father, hoping it is greater than his obsession to control. We pray he will not come after us, choosing instead to invent a story for the townspeople rather than risk dragging Minnie and Susan back to tell their own version.

One wagon suffices for the long journey west. We take turns walking and riding. I find myself spending more and more time with Solomon, and as the dust stirs around us by day and the beans simmer over the fire by night, my respect for this man grows. He knew my grandmother—called her Granny C—and he tells me her stories. I smile as I sleep under the stars, surrounded by love and family and the hope of new beginnings.

Thaddeus finds me walking a pace slower than the others and falls into step beside me.

"You alright?" he asks.

I nod. "Just thinking 'bout how much my life has changed in such a short time." I pull my shawl tighter around my shoulders as a cool breeze nuzzles my neck.

"Are you happy?" He dips his head to meet my eyes, to look deep. "You can be happy? Even th-though…Minnie and I…"

I place a hand on his arm and give a reassuring smile. "I'm happy."

My gaze jumps around like a rabbit, landing on all the people I love in the world. Mama, Mingo and Mayme, Daffney and her babe, Omey, Mirsa, Kolle, Ayda, Minnie, Jonah, Susan. It lands on Solomon and rests there awhile.

Thaddeus chuckles.

My face warms, and I flick my eyes away.

"He's a good man. Minnie speaks highly of him, as d-does Jonah."

My eyebrows rise. "You've been asking around?"

He winks. "I've got to look out for my Liberty."

My heart swells. This relationship between us is not what I had wanted, but it's warm and soft. It fills me with satisfaction. Yes, I am happy.

~

We arrive in Nebraska to a chill in the air that my body doesn't know what to do with. I've never been so cold in my life. With what little money we have left, we must decide between food and fabric for warmer clothing and blankets. This foreign land has little for firewood. Grass fills the horizon. So strange. So different from all I've known.

Thaddeus's cabin is small but provides adequate shelter. All twenty of us cram inside and hunker down while the men claim land for Jonah and Mama, Mingo and Mayme, Solomon and the others. Then they set to work building cabins out of sod, laboring long hours in bitter wind to get walls up before the first snowfall. The women set to washing and cleaning, sewing and quilting. We've arrived at our new home just in time to see all the land dead and barren. Cold and lifeless. I'm hungry and tired. I pray for food and strength.

I reach into my bag and pull out Mama's journal. How providential that I took it with me to the chapel that night. While the cabin burned, the journal and Mama's letters were safe with me. Susan's letters were safe with Minnie. Out of everything I've ever owned, nothing could be as precious. No hat with a peacock feather. No scarf. No shoes. The things I thought I needed to feel like I was somebody…I'm no worse off with them in ashes. But these pieces of Mama's journey led me to her God, who became my God. I hug the journal to my chest, gratitude welling up within me again.

A knock at the door startles me. I rise to answer.

Thaddeus's neighbor stands there, basket in hand. His moustache twitches as he smiles and lifts the towel covering the top. Food! Bread and preserves. Smoked meat and cheese. Eggs and milk. Flour and coffee.

I fling my arms around his neck. The basket wobbles between us. "Sorry." I wipe my wet cheeks and take it from his waiting arms. "Thank you. Thank you so much."

Minnie and Ayda are beside me now, eyes and smiles bright. I glance behind to see Susan, her countenance beaming.

The neighbor's laugh rumbles up from his belly. "Tell Thaddeus that I am grateful for him allowing me to work his land these past couple years. It brought in a good harvest. I'll share what I have with you this winter, until you can eat from your own planting."

Minnie presses her hands to her cheeks. "I don't know what to say. We are so grateful."

"No need to say a thing." The man stuffs his hands in his pockets and rocks back on his heels. "It's called being neighborly. Feel free to visit my wife anytime. She could use the lady company." With a wink, he turns to leave.

Daffney, Omey, Mirsa, and Mayme swarm about the basket as well, and we squeal as we sift through the contents. The Lord answered my prayer. Far above what I even dreamed. In the clamor, something bumps into me. Mayme's belly. I grin. "My little niece or nephew is sayin' hi again." I press my hand to her middle, returning the greeting. My sisters' smiles and laughter dance around me, lifting my spirits high and higher still.

Something catches my eye. Out the window, the neighbor walks toward his farm. His right hand is clamped on his head to keep his hat from blowing off. *Thank you, Lord, for him.*

I squint. Frown. In the far distance, a group of people trudge forward into the wind, bent low. What's that on their heads? On their clothing? I grab Minnie's sleeve and pull her next to me. "Is that—"

"Indians." Her mouth purses. "Such a shame, isn't it? Thaddeus says the government is making them leave their land and move to reservations. Little by little, more and more of them have to leave."

"Their land? Where?"

"Here." She gestures to the plains out in front of the cabin. "All over Nebraska."

"We took their land?"

She crosses her arms. "The government took their land. Then they gave it to us."

A sick feeling arises. I know what it's like for the government to take my land and give it to someone else.

"Oh, don't look at me like that. It's not our fault. There's nothing we could do about it. They'd send the Indians away whether we claimed homesteads or not. It's just one of those things." She shrugs and walks away.

I place my hand against the cool glass windowpane. My heart reaches after those people, displaced and oppressed. Why does my liberation have to mean someone else's oppression? When will we all be free? *Oh Lord, justice! Bring justice.*

I watch until I can't see them anymore. Pray until my mind can't form another word. Mama spent her life praying for the end of slavery, for my freedom. Perhaps I can give mine to pray for theirs.

My gaze again scans the expanse of my new patch of earth. We will work the land together, each relying on the other. Something within me leaps at the thought of living for something bigger than me, of giving myself for a greater purpose. Maybe there's some Mercy in me after all. I smile wide. *We live and die together.*

33

———

June 2020
Chicago, Illinois

"Psst. Wake up." Mercy nudged David's shoulder. He rolled onto his back, still snoring, eyes clamped shut. Streaks of light glimmered on him from the moon and the spotlight on the building across the street, making stripes along his chest, knees, and feet. He looked like a zebra. Mercy chuckled.

"David." She hunched over him and shook his arm, whispering as loud as she dared. "Wake up, already."

He didn't even flinch.

Time for a good tickle on the tummy.

David startled awake. "What?" He swatted the air. "Mercy? What's going on? Is everything alright?"

She held up a box of chalk she'd found in Java's room earlier. "I need you to sneak out with me so I can draw on the sidewalk."

"Now?" David rubbed his eyes, then squinted at her. "Are you crazy?"

"I want to surprise DeAndre. I want him to wake up and look out the window and see my artwork." She lifted the corners of her mouth. Had she convinced him?

He frowned up at her.

She switched to her puppy dog face. "Please?"

"Oh no. I'm done getting into trouble for you. You're going to have to ask DeAndre and Janell in the morning."

Mercy threw her head back. "But if I ask them, it won't be a surprise."

"Tough, Sis. Go back to bed." David pulled the blanket over his head and rolled over, putting his back to her.

"Fine. You're not my favorite anymore."

No response.

Mercy bit her lip. Saying *I'm sorry* had always been easier than asking, *please*. *I'm sorry* got her a hug and a reminder that she was loved. *Please* almost always ended in a *no*.

She was tired of *nos*.

DeAndre said that she would change the world, but Mom wouldn't even let her ride in the car without a booster seat.

~

"Cereal okay this morning, sweetheart?" Janell smiled at her from across the kitchen island.

"Sure."

A clink, and then Janell set the bowl in front of her and filled it to the brim with Froot Loops. When she poured the milk, some of the colorful *Os* spilled over onto the island. Janell didn't seem to mind. She just plunked in the spoon and said, "Be careful carrying that."

Mercy slurped some milk from the side of the bowl. She should ask right now, before her courage galloped away like a horse. Her heart beat loud in her ears. She licked her lips. *Here goes nothing.*

"Janell, can I do some chalk art on the sidewalk this morning? Before my parents get here?"

Janell wiped the spilled cereal with a rag. "Sure." She smiled. "Right after breakfast?"

"That'd be great!" Mercy beamed at her. She couldn't believe Janell had said yes. Just like that. Without even thinking about it. Now, how was she going to keep it a secret from DeAndre? Maybe she'd just tell him not to look until she was done. Mercy grabbed her bowl and tiptoed to the table, trying not to spill. Only a little sloshed out the sides. She sat next to Java.

"Good morning." DeAndre breezed into the kitchen and headed straight toward the coffeepot. He kissed Janell on the cheek. "I'm going to head to the studio for a bit. To work on what we talked about last night."

The two of them exchanged a look. A secret look. Mercy's insides twisted. She hated secrets.

He poured coffee into a tall travel mug. "I'll be back by ten."

Janell's face scrunched. "Breakfast?"

"I'll take a bar. I want to get started."

Janell rustled through a cabinet and came out holding a protein bar. She tossed it at him, and he caught it.

DeAndre came around to her and kissed the top of her head. "Love you, Mercy Girl. I'll see you in a bit." Then he kissed Java's head. "Love you, Java Bean. See you soon."

He spun back around to Janell. "Joe's still sleeping?"

She poured some boring cereal into her own bowl. "Wonder of wonders."

"Alright, I'm out." DeAndre waved. "Bye, David," he called to the couch.

David still lay like a lump, covered from head to toe in his blanket, unmoving.

As the door clicked shut, Mercy felt a jolt shoot through her like lightning. She *would* get to surprise her dad. One of her dads. The one who cared about her art. She shoveled a giant bite into her mouth, chewed twice, and gulped it.

"Whoa. Slow down. No choking." Janell brought her bowl to the table, settling into the chair on the other side of Mercy. "Here's the plan. We finish eating, then I wake your brother and have him keep an eye on Java. He can text me when Joe wakes up."

Mercy nodded, grinned, then spooned another full bite into her mouth.

~

It was a bit tricky, but she figured out how to color one half of the drawing first and then the other half so that people always had a place to step. Who did she want to be? What did she have to give? This is what she wrote and drew, down to each tiny nub of chalk. She nearly covered the whole strip in front of DeAndre's apartment. When Janell needed to nurse Joe, David came and sat with Mercy.

Several people complimented her as they passed. "How beautiful."

But it wasn't until she got upstairs that she saw the effect of her artwork.

Sitting on the couch, peering at the kaleidoscope of pastel blue, purple, orange, yellow, and pink, she watched people walk by. Pause. Look down.

You Are Chosen. You Are Strong and Brave. You Can Give Love Away. You Can Change the World!

Her words were surrounded by pictures of shooting stars and rainbows, of wispy clouds and a sunrise.

She watched the passersby look, then back up to see more.

And their expressions changed. Frowns turned into smiles. Worry turned into peace. Their shoulders and backs straightened. They held their heads higher. They walked like they believed it was true.

With each person transformed before her eyes, hope sprang within her. She *could* change the world. She *was* changing the world. For that person…and that one…and that one. She wasn't too little or too broken or too black or too white.

A man crouched down, studying her work, as if taking in every detail. A woman stepped beside him. Wait, was that Mom? And Dad? As if on cue, they looked up, searching the tower of windows for her face. She waved until their eyes landed on her. Dad pointed to the colorful sidewalk, then tapped his heart, his smile wobbly. Mom tried to make a heart with her hands. She wasn't doing it right, and Mercy spit out a tear-choked laugh. They were proud of her! Even from way up here, it was obvious. It nearly gushed out of them.

All her life, she'd felt like she didn't belong anywhere, that she never really fit. That maybe no one really wanted her anyway. But it was all a lie. She belonged everywhere. With Mom and Dad. With DeAndre and Janell. With Hope, Faith, David, and Daniel. With Java and Joe. With Bethany and with MeeMaw. At white church and at black church. No matter where she went, she would belong because no matter where she went, she was loved. She wasn't half of anything. She was one hundred percent of who God made her to be. She could open her heart and take in the love that came her way.

And she could give love away.

34

June 2020
Chicago, Illinois

DeAndre squirted an array of brightly colored oil paint across the top of his palette. Streaks of skin-colored tones filled the sides. He set to mixing colors and brought his brush to the canvas, bringing his own form to life.

He leaned back, tilting his head. No. It wasn't right. *It's missing something.* His goodbye present to Mercy needed to be perfect, needed to convey to his daughter what he could never fully put into words—how much he longed to gather her in his arms and keep her close to him forever.

Whenever Natassa and Brandon decided to leave, they would take Mercy with them. For good. As much as they'd bonded in the last few days, neither Brandon nor Natassa had spoken a word about continuing a relationship once their car rolled out of Chicago. Natassa's last words on the matter—*Do you know your place? Because it's not in her life.* —resonated as the final say on the subject.

His girl wouldn't have his words of love to reassure her over the tumultuous years ahead. Preteen angst, her first boyfriend, friend drama, prom, graduation, choosing a college—she'd navigate all of it without him. Whatever came down the line for people of color in their nation, she'd have to figure it out without his guidance. But he could leave her this—a painting to remind her that he would always love her no matter what.

He needed it to speak all that was in his heart.

How could he do that?

He puffed out his cheeks and went to work on Mercy's form.

He smiled as he outlined the perfect upturn of her mouth. That girl had a way of filling the entire room with the light of her smile. Could she be more beautiful? He painted her in her Wakanda costume, beaming up at him as he grinned down at her. He'd come back and fill in details later. Now for the fun part.

An explosion of color all around them, a rainbow of brilliance. DeAndre blended one bright color into the next, bursting around father and daughter. It looked like joy. Hope. Love.

DeAndre took a step back and rolled his neck back and forth, stretching his tight muscles. He picked up a smaller brush, ready now to return to the faces.

The bell above the door jangled, and DeAndre stilled. *A customer?* He set his palette down, wiped his hands on a rag, and slipped through the dividers.

A man stood, back to him, observing the displayed canvases.

"Can I help you?"

He turned.

"Rob?" DeAndre shook his head as if to jar himself into reality. His old friend from Crawford County and Java Joe's stood in his studio. "What are you doing here?"

"Hey, DeAndre." Rob chuckled nervously. "Nice to see you."

DeAndre stared, waiting for an answer to his question.

Rob's gaze swept the room. "I was in town for work. Thought I'd stop by."

He opened his mouth, but nothing came out. What was there to say?

Rob closed his eyes and sighed long and deep. Then he locked his gaze on DeAndre. "Look, I screwed up. I know it. I was supposed to be your friend, and yet I ditched you when you needed me. I should have visited you in jail or at least written to you."

DeAndre wanted to look away but forced himself to keep eye contact. What should he say? *No problem, man. No biggie?* Rob's actions, or lack of them, had twisted like a knife. DeAndre's throat went dry.

Rob tented his hands in front of him, his eyes earnest. "I came here to ask for your forgiveness. How I acted…well, it's not like Jesus. He doesn't duck His head and refuse to associate with us when we screw up."

DeAndre swallowed and closed his eyes. The note he'd written to Natassa was seared on his conscience. *Please forgive me.* And the note she'd written in return. *I forgive you. God will forgive you, too.* Could he really look Rob in the eye and deny him what DeAndre himself had so freely received?

"I'm not gonna lie." His throat burned. "It hurt man. You and James and Patrick, you guys represented something like hope to me. New beginnings and freedom. Then y'all dropped me like that." He snapped his fingers. "What happened to that hope then?"

Rob dipped his head. "I am so sorry."

"I'll tell you what happened to it. I found that I couldn't put my hope in any man, in any person. Only in God. He's the only perfect One who will never let me down."

"You got that right." Rob scrubbed the back of his neck.

DeAndre took a deep breath. "So, I forgive you, man. I forgive all you guys." He released the tension in his shoulders.

The corner of Rob's mouth tipped upward. "Whoa, man. Thank you. You don't know what a weight you've lifted."

He nodded. He could imagine.

"Nice place you've got here. Scott Studios. Your very own studio named after you."

DeAndre tilted his head. "It's actually Janell's. Named after Mrs. Scott. I'm just a humble employee."

Rob pressed his lips together. "Good thing you married up, then."

He laughed. "Yeah. Good thing."

"Can we sit. Chat a bit?" Rob gestured to the chairs.

"Sure."

"I've been reading some stuff, learning, and I've come to realize that we—all of us at Java Joe's—meant well, but we didn't necessarily go about things the right way. With you, I mean. Didn't see things the right way." Rob fidgeted in his chair.

"Oh, you mean how y'all slid into the white savior role?"

The corner of Rob's mouth quirked up. "Something like that."

"Look, you boys were clueless. For sure. But you were also my friends. I can give you grace." Could he blame them for not knowing how to navigate something they'd never been trained in? "Thank you for acknowledging that, though. And for stepping up your game."

"What is it they say? You know better, you do better?"

He nodded. "We're all learning."

Rob and DeAndre caught up on the last few years. Then DeAndre opened up about Mercy.

"I just found her, and I'm about to lose her for good."

"Nah, man. You didn't find her; *she* found *you*. That's amazing. It sounds like God's fingers were all over that." Rob leaned forward, resting his elbows on his knees, his gaze locked on DeAndre's. "If she found you once, who's to say she won't find you again? Can you trust the Lord with your little girl?"

DeAndre shifted in his chair. *She found me once. She can find me again.* He closed his eyes. Inhaled that assurance. Confidence rose within him. *If she found me once, she will find me again. It's just a matter of time.* Could he trust God with his little girl? Could he trust God with the timing of everything? He pressed his hand to his burning heart and nodded.

~

When Rob left, DeAndre returned to his painting. He could see now what the painting was missing, what his face was devoid of. *Peace.* His portrait showed his love for his daughter but no rest in that love. Although his mouth smiled, his eyes looked angsty and troubled. If he gave that picture to Mercy, it would haunt her instead of comforting her. But he hadn't been able to paint what he didn't have inside of him.

Now he could.

He picked up his brush and softened the lines around his eyes, around his mouth. He transformed the dark countenance into one of calm trust.

He stepped back and angled his head.

There. Perfect.

He wiped his brush on a rag and then dropped it into a bowl of solvent. After grabbing a piece of paper and a pen from the desk drawer, he began to write, chuckling as smudges of paint rubbed off onto the paper from his fingers. Something to remember him by.

35

____

June 2020
Chicago, Illinois

Natassa knelt on Mercy's air mattress in front of the printer. The machine spit out sheet after sheet of what might as well have been pure gold. Her massive belly jiggled slightly as she bounced with nervous energy. Such a good idea to look for further records regarding Mercy and Susan. Why hadn't she thought of that?

Finally, the printer's hum silenced. Natassa snatched the stack of papers from the tray and used the desk to hoist herself to standing. She rushed out of Mercy's room as fast as her penguin waddle could take her.

"I've got it." She waved the stack in the air, then dropped it on the dining room table.

David, DeAndre, Janell, and Brandon swarmed the pile. They each took a page and sat. For several moments, the only sounds were those of the children playing in the background and an occasional rumble from the street below.

"Hmm." Brandon broke the silence. "I thought we were looking for records around Georgetown, but all of these people lived and died in Nebraska."

Natassa's brow furrowed as she searched through unfamiliar names and dates. "You're right. Do you think it's the wrong Susan Renald?"

"No." Janell pointed to the paper in front of her. "Right here, it says that Susan was born in Hamburg, South Carolina. That's not far from Georgetown, is it? A lot of people moved west."

Natassa took the stack of papers and riffled through them, searching for something other than genealogies. There in the middle of a page. A few pictures. She held them up. Squinted at the script scribbled on the bottom. Gasped.

"What?" Brandon and David asked in unison.

"It's the right people. Look." She turned the picture toward them. "It says this is Minnie and Thaddeus Wyndom, this," she said while pointing, her grin spreading, "is Liberty and Mercy Miller, and this is Susan and Mercy together."

Janell squealed and rushed around the table to peer over Natassa's shoulder. "Let me see."

Natassa handed it to her, and she held it close to her face. "I hate how old pictures are so grainy."

"Liberty was one of Mercy's daughters, right?" DeAndre asked.

"Yes. One of the middle ones, I think," Natassa said.

David held out his hand for the picture. "And who is Minnie? Susan's daughter?"

"Yes."

Natassa returned to weeding through the stack. More names and dates. They'd have to sit and make a family tree at some point. It was all getting jumbled in her brain, but—her breath caught as her gaze brushed over *Dear Mercy*. She snatched it from the pile.

"Oh my goodness! Letters from Susan to Mercy."

"What?"

"Are you serious?"

The paper shook in Natassa's hand as she read out loud Susan's words to Mercy. Janell read the next page of letters, and they traded off from there. When they finished, they sat in stunned silence.

Finally, DeAndre spoke. "Whoa. So, at that point, Mercy hadn't come back to see Susan. But we have a picture of them together, so she must have eventually."

Brandon rubbed his temples. "And somehow they all got to Nebraska?"

"Look." Janell held out a paper to Natassa. "It's a newspaper article from 1905 in the *Omaha Daily Bee* featuring Liberty. She spoke at some Friends of the Indians conference. Looks like her views differed a bit from the norms of the time."

"How so?" Brandon asked.

"Says she wanted them to be able to retain their cultural heritage. Others wanted to"—her finger trailed the lines of print— "strip them of their heathen ways."

Natassa took the article. "It says her name was Liberty Lincoln. She must have married by this time."

David sifted through the papers in front of him. "Yes, she married Solomon Lincoln in"—his eyes scanned the page— "1872."

"What's this?" DeAndre's brows rose as he took in the pages in front of him. "*Nebraska: My Journey to You* by Liberty Lincoln."

"A book?" Natassa leaned over the table as far as her belly would allow.

He flipped through. "Not long enough to be a book. More like a pamphlet or a journal. It starts with her telling about living in Louisiana."

"Read it to us, will you?" Janell angled her chair toward him and sat forward expectantly.

DeAndre read of how Liberty fled from New Orleans due to threats by night riders. Of a Union soldier befriending her.

"Thaddeus? The same man who married Minnie?" Natassa sifted through the mess on the table and found the picture again.

DeAndre shrugged and kept reading of Liberty's journey to Georgetown. Of her connecting with Susan and Minnie. Of Thaddeus going back for Mercy and her family. Of all of them migrating to Nebraska.

Natassa sat back in her chair, a satisfied smile spreading. "It all makes sense now."

"Hey, look." Janell held up another newspaper clipping. "It's Mingo in front of an AME church."

David quirked a brow. "AME?"

"African Methodist Episcopal," Janell explained. "Pastor Mingo Freeman founds Liberty Road AME Church in Renada."

DeAndre's head snapped up. "No way. I've heard of that church."

"Why was Mingo's last name Freeman?" David asked.

Natassa gave her son a reassuring smile before taking the article from Janell's outstretched hand. "They all got the chance to choose last names after the war. Most chose the name of their masters like Jonah did, but some didn't. Solomon chose the last name of Lincoln. Many former enslaved people did that to honor the president. Mingo chose the last name of Freeman, likely to mark his new status."

"What did Mercy choose?"

"I'm not sure." Natassa studied the fuzzy photograph of a grinning tall, handsome man in a suit standing in front of a church sign.

A giggle bubbled forth from Janell. "Follows." She smacked her hand on the table. "Can you believe it? She chose the last name Follows. It lists it right here on her marriage certificate as her maiden name. Mercy Follows."

Laughter ping-ponged around the table.

"Uh, Mom?" David's voice shook her from her happy haze.

"What?"

"Why is your name on this paper of Susan's relatives?"

Natassa leaned forward, propping her elbows on the table. "Huh?"

He slid a sheet across to her. "Look. Natassa Wyndom. A child of Minnie and Thaddeus."

Her mouth parted as her eyes found her first name listed in front of her. "Strange."

Brandon folded his hands together on top of the table. "What an unusual coincidence."

She'd never heard of another person with her name. Never. "I don't think I believe in coincidences."

~

When her mother answered the phone, Natassa didn't even bother making small talk first.

"Why did you name me Natassa?"

"Well, hello, dear." The pinched formality in her mother's voice wouldn't deter her today.

Natassa paced back and forth in the hallway, phone pressed tight against her ear. "Why?"

"It's an old family name. I always loved the sound of it."

"A family name?" Her brows rose. "From whom?"

"I don't know. Several women in our family line were named Natassa. Your great-great-grandma, I think? An aunt somewhere back at the turn of the century. I think the name first appeared on the family tree in the late 1800s or thereabouts."

Her mother paid attention to the family tree? Natassa had never given it a thought. "Does the name Renald sound familiar?"

A sigh. "I don't remember."

"Where is this family tree?"

"Why are you all of a sudden so concerned with genealogy?"

"Tell me, Mother. I have to know." She closed her eyes and softened her tone. "Can you scan it and email it over to me?"

"I'll see if your aunt can. Honestly, what's gotten into you?"

"Aunt Chrissy? I'll text her. Thanks."

Laser-focused on finding answers, she nearly hung up, but a niggle inside stopped her. She lifted her phone back to her ear. "Mom?"

"Yes?"

"Thank you. For watching the children all this time. For allowing us to make this trip. For always being there."

"Of course. That's what mothers are for."

~

"Well, I'll be." Bethany's voice held a hint of awe.

Natassa cradled the phone to her ear while she scanned the two papers laid out on the patio table in front of her. "Remarkable, isn't it?"

She sat on DeAndre's back porch, basking in a few peaceful moments under clear, blue skies. A fresh breeze rustled the end of her family tree. The one her aunt had emailed over. She clamped her hand on top of it. She would not let this miracle blow away.

"They line up exactly. You're sure?" Natassa could picture Breanna's open-mouthed gape.

"Except for a few minor spelling discrepancies here and there—likely due to illegible handwriting—yes. The family tree we pieced together from Susan's family lines up precisely with mine." Her toes curled. She was part of this story—this grand, big, beautiful story—and connected to Bethany. Not by blood but by friendship through the generations. How amazing was that?

"You seriously had no idea?"

A car horn resounded from the street, followed by shouts and curses from an angry driver. The squealing of tires.

"I knew Minnie had a daughter named Natassa. It's why I was so intrigued by your name. Then when you told me you was naming your baby Mercy, I felt led to give you the journal. But I didn't know that you were related to Susan."

A laugh bubbled up. "How is this possible?"

"With God, all things,"

Natassa chimed in, "are possible." The memory verse was no longer words on a page. They were live to her.

But then she sobered. "So…my family owned your family." She pressed her lips together. What a hard reality to digest. She'd mulled it over all night. "Horrible, isn't it?"

"Oh, sugar. The way I see it restoration has come full circle."

Natassa pressed a hand to her burning heart. "That's beautiful."

"He makes all things beautiful in time, sugar. All things. Now you tell everyone hi for me. And have a safe trip home."

Home. She'd be going home tomorrow. And leaving here so much different than when she came.

36

———

June 2020
Chicago, Illinois

DeAndre awakened to a stiff neck and pain cramping his back. He rubbed his eyes, wincing from the glare of the sun. Where was he? He shifted and felt the weight of Mercy's head against his chest. *We must have fallen asleep watching the movie last night.* He rolled his neck to one side and carefully slid his feet from their propped position on the coffee table, trying not to jostle his girl.

While he had slept in a half-sitting, half-slouching position all night, Mercy had nestled into him, stretching her legs long on the couch and using his chest as her pillow. DeAndre ran a hand over her hair, treasuring this last moment of togetherness. He glanced at his watch. Natassa and Brandon would be there in an hour and a half to snatch her away.

David snored on the other couch, flat on his back with his mouth gaping open.

DeAndre smiled. He'd miss that boy, too.

How had these two become a part of him in such a short amount of time? Soon he'd watch their cars pull out of view. Life would go back to normal. His heart squeezed.

Mercy wiggled and buried her head deeper into him, pulling the blanket over herself as if she didn't want to let go of the moment any more than he. Though his body screamed to get up and stretch, he remained still. Holding his breath. Holding on to this moment in time.

"What time is it?" Mercy mumbled.

DeAndre lifted the blanket off her head. "Eight."

She groaned.

"How about some pancakes?"

Her eyebrow lifted. "You're cooking?"

"The microwave kind." He winked.

"Sure." She lifted herself up and stretched her arms over her head, yawning.

DeAndre stood and pumped his legs to banish the pins and needles that crept up his calves. He marched his way to the kitchen, knees high.

"What in the world?" Janell breezed into the kitchen in her pink pajama set and Minnie Mouse robe.

"Couldn't feel my feet." He kissed the top of her head.

She leaned into him. "I missed you last night."

"Sorry."

"Not a problem. Just wanted you to know that I kind of like you." She grinned up at him.

He planted another kiss on her forehead. "Go sit, woman. I'm cooking."

She quirked an eyebrow.

He dug through the freezer and pulled out a bag of pancakes, presenting them triumphantly.

Janell threw her hands up. "Okay. Okay. Go right ahead, Chef Scott."

Mercy giggled from her spot on the couch.

Janell turned and opened her arms to Mercy. "Come here, you."

Mercy ran into Janell's embrace. Janell lifted Mercy off her feet and twirled her around, eliciting giggles and squeals.

"My turn!" Java crashed into Janell from behind.

Janell scooped him up and spun him in circles.

DeAndre popped a plate of pancakes in the microwave.

"What's for breakfast?" David sat and covered a yawn.

"Good morning, sunshine." DeAndre drummed his hands on the kitchen island. "Pancakes by yours truly."

David snickered.

Punk.

DeAndre grabbed butter and syrup from the fridge and placed them on the island.

"Wait!" Mercy looked up at him with pleading eyes. "Before we get sticky, I have something to give to you."

He stared at her. Was there any end to her sweetness? "Something to give me? But you already gave me that beautiful chalk mural on the sidewalk." He put a hand over his heart. "That was a remarkable gift."

"But this is for you to keep forever. I want to give it before Mom and Dad get here. I don't know…" She bit her lip. "Hold on." She dashed to her room.

Mercy returned clutching an 11 × 14 in. canvas to her chest. "I asked Mom to take me to the store for supplies, but I forgot to buy wrapping paper or a bag." Her gaze dropped to the floor.

"It's fine. You painted something for me?" DeAndre came out from behind the island and crouched before her.

Mercy nodded, then flipped the canvas around, revealing a painting of the two of them standing hand in hand on top of a rainbow. Iridescent raindrops sparkled around them like jewels.

"So we can always be together." She pulled her bottom lip in.

DeAndre's breath caught. His eyes burned, and he pulled Mercy into a hug before she could see them water. "It's the most beautiful painting I've ever seen." He sniffed. "I'll treasure it forever."

Janell held her hand over her heart, and her eyes shimmered with tears.

He blinked his own away and cleared his throat. "As long as we're giving gifts, I might as well let you have the one that I made for you."

He spun around and retrieved it from his bedroom.

He knelt in front of Mercy, the backside of the canvas facing her. "I didn't have any wrapping paper either."

Mercy smiled.

He turned his canvas around to display the two of them together surrounded by explosions of color.

Mercy's mouth fell open. "Wow!" Her hand gravitated toward the faces as if she wanted to touch them, but she held back. "It looks so real."

"The love I have for you is real, Mercy." He swallowed. "It will always be there. No matter what."

Sidestepping the painting, she flung her arms around his neck.

He clutched her to himself. If only he could hold on forever.

A knock sounded at the door.

Janell rushed to answer it as Mercy's grip loosened.

"Sorry we're early." Natassa's chipper voice invaded the space between them. "We're eager to get home."

Mercy pulled away.

~

Mercy kept her hand planted on the car window until Dad turned the corner, and DeAndre couldn't see them anymore. She swiped her cheeks with her sleeve. Stupid tears. They wouldn't stop coming no matter how hard she tried to press them down.

She pulled out the letter DeAndre had given her as she walked out the door.

Dear Mercy,

I want you to know that I will always treasure this time I got to spend with you. You are a delight. You're smart, talented, funny, sweet, a great helper, and a wonderful sister to the boys. I am proud to be one of your dads. Even though we may not see each other, know that I will always be thinking about you and that I will always love you. You have so many people who love you. Believe that you are strong and brave. A warrior princess.

Love forever,
Dad

Great. Now big splotches blurred some of the words. She hiccupped, trying to swallow back the sadness.

Or was it all sadness?

No, there was something else swirling around inside of her too, alongside the sad. Maybe a bit of happy that she had found DeAndre. That she'd met him and loved him. That he loved her and would miss her. *I don't know what I'm feeling. It's all so confusing.*

So, she did what she always did when she couldn't sort out what was going on inside of her. She grabbed her sketchbook and colored pencils and began to draw.

~

Deflated, DeAndre lay on the couch gazing up at the shifting shadows on the ceiling. Glints and glimmers of light.

"Daddy, will you be the bad guy?" Java thrust Darth Vader in his direction.

"Not now, bud." DeAndre sighed. He was so tired of being the bad guy.

His phone buzzed on the coffee table, and he stretched out his hand to pick it up. Mama.

"Hey."

"Hi, Dre. How you doin?" Her voice was laced with compassion. He pressed his lips together, willing himself not to crack under the weight of it.

"Been better."

"I'm sure."

He could use one of Mama's hugs right about now.

"I wanted to tell you that I got something for you. I ordered you a subscription to those travel magazines you love so much."

A calm settled inside him. "Yeah?"

"Yeah. Mine came in the mail today, so yours probably did, too. Have you checked your mail?"

"Not yet."

"Well, I just wanted to let you know. Those magazines helped me through some dark days, and I figured you could use that right about now."

Could he ever. "Thanks, Mama."

He lifted himself from the couch and jogged to his mailbox to check, sloughing off the heaviness that had engulfed him. Sure enough, it was there. Just like he remembered from his childhood. Pictures of far-off lands and adventures. Those magazines had lit a fire in his imagination all those years ago. He smiled as he flipped through the pages.

An idea sparked.

Once upstairs, he grabbed a pen and began to doodle, right there on a photo of the Grand Canyon. The picture showed tourists taking mules into the canyon. Next to them, DeAndre drew a unicorn, and on top of the unicorn, he drew Mercy and himself. Walking in the background, he drew Java and David, Mama and Harlem, Janell holding Joe.

He flipped a few pages to a photo of the Mojave Desert. In the clear blue sky, DeAndre drew a pterodactyl flying with Mercy and himself on its back. He grinned, giddy at the possibilities strewn throughout the magazine.

His knee bounced as he picked up his phone. What if she said no? But he had to try.

He shot a text to Natassa. *Can I have permission to mail Mercy some drawings from time to time?*

His finger trembled as he pressed send.

He drummed the table with his fingers while he waited for a reply, his eyes on the clock. Ten seconds. Twenty. Thirty. A minute. Two.

His phone buzzed.

Sure.

Smiling, he tore out his two pictures from the magazine. He then grabbed an envelope from the office and placed the pictures inside. At least he could have some contact with his little girl. His girl? Yes, his girl.

37

———

July 2020
Renada, Nebraska

"**M**om! Look. I got a letter from DeAndre." Mercy thrust the envelope in front of Natassa's face, her grin radiant.

Natassa's throat burned, but she forced a smile. "That's great." She shuffled through the rest of the mail on the kitchen island, feigning interest in bills and coupons.

The sound of Mercy tearing open the envelope grated on her nerves. Was she grinding her teeth? She loosened her jaw.

"Oooh. Look at that! He drew me and him on the magazine picture. Cool!"

Natassa dropped the pile of mail on the granite surface. "I need to do some wash."

She retreated to the laundry room and scooped warm clothes from the dryer. What was wrong with her? She'd told DeAndre he could send the pictures. She'd spent two weeks with the man and his family. Two good weeks. They'd laughed together, cried together. Bonded in some strange way.

So why did she feel like something was off now?

She dumped the clothes onto the laundry room table and began to sort and fold into piles. Daniel's jeans. Hope's T-shirt. Faith's sweater. If only she could sort through the web of feelings inside of her so easily. Compartmentalize and examine. Tuck them away neatly into drawers. She put the girls' clothes into a basket, then climbed the stairs.

When she entered Mercy's room, her breath caught. DeAndre's painting hung front and center, the bright colors jumping out, entwining themselves around the crevices of her heart. She stopped and stared, her eyes glued on the expressions in those painted faces. Love. Belonging. She nearly doubled over with the ache of it.

A groan crawled up her throat, clawing its way out. She dropped to her knees, basket tumbling, clothes spilling out over her big belly and onto the carpet. *Oh God.* She rocked back and forth. *Have I done the right thing?*

She was keeping this man from her daughter, holding him back from fully embracing her into his life. And why?

Why, Lord?

All of the answers she'd spouted off to DeAndre, to Brandon, to herself…were they truth? She wanted to know the truth.

Because you're afraid.

She nodded, agreeing with the small voice inside. She hung her head and ran her fingers through the plush carpet.

Look to Me.

Natassa closed her eyes and lifted her head, picturing her perfect Heavenly Father. Her Daddy God who never held back any good thing from her. Did she believe that? Could she believe it after all she'd been through?

"No good thing will He withhold from them that walk uprightly," Psalm 84:11.

It might not always feel true, but God's Word always stood true, no matter what. God wasn't the author of evil. He didn't take her babies from her or cause her to get raped to test her faith. All good things came from Him. Only good things. And when bad things came from another source—the enemy of her soul—God somehow redeemed them and brought light into the darkest night.

Lord, if You don't hold good things back from Your children, who am I to hold a good thing back from my daughter? DeAndre is good for her, isn't he? I can see that he is. I feel that he is.

Natassa sniffed and wiped her face with her sleeve.

God, You don't hold back on me. You love me so fully, so completely. Without reservation. Help me to receive that love right now, Lord. Let it drive out all fear.

As she knelt still and silent, she felt God's love wash over her. Cleansing. Refreshing. Infusing strength and courage into her core. She inhaled deeply. Charity danced within her belly.

She could do this. She could share her daughter without fear of losing Mercy's affection. Without a cloud of anxiety causing her to question if she'd done something wrong or why she wasn't enough. She could simply give space for love and trust that God held Mercy in His hand.

Natassa scooped up Mercy's clothes and heaved to her feet. She nodded to the DeAndre in the painting, placed the clothes in the drawers, and went downstairs to see the magazine pictures.

~

Glass crunched under Natassa's feet as she walked around the perimeter of the remains of St. Anthony's Baptist Church. Gaping holes yawned where the stunning stained-glass windows used to be. It looked as if someone had painted half of the bricks a dark gray. Dozens of men hauled wooden beams out of the interior and piled them in the parking lot. And…was that a pew? Flames had devoured half of the wooden structure, but the curve of it betrayed its original purpose.

"It's just a building." Bethany spoke near Natassa's ear.

She jumped, then wrapped her arms around herself. "Yeah." But it was a good one.

"We're the church, sugar. You know that." Bethany patted Natassa's back before retreating to the hollowed-out interior.

The people of St. Anthony's—the church—had come together to clean up and then rebuild. A new structure would be built on top of the ruins of the old. New beginnings. A fresh start. Several other churches across the city were taking offerings and lending resources to help with the effort. There was talk of cushioned pews and perhaps even a keyboard instead of an organ. This new St. Anthony's would look quite different from the old, according to the sketches Natassa had seen. But Bethany would be there, and Old Ezra, and Mazy. As long as her church family was there, it would be a home to her.

"Mom! Look what we found." Mercy waved Natassa over to where Brandon and the children stood by a charred half wall.

Natassa scrunched her nose. She nearly said, "Be careful," but held her tongue. Brandon was watching them, and he was competent. She crunched her way over to them.

David smiled at her. "This windowpane is still intact." He pointed downward.

Natassa gasped. The yellow cross she had seen the first time she'd driven by this church. The one that had drawn her to this place, that led to her journey here. "How?" She looked around her. Nothing else seemed to be in one piece.

Brandon shrugged. "I don't know. I thought you'd like it. You know, since you have a thing for stained glass."

Natassa bent over and ran her fingers over it. A layer of dust rubbed off, and she brushed her hands together. She blew gently on the glass, and the sunny hue sparkled to life. "I can't believe it." She turned to Daniel. "Go get Bethany. See if they want this. To display it in the new building or something."

He pivoted and disappeared.

Bethany emerged moments later. "Well, would you look at that. Hope in the midst of ashes." Her grin spread. "Why sure, sugar. We can use this in the new church. Display it for everyone to see. Then you'll always have it there to remember."

She would never forget.

~

Mercy made a silly face at the screen.

Java rewarded her with a fit of giggles.

"And how's my JoJo?" She grinned at her baby brother's drooly face.

"He's great." Janell bounced Joe on her lap. "He can't wait to see you next month."

"We all can't wait to see you." DeAndre leaned forward, and his face filled most of the screen.

Mercy beamed. She enjoyed her weekly FaceTime dates with her other family. She had two families now, and they both loved her. She loved both of them, too. Mom and Dad were letting her stay with DeAndre and Janell for the whole month of August. Well, at least until school started. And they said she could spend two whole months every summer in Chicago, and some time on winter and spring break, too.

"Hold on. Let me show you what I'm working on." Mercy set the tablet on the couch and raced upstairs to grab the canvas off her easel. She dashed back down the steps and slid into the living room, hopping back onto the couch. She propped the canvas up and then angled the tablet toward it. "Can you see it?"

"Hey." Was that pride in DeAndre's voice? Mercy's chest puffed out. "That looks familiar."

Mercy chuckled. "I copied the magazine page you sent me of the unicorn."

"Wow. Did you use acrylics?"

Mercy nodded.

"Great job showing the depth of the canyon. Your technique has really improved. I'm impressed."

"You taught me a lot." Mercy ducked her head.

"You taught me a lot too, kiddo."

Her head snapped up, forehead scrunched.

"No, for real. You did. I love you, sweetheart."

"Love you too, Dad. Always and forever."

MERCY WILL FOLLOW ME

Book One of *The Mercy Series*

Natassa seems to have it all – a devoted husband with a good income, beautiful children, a faithful best friend- but it only takes one night for her world to crumble, catapulting her into a journey of trauma and healing, old pressures and new friendships. Will she learn to stand her ground or will she always live in someone else's shadow?

DeAndre longs to break free from the neighborhood that keeps dragging him down, but the streets are made of quicksand. Dreams can hardly take flight there, even if he paints them wings. And when he does the unthinkable, could mercy ever be a possibility?

In the 1800s, a mulatto enslaved girl is torn from her mother and left to figure out who she is on her own. Through her time as a house slave in Tennessee and Kentucky, Mercy grapples with her deep ache for her Mama and her understanding of black and white. Which is more important to her? Freedom or loyalty?

Join these three characters, see how their stories intertwine, and dare to believe that mercy will follow you.

Available in Paperback, Kindle, and Audiobook.

MERCY'S SONG

Book Two of *The Mercy Series*

Natassa has settled into a "new normal" three years after the assault that changed her life. Marriage, family, and a new career have brought changes that she never thought were possible, and love like she'd never known before. But any semblance of peace shatters when a new development occurs in her case. Flooded with emotion she thought she'd long put to rest, Natassa must navigate strained relationships. Will she find the truth that can set her free?

DeAndre returns to Crawford County after dropping out of art school and finds an opportunity for romance. His past continues to haunt him, even as he and his new love seek to piece the broken shards of their lives together. Soon, a shocking discovery sends DeAndre reeling and forces him to choose between the woman he loves and his integrity. Will he end up losing everything or can he cling to hope despite it all?

In the 1840s, Mercy labors next to her mother in the rice fields and discovers a spark of affection growing between herself and Jonah, another slave. But Mama's health begins to fail, and the missus makes an announcement that will alter their lives forever. Will Mercy's plan to save them succeed? Or will they lose everything, including each other?

Available in Paperback, Kindle, and Audiobook.

ABOUT THE AUTHOR

Sarah Hanks is an award-winning author of Christian fiction in both the contemporary and historical genres. After spending over a decade mostly writing and teaching Sunday school curricula for churches in her community, she finally jumped into writing fiction full time.

She and her husband have eight children of their own, a couple of whom seem to have inherited their mother's love for playing with words and crafting stories. Though Sarah dreams of a cabin by the beach, the family of ten lives jammed together in beautiful chaos near St. Louis, Missouri. She buys ear plugs in bulk.

You can find Sarah Hanks on Facebook and Instagram as @authorsarahhanks, or connect with her on sarah-hanks.com. She also loves to combat the swarm of negativity with hope-filled emails. You can sign up for her email list on her website.